"Hold out your arms and I'll hand him over to you," Hannah said with a reassuring smile.

Garrett did as she said, feeling an overwhelming sense of awe as she settled the babe into his outstretched arms. So, this was what becoming someone's father would have felt like.

"Now bring him to your chest," Hannah coached softly.

As he settled the towel-swaddled infant against his chest, Garrett felt his heart swell.

"I'd like to name him after you," Hannah said, her eyes drifting shut.

Garrett's gaze snapped up, her words taking him by surprise.

"That is, if it's all right with you," she mumbled sleepily.

"I'd be honored," he said. Truth was, he couldn't have been more honored. It wasn't as if he'd ever have children of his own to pass his name down to.

"Garrett Austin," Hannah said with a sigh. Her soft, even breathing told him she had finally fallen into an exhausted slumber.

Garrett looked down at the precious bundle he held in his arms and smiled. "Welcome to the world, Garrett Austin Myers."

Kat Brookes is an award-winning author and past Romance Writers of America Golden Heart® Award finalist. She is married to her childhood sweetheart and has been blessed with two beautiful daughters. She loves writing stories that can both make you smile and touch your heart. Kat is represented by Michelle Grajkowski with 3 Seas Literary Agency. Read more about Kat and her upcoming releases at katbrookes.com. Email her at katbrookes@comcast.net. Facebook: Kat Brookes.

Award-winning author **Stephanie Dees** lives in small-town Florida with her pastor husband and their two youngest children. A Southern girl through and through, she loves sweet tea, SEC football, corn on the cob and air-conditioning. For further information, please visit her website at stephaniedees.com.

The Rancher's
Baby Surprise

Kat Brookes

&

The Cowboy's
Unexpected Baby

Stephanie Dees

LOVE INSPIRED
INSPIRATIONAL ROMANCE

LOVE INSPIRED®
INSPIRATIONAL ROMANCE

Recycling programs for this product may not exist in your area.

ISBN-13: 978-1-335-46277-0

The Rancher's Baby Surprise and The Cowboy's Unexpected Baby

Copyright © 2021 by Harlequin Books S.A.

The Rancher's Baby Surprise
First published in 2018. This edition published in 2021.
Copyright © 2018 by Kimberly Duffy

The Cowboy's Unexpected Baby
First published in 2020. This edition published in 2021.
Copyright © 2020 by Stephanie Newton

This edition published by arrangement with Harlequin Books S.A.

For questions and comments about the quality of this book, please contact us at CustomerService@Harlequin.com.

Love Inspired
22 Adelaide St. West, 40th Floor
Toronto, Ontario M5H 4E3, Canada
www.Harlequin.com

Printed in U.S.A.

CONTENTS

THE RANCHER'S
BABY SURPRISE

Kat Brookes

I'd like to thank Harlequin for the opportunity I've been given to share my stories with so many of its wonderful readers. It was a dream of mine for a very long time to write for Harlequin, and now I am living that dream. I'd like to thank Melissa Endlich for bringing me into the Love Inspired family, the editing department, my cover artist and Harlequin's fabulous marketing crew. Lastly, I'd like to extend a very warm welcome to my new editor, Carly Silver. Thank you for your time and input with this story. I look forward to publishing many more books with you in the future.

And they that know thy name
will put their trust in thee: for thou, Lord,
hast not forsaken them that seek thee.
—*Psalms* 9:10

Chapter One

Hannah Sanders eased her foot off the gas pedal as she struggled to make out the winding country road ahead. The overcast day had turned as black as night when she'd driven into the storm. Even her car's high beams struggled to push through the wall of rain before her. Deepening puddles along the barely visible road pulled at her tires, causing Hannah to tighten her grip on the steering wheel even more.

"Dear Lord," she prayed, resisting the urge to run a hand over her rounded abdomen, knowing she needed to keep both hands firmly wrapped about the steering wheel, "please don't let anything happen to this baby." *Her sister's baby.*

The wipers, set on high, pushed water to and fro on the windshield, but the deluge outside rendered them nearly useless. Why hadn't she turned around when she'd seen the approaching storm? As if in answer to her question, the cramping in her lower back returned, this time wrapping around to her swollen abdomen. She hadn't turned around because, according to her GPS, Bent Creek, Wyoming was the closest town in any direction to seek shelter from the storm she was driving through.

Hannah clenched her teeth as the cramping sensation, one she still hoped was nothing more than false labor pains, settled low in her abdomen. Tears pooled in her eyes. "This can't be real labor," she uttered in denial as she fought to push away the sense of panic threatening to overcome her. It was too soon. The baby, the tiny little blessing her older sister and her husband had entrusted her with, wasn't due to arrive for five more weeks. A child that, following the multicar pileup that had taken her sister's and brother-in-law's lives three months earlier, would be Hannah's to raise. To love.

And love this baby she would. With all her heart. He was all she had left of Heather, her only sibling. She told herself to stay calm. That stress wasn't good for the baby, and what she was experiencing was nothing more than false labor pains. But what if they weren't? She couldn't give birth to Heather and Brian's son on the side of some rain-soaked road alone. There could be complications? What if—

A crack of thunder erupted in the looming clouds above just as Hannah started across an old wooden single-lane bridge, yanking her from her fearful thoughts. The Honda Civic shuddered almost violently below her. Then, before she could fully process that the rumble she'd both heard and felt wasn't thunder, the bridge gave way beneath her car.

A panicked cry escaped her lips. She jammed her foot on the brake, not that it made any difference as the nose of her Civic dipped downward. The creek's rampant flow immediately crested over the front end of the hood on the driver's side, mixing with the deluge of rain still coming down around her. Hannah's stomach dropped, and it had nothing to do with the life growing inside her. It was an instantaneous fear of what might very well be her last few moments on this earth. Was this how her sister had felt in the milliseconds before the deadly crash that took her life?

Guilt rose up, overtaking that fear. Her decision to drive on through the storm instead of pulling off onto the side of the road to wait it out would cost her not only her life, but that of the innocent babe she carried inside her. Thick, hot tears of regret rolled down her cheeks. Just when she thought her car was about to be swept away, the rear of the vehicle caught on something, causing it to hang up on the rain-soaked hillside behind her. The car now hung partially submerged in the rushing water of the creek. Thankfully she hadn't been going fast enough for the front air bags to deploy. There was no telling what kind of injury that might have caused to the baby this far along in her pregnancy.

However, the seat belt she'd secured herself in with, thanks to the downward slant of the vehicle, now pulled taut against her swollen abdomen. While it kept her from sliding forward into the dashboard, it also made it harder to breathe and nearly impossible to move.

The engine sputtered and died as water pushed through the partially submerged hood of the car, causing the headlights as well as the inside lighting to go out. Fearing that any movement she might make would dislodge her car from the creek's hillside, Hannah sat perfectly still. If one could call it sitting, with gravity wanting to pull her body downward toward the nose of the car.

Darkness shrouded the world around her as she sat listening to the sweeping rush of the water around her. Rain drummed against the car's roof, the sound drowning out the furious pounding of her heart as the reality of the situation she suddenly found herself in settled into her panic-stricken mind. She was caught up in a flash flood. She'd seen enough news coverage on them over the years to know what they were capable of. Less than two feet of rushing water could sweep vehicles away as if they were nothing more than weightless toys.

A damp chill began to seep into the car, making Hannah shudder. She had to do something. But what if her movement caused the Civic to break free of whatever it was that had hung it up? The car bobbed against the water's force and she knew time was running out. With the water rising as quickly as it was, the flooding creek would soon sweep her—*them*—away. Two more lives gone far too soon.

Her thoughts went to her sister's child and the life he would never have the chance to live. And what of her father? What would become of him? He was still grieving over the loss of his oldest daughter. She couldn't do this to him again. Wouldn't do this to him. Forcing one hand's iron-banded grip to loosen on the steering wheel, she released it and then eased slightly numb fingers across the center console, searching the front passenger seat for her purse and the cell phone she'd left lying on the seat next to it. She only prayed she would have signal out there in the middle of what felt like nowhere.

Her fingertips danced over the empty passenger seat and Hannah groaned. Her purse must have slid onto the floor when the bridge dropped out from under the front of her Honda. There was no telling where her phone had ended up.

"Dear Lord, please keep us safe until help arrives," she prayed, determined to cling to her faith despite the gnawing fear that no one would be out in a storm like this. Why would they be?

She turned her head slowly from one side to the other, trying to assess her situation. Through the heavy downpour, she was barely able to make out the hazy outlines of tree trunks along the creek's bank on either side of her car. Below her, angry whitecaps churned in the rising creek as fallen logs and other debris swirled past.

To think that she'd made the conscious decision to take less-traveled roads on her way back from Idaho to Steamboat Springs, believing the fewer vehicles on the road the safer she and the child she carried inside her would be. She'd been so wrong.

The force of the rising water, surging in a constant push against the side of her Civic, had Hannah's panicked gaze shifting toward the driver-side window. There would be no leaving out that door, which was taking the brunt of the creek's rushing flow. She looked frantically to the passenger side, which, much to her dismay, had water lapping up along its side mirror as well. With no power, she couldn't lower the windows. That left her with only one other option: getting her very pregnant self into the backseat where she might be able to, if the car remained where it was, make her way out onto the bank of the swollen creek through one of the rear doors. Then she would have to pray she didn't lose her footing on the wet, muddied ground.

The vehicle shifted again beneath her, making Hannah gasp. By the grace of God, it remained where it sat, precariously suspended on the side of the bank. Whatever she was going to do, she needed to do it now. If her car were to dislodge and be taken away by the rushing water, her life would end, right along with that of the innocent baby tucked so trustingly in her womb.

Heart pounding, she moved to unlatch her seat belt. With trembling fingers, she jabbed at the button, but it refused to release. She tried again to no avail. "No," she gasped, a deeper panic setting in. She tried to push free of the strap, but her protruding abdomen made that impossible. Nausea roiled in her gut. Closing her eyes, she tried to calm down. She needed to think.

Another pain, this one sharper than the previous ones had been, caused her stomach to clench. A hazy darkness began to skirt the outer edges of her vision. Hannah's thoughts went to her sister and the babe that should have carried on his parents' legacy. She thought of her widower father back in Steamboat Springs, who would be utterly devastated to lose yet another daughter, another grandchild.

"I'm so sorry," she sobbed softly. Then, letting her fear go, she turned herself over to the Lord's safekeeping as the darkness claimed her.

"I've driven in storms before," Garrett Wade muttered into the phone as he pulled away from his ranch house.

"I'd rather lose a horse than a friend," Sheriff Justin Dawson said worriedly from the other end of the line. Justin, the best friend of Garrett's younger brother Jackson, had property that bordered the Triple W Rodeo Ranch, which Garrett and his brothers shared with their parents. Shortly after the storm had begun, he'd called to ask Garrett for advice regarding one of his mares that was having birthing complications. While he could have possibly talked Justin through the birthing, Garrett felt better seeing to it himself. After all, as a veterinarian, that's what he'd devoted his life to—caring for animals, horses in particular. He'd delivered dozens of foals over the years, and it appeared he'd be adding another to his list that dark and stormy afternoon.

The storm worsened, slowing his travel to what felt like a mere crawl. Rain deluged the windshield of his truck, making it almost impossible to see more than one or two cars lengths ahead. He rounded the curve that cut through one of the smaller wooded hillsides on the property, wondering if he might be better off turning around at the bridge just beyond and help Justin with the delivery of the foal via the phone.

He knew far too well how helpless one could feel when a life hung in the balance. Even if the life in jeopardy that afternoon belonged to a horse. He was still driven to do whatever he could to make certain Justin's mare and its foal survived whatever complications had arisen. As he hadn't been able to with Grace. Not that there was any comparison to the loss of a human life. But if he had the ability to make a difference where he hadn't been able to in Grace's case he would. Be it animal or human.

Grace. It had been a stormy afternoon very much like this one when he'd lost the other half of his heart. His high school sweetheart. No, not lost. She'd been taken from him—by cancer. Seventeen years old, with so much life ahead of her, a life she was meant to spend with him, she had slipped away with him holding her hand.

Pulled abruptly from the painful thoughts of his past, Garrett stepped hard on the brake as he eyed the road ahead. He sent a prayer of thanks heavenward as he took in the sight before him. Had he been traveling any faster, he might not have noticed the bridge had been washed out until it was too late.

The bridge had been old and in need of replacing anyway, but its loss had effectively cut off his family's fastest route into town. Shifting the car into Reverse, he started to back away, preparing to turn his Ford F-450 around and head back to the ranch. However, something protruding from the space where the bridge had once been caught his eye as his truck's headlights passed over it.

Leaning forward, Garrett squinted, trying to make out what that something was through the heavy rain. Part of the bridge, perhaps? He slowly drove toward the creek until the blurred outline became clearer. The moment he realized the back end of a car was jutting up from the sloping hillside, Garrett threw his Ford into Park and jumped out into the rain. Had the vehicle's passenger, possibly even passengers, managed to escape before the car settled so precariously over the rapidly rising creek? Or were they trapped inside, on the verge of being swept away by the swirling water? Heart pounding, he raced toward the collapsed bridge.

"Hello?" he hollered. "Is anyone in there?"

When he received no response, he ran toward the upended vehicle, stopping just far enough away from the creek's edge not to accidentally slip into it. Water was halfway up the front doors, but by some Providence the car's rear held fast against the muddied hillside. Thunder and lightning crashing around him as he pulled his cell from the front pocket of his jeans and switched the flashlight app on. It wasn't as good as having the real thing, but at that moment it cast enough light into the vehicle to see that the Honda wasn't empty. The shadowy outline of a slight female form lay limp against the taut harness of the driver's side seatbelt. He couldn't see her face, as the woman's head faced the opposite direction, but she appeared to be unconscious.

The vehicle creaked and groaned as the rushing water threatened to tear the car free of whatever it was that held it to the bank. His gaze shifted immediately toward the rushing water below as it crested over the car's hood. There was no time to waste. Garrett broke into a run for his truck, heedless of the stinging rain. *Dear Lord, please don't let me have arrived too late.*

He grabbed a heavy-duty flashlight along with the recovery towrope he kept in his truck in case one of their horse trailers got stuck in mud and secured the rope to the front of the F-450. Then he hurried back to where the Honda hung precariously atop the hillside and kneeled on the ground where the back end teetered. Shining the light under the car's carriage, he found a secure place to latch the towrope.

He ran back to his truck. Throwing the oversize vehicle into Reverse, he eased backward until the rope grew taut. Then he gave it a little more gas and began pulling the smaller car back up the bank. It caught for a moment, refusing to budge, which sent Garrett into another round of fervent prayers. Then, as if in answer, it let loose, sliding in the slick mud as it ascended the remainder of the way up the side of the flooding creek.

It wasn't until he'd gotten the car safely away from Bent Creek's rising water that Garrett realized he'd been holding his breath. Exhaling his relief, he grabbed once more for the flashlight and then went to check on the driver inside the other vehicle.

When he reached the car, he pulled on the front door handle, only to find it locked. Aiming the beam of the flashlight directly inside, he saw the unconscious woman now lying back against the seat. A surge of urgency filled him. He pounded on the window as the driving rain beat down on him.

The woman shifted slightly and then her eyes fluttered open. Light green eyes, the color of peridot, looked up at him. The expression on the young woman's face, one of both fear and relief, had him wishing there wasn't a solid metal door separating them. He wanted to tell her she was all right. Needed to know that she truly was all right. Needed his pounding heart to settle back into its normal rhythm.

"You're safe!" he hollered over the storm.

Wide-eyed, the woman looked up at him pleadingly, but she made no move to open the door. Was she suffering from shock? It was understandable if she was. A slender hand rose to flatten against the window in a silent plea and then dropped away as an expression of pain moved across her face. Had she been injured when the car had gone down over the bank?

"Unlock the door!" he instructed, motioning toward the door beside her.

She moved then, just enough to reach for the manual lock button. Then the door clicked.

"Thatta girl," he muttered as he eased the door open. Rain spilled off the brim of his cowboy hat as he leaned in, keeping the beam of the flashlight averted as not to blind her with it. Looking down into her tear-stained face, he asked, "Where are you injured?"

"I'm not," she said shakily.

Maybe she didn't realize she'd been hurt, because there had been no mistaking the pain he'd seen etched across her face as he'd peered down at her through the rain-splattered window.

Before he could respond, she added, "I think I might be in labor."

Labor? She had that part all wrong. Justin's mare was in labor. *She* was recovering from the shock of nearly being swept away by a flash flood. His gaze dropped down to where the shaft of light from the flashlight crossed over her midsection. Her very swollen midsection. *Dear Lord.*

His calming heart kicked up again. "Are you sure?"

"No," she answered with a sob. "But I've been having pains on and off for the past few hours. It's got to be false labor. Please tell me it's false labor," she pleaded, fear in her eyes.

He didn't want her to be afraid. Didn't want her to be in labor, for that matter. Not here. Not now. Memories of that awful, stormy day years before threatened to rush in, but the woman's soft whimper kept Garrett anchored to the present. "When is your due date?" he asked with another glance down at her protruding abdomen.

"Not for five more weeks," she replied, biting at her quivering lower lip.

It was at that moment he realized she was shivering. The inside of the vehicle had grown chilled as it hung partway in the water. The cold rain hadn't helped matters, either, causing that afternoon's temperatures to drop. "Wait here," he told her. "I'll be right back."

"Please don't leave me," she cried out, panic filling her voice.

"I'm going to get my poncho from the truck," he told her. "You're already chilled. We don't need you getting soaked to the bones on top of that."

She eased back against the seat and nodded slowly, another shudder racking her form.

Garrett raced back to his truck, sending up a silent prayer of thanks to the Lord for placing him there when he had. Collecting the oversize poncho, he hurried back to the frightened young woman. *Five more weeks. Please let it be false labor pains and nothing more.*

Opening the car door, he called out, "Slide out and I'll cover you with this." He shook out the folded rain poncho and held it up over himself and the top of the car.

"I… I can't."

His brows drew together. "We're far enough away from the water. It's safe for you to leave your car." But not for a whole lot longer, if Bent Creek kept rising the way it was.

"M-my seat belt is stuck."

"Sit back," he told her. "I'll give it a try."

"Okay," she managed with a weak nod.

Leaning into the car, he reached around the rounded mound of her stomach and jabbed at the release button. Just as she had said, it wouldn't budge. Chilly rain seeped into his clothes as he worked at the latch. Finally, he pulled back with an apologetic frown. "It's not going to give."

Fear lit her eyes. "Are you going to have to leave me here?"

"Not a chance," he said, wanting nothing more than to quell the panic he heard in her voice. "I'm going to cut the seat belt away."

"C-cut it?" she stuttered, the chill she'd taken on seeming to get worse. "Wouldn't oiling the latch be better?"

"I don't have any oil handy," he told her and then with a regretful frown said, "I know you'd rather I didn't damage your car, but with the bridge out and other possible flash floods hitting the area, there's no telling how long it would be before 911 could get anyone out here."

"After having creek water rush through the hood of my car, I think the worst of the damage has already been done."

He nodded in agreement.

Suddenly, her expression changed, her breath catching as her hand moved to the pale yellow shirt stretched taut across her stomach.

"The baby?" he inquired worriedly.

"Yes," she gasped. "Cut the belt," she blurted out. Then, as if suddenly realizing the forcefulness with which she'd made her request, added, "Please."

Hearing the urgency in her voice, Garrett reached into the front pocket of his jeans and withdrew his pocketknife. "I'm coming in from the other side," he said as he stepped back and closed the door, wanting to keep her as dry as possible.

He hurried around and slid into the passenger side,

yanking the door closed behind him. Shoving the rain poncho aside, he shifted to face the woman trapped behind the wheel. "Do you think you could hold the flashlight for me? It's heavier than your average household flashlight."

"Y-yes." She reached out to take it from him, holding it firm despite the trembling he'd seen in her hand as she'd done so. With a slight adjustment, she centered the beam on the point where the belt and the latch met. It danced around slightly, but she did her best to steady it.

"Thatta girl," he cooed again, as if talking to a wounded horse. Turning in the seat as much as his long frame would allow, he unfolded the razor-sharp blade. Seeing her tense, he said calmly, "What's your name?"

"H-Hannah. Hannah Sanders."

"Just hold real still for me, Hannah. This should only take a second."

Her gaze dropped to the blade and she swallowed hard. "Y-you didn't tell me your name."

"Garrett Wade," he replied, noting the fear in her eyes as she looked down at his knife. "No need to worry. I grew up on a ranch." He worked the tip of the knife gently beneath the stubborn strap. "My father taught all three of his sons at an early age how to handle a knife properly."

Her gaze lifted. "How old are you now?"

"Thirty-four," he answered as he focused on the troublesome belt, carefully slicing into it.

She exhaled a sigh of relief. "So you've had lots of time to p-perfect your knife skills."

"Enough," he agreed, her reply causing a grin to tug at his lips.

A scant few moments later, he had freed Hannah Sanders from her restraints. She inhaled deeply, closing her eyes.

Garrett stilled. "You okay?"

Opening her eyes, she met his worried gaze. "Yes. It's just such a relief to be able to breathe fully again."

He nodded in understanding, and then he folded and put away his pocketknife as his racing heart slowed. To think of what might have happened if he hadn't gotten there when he had. "Now we just have to get you somewhere warm and safe."

"Safe?"

He inclined his head toward the creek. "The water's still rising. Best to clear out, just in case it spills over and tries to sweep your car away again."

The look of relief he'd seen on her face faded away with his words.

Garrett silently chided himself for not giving more thought to the words he'd spoken. While they'd been truthful, he supposed he could have kept his concerns to himself. Unlike his brothers, he'd never been any good at saying the right thing when it came to women. Most likely because a majority of his time was spent in the company of animals. Not the best learning ground for social interaction.

"I'm not going to let anything happen to you," he said. "And I'm a man of my word. Now just sit tight while I come around to help you out."

"M-my purse," she said, shivering. "It fell to the floor."

Glancing down by his booted feet, he frowned. "I'm afraid I got mud on it."

"That's okay," she assured him with a weak smile. "It'll wipe clean."

With a nod, he reached for it and then handed it over to her. "I'll be around to get you." Drawing the poncho up over his head, he slipped back out into the storm.

Hannah looked out into the darkness, the flashlight still gripped tightly in her hand. Its beam still directed downward. She watched through the pouring rain outside as her rescuer made his way around the front of her car.

Thank You, Lord, for sending this man to help us. She placed a hand against her stomach, feeling the life stir beneath it. "We're going to be all right, little one." While she didn't know this cowboy who had rescued them, Hannah knew in her heart that he would keep them safe.

Her rescuer stepped up to the driver's side door and eased it open. He had the poncho draped over his head, one long arm holding the outer edge of it over the Civic's roof to help shield her from the rain when she slid out.

Clutching her purse in one hand and the weighty flashlight in her other, Hannah turned, easing a foot out the open door.

"Let me get that," he said, taking the flashlight from her. "Now, careful you don't lose your footing," her said, his words nearly drowned out by the loud pulse of rain hitting the poncho he held extended over them.

Nodding, she pushed to her feet. Only it wasn't the water under her shoes that had her going down. It was her trembling legs which promptly gave way beneath her. The next thing Hannah knew, she was being swept up into a pair of strong arms and carried away from her car and the raging creek beyond.

"I c-can walk," she protested.

"I can see that," came his reply, concern lacing his words. "But I'm not taking any chances. Not when you're having abdominal pains."

"I'm not having them now," she told him, closing her eyes, too exhausted to say any more. When they reached his truck, she expected Garrett to set her on her feet, but he held her securely against him as he opened the passenger door and placed her, as if she weighed nothing at all, up into the spacious bucket seat.

"Don't take the poncho off until I close the door," he told her. "I've got to go unhook the towrope from the truck and then we'll get going."

As soon as the heavy door slammed shut beside her, Hannah worked her way out from under the poncho, her gaze searching the curtain of rain coming down outside for the man God had sent in answer to her prayers. She latched on to his shadowy outline, this kindhearted cowboy who had become her lifeline when she'd thought all was lost. By the time he'd climbed into the driver's seat, Garrett was soaked from his wide-brimmed cowboy hat to his muddied boots. Beneath the fading glow of the truck's dome light, she could see the beads of water dripping from the damp tips of his wet, wavy hair.

"I'm so s-sorry you had to get out in this storm," she said as he reached between them to place his wet cowboy hat onto the floor behind her seat.

"Given the alternative outcome, I thank the good Lord above for putting me in the right place at the right time," he replied as he reached back between the seats to grab a thick woolen blanket. Handing it over to her, he said, "Shove that wet poncho to the floor and wrap up in this. I can hear your teeth chattering from over here."

Nodding, she draped the blanket over herself, relishing the warmth it provided. "I c-can't thank you enough for coming to my rescue." Her hand moved to her swollen belly. "Our rescue."

His gaze dropped to the rounded, blanket-draped mound and then back up to her face. "It's going to be okay. I'm going to take you to my brother's place, where you can warm yourself by the fireplace," he said as he threw the truck into gear. "It's closer than mine. We'll hole up there until the storm lets up. You sure you're all right?"

"I'm alive," she replied with a grateful smile. "I'd say that's far better than all right."

He nodded.

"Do you think your brother will mind?" she asked, the chattering of her teeth easing somewhat as the blanket, along with the heat blasting up from the truck's floor heater, began to ease the chill from her body.

"Jackson?" Garrett said, glancing her way. "Not a chance. The man is a social butterfly. He always welcomes company." He turned the vehicle around and started back along the rain-soaked road.

The warmth filling the truck's cab cocooned her as they drove through the storm. The farther away from the flooding creek they got, the more relaxed she felt. And tired. So very tired. She needed to stay awake. That was her first thought. But, as her eyelids grew heavier, she knew she was fighting a losing battle. While Garrett Wade was little more than a stranger to her, Hannah knew he'd been guided to that washed-out bridge by the Lord in answer to her prayers. He would keep her and the baby she carried inside her safe from the storm outside. Comforted by that knowledge, she closed her eyes and gave in to the exhaustion.

"Are you sure she's only sleeping?"

"She's been through a traumatic experience," a vaguely familiar voice replied. "That sort of thing would wear anyone down."

Hannah struggled to push away the haze of sleep as arms moved beneath her, lifting her. "Garrett?" she said sleepily, trying not to wince as her abdomen suddenly constricted, the pain slightly more intense than it had been before.

"I've got you," he replied.

"You need me to take her?"

"I've got her," Garrett said as he pivoted away from the truck. "Can you see to the door?"

"She doesn't look to weigh much more than a bale of hay. I think my bum leg could have handled it."

"Maybe so, but I promised to see her safely to your place and I intend to do just that."

The passenger door slammed shut behind them as Garrett carried her toward what she assumed was his brother's house, rousing Hannah more fully. She forced her eyes open, her gaze first settling on Garrett and then drifting over to the man keeping pace beside her rescuer. He was holding a large umbrella up over her and Garrett, heedless of the rain soaking into his flannel shirt.

As they neared the house, light from the porch spilled out across the man's face. A face very like the man who held her in his arms. "You must be the butterfly," Hannah said, trying not to show the worry she felt as the possibility that she might truly be in labor settled in.

He looked down at her in confusion and then cast a worried glance in his brother's direction as they ascended the wide porch steps. "Are you sure she didn't hit her head on the steering wheel or something when the bridge dropped out from under her car?"

Garrett hesitated, glancing down at her. "I don't think so."

"I didn't," Hannah replied with a slight shake of her head.

"But you heard what she just called me, right?" the younger man insisted. "Butterfly."

"Oh, that," Garrett said as they stepped beneath the protective covering of the porch roof. "She got that from me," he explained as they crossed the porch. "I said you were a social butterfly," Garrett added in clarification and then added impatiently, "Can you get the door?"

His brother yanked the screen door open and then stepped aside, holding it in place until Garrett had her safely inside the house. Then he followed with a frown. "You couldn't have compared me to something else, like a wolf, for instance?"

Ignoring his brother's muttered complaint, Garrett carried her into one of the rooms off the entryway, where he lowered her onto a large brown overstuffed sofa. Then he kneeled to slide the rain-soaked sneakers from her feet. "Best get these wet shoes off you." He glanced back over his shoulder at his brother. "Got a thick pair of socks she could borrow?"

"Be right back," his brother said.

"I don't need…" she began, but he was already moving through the entryway in long-legged strides, his gait somewhat off.

"Yes, you do," Garrett said firmly as he set her wet shoes aside and then adjusted the bottom of the blanket to cover her stockinged feet. Then he stood and took a step back. "You can't afford to catch a chill."

Too tired to argue, she said, "No, I suppose not."

His brother hurried back into the room, a thick pair of wool socks in hand. "These might be a little big on you, but they'll be plenty warm."

She reached for them. "Thank you."

"If you haven't already figured it out," Garrett said as she removed her socks and pulled on the pair she'd been given, "this lanky cowboy beside me is my brother Jackson Wade. Jackson—" his introduction was cut off as Hannah let out a soft gasp. His worried gaze shot to her face. "Hannah?"

She sank back into the sofa, a hand pressed to her swollen belly. "It's okay," she said shakily. At least, she prayed it was.

"Another pain?" he asked with a frown.

Jackson's gaze dropped to the blanket covering the rounded swell of her stomach and his thick brows shot upward, clearly noticing her condition for the first time since she'd been carried in. "Is that… I mean is she…?"

"Pregnant?" Garrett finished for him. "Yes. And, despite her reassurance otherwise, I think she might be in labor." He looked down at her. "Hannah? Should I call 911?"

His brother's eyes snapped up, some of the color

leaving his tanned face. "Labor? As in, having her baby right now?"

Dear Lord, I hope not. Hannah shook her head, refusing to believe that was the case. "I don't think there's any need to do that. I've been under a lot of stress lately. And then getting caught up in that flood, well, I'm sure they're just false labor pains. I'm not even close to my due date yet."

Jackson looked relieved. Garrett, on the other hand, didn't appear to be as accepting of her reply.

"We should call your husband," Garrett said. "Let him know you and the baby are safe."

"I'm not married," she replied.

"I see," he said with a quick glance at her rounded abdomen.

Warmth blossomed in her cheeks. "The baby's not mine." The second the words left her mouth she realized how untrue they were. The child growing inside her womb was hers now, for as long as the good Lord willed it to be.

The two men exchanged glances. Not that she blamed them. She knew how that last statement had to sound to them.

"The baby was my sister's," she explained, tears filling her eyes. "She and her husband had tried for so long to have a child, but she could never carry to term. So, when the doctor suggested they look into finding a gestational surrogate to carry their baby for them, I knew I wanted to do this for her."

"*Was* your sister's?" Garrett replied with a gentle query.

Her hand went protectively to her stomach as she choked out the words, "Heather and Brian died three months ago in a car accident."

"Hannah," Garrett groaned. "I'm so sorry."

She brushed a stray tear from her cheek. "I'll manage."

"Alone?"

"Women raise children alone every day." She ran her hand over her stomach, a knot forming in her throat. "This child is all I have left of my sister. I'll do whatever it takes to make his life one filled with love and happiness."

"Is there someone else we could call for you?" Jackson asked.

Her gaze dropped to the floor between them. "No."

"No one?" Garrett pressed worriedly.

"It's just my father and me, and he's been really sick with a virus. Probably brought on by all the stress of dealing with my sister's recent death," she said. "It's been so very hard on him. Especially since we lost my mother a little over a year past. I won't have him worrying himself even sicker over me when I'm perfectly fine. Just carless."

Garrett nodded in understanding, yet the worried frown remained fixed on his handsome face. "We'll see what we can do in the morning about getting your car out of there."

"If it's still there," she said with a shudder.

"Either way," he agreed, "it's not going to be drivable. You'll be needing a rental car to get back to…"

"Steamboat Springs," she supplied.

"You're a ways from home," Jackson said.

Hannah felt another twinge starting. *Please, oh, please, make it stop.* "There was something I needed to do," she said, trying to keep her voice calm when she felt the panic washing over her. "If you don't mind, I'd like to freshen up a little bit." And take a moment alone to collect herself. Stress wasn't good for the baby and she'd been under so much of it. Was it any wonder she was experiencing premature labor pains?

Jackson motioned toward the doorway. "Take a left down the hall. The bathroom will be the second door on your right. In the meantime, can I offer you something to drink?"

"I think I might have a few packets of tea left in the cupboard," Jackson replied. "Can I fix you a cup of chamomile tea?"

"It would help to take the chill off," she said, another sharp pinch squeezing at her abdomen. Maybe she should ask Garrett if he could drive her to the hospital once the rain slowed, just to be sure she wasn't in true labor. "But I hate to impose on you any more than I have already."

"You're not imposing," he replied. "I like having company. I'm a social butterfly, remember?" he said with a glance in Garrett's direction, causing his brother's mouth to quirk in a barely suppressed grin. Then he turned back to Hannah. "That being the case, I just wish we had been able to meet under better circumstances."

She nodded. "Agreed." When the viselike grip took hold of her stomach, Hannah fought the urge to groan aloud. Shoving aside the blanket Garrett had lent her in the truck, she made a quick adjustment to the leather strap of her purse, securing it atop her shoulder as she pushed awkwardly to her feet.

Garrett reached out to steady her.

"Thank you."

"Do you need me to walk you down the hall?"

Shaking her head, she lifted her gaze to meet his. "There's no need. I'll be fine."

"I don't think—" he began, only to be cut off by his brother.

"Why don't we go fix that tea Hannah said she'd like to help take the chill away?"

"It doesn't take two of us to make a cup of tea," Garrett argued with a frown.

His younger brother arched a warning brow.

Reluctantly, Garrett stepped aside, watching worriedly as Hannah made her way past him and out of the room.

"I'll tell you right now," she heard him say as she walked away, "The cowboy in me doesn't like leaving her to fend for herself in her condition. Not one little bit."

Thank the Lord for cowboys. If not for men like Garrett Wade, she might have lost more than her own life. She would have lost the baby Heather had prayed so long for.

Chapter Two

Garrett glanced up from where he sat at the edge of the sofa, waiting on Hannah's return, when his brother came back into the room carrying a steaming ceramic mug.

Jackson glanced around. "Not back yet?"

"No," he muttered with a frown, his gaze moving past his brother to the entryway.

He followed the line of Garrett's gaze with a deepening frown. "Maybe you should go check on her."

He wanted to. Would feel a whole lot better if he did. But Hannah had assured him that she was fine. He had to take her word for it. "Best give her a little time," he told his brother. "She's been through quite an ordeal. I'm sure she just needs a little extra privacy to sort through all of her emotions."

"You're probably right," Jackson agreed with a nod as he placed the mug onto the coffee table and then settled into a nearby recliner.

Garrett sat staring at the paper tag that dangled over the rim of the stoneware cup as the tea steeped. Rain pinged against the windowpane as the storm continued on outside. Beside him, the clock over the fireplace mantel ticked away the minutes. Too many minutes. What if Hannah's legs had given out on her again? What if she'd fainted from all the stress she'd been under? Losing her sister and brother-in-law, suddenly finding herself in the role of mother-to-be, nearly dying in a flash flood.

"Maybe I will go check on her," he announced and was just about to shove to his feet when Hannah, face alarmingly pale, stepped into the doorway.

The sight of her wan complexion and fearful eyes had both men shooting to their feet.

"Hannah?" Garrett inquired as he moved toward her.

She looked up at him, tears in her eyes. "I think my water just broke."

It took a moment for her words to sink in. *Dear Lord.* "You think?" Maybe she was mistaken.

"I'm pretty sure it did," she said shakily.

He crossed the room to where she stood trembling. "Everything's going to be okay." He prayed he sounded more confident than he felt at that moment.

"I'll call 911," his brother said as he pulled his cell phone from his jeans pocket.

"I'll take her to the guest room," Garrett replied with a worried frown as he scooped Hannah up into his arms, using the utmost of care. Since her water had broken, he thought it best she not walk around.

She trembled against him as he carried her back down the hall to one of the guest rooms.

"I'm so sorry," she said against his shirtfront with a hiccupping sob.

"There's nothing to be sorry about," he assured her

as he lowered her quaking form onto one of the twin beds lining the walls. "Are you in pain?"

"Not at the moment," she choked out as she curled up on her side.

"But you're still having contractions?" he deduced.

"Yes," she confirmed, tears streaming down her cheeks. "And they're coming closer together."

He didn't have the means to stop, or even slow her contractions. And with her water having broken, there was no turning back. Hannah was having her baby whether she was ready for it or not. "Looks like you're about to bring that little one into the world. We'll need to start timing them."

Her hand shot out, grasping at the sleeve of his shirt. "He can't come yet. It's too soon."

"Babies come early sometimes," he said calmly when he was anything but. Still, he felt the need to say something, anything, to ease the fear he saw in those large, green eyes of hers. "They just need a little extra seeing to. As soon as the ambulance gets here…" he began, the words drifting off as her troubled gaze left his. Garrett turned to see his brother standing in the open doorway, looking nearly as pale as Hannah had only moments before.

"There's a tree down across Miller Road," his brother said evenly. "No through traffic."

"We've got chainsaws," Garrett said determinedly. "We can see to it."

"Please don't leave me," Hannah blurted out, her grasp on his shirtsleeve tightening.

Jackson stepped farther into the room, shaking his head. "We won't." He looked to his brother. "Can't actually. The tree brought several wires down with it, some of which are hot. The electric company is sending out an emergency crew. Once that's been taken care of, the tree can be safely cleared away and the ambulance can get through. Until then…" He let the words trail off.

"We're on our own," Garrett muttered in understanding.

Another gasp pushed through Hannah's pinched lips, drawing both men's gazes her way.

"Aren't you going to do something?" Jackson demanded of his brother.

Garrett forced his gaze to his brother. "Me?"

Jackson glanced over at Hannah, his expression one of concern. "You're a doctor. Help her."

"You're a doctor?" Hannah repeated, sounding so hopeful.

He shot his brother a chastising look before turning back to Hannah. "I'm a veterinarian. The only babies I have ever delivered are the four-legged kind." He glanced back over his shoulder. "Jackson, head on over to Mom and Dad's and let them know what's going on. Bring Mom back with you. If anyone knows about birthing babies, it's her." She had chosen to deliver her two youngest sons at home with only the help of Mrs. Wilton, a friend of his mother's who was a midwife.

"Garrett, I would never forgive myself if they got caught up in a flash flood on their way back here to help me."

"They'll be fine," he assured her. "Go," he said to Jackson. As soon as his brother took his leave, Garrett turned back to Hannah. "Our parents live just a short distance up the road in the direction opposite from the rising creek."

"Jackson will have Mom back here in no time. In the meantime, we'll need to give your ob-gyn a call to let him know what's going on."

"Her," she said with a soft sniffle. Releasing the hold she probably hadn't realized she still had on his sleeve, she reached into her purse to retrieve her phone. Her hands were trembling so hard, it appeared to be all Hannah could do to hold on to it as she brought up her contact list. She lifted her gaze to his. "Would you mind calling for me?"

He reached for the phone and glanced down at the names on the screen. "Dr. Farland?"

"Yes. That's her," she said.

As he made the call, Garrett prayed the Lord would continue to keep her and her unborn child safe. He had told her everything would be all right, but that decision lay in far greater hands than his own.

"Garrett?" he heard his mother call out as Jackson's front door banged open. Scurrying footsteps followed.

He looked up from where he sat in a chair next to Hannah's prone form to see his mother, followed by Jackson, spill into the room, twenty minutes after his brother had gone to get her.

Hannah, whose long, dark russet hair now hung in sweat-dampened ringlets around her face, accentuating her large, pain-filled eyes, attempted to sit up.

"Don't get up on my account," Emma Wade immediately protested with a staying hand as she crossed the room. Then, after taking a good look at the woman Garrett had rescued from near tragedy, said, "You must be Hannah."

"Yes."

"Such a pretty name." With a warm, motherly smile, she introduced herself.

Hannah nodded, unable to speak as a groan slid past her tightly compressed lips.

Garrett couldn't suppress his worried frown as he looked up at his mother. "Her pains are coming about six minutes apart."

"Then I'm here just in time to take over," his mother said, giving his arm a comforting pat.

"I'll just wait out on the front porch," Jackson said as he backed out through the open door.

Garrett started to stand, to join his brother, but Hannah latched on to his hand, her grip firm. He glanced down to find glistening, fear-filled eyes staring back at him, and he couldn't bring himself to leave her side.

"It's going to be okay," he said, giving her hand a comforting squeeze. Just then, thunder rumbled outside, rattling the windowpane and Garrett was pulled back to the past.

"I'm scared."

"You're going to be okay, Grace. I won't let anything happen to you," he promised. And then she was gone.

A firm hand came to rest on Garrett's shoulder, pulling him back to the moment. "Honey," his mother said softly beside him, "I'll see to Hannah now. Why don't you go wait with your brother and watch for the ambulance to get here? They might get the road cleared sooner than expected."

He looked to Hannah, torn between the need to stay with her and the need to distance himself from the bad he knew could happen so unexpectedly.

"It's okay," Hannah said, slowly slipping her hand

from his. "I'll be fine." She sent an appreciative smile to his mother.

If it was *okay* then why did he feel like he still needed to do more?

Before Garrett could respond, Autumn, new bride of his youngest brother, Tucker, stepped into the room. "Water is heating on the stove."

"Thank you, honey," his mother replied.

"Jackson called you and Tucker, too?" Garrett asked with a frown.

"He didn't call them," his mother replied as she returned to Garrett's side. "I did. I thought it would be good to have another woman here to help out, just in case the ambulance hasn't arrived by the time Hannah's little one is ready to make his grand entrance into the world."

"And Blue?" he asked, referring to his niece, Tucker's little girl.

"Is back at the house, coloring with her grandpa," Autumn answered.

"Hannah, honey," his mother said, "this is my daughter-in-law, Autumn."

"I'm so sorry you all had to come out on a day like this," Hannah said, tears filling her eyes. Before either Autumn or his mother could reply, she gasped, and then clutched at the mound beneath the blanket he'd covered her with while they had waited for his mother to get there. Her pretty face contorted in pain, and her breaths became panicked, coming short and fast.

His mother nudged him from the chair. "Time for you to go join your brothers out on the porch."

He nodded and stood, knowing his mother was right. He needed to leave the room, but it was killing him to do so. His gaze moved once more to Hannah and the pain he saw there grabbed at his heart. *Lord, please find it in Your heart to ease her pain.* He looked to his mother. "Call me if you need my help."

"I will," she said calmly.

"Garrett," Autumn said softly from behind him.

He turned to look at his sister-in-law.

She offered a calming smile and said in that sweet, Texas-accented voice, "Your momma and I are gonna take real good care of Hannah and her little one."

"Honey," his mother said as she settled into the chair he had just vacated, "ask Jackson if he has a hair dryer. I don't want Hannah catching a chill with her damp hair. We're going to be needing some clean towels, and something to cut and then clamp the umbilical cord with. Sterilize them with rubbing alcohol, if your brother has a bottle of it on hand. And please ask Jackson to bring us that water Tucker put on the stove to boil."

"I'll see to it," he replied, grateful to have something to do other than just stand around wondering when the ambulance was going to get there. He just prayed it would be soon.

"Thanks for calling to let me know," Garrett said, relieved to hear that Justin had been able to help his mare deliver her foal safely into the world. Now he just prayed Hannah would be able to do the same with her baby.

"Keep me updated on Miss Sanders," Justin said. "In the meantime, I'll see to it the road to the washed-out bridge is closed."

"I will," Garrett said, ending the call. Then he turned

and started back across the porch, shoving his cell back into the pocket of his jeans.

"You're going to pace a hole right through my porch floor," Jackson grumbled as Garrett passed by the rustic wooden chair in which his brother was seated.

Tucker nodded in agreement from where he sat stretched out in the matching high-back bench. "If he paces any faster, the floorboards are likely to spark into a trail of flames."

How could his brothers just sit there, sipping at their coffee and making jests as if it were just another ordinary day? It wasn't. Truth was, riding bulls and climbing atop broncs during his rodeo days had been less nerve-racking then this. "Do either of you realize how serious this situation is?" Garrett demanded as he continued pacing. "It's not time for her baby to come." He looked toward the door. "I should be in there with her."

"She's in good hands," Tucker said soberly.

"Best thing you can do for her right now is pray," Jackson suggested.

"And what if those prayers go unanswered?" he asked, as they hadn't been with Grace. "Hannah's too young to die."

"Hannah isn't going to die," Jackson said firmly. "She's young and healthy."

"She's been in labor for nearly three hours."

"Babies come out when they're good and ready," Tucker replied, "If God planned to call Hannah home, He wouldn't have seen to it that you were there to save her and the child she's carrying from those flood waters."

He prayed his brother was right. Yet, despite his brother's reassuring words, Garrett couldn't quell the restless energy that filled him. So, he continued pacing the length of the porch which ran all the way across the front of the cedar-sided ranch house.

The front screen door creaked open, bringing Garrett's steps to a halt and drawing all three men's gazes that direction. Autumn stepped out onto the porch and Garrett swallowed hard. It had only been forty-five minutes since he'd left Hannah in his mother's and Autumn's safekeeping, minutes filled with searching glances toward the distant road for an ambulance that had yet to arrive, minutes filled with anxious pacing and fervent prayers. Why wasn't his sister-in-law still inside helping his mother? Unless...

Garrett's heart thudded as he zeroed in on Autumn's face. Hannah had said herself that it was too soon for her baby to be born. Not that babies didn't arrive early all the time, but usually they were delivered in a hospital with medical equipment readily available to care for a premature baby. His fears were laid to rest the moment he realized that his sister-in-law was smiling.

"Hannah?" Garrett asked, the word coming out of a raspy croak.

"Tired, but doing well."

Jackson sat upright and pushed to his feet. "And the baby?"

"He's tiny," she said, and then seeing Garrett's worried frown, added, "but that's to be expected seeing as how he came early. And he's breathing on his own."

"Thank the Lord," all three men muttered in unison.

"No sign of the ambulance?" she asked.

"Not yet," Tucker answered with a shake of his head.

A slight frown pulled at her lips at hearing that.

"I'll call and see if I can find anything out," Jackson offered.

"That would be good," she said with a nod. Then she looked to Garrett. "Hannah's asking for you."

"She is?" he said, feeling a surge of something he couldn't explain move through him. And then, without waiting for a reply, he hurried into the house. Long strides carried him down the hallway to his brother's guest room. He needed to see for himself that Hannah was all right. That her baby was all right.

His mother looked up from where she sat watching over Hannah when he stepped into the room. "Perfect timing," she said with a smile as she rose from the chair. "I'm parched. While you sit with Hannah and her little one, I'm going to go fix Autumn and myself a cup of tea and call your father."

Garrett looked to the bed where Hannah lay, her face blessedly pain-free. She looked tired—understandably, after all she had been through—but there was a glow about her that hadn't been there before. Her long hair, now dry with the exception of a few sweat-dampened spirals, fell about her face and down over her shoulders. It was the most vibrant shade of copper-red he'd ever seen, reminding Garrett of a fall sunset. Something he hadn't picked up on in the dark of the storm.

His gaze fell to the towel-wrapped bundle Hannah held in her arms as she lay there and the tiny face peeking out of it. So very tiny.

"He doesn't bite," Hannah said with a sleepy smile as she looked down at the babe in her arms. "You can come closer."

"He's perfect," Garrett said in awe as he moved to settle into the straight-backed chair his mother had just vacated. Despite his slightly wrinkled, blotchy red skin and scrawny little limbs, her son was perfect. The baby had a dusting of strawberry blonde hair on his head and big, slate blue eyes.

"He's so small," Hannah said with a worried frown as she looked down at her son. Then her gaze lifted to meet Garrett's. "But he's here. Without you, he might have…" Tears filled her eyes. "We might have…"

"But you didn't," he said, not wanting her to dwell on what could have happened. It hadn't. "And I think the Lord played more a part in it than I did," he added with a warm smile.

"That might be the case," she agreed. "But you were the one He sent to save us. The man who risked his own life to save ours. The man who helped to calm me, finding us shelter during the storm. I can never thank you enough for what you did for us."

"Seeing that you're both all right is enough for me," he said, noting that she could barely keep her eyes open.

"I should leave you to rest," he said.

"I'm so tired," she admitted with a soft sigh.

"Then close your eyes and get some sleep," he told her.

Worry creased her brows. "I don't dare. Not while I'm holding him. He could fall from my arms if I relaxed in sleep."

"I could hold him for you," he heard himself offering before he thought things out thoroughly.

"If you don't mind," she agreed with a sleepy yawn. "I know he'll be safe with you, and I'll only close my eyes for a short while."

She was trusting the most precious thing in the

world to her into his safekeeping. Garrett's gaze came to rest on the sweet face of her newborn son. He was so small. Hardly bigger than his own outstretched hand, he thought with a surge of panic. Not that he hadn't handled other small newborns before, but those had been in the form of bunnies and puppies and kittens. *This* was a baby, and he would never have one of his own.

"Garrett?"

He looked up at Hannah. "I've never held a baby before. I'm not sure I would even know how to go about it."

"That's how I felt when your mother laid him in my arms. But it's much easier than you think," she said with a reassuring smile. "But you'll need to wash your hands first."

Of course. He knew that. He should have done so before ever coming into the room, but he'd been so eager to see for himself that Hannah and the baby were all right. "Be right back," he said, hurrying off to the washroom.

When he returned, Hannah smiled up at him. "Ready?"

"Ready."

"Okay, now hold out your arms and I'll hand him over to you."

He did as she said, feeling an overwhelming sense of awe as she settled the babe into his outstretched arms. So, this is what becoming someone's father would have felt like.

"Now bring him to your chest," Hannah coached softly. "It will help to keep him warm. Just make sure his face isn't covered. He doesn't have as much body fat on him as a full-term baby would have had."

As he settled the towel-swaddled infant against his chest, Garrett felt his heart swell.

"I'd like to name him after you," Hannah said, her eyes drifting shut.

Garrett's gaze snapped up, her words taking him by surprise.

"That is, if it's all right with you," she mumbled sleepily.

"I'd be honored," he said. Truth was he couldn't have been more honored. This child she'd given birth to was all she had left of her sister and he was going to carry Garrett's first name. And it wasn't as if he'd ever have children of his own to pass his name down to. His heart had died with Grace that day, along with his dreams of having a family of his own.

"What's your middle name?"

"Austin," he replied, his attention centered on the tiny face before him.

"Garrett Austin," Hannah said with a sigh. Her soft, even breathing told him she had finally fallen into an exhausted slumber.

Garrett looked down at the precious bundle he held in his arms and smiled. "Welcome to the world, Garrett Austin Sanders."

He sat holding the infant for nearly half an hour, his mother and Autumn popping in and out to check on Hannah who was still sound asleep. Both had offered to take the baby, but he'd refused to part with the sleeping infant. While holding something so small—a living, breathing little something—terrified him, Hannah had entrusted him with her baby's safekeeping. He would keep her son cradled in his arms until she awakened.

That determined thought had no sooner passed

through his mind when the sound of the baby's breathing changed. Not significantly. If he hadn't been holding the bundled infant against his chest, he might not have even noticed. But it had definitely quickened, the urgent little breaths enough to stir unease in his gut.

He crossed the room and stepped out into the hallway. "Mom," he called out softly, not wanting to startle the baby.

A second later, she was in the hall, moving toward him. "Honey? Is something wrong?"

"I'm not sure," he answered with a worried frown as he looked down at the baby. "His breathing seems a little off. I wanted to see what you thought before overreacting." Preemies might have issues with underdeveloped lungs, but that wasn't always the case.

Concern lit her features as she leaned in to check on Hannah's son. That concern remained as she lifted her gaze back up to his. "His coloring doesn't look good. We need to get him some immediate medical care."

Care that Garrett couldn't provide. "Take the baby and have Autumn get Hannah ready to leave." He started for the front door.

"What are you going to do?" she called after him.

"Whatever it takes," he answered as he let himself outside.

Minutes later, Hannah was lying across the backseat of his truck, her newborn son held securely in her arms as they drove across the range, along the fence line that ran parallel to the temporarily impassable road. He hated that they didn't have a car seat for her son, but there was no time to wait for the ambulance to be able to get through. Jackson and Tucker had gone on ahead of them to take down a section of the fence for them to drive through in order to safely access the road beyond the downed wires.

"Garrett," Hannah said, "I'm scared."

That made two of them, but he wasn't going to tell her that. "We'll be at the hospital before you know it. Tucker's calling to let them know we're on our way." He followed his words of assurance up with a silent prayer. One for the baby and one for himself, because he was going to have to step through those dreaded hospital doors.

They were met by hospital personnel with a wheelchair for Hannah at the emergency room pull up. Her son, now laboring for breath, was quickly whisked away ahead of them. Hannah looked up at him, tears in her eyes.

He squeezed her hand reassuringly. "It's going to be all right."

As soon as she was settled, the hospital attendant wheeled her in through the automatic sliding doors.

Garrett, heart pounding, nausea roiling in his stomach, stood staring at those same doors as they slid shut behind the departing wheelchair. Hannah needed him. But so had Grace. *Please, Lord, let us have gotten here in time.*

Gathering his courage, more courage than he'd ever needed back when he was riding bulls and broncs professionally, Garrett followed them inside.

Chapter Three

Fighting a yawn, Garrett pulled out his cell phone to check the time—9:37 a.m. He wondered if Hannah had awakened yet. The previous day's events had clearly left her spent, and understandably so. And what about her son? Lord, he prayed the infant that he'd held in his arms shortly after his birth was faring well. The emergency room personnel had taken him straight to the neonatal intensive care unit as soon as they'd arrived at the hospital and he hadn't gotten to see the baby again before he'd left to head home.

Hannah hadn't been the only one under emotional stress when they'd arrived at the hospital the day before. Garrett hadn't stepped foot inside the place since the day Grace had taken her last breath there. Truth was, he dreaded ever having to return there again, but none of that had mattered when Hannah's son's life was at stake.

Once Hannah had been examined, she'd been placed in a private room just down the hall from the NICU. Garrett had then done his best to calm her fears, pushing his own aside. Despite the doctor's reassurance that it was common for a baby born five weeks earlier than expected to need a little help breathing, that his lungs would strengthen in the days and weeks ahead, she'd been beside herself. So much so, that Garrett had ended up staying by Hannah's bedside until late into the night, talking to her about anything and everything to keep her mind from going into the dark places he knew all too well. Places he'd gone to when Grace had taken a turn for the worse, with all the whys and what-ifs.

Exhaustion threatened to drag him down. He had remained seated at Hannah's bedside the night before until sleep had finally claimed her. And that hadn't been until well after midnight.

"Morning," Garrett muttered as he stopped by the corral on his way to the barn.

"Morning," Tucker replied. His brother stood in the center of the corral, working with a green mare they'd purchased to use as a saddle horse. Breaking in horses was one of his brother's specialties. "Didn't expect you in this early. Not after the late night you put in."

Garrett raised a brow. "How did you know about that?" He'd been in touch with his family from the hospital to update them, but he hadn't called anyone when he'd finally headed home. It had been too late.

"Couldn't sleep," his brother admitted. "I was sitting on the porch when you drove past. How was Hannah doing when you left?"

"As well as can be expected, under the circumstances." Garrett glanced around, seeing their other brother's truck parked beside the far end of the barn. "Where's Jackson?"

"In the barn," Tucker replied, his gaze remaining

fixed on the young mare. "Just got back from running feed out to the veteran horses."

Unlike a lot of rodeo stock companies that unloaded their retired stock once the animals' profitability was gone, the Triple W Rodeo Ranch kept theirs. They had a special section of land fenced off specifically for the older horses where they could live out the remainder of their lives in leisure, being grain-fed daily. They had worked hard during their rodeo years. In his opinion and his brothers', they deserved no less.

Garrett nodded, not that his brother had seen him do so. Tucker's visual focus remained solely on the mare he was coaxing to pick up her pace as she ran around the outer edge of the fenced-in enclosure.

Shoving his phone back into his jeans, he leaned against the fence, watching his little brother at work.

"Didn't expect to see you here this morning." Jackson's familiar voice came from behind him.

Garrett glanced back over his shoulder to see his brother striding toward them. "Why wouldn't I be here?"

"You having had such a late night and all," his brother prompted.

Garrett's gaze shifted back to Tucker.

His youngest brother must have felt his accusing stare, because there was no way Tucker could have seen it with his back to them the way it was. Yet he called back over his shoulder, "I might have mentioned to Jackson that there was a good chance you'd be hitting Snooze on your alarm clock today."

"Well, I didn't," he said in irritation. At thirty-four he could still manage a late night here and there and still get up in time to help his brothers with ranch duties. How was he supposed to sleep in, anyhow, with thoughts of Hannah and her son weighing so heavily on his mind? "I have blood draws to do today."

Every six months, they needed to draw blood from the rodeo stock to keep their health certificates up-to-date. Otherwise, they wouldn't be able to transport the broncs from state to state to the various rodeos. Having an in-house vet on the ranch also saved them money.

Jackson lifted a brow. "Someone's a little on the touchy side this morning."

"Maybe a little," he grumbled. "Lack of sleep, and then receiving some bad news, has a tendency to bring that about."

Jackson's head snapped around. "Hannah?"

He shook his head. "No. She and the baby are okay. Or, at least, they were when I left the hospital last night. The bad news is business related."

That grabbed both of his brothers' attention.

"Kade called this morning," he explained. "He had to put Little Thunder down last night." Kade Owens owned the Breakaway Ranch in Oklahoma where, along with raising beef cattle, he bred and raised bucking bulls. Little Thunder was one of Kade's top, prize-winning bulls. The Triple W had partnered up with Kade a few years back to allow them, as a joint partnership, to qualify for a PRCA stock contractor card, which required the stock provider to own a minimum of twenty-five bareback horses, twenty-five saddle bronc horses and twenty-five bulls.

"What happened?" Tucker asked.

"Thrombosis of the inferior vena cava."

"Which is what?"

"A liver abscess," Garrett explained, "which led to a serious infection near the heart."

Jackson shook his head. "A real shame. He's been a good bull. Hopefully, The Duke and Wise Guy will come into their own this year."

"They showed promise last season, so maybe this will be their year," Garrett acknowledged with a nod, recalling the two newest additions to Kade's rodeo bull lineup. "At least, Kade still has some top contenders that rank right up there with Little Thunder for the upcoming season." Their first scheduled rodeo fell during the second week of June. Without having promising stock to offer for rodeo competition, contractors risked losing out on future contracts. That's why they made sure their stock stayed strong and healthy, sending the best they had to offer out to the various rodeos.

"True," Jackson agreed with a nod as they watched Tucker move in slow, fluid circles from where he stood in the center of the corral, following the movement of the mare as it made its way in larger circles around him.

Garrett slid his cell phone from his jeans pocket once again. A quick glance told him there were still no messages from Hannah or the hospital. That had to be a good thing. At least, he prayed it was. If something had happened, surely someone would have contacted him. Hannah had placed his name on the very limited visitor's list, along with his cell phone number.

"You don't need to be here, you know," his brother said, his tone no longer teasing. "Tucker and I can handle things here if you want to go to the hospital to check on Hannah and the baby."

"You and Tucker can't see to the blood draws," Garrett pointed out. "Besides, it's not my place to be there with her," he muttered, despite the pull he felt. The last thing he wanted to do was force himself in her life.

"You're right," Tucker agreed as he turned, following the horse's path. "Best you stay here and be useless, because your focus is anywhere but on what you're supposed to be doing this morning."

"And I'm sure Hannah prefers to be alone in that big old hospital with no one to turn to if she starts feeling overwhelmed with everything," Jackson tossed out. "And with her baby being in neonatal ICU, you can pretty much bet she's at least a little fearful—"

"Point made," Garrett grumbled. If he wasn't already worried about Hannah, he would be hard-pressed not to be after his brothers' guilt-inducing comments. But she'd refused to let him call her father the night before. She'd said she'd needed a little time to let everything sink in, and that even if her father had wanted to come to the hospital to be with them he couldn't. Not while he was sick.

"Someone should be there for her."

"I could go after I'm done here," Tucker volunteered as he relaxed his posture, signaling for the horse circling about him to slow down. "Seeing as how you're digging in your heels at the thought of doing it. I could pick up Autumn on the way. I'm sure she'd like to know how Hannah's doing, her having helped with her baby's birth and all."

Garrett shot his youngest brother an incredulous look. "Appears I'm not the only one lacking focus today. Yours is supposed to be on that horse right now, not on other people's conversations."

Tucker chuckled. "What can I say? The good Lord

blessed me with the ability to be a successful multi-tasker."

"He is, at that," Jackson agreed. "Listen, I'm almost done here. Why don't I run over to the hospital and sit with Hannah for a few hours, seeing as how you and Tucker are going to have your hands full for a while with breaking horses and performing vet duties?"

His brother's suggestion immediately had Garrett rethinking his decision to put off going to the hospital until after he'd done blood draws. There was no reason he couldn't finish them up on the remaining horses later that day, or even tomorrow, for that matter.

"I rescued Hannah and her baby from that rising creek," he said determinedly. "That makes them my responsibility. So, if anyone's going to the hospital to sit with her, it's going to be me. I can see to the blood work later."

Jackson's mouth tugged up at one side, displaying the lone dimple all three brothers had inherited from their father. "Far be it from us to try and usurp your *responsibility*, big brother." He started for the barn, calling back over his shoulder, "Tell Hannah she's in my thoughts."

"Give her my regards as well," Tucker called out as he turned, gaze fixed on the young mare he was working with as he queued her to speed up.

With only a wave of acknowledgment, Garrett walked away. He would go to the hospital, but he was only going to stay long enough to make certain Hannah and the baby were doing all right. He didn't want to feel as if he needed to be there with Hannah and her son. Didn't want to care more than he already did in the brief time since he'd come across Hannah's partially submerged car at the washed-out bridge. Because other than the love he held for his family, he preferred not to care with any real depth for anyone else ever again.

He had just reached his truck when his mother called out to him from the chicken coop, "Garrett!"

Turning, he started toward her, meeting her halfway. "I was just—"

"Heading to the hospital," she finished for him as she switched the basket of eggs she'd collected to the crook of her other arm.

"How did you know?" he asked in surprise.

"Because I know you, and you're not the type of man to leave something unfinished."

He looked at her questioningly.

His mother tilted her head to look up at him, the morning sun glinting off her smiling face. "You're the reason Hannah and her son are alive today, with the good Lord's guiding hand, of course," she was quick to add.

"He's not her son," he said. "She was carrying that little boy for her sister who died in a car accident a few months ago."

"I know," she said, her eyes filled with compassion. "Jackson explained things to me when he called for us to come over and help with the baby's birth. And then Hannah filled in the rest when Autumn and I were helping to deliver her baby. Such a heartbreaking way to become someone's mother. And that's what she is now—that boy's mother. Something Hannah might not have even had the chance to experience if you hadn't come along when you did."

He nodded in agreement.

"That being the case," his mother went on, "it only

stands to reason that you would feel the need to look in on them today and for however long they'll be in the hospital. The three of you will forever share a very special connection."

"What if I'd rather not feel any sort of connection to them?" he muttered with a frown.

His mother's expression softened even more. "Honey, I know you'd rather live your life free of any sort of emotional entanglements, but they're a part of life. No matter how large or how small, they help to shape the man you are and the man you will become."

He was content with the man he was now. He had a good life. A supportive family. A successful veterinary business. Part ownership of a thriving rodeo stock company. He didn't need shaping, and he certainly didn't want entanglements of any sort.

"Your needs aside," she said in that motherly tone he knew so well, "you and I both know there are still going to be some hard days ahead for Hannah. Not only with her own physical and emotional recovery, but with the baby's health as well."

"Garrett Austin," he said, recalling Hannah's words the afternoon prior.

His mother looked up at him in confusion. "What?"

"Hannah asked if I would mind if she named her son after me."

His mother's eyes teared up. "What a truly touching thing for her to do."

Ignoring the lump that formed in his throat, Garrett muttered, "I just hope Hannah doesn't regret that decision down the road."

"Whatever makes you think she'll regret it?"

"Because she's been through so much," he explained. "Losing her mother, and then her sister and brother-in-law so close together. Then having to come to terms with the knowledge that she's going to be the one raising her sister's son. And if that wasn't enough for one person to shoulder, she got caught up in a flash flood while in labor. She might have second thoughts on a name she chose when her emotions were so taxed."

His mother nodded. "It's true. That poor dear has had more than her share of tough times. But she's here, her son's here, because of your selfless actions yesterday. You and I both know how easily that ground along the side of the creek could have given way while you sought to rescue Hannah from her car. Garrett, you took such a risk to save them."

He could hear the worry in her voice. "But it didn't. Although I admit I did a fair amount of praying yesterday." The second he'd realized someone was trapped inside that partially submerged car, he knew he would have done whatever he could to help. "From the moment Hannah looked up at me through the driver's side window, her eyes wide with fear, I knew I couldn't—*wouldn't*—let her die. Not like I had Grace."

"Oh, honey," his mother said, her eyes now filled with unshed tears, "your love kept Grace with us longer than she might have been without it. I truly believe that in my heart. But it was her time to go. Just as it's time for you to let go of the guilt you've held on to for so long. Guilt that's not yours to harbor."

His mother became a hazy blur in front of him as moisture gathered in Garrett's eyes. "I don't know if I can."

She reached out and placed a gentle hand atop his forearm. "You'll never know unless you try. And I will say that if Hannah chooses to honor your act of self-lessness by naming her son after you, accept it graciously. That little boy couldn't be named after a finer young man."

Garrett cleared the emotion from his throat. "I am the man I am today because of you and Dad." Leaning forward, he kissed his mother's cheek. "Love you."

"Love you, too."

He drew back. "Don't hold supper on my account if I'm not back in time. I'm not sure how long I'll be staying at the hospital." If Hannah was having a day even half as emotionally trying as the one before, then he would stay and do whatever he could to lift her spirits. Because, like his brother had pointed out, she was all alone.

His mother looked up at him with a tender smile. "Please let Hannah know she and the baby are in our prayers. And, if she needs a place to stay until she's recovered enough to go home, she's more than welcome to stay here at the ranch."

"I'll be sure to let her know," he said and then started back toward his truck.

"Garrett…"

He stopped, casting a glance back at his mother.

"If things get too hard for you, being there at the hospital and all, call me. I'll come relieve you and keep Hannah company."

"I'll be fine," he said determinedly. Because this time it wasn't about him. It was about Hannah and what she needed. That meant pushing past his own emotional hang-ups and proving that he was the man his daddy had raised him to be. With a wave, he strode off, thoughts of Hannah and her precious son front and foremost in his mind.

* * *

Hannah paused in the doorway of the hospital's neonatal intensive care unit to cast one more glance back at the incubator that held her sister's precious little son. No, she had to think of him as *her* son now. But guilt kept her from accepting it fully. Austin, as she was calling the child, was Heather's. It didn't seem right claiming him as her own, especially after reminding herself throughout the entire pregnancy that the baby she carried inside her wasn't hers. But her sister and Brian were gone, and their son needed, at the very least, to have a mother in his life. And truth was she needed him, too. So very much.

If not for Garrett Wade, she and Austin would have become yet another flood statistic. Brushing a tear from her cheek, she sent a silent prayer of thanks heavenward. The Lord had sent her a real-life hero if ever there was one. He had come to her rescue not once, not twice, but three times.

First, when he'd pulled her car from the rushing floodwaters and got her to safety. Then when he'd brought his mother and sister-in-law in to help with her baby's untimely arrival during the storm. And then afterward, when the ambulance couldn't get through because the main road remained cut off and the baby had begun having problems breathing. Garrett had gotten them to the hospital—to the medical care her son desperately needed.

"I thought you were supposed to be resting."

As if he'd stepped right out of her thoughts, Hannah turned to find Garrett standing in the hospital corridor, a worried frown on his handsome face. She managed a small smile, even though her heart wasn't in it.

His brow creased as his gaze lit on her face. "Hannah?" Looking past her, he said, the words strained, "The baby?"

"He's holding his own," she answered.

With her reassurance, his focus returned to her. "Thank the Lord."

"I was just going back to my room," she said, feeling drained.

"I'll walk you there."

"Thank you."

Garrett stepped around to place a supportive arm around her waist as he accompanied her. "How are you feeling?"

"I've been better."

He nodded in understanding. "Should you be up moving about on your own?"

"They encourage it," she replied as they made their way down the corridor.

Garrett, bless his heart, didn't look happy about it, but kept his thoughts to himself. "Can I get you anything?" he asked as they turned into her room. "A glass of water? Crackers?"

"No, thank you." She wasn't certain she'd be able to keep anything down.

He turned his back to her as she settled herself into the hospital bed and drew up the covers.

"You can turn around now," she told him.

He did and then stood there looking anything but comfortable.

"You don't have to stay."

He shook his head. "I want to. That is, if you want me to stay."

"I…" The tears she'd been holding back spilled down her cheeks.

"Don't cry," he said with a groan. "I don't have to stay. I probably shouldn't have come." He started for the door.

"Please don't go," she said with a hiccupping sob, futilely trying to brush the tears from her cheeks.

Garrett stopped and then turned, hesitating for a moment before finally making his way over to stand next to her hospital bed. He looked unsure of what to do. Like he wanted to be anywhere else but there, and she couldn't really blame him.

"They're sending me home tomorrow," she explained between tearful gasps.

He exhaled in relief, the worry leaving his face. "So those are happy tears. For a minute there, I thought…" His words trailed off as she began sobbing again. "Hannah?"

"Garrett, I don't have a home to go to," she said. "Not here, anyway."

"Yes, you do," he told her. "Mom wanted me to tell you that you're welcome to stay with them until you're feeling up to traveling back to Colorado."

"That's so kind of her," she said, her voice cracking with emotion. "But how can I even think about leaving Austin? That's what I'm going to call him, even though his given name will be Garrett Austin Sanders."

"I like it," he told her. "But then I'm a bit partial to the first two names, having had it myself for the past thirty-four years. And, just to be clear, the invitation from my mom was for the both of you. She's raised three sons of her own. She'll be more than happy to help you with the baby."

"That's just it," she said with a sob. "They want to

send me home without him. Because he came early, he's not ready to leave the hospital yet."

"Then you should stay here with him."

"I already asked, but there aren't enough available beds for me to continue staying on here." She looked up, meeting his gaze, her heart breaking. "Garrett, I can't leave my baby here all alone. Not while he's hooked up to all those machines."

He placed his hand over hers, giving it a comforting squeeze. "He's in good hands, Hannah. You need to focus on that. Did they say how long until he can go home?"

She shook her head. "It's too soon to know, but it could be weeks."

"Whatever it takes to get your son strong enough to come home to you," he told her, his determined words touching Hannah deeply. "In the meantime, I'll bring you to the hospital anytime you want and pick you up whenever you're ready to come home. I'll even stay when I can."

"Garrett, I can't ask that of you," she said, shaking her head in refusal.

"You didn't," he said with a warm smile. "I offered."

"But your job…"

"Isn't going to be an issue," he assured her. "Most of my income comes from my share of the rodeo stock contracting business I co-own with my brothers, and we aren't into the start of the rodeo season yet, so there is no issue there. As for my being a vet, I work mostly with our horses, but make a few large animal calls here and there. We have another vet in town who can cover for me if the situation arises."

Her fingers curled around his hand. "You are such a

good man, Garrett Wade. I'm so thankful God brought you into my life." She thought about the precious little boy she'd given birth to and added with a teary smile, "Our lives."

Before he could respond, her cell phone, which was lying atop the wheeled side table, rang out. With his free hand, his other still held in Hannah's determined grasp, Garrett reached for the phone and handed it over to her.

"It's my father," she said with a worried frown. "What do I tell him?"

"Probably best to start with the truth," he answered. "He's bound to pick up on your emotional state and will worry more if he thinks you're keeping something from him."

She nodded. Garrett was right. She needed to tell her father what had happened. Bringing the phone to her ear, she answered, "Hi, Dad."

Garrett mouthed, "I'll step out and give you some privacy."

She shook her head, praying he would stay. His being there gave her comfort and helped to calm her fears.

Thankfully, Garrett nodded, falling silent as she took the call.

"Hi, Dad."

"Hi, honey," her father replied and then paused to cough, the sound clearly coming from deep in his chest.

She gasped. "Dad, you sound terrible. Have you seen your doctor yet?"

"Not yet," he admitted. "I was hoping the cough would start to ease up now that the cold's finally out of my head, but it hasn't. I'm going to call Dr. Mason today."

"I'm glad." She had enough worries on her plate without adding her father's ailing health to them.

"I wasn't calling to talk about me. I was worried about you," he said. "I thought you were supposed to get home last night, but when I woke up this morning and realized you hadn't made it home… Well, all sorts of things went through my mind."

"I'm sorry to have caused you worry, Dad," she said. "I never meant to. I really thought I'd be home last night."

"It's all right, honey. All that matters is that you're all right," he said, unable to keep the emotion from his voice. "I know how hard it had to be for you to take your sister's and Brian's ashes to Shoshone Falls. I wish you would have let me ride along with you."

Having lost both his wife and his daughter in just over a year's time, the task of delivering Heather's ashes to a place that was very special to her would have been unbearably hard on him. Especially with him not feeling up to par. "You weren't feeling well, and taking Heather and Brian's ashes to the falls was really something I needed to do on my own." In truth, the long drive had given her time to reflect, to mourn, to start to plan her future. One that now included raising a child.

"I understand," he said. "When do you think you'll get here?"

"About that…" she began.

"Hannah," he said worriedly. "What's wrong?" The question was followed by another round of coughing.

This was something she would rather have told her

father in person, so he could see that she and the baby were all right. But that wasn't an option. Not with her son needing to remain in NICU for an undetermined amount of time. "I'm in the hospital."

"Dear Lord," he groaned.

"I'm fine, Dad," she hurried to assure him. "But I was in labor when Garrett rescued me."

"Rescued?" her father gasped between coughs.

Hannah cringed. Why had she even brought that part up? Her father hadn't needed to know about that. "Dad? Are you okay?"

"I've been better," he rasped out as his coughing subsided. "Hannah, what happened? Where are you?"

She went on to explain everything that had happened in a shortened version and with far less detail to spare her father any further stress.

"Well, thank the good Lord for sending that young man there. I couldn't bear to lose you, too."

"You won't."

"How is the baby?" he asked hesitantly, as if fearing what her answer might be. "I know my grandson wasn't due to arrive for another month or so."

"Apparently, your grandson was tired of waiting. Garrett Austin came into the world wailing loudly." And he had, but that was before her son's breathing issues began.

"You named him after the man who rescued you from the flood," he acknowledged, his words filled with emotion.

"Yes," she answered. "If not for Garrett, we wouldn't be here today." She felt Garrett tense up beside her. Her praise might embarrass him, but it was true all the same. "Your grandson is small, and in need of a little extra care, but he's going to be fine," she said determinedly. He had to be. Like her father, she didn't think she could bear the loss of yet another person she held dear.

"That explains why you didn't call."

"I was waiting to talk to the doctor this morning before I called you. He came by a little while ago to tell me that they're releasing me tomorrow, but Austin has to remain in the neonatal intensive care unit until he's strong enough to go home. Do you mind watching the boys until I can get home?"

"You don't even have to ask," he answered with a wheeze. "But I'd prefer to be there with you and the baby."

Her frown deepened. "Dad, listen to you. You sound awful. As much as I would love to have you here with us, I have to ask you not to come. It's too risky for the baby. And if I get sick, I won't be able to be around him either."

"Ah, honey, I understand. I just hate the thought of the two of you being there all alone."

She looked up at Garrett and managed a small smile. "We won't be alone. We have Garrett and his family here to watch over us. Mrs. Wade has even offered her home to me during my stay here. So, please, go call your doctor and get yourself well, so you can love up your grandson when the time comes for me to bring him home."

"I will," he said with a resigned sigh. "Make sure you keep me updated with how things are going. You and my grandson are all I have left in this world, and as soon as the doctor considers me well enough to be around the two of you, and I can find someone to watch over the dogs, I'll be there."

"You're all we have," she replied. "So please take care of yourself."

"You can count on it. And tell that young man who rescued you that I look forward to meeting him someday soon. I want to thank him in person for what he's done for you and my grandson."

"I'll let him know. I love you, Dad."

"I love you, too, honey."

Hannah hung up and looked to Garrett. "He sounds awful."

"A cold?" Garrett surmised.

"Yes," she said with a worried frown. "It's pretty deep in his chest, but he assured me he's going to get in to see his doctor."

"Then you need to set that worry aside and focus on getting your strength back, and on that little one of yours, so we can get him home with his big brothers as soon as possible."

"Brothers?" she repeated in confusion.

He looked chagrined. "I wasn't trying to listen in, but I heard you ask your father if he'd mind watching over your boys for a little while longer. I know how hard being away from your boys for any length of time is going to be for you."

She smiled. "Oh, it will be."

He studied her, as if trying to find the humor in the situation. "I'm sure Mom wouldn't have a problem with them coming here to stay with you until you can go back to Steamboat Springs. Unless they're in school. I have no idea how old your boys are."

"Garrett, you're sweet to think of my boys, but you

should know that Buddy and Bandit already graduated from school."

His chestnut brows lifted.

"Puppy school," she added with a grin. "They're my two-year-old golden retrievers."

He let out a husky chuckle. "You had me worried for a moment. I was wondering what mother would ever think to name her son Bandit."

"He likes to take things and hide them," she explained, the temporary redirection of her thoughts to something other than the seriousness going on in her life helped to lighten her heavy heart. Hannah sighed. "I'm really going to miss having those two underfoot."

Garrett squeezed her hand. "It won't be for long. We'll have you home with all three of your *boys* before you know it."

The conviction in his words made her believe that no matter what the coming weeks brought about everything would be okay. Garrett would make certain of that. Hannah sent up a silent prayer of thanks to the Lord for sending her this unexpected pillar of strength in the form of this kind, lone-dimpled cowboy.

Chapter Four

Garrett glanced again at the clock on the kitchen wall. It was five minutes past the last time he'd looked. It had been five minutes the time before that. He should have taken his mother up on her offer to pick Hannah up from the hospital that morning and bring her home. He hadn't. And, for the life of him, he couldn't say why.

Every trip he made to that place stirred up memories. At first, they were of Grace and those final days he'd had her in his life. But then other memories took over. Memories of the storm. Of Hannah's pretty, fear-stricken face looking up at him from where she sat trapped in her car. Of the trust he'd seen in her eyes when he'd told her she was going to be all right. Of her brave smile.

Frowning, Garrett shook his head and crossed the room to grab his cowboy hat from the end table, settling it onto his head. Guilt pricked at his conscience. How could he allow his memories of the only woman he'd ever loved—girl, actually, because that's what Grace had been when she'd died—to be so easily set aside?

Not that he hadn't gone out a time or two during his

rodeo days. But he'd done so, knowing those women were more interested in snagging themselves a professional rodeo rider than in dating the man he was inside. They'd been safe, because he knew feelings would never come into play. When he would tell them he wasn't interested in starting a real relationship, they would simply move on to another. But Hannah, in what little time he had known her, had made him feel so many things—fear at the thought of her or the baby she'd been carrying dying, determination to save her like he hadn't been able to with Grace, the need to protect her and admiration for the strength he saw inside of her.

His cell phone rang, pulling Garrett from his troubled thoughts. He hurried to dig it out of his jeans pocket, praying, as he did every time his phone rang, that it wasn't the hospital calling to say he needed to get there right away. Only in Grace's case, it had been her father who had made the call, telling Garrett to get to the hospital right away. His trepidation eased when he saw the caller ID on the screen.

"Justin."

"Garrett," his friend said in greeting.

"How's the new foal getting along?" Thankfully, it had survived what sounded like a rough delivery. One Justin had tended to on his own, thanks to the poorly-timed storm.

"Couldn't be better," the sheriff replied. "The reason I was calling was to let you know where Miss Sanders's car was towed to, and to let you know that they found a small overnight bag in the backseat. I picked it up and was going to run it over to her, but I wasn't sure if she was still in the hospital, or if she had already been released. I know they don't keep anyone in for long these days."

"I was just about to leave for the hospital. Hannah's being released today. Are you at the office?"

"For another hour or so."

"I'll swing by and pick the bag up on my way to the hospital. Hannah might want to wear something else to come home in." At least, this way she would have a choice. His mother had taken the clothes Hannah wore the day before when she'd gone to visit her and the baby at the hospital and had washed them for her so she would have something clean to wear when she was released. They were already in his truck, all neatly folded inside of a canvas tote.

"How's the baby?"

"Unfortunately, he's not able to come home yet," Garrett replied with a frown, hating that Hannah had to be separated from her son. "But it won't be long. She'll be staying at my parents' place until her son is able to travel back to Colorado with her."

"I didn't realize she was so far from home," Justin said. "I need to fill out a report, but I can do that once she gets settled in at the ranch. In the meantime, I'll be sure to keep her and the baby in my prayers."

"I'm sure Hannah would appreciate that. See you soon." After hanging up the phone, Garrett grabbed his truck keys and headed out.

He stopped in the building he'd constructed next to his house that served as both a clinic and supply storage to double-check his schedule before setting out. Thankfully, he only had a few appointments scheduled for the next week or so, vaccination updates and such, since he'd be making a fair number of trips to the hospital with Hannah to see her son.

Her son. That tiny little blessing Garrett had held in his arms; perhaps he would have had his own son if Grace had lived to give him the family they'd talked about having someday. Who would have thought a baby could have such a pull on a man's heart? But Hannah's son had done just that.

Lord, please keep that precious little baby safe, he prayed and then headed for his truck.

Fifteen minutes later, Garrett pulled into a parking space outside of the sheriff's office. He stepped from his truck just as the building's front door swung open and Justin, dressed in his uniform, came out to greet him, a quilted floral travel bag held in one hand.

"Cute bag," Garrett remarked with a grin, as he moved toward his friend. "The pink roses go remarkably well with your uniform."

Justin held it up, turning it to and fro. "Thanks. I thought so, too." He handed the bag over to Garrett, and then extended his hand, giving Garrett's a firm shake. "How are you holding up?"

"Me?"

Justin nodded. "You. It's no secret that you've had an eventful few days. Flood rescue, baby delivery and then personally taking on the responsibility of looking in on Miss Sanders and her little boy."

"I see you've been talking to Jackson," Garrett said.

"Your father, actually," the sheriff admitted. "I ran into him this morning at Abby's. He snagged the last crème-filled donut, leaving me with the remaining selection of cake donuts."

"Not surprised," Garrett replied with a chuckle. All the Wade men had a sweet tooth.

"He was on his way out, so we didn't have much of a chance to talk, but he did tell me that you were spending a lot of time at the hospital with Miss Sanders." His expression sobered somewhat. "I know that can't be easy for you."

He nodded. As Jackson's best friend, Justin had been around when Grace took ill. He knew what Garrett had been through. "It hasn't," he answered honestly. "But Hannah's father is sick and can't be here with her."

"What about her mother?"

"Passed away. And then her sister died a few months ago. And being miles from home doesn't make things any easier."

Justin's teasing grin flattened. "And now she's going through all this." He shook his head. "The Lord knew what He was doing when He placed her in your family's lives."

Before Garrett could reply, one of the deputies came out to let Justin know that his sister was on the line and that she sounded upset. Excusing himself, he immediately went to take the call.

Garrett understood the look of concern he'd seen on his friend's face as he'd strode off. A little over a year earlier, Lainie, Justin's little sister, lost her husband when a drunk driver struck their car. She and her seven-year-old son had remained in Sacramento, despite the urgings of Justin and his parents for her to move back home.

Though he'd never made mention of his suspicions to anyone, Garrett thought that at least part of the reason Lainie hadn't come home was because of Jackson. While she and Jackson never dated, there had been a time when Garrett thought his younger brother might have feelings for Lainie and her for him. But then Jackson went off to ride in the rodeo and Lainie headed to college, finding love elsewhere. Now, with no husband to take care of her and her son, Justin was determined to be there for them. Just as Garrett would be there for Hannah and hers. For now.

"Morning," the two nurses on duty in the NICU said in quiet greeting when Hannah stepped into the room.

"Morning," she replied, keeping her voice low as well. Only Austin and one other newborn, a little girl born two months too soon, were being cared for in the neonatal intensive care unit at that time. Seeing that fragile little girl, so much smaller than her own son, made Hannah want to cry. Life could be so unfair sometimes.

She had taken only two steps across the room, in the direction of the incubator that held her newborn son, when she noticed an odd glow filling Austin's temporary crib. A sense of unease filled her as she hurried over to it. Inside, her son, dressed in only a diaper, his eyes covered with a small white mask, was bathed in the glow of a deep blue light.

With a worried gasp, Hannah pressed a hand to the clear side of the incubator.

"It's called a bili light," a soft voice from behind her stated.

Hannah glanced back to find the younger of the two NICU nurses, Jessica, if she remembered correctly, standing there, an empathetic smile on her face. "What is a bili light?" she asked anxiously, her attention returning to her son.

"A type of phototherapy used when a newborn is jaundiced," she explained.

"Why is he jaundiced?" Hannah asked, her panic growing. Why hadn't she read up on more than just what could happen during pregnancy? Maybe because what happened after were the things her sister should have known about. Not her. And when Heather and Brian had died, her focus had been on getting through the grief.

"Jaundice occurs when a baby's blood has more bilirubin than it can get rid of," the young nurse said calmly.

"Is it serious?" Hannah asked, her heart pounding.

"It can be," she answered honestly. "But not in most cases. This type of jaundice is quite common in newborns because their organs aren't able to get rid of the excess bilirubin very well, giving them a tinge of yellow to their skin coloring and to the whites of their eyes. The lights you see above your son are able to pass through an infant's skin and break down the bilirubin into a form that the baby can eliminate. That's why we have him lying there in only his diaper. To expose as much of his skin as possible."

"How long will he have to be under these lights?" Hannah asked, trying not to let her fear show.

"Typically, twenty-four to forty-eight hours. At that point, the newborn's liver can usually handle the bilirubin itself."

"And if it can't?" she heard herself asking, unsure if she really wanted to know the answer.

"Depending on the severity of the jaundice, the infant could require a blood transfusion. Sometimes, they just need more time under the lights and plenty of hydration." She moved to stand next to Hannah. "But your little one's case isn't severe. So try not to worry."

If only it were that easy, she thought with a frown. "I'm his mother," Hannah said, still mentally trying to come to terms with that fact. "It's my job to worry over him. Wouldn't you if you had a child hooked up to all these wires and tubes, and now *this*?"

Jessica nodded. "I would, and I did."

"You did?" Hannah repeated.

"I know firsthand what you're going through," the young nurse answered, her gaze settling on Hannah's son. "My son was born six weeks early. There were complications with my delivery and I nearly lost Dustin. But my son is a fighter, thank the Lord, and stubbornly clung to life while being hooked up to all of these tubes and wires. Just as your son is now," she noted. "He struggled to breathe. His body couldn't regulate its temperature. Like Austin, he was jaundiced and had to lay for days under the bili lights." She looked to Hannah. "Today my son is a healthy, happy seven-year-old."

"Thank you for sharing that with me," Hannah said with a grateful smile. Knowing that Jessica had gone through what she was going through now, and that her son had grown into a healthy little boy, helped to calm her fears.

"I wanted you to know that I truly do understand what you're going through right now, beyond the knowledge I've gained as a medical professional. In fact, my son is the reason I decided to get my GED and then pursue a degree in nursing, my focus on neonatal care."

That meant Jessica hadn't graduated from high school. She had to assume it was because of the baby, because she didn't look to be much more than twenty-five and she'd said that her little boy was seven. It was so hard to think of children having children, but Jessica had made something of her life for the sake of her son. Her story was a reminder to Hannah that she wasn't alone when it came to surviving life's hardships.

"I'm so glad things turned out the way they did for you," Hannah said with a soft smile.

"If they hadn't, I would have spent the rest of my life blaming myself for it," Jessica admitted as she reached into the incubator to check Austin's vitals. "When I found out I was expecting, I spent months in denial when I should have been having prenatal visits and taking vitamins, and putting my baby's needs first."

"You were young," Hannah said sympathetically.

"I'm twenty-seven, and discovering that I was going to be someone's mother was more than a little overwhelming for me. It's something you know is destined to change your life forever."

Jessica nodded in agreement as she adjusted the position of Hannah's sleeping son. "More than I ever imagined. However, I wasn't as blessed as you. Dustin's father wanted nothing to do with us, unlike your son's."

Her son's father? She had to be referring to Garrett. There had been no one else there for her. The memory of seeing Austin cradled ever so tenderly in those big, strong arms came rushing back. Watching the cowboy's worried expression fade away, to be replaced by one of awe and wonder, had touched her deeply.

"Garrett isn't Austin's father," Hannah explained, and then added sadly, "His father is dead. He and my sister, Heather—Austin's biological parents—were killed in a car accident a few months ago. I had offered to be a surrogate mother for them, because Heather couldn't carry a baby to term."

Jessica's expression changed instantly. "I'm so sorry. I just assumed…"

"Please, don't apologize," Hannah said. "I can see where you might have gotten that impression, seeing as how Garrett brought me to the hospital and has been here with me every day since I was admitted. But he and I only met a few days ago."

Surprise flashed across Jessica's face.

Hannah went on, "Garrett rescued me from a flash flood I got caught up in while driving through Bent Creek, after which I went into full labor. If not for him, my son and I might not be here today."

"That had to be so frightening," Jessica said, a hand pressed to her chest. "I'm so glad he was able to reach you in time."

"My prayers were definitely answered that day," she said.

"Morning," the other nurse said from a small desk near the doorway.

"Good morning," a familiar male voice replied, immediately drawing Hannah's gaze.

With a warm smile aimed in her direction, Garrett crossed the room to where Hannah stood with Jessica.

"Morning," Hannah greeted, surprised by how happy she was to see him. Maybe it was seeing a somewhat familiar face when she was feeling so alone. All she knew was that Garrett's presence seemed to wrap around her like a security blanket, instantly soothing some of her growing fears. Realizing she was still staring up at him, she turned her attention back to her son, who looked so incredibly small and fragile inside the lamp-lit glass enclosure.

"I need to go update your son's records," Jessica told her. "I'll be back in a little bit to look in on him."

Garrett moved to stand beside her when Jessica walked away. "How are you holding up?"

"Not well, I'm afraid," she admitted, wrapping her arms about herself. "I don't know how I'm supposed to leave him."

"I know it won't be easy," he said, his tone filled with compassion, "but he's got to stay here and grow strong. You'll see him every day until he's ready to come home with you."

She nodded. "I know." But the thought of leaving Austin tore at her heart.

"We don't have to leave just yet," he told her. "I don't have anything I need to be doing today."

Hannah fought the sudden sting of unshed tears. "If it's all right with you, I'd like to stay for a little while longer. Austin's had a setback."

With a worried frown, Garrett looked down into the incubator. "What's happened?"

"He's jaundiced," she answered. "That's why they have him under these special lights."

He gave a nod of understanding. "It's not uncommon for a newborn, especially one that was born prematurely, to have issues with jaundice."

Hannah sniffled softly, fighting to hold back the tears. "A mother is supposed to be able to make everything all right. Because that's what I am now, aren't I?

His mother? But my son is so tiny and helpless, and there's nothing I can do to help him."

His hand moved to wrap around hers. "You are his mother, Hannah. And you need to stay strong for him. Don't let your fears push your faith aside. Trust in the Lord to heal Austin and give him the strength he needs."

"I'm trying, Garrett," she said with a soft sob, clinging tightly to the hand holding hers, as if doing so would help give her the strength she would need to get through this. "But sometimes it gets so overwhelming, and I feel so alone."

"I know," he said, giving her hand a sympathetic squeeze. "But you're not alone, Hannah. You have me, and you have my family here to support you while you are going through this. We'll weather this rough patch together. I promise."

She was not alone. Garrett hadn't abandoned her. A woman he didn't even know, had no obligation to. No, he'd come back to check on them. Offering her comfort and support. He was a good man. The kind a woman dreamed of coming into her life someday. Only, her life was far too complicated now, and that "someday" had been pushed aside by the need to focus solely on the baby she would be raising on her own.

When Garrett's hand left hers, Hannah found herself wishing he hadn't pulled away. His gentle touch was comforting, giving her a strength she couldn't seem to find on her own right now.

"Have you eaten?" he asked.

"They brought a breakfast tray to my room this morning."

"But did you eat?" he pressed.

Hannah shook her head. "No. I wasn't hungry."

"I figured as much," he replied. "Hannah, you need to eat to keep your strength up, or you won't be any good to your son. Tell you what, how about you and I take a walk down to the cafeteria?"

"He's right," Jessica said, joining them once more alongside the incubator. Reaching inside, she shifted Austin slightly. "You need to keep your strength up. Trust me, I know. Go on and get yourself something to eat. I'll be here to watch over your son for you."

She had no doubt that her son would be in capable hands, but it was still hard to walk away. But Garrett and Jessica were right. She needed to keep up her strength. For Austin's sake, if not her own. "Thank you," Hannah said. "We won't be long."

"We'll be here," Jessica replied with a smile as she cast a glance toward Hannah's son.

Garrett escorted Hannah from the room, a supportive hand placed at the small of her back as they made their way down the corridor. "Should I get you a wheelchair? It's a bit of a walk to the hospital's cafeteria."

She glanced over at him with a grateful smile. "I don't think that will be necessary. As I said yesterday, they prefer me to be up and moving about. Even if a bit more slowly than my normal pace."

"I'm sorry," he replied with a frown. "I do remember you mentioning that. Truth is, I don't have much experience with this kind of thing. There's a big difference between a horse and you giving birth."

Much to her surprise, a soft giggle pushed past her lips. "I would hope so."

Color flooded his tanned cheeks. "That didn't exactly come out the way I meant it to. What I was trying to say was—"

"You don't need to explain yourself," Hannah said, cutting him off. "This is all new to me, too."

They stopped at the elevator doors and Garrett reached out to push the down button. "Fortunately, my mother has a lot of experience with having babies. She'll be able to help you navigate this new part of your life. Even Autumn will be able to answer a lot of your questions. She helped with the raising of Blue for most of her young life."

The elevator doors slid open and they stepped inside. "Blue?"

"My niece," he answered as the doors closed. He jabbed at the floor button that would take them to the cafeteria. "Tucker eloped with Autumn's sister back when he was riding the rodeo circuit. But they were young, and things didn't work out the way he thought they would. In fact, Summer walked out on him without even a note of explanation, and it wasn't until just recently that he learned of his daughter's existence, when Autumn came to tell him of her sister's passing. Blue's five now."

"She kept his daughter from him all those years?" she said, her heart going out to Garrett's brother.

"Summer had her reasons for doing what she did," he said. "Not that I agree with them, but then, I didn't grow up in a broken family the way she had. My brothers and I were raised with the love of both parents, who are still happily married today."

"I can't even imagine what it would have been like to grow up without two loving parents." Like her son would have to do, she thought sadly. But she would do everything in her power to make certain he always felt loved. Something else struck her at that moment. Looking to Garrett, she said, "So your brother married his wife's sister?"

"Her twin sister," he answered as the elevator arrived at their floor. "While they grew up together down in Braxton, Texas, Autumn and Summer are, or I suppose that should be *were*, two very different personalities. Autumn is a better fit for the man my brother has grown into. And she loves his daughter, her niece, as if Blue were her very own."

Just as I will love my nephew, Hannah thought to herself. He would never doubt her. She'd make certain of that.

Garrett's worried gaze slid over to Hannah who was seated in the passenger seat of his truck. "You doing okay?"

She hesitated before nodding her reply. "A little tired. That's all."

"I think that's to be expected," he assured her, his attention returning to the road ahead. "You've been through a lot these past few days. And hospital beds aren't known for inducing the most restful night's sleep."

"To be honest, I am looking forward to spending the night in a real bed again," Hannah said, looking out the passenger side window. "I just wish…"

"That Austin were here with you," Garrett finished for her, his tone gentle.

"Yes," she replied with a heart-wrenching sigh.

"It won't be long," he said. "And I'll take you back to see your son after supper." The hospital was in the next town over, so the drive wasn't overly long. Twenty-five minutes at the most.

"I've taken you away from your responsibilities enough for one day," she said, looking his way.

"Right now, you're my responsibility," he said, wondering the second the words left his mouth where they had come from. While he had every intention of helping Hannah out while she was there, a position he had set his mind never to put himself in again after losing Grace, he would do so without any sort of emotional commitment. Cut and dry was how he preferred things when it came to his emotions. It was safer that way.

"As soon as I can arrange it, I'm going to have a rental car delivered. That will allow me to travel to and from the hospital without having to impose on you or your family."

A frown tugged at his mouth. "Are you sure that's a good idea? Driving so soon after giving birth? I know I'm a vet, but I would think your body would need a little healing time before doing so." Steering a car used abdominal muscles which had to be weakened from carrying a baby. Not to mention all the physical strain a body went through giving birth.

Her lips pressed together.

"Hannah?"

"It might be a little sooner than the doctor suggested," she confessed, avoiding his gaze.

"I thought as much," he replied with a sigh. "Look, I know you don't want to have to depend on others to help you with things you've always been able to do on your own. But this isn't a normal situation. Your car was totaled in a flood. You went into labor sooner than expected. Your son requires additional medical care.

Your father is sick and unable to help you out right now. Let my family help you through this. Let *me* help you."

Garrett couldn't take the words back. He wanted to help Hannah. It was the Christian thing to do. And there was no risk of getting emotionally caught up in the situation as he had with Grace. His heart would have to do more than beat for that to happen, but the organ had been numb for pretty much half his life.

"You're a stubborn man, Garrett Wade," Hannah told him with a small smile.

"Determined," he countered with a grin.

She sighed softly. "I suppose there will be plenty of time to practice being self-sufficient once Austin and I go home. And you needn't worry about us financially. My insurance will cover most of our care, and, besides the money I have put away in my savings, we have the life insurance Heather and Brian left to me, along with the sale of their house."

"What if your insurance doesn't cover Austin's care?" he asked.

"It will," she assured him. "With no surrogacy contract between my sister and her husband and myself, something we felt no need to have, and with their passing, I can legally claim him as my own."

"And what about your sister's husband's family? Do you think they'll try and fight you on this?"

She shook her head. "Brian didn't have the best home life growing up and hadn't been in contact with his family since leaving home at seventeen. Heather and Brian had made their wishes clear to me, that if anything were ever to happen to them they wanted me to take over the raising of their child, or children, if the Lord saw fit to bless them with more than one."

"You might not need help financially, but you might find yourself in need of other forms of assistance while you're here. So, until you're able to go home to Colorado, consider yourself tucked securely beneath the Wade family wing."

Moisture filled her eyes. "Thank you."

He looked away, not wanting to see the tears pooling in her eyes. Hannah's tears had a way of getting to him, making him feel things he'd just as soon not feel. Like connected and vulnerable and protective, all at the same time. "You're welcome."

Silence fell between them for several minutes. Hannah's attention was fixed on the land that stretched out around them. His family's land. While Garrett struggled to focus on anything but the woman beside him. He'd never felt so distracted.

"That's my place," he announced as they drove past the barn-style ranch house that sat off in the distance. "The smaller building next to the house is my vet clinic, not that it gets used too often. Most of my work is done on-site, rather than having my customers transport their cows and horses."

"I love how the house, barn and your vet building are all the same shade of red trimmed in white."

"Chili pepper," he said. "At least, that's what the builder said the shade was called when I chose it from the color strips he gave me to look over. The white was listed as marshmallow. Not sure when paint selections became centered around food, but I'd rather go back to having it referred to as just plain red or basic white. No way was I going to tell my brothers I had decided to trim my house in marshmallow. Takes the cowboy right out of a man."

Hannah laughed, the sound beyond sweet to Garrett's ears. "I think you still have plenty of cowboy left in you."

He chuckled. "Appreciate that. Sorry to have rambled on about house paint of all things. I'm not the best conversationalist. Truth is, most of my time is spent with animals."

Her sweet smile widened. "I think you converse quite well. And I'm grateful for any conversation that helps keep my thoughts from straying to things I have no control over."

He was glad to hear her say that. He'd been trying to do just that, knowing how upset she'd been when they'd left the hospital that afternoon. After another mile or so, Garrett pointed off to the side. "That's Tucker's place." A one-story log house with a sprawling cottonwood shading a section of the front yard. Garrett smiled as his gaze passed over the swing he and Jackson had hung from one of the thick cottonwood branches when Blue had first come to Bent Creek. Their niece had spent countless hours on that swing, much to Tucker and Autumn's dismay, as they'd been the ones who'd had to stand there, pushing her for hours on end.

"Jackson's place, which I took you to during the storm, is a few miles down the road, just before the bridge. Or, at least, what used to be the bridge," he corrected.

"Do many people use that bridge?" Hannah asked.

"A few, but it's mostly my family, since the road cuts through our ranch," he told her. "We've all built our homes along this road."

"I'm sorry you lost your quickest access to town."

He shrugged. "Not a big deal. The bridge has been washed out a couple of times before. We're used to it. We'll just have to allow ourselves extra time to get to town, since we'll have to take the long way in until they get a new bridge up in its place."

"It's nice that you all live close by each other," Hannah said with a sad smile. "Heather and Brian lived on the outskirts of Steamboat Springs, so we were able to see each other often. I'm thankful now for the time we were able to spend together."

"I never really gave it any thought," he admitted. "It's all I've ever known, where they're concerned. We grew up together, rode in the rodeo together, at least for a while, work together, and live on the same stretch of land. I suppose we just take being together for granted." Something he should have known better than to do. Mari, his baby sister, had been taken from them far too soon after she'd contracted meningitis. Only six years old. And then his high school sweetheart, who had been on the verge of adulthood. Even Summer had died far too young.

"Life has no guarantees," Hannah said with a frown.

Garrett nodded solemnly. "That I know."

"You've lost someone close to you?"

His gaze pinned to the road, he replied, "Haven't we all?" Needing to redirect their conversation to something that touched less upon his own painful past, he nodded in the direction they were traveling. "The Triple W is about a half mile down the road."

"The Triple W?"

"The Triple W Rodeo Ranch," he clarified. "It's the property my brothers and I grew up on. My parents still live there, while my brothers and I have built our own houses elsewhere. The main ranch is where we keep the livestock trailers, supplies for the rodeo as well as feed and medical supplies. It has the largest barn and several smaller areas of fenced-off land that allow us to keep the horses we will be taking to upcoming rodeos in a more contained area. Saves us from chasing them all over creation."

She looked to him questioningly. "Shouldn't that be the Four W Rodeo Ranch? You, your brothers and your father."

If he and his brothers had gotten their way, it would have been. But their father preferred to remain in the background, helping when needed, but not actually being a part of their growing business.

"When Dad retired from the rodeo, he spent years building this place into one of the most respected horse ranches around. People knew they could be assured of purchasing quality horses from the Big W Horse Ranch. So, by the time the three of us boys were grown and done riding the rodeo circuit, he was more than ready to take a step back from the business, turning everything over to us. We began taking in, as well as breeding our own, horses for rodeo competition."

"I never really gave any thought to where rodeos get their livestock from," she said. "I've never even been to one."

"You haven't?" he said in surprise. It was hard to remember that going to rodeos wasn't just the norm for some families. But it was all he had known.

Hannah shook her head. "No. I was more the stay-at-home, bookworm type."

He took a moment to study her before glancing back at the road. "Bookworm type, huh? Not sure I see it."

She arched a questioning brow. "Why is that? Because I'm not holding a book?"

He shrugged. "Maybe because you were traveling all alone, even when you were so far along in your pregnancy. Throw in your braving a raging flood, and I see you much more as an adventurer."

Her smile withered away, making Garrett wonder what he'd said wrong. "I didn't set out seeking adventure. I drove to Shoshone Falls in Idaho to spread my sister's and her husband's ashes in a place that held special meaning for them. And I was only alone because Dad was feeling under the weather. Not that I minded making the drive by myself. It gave me time to work on coming to terms with things."

"I'm sorry you had to do that," he said regretfully, wishing he hadn't taken the conversation in that direction. No matter how unintentional it had been.

"It was hard," she admitted. "But doing that for my sister gave me a sense of peace that I had been struggling to find. Partly because I was seeing my sister's wishes carried through, but some of that peace came from the untouched beauty of mountains and prairies that surrounded me during my drive to Shoshone Falls." She glanced around. "I would imagine that living here, surrounded by such a picturesque view of nature, offers the same kind of inner peace."

He'd never thought of it that way, but after Grace had died he'd spent hours each day riding across the ranch, stopping at times to just sit and take in the view. He hadn't thought so at the time, because the pain had been too great, but looking back he supposed he had found some sort of solace back then as he'd sat looking out over God's land.

"It does," he answered with a nod as he turned into the drive leading up to his parents' house.

Garrett's mother stepped out onto the porch, waving as she welcomed them home. Autumn followed, smiling warmly, and Blue came hurrying out behind them, her long, chestnut curls bouncing wildly around her tiny shoulders.

"Looks like you have a 'welcome home' committee awaiting you," he said, casting a look in Hannah's direction. "Should I apologize now? My family can be somewhat overwhelming at times."

Her expression softened, and tears immediately filled her eyes.

"Hannah?" Garrett said worriedly.

"That's so kind of them," she said with a sniffle.

Relief swept through him with her response. She wasn't upset. She was touched. "Prepare to be smothered by kindness," he warned with a grin as he came to a stop in the drive.

Chapter Five

"Hello," Hannah said, feeling slightly anxious as she and Garrett stepped up onto his mother's porch, the overnight bag he'd managed to salvage from her flood-totaled car clutched in his large, sun-browned hand.

"Welcome to our home," his mother greeted with a warm smile.

"Thank you for having me," she replied.

"Don't be too grateful," Garrett said with a charming grin. "She might never let you leave. Mom loves to coddle people."

Garrett's sister-in-law, Autumn, laughed. "He's right. In fact, her homemade cookies, of which I've eaten plenty of since coming here, are one of the reasons I stayed."

"Me, too!" the little girl Hannah presumed to be Tucker's daughter chimed in.

"Tucker and my granddaughter being the biggest reasons Autumn decided to stick around," his mother said with a knowing smile.

Blue nodded. "Daddy, too. He loves Grandma's cookies."

They all laughed.

"I meant that your aunt Autumn stayed not only because of my cookies, but because she fell in love with your daddy."

The little girl's head swung around, her gaze lifting to Hannah's face. "If Grandma gives you cookies, will you fall in love with my uncle Garrett? He has to live in his house all by himself."

Hannah tried not to smile overly big at his niece's innocent query. It was clear she loved her uncle and worried about him being lonely. Before she could respond, Garrett answered for her.

"Cookies can't make two people fall in love," he gently explained.

"I beg to differ," his mother replied. "My oatmeal raisin cookies won your father's heart over."

Blue giggled.

"You had his heart from the first day he met you," Garrett promptly reminded her.

"I had his attention," his mother corrected. "But it was my oatmeal raisin cookies that convinced your father that his heart was indeed on the right track."

"I can see that there is no use trying to set Blue straight on her cookies-and-love misconception." He turned to his niece. "Miss Sanders will be going back to where her family lives in Steamboat Springs when her baby is big enough to travel. So, cookies or not, she isn't going to be sticking around for long." He turned to Hannah. "If you haven't guessed already, this adorable little chatterbox is my niece, Blue Belle Wade."

"What a pretty name," Hannah said.

"My mommy named me after a flower," Blue, the spitting image of her father with her chestnut-colored hair and lone dimple that dipped into her cheek whenever she smiled, announced with a measure of pride.

"Her very favorite flower," Autumn added with a pained smile.

Hannah understood what Autumn was feeling. They had both lost sisters that they loved dearly. They were each now responsible for the raising of their niece and nephew. At least Autumn had a husband to turn to for support.

"Let's not keep you standing out here on the porch," Emma Wade said, her short, auburn curls dancing atop her shoulders as she leaned forward to open the screen door. "Come on inside."

They all moved into the house with Blue in the lead.

Hannah glanced around, finding Garrett's parents' place to be warm and welcoming. From the pictures displayed on the walls to the crocheted throws draped over the sofa and recliner. The staircase wall had been stenciled in large black script that read Family, Faith & Love. Exactly what she would have expected from the people who had raised a man as kind and caring as Garrett.

"I wasn't sure if you would have anything to wear other than the clothes you had on when Garrett found you," Autumn said, "so I brought a few of my things for you to make use of while you are here, or until you have a chance to pick something up that suits your taste better."

Hannah was beyond touched by the gesture. "That was so kind of you, Autumn. I only had one change of clothes with me when I drove to Idaho, because I was only planning on being away for a night. So, thank you for thinking of me."

"How could I not?" she said with a warm smile. "I helped deliver your son. I can't help but feel as though we will always have a special bond."

It was true. While her own sister hadn't been able to be with her for Austin's arrival into the world, she had been blessed to have two wonderful women at her side. "I agree. I am so thankful that you and Mrs. Wade were able to be there."

"You and me both," Garrett chimed in with a grin as he removed his cowboy hat. "Barn deliveries are more my specialty."

Everyone laughed, Hannah included. Some of her sadness and fear from that morning eased with their lightheartedness.

"Let's get you settled," Emma said with a smile. "The clothes Autumn brought for you are in a bag on the bed. Come on, I'll show you to where you'll be sleeping during your stay here. It's Garrett's old room."

"I wanna show her!" Blue exclaimed as she raced to the staircase and bounced excitedly up the steps.

"Walk," Autumn called after Blue.

Garrett turned to Hannah. "I'll run your bag up, and then I'll head out to the barn while you ladies proceed with your tour."

"Your brothers have everything under control," his mother assured him. "Stay and help Hannah up the stairs, just in case she's a bit unsteady. Once we've shown her around up there, we'll go down to the kitchen and have a piece of peach pie." She smiled knowingly at her son. "I just pulled it out of the oven before you got here."

"I had intended to give Hannah a chance to settle in and get to know you and Autumn a little better without me around," he admitted. "But how could any man turn down peach pie fresh out of the oven?"

"Your brother wouldn't," Autumn said with a smile. "That's for sure."

"You don't have to worry yourself over me," Hannah protested, not wanting Garrett to change his plans again because of her. But inside she was thankful to have him there. She liked spending time with Garrett. Liked the low, soothing tone of his voice. The kindness in his smile.

He shook his head. "Can't be helped. And Mom's right. You've just had a baby. Best to take things slow. That being said, why don't we see how you handle the stairs before you try and tackle them on your own?"

She relented with a sigh, admitting, if only to herself, that she did seem to tire more easily since having her son. She supposed her body did require a little more time to recover from all the changes that it had gone through.

Placing a supportive hand at Hannah's back, Garrett escorted her up the steps behind his mother.

Autumn took up the rear.

Hannah looked up at Garrett with a grateful smile and nearly missed a step in her distraction.

"I've got you," he said, wrapping a supporting arm around her back.

She found herself leaning into his strength when what she should be doing was insisting she do this on her own. Because that's how things were going to be once she and Austin went back to Colorado. Her father had already raised his family, and he wouldn't ask him to help her raise another. Not that he wouldn't do plenty of doting on his grandson; of that, she was certain, just as Garrett was determined to dote on her. Truth be told, it was nice having someone look after her the way he had been since coming to her rescue.

"This is the bathroom," Garrett's mother said, pausing to point it out to Hannah. "The linen closet with fresh towels and washrags is right there." She motioned toward a tall, narrow, oak cabinet door next to the bathroom's entrance.

Hannah nodded and then followed them into what Emma announced was to be her guest room during her stay there. Three walls were beige with the remaining one behind the bed done in a navy and beige plaid wallpaper. The bag Autumn had left for her sat atop the bedspread, which matched the wallpaper almost exactly. The only difference was that the quilt was edged in beige with embroidered miniature cowboy boots with spurs, and a lone boot inside a circle of beige embellished each of the two pillow shams. The bedside lamp was an antiqued bronze statue of a cowboy atop a bucking horse. A smile moved across Hannah's face as she turned to face Garrett.

"Your room is so cute."

"Let it be known that my room was not *cute* when I lived here," he said defensively. "This was all done *after* I moved out."

"I confess," his mother said. "I redid all of the boys' rooms after they moved out with things that reminded me of my sons."

"You should have seen Tucker's reaction when he saw his momma's most recent makeover to his old room," Autumn said, laughing softly.

"It's a princess room!" Blue declared, her face beaming with delight.

His mother nodded. "We added a frilly pink bed-spread to Tucker's old bed, and then hung shimmery pink netting over it. But there are still reminders of Tucker in there. A wall displaying some of his rodeo pictures and ribbons, and a few framed newspaper clippings."

"Which go perfectly with the miniature crystal chandelier you switched the overhead light out for," Autumn teased with a smile.

The corner of Garrett's mouth hitched upward. "I forgot about all of that. I guess little boots aren't so bad after all."

Hannah laughed. And then she thanked the Lord for bringing the Wades into her life. Their kindness, and their humor, would undoubtedly see her through the emotional days ahead. But she was most thankful for Garrett and the happiness he stirred in her heart—one that had suffered so much hurt in recent years—whenever she was with him.

The next morning, Hannah walked into the kitchen. Emma glanced back from where she stood at the sink, washing dishes. "Good morning, dear."

"Good morning, Mrs. Wade," Hannah replied as she stepped into the room, and then catching sight of Garrett's father seated at the breakfast table, added, "Morning."

"Hannah," he greeted with a warm smile, and then stood, placing his cowboy hat atop his graying head. He walked over to plant a quick kiss on Emma's cheek. "I'll be out in the barn. Give a holler when you're ready to leave for church." With a tip of his hat to Hannah, he strode from the room.

"Emma," Garrett's mother said, drawing Hannah's attention back in her direction. "No more 'Mrs. Wade.' I've already told you there's no need for formalities here. How did you sleep last night?"

Hannah had mentioned at dinner the night before that she hoped she would be able to sleep that night, because her troubled thoughts had kept her tossing and turning until the wee hours of the morning the night before. Garrett's mother had then fixed her a cup of chamomile tea right before she turned in for the night, and it seemed to have helped. "I slept much better. Thank you again for the tea."

"You're quite welcome. I'm glad it helped." She motioned toward the kitchen table. "Have a seat. The tea water is still warm. I'll fix you a cup. Unless you'd prefer coffee instead."

"Tea is fine." She'd never acquired a liking for coffee, which she had tried a few times during her college years.

"Sugar or honey?"

"Honey."

With a nod, Garrett's mother set to making her a cup of tea. "How are you doing?"

"I'm getting my strength back," Hannah told her.

Emma looked to Hannah, a soft smile on her face. "I meant emotionally. I know you try and put up a strong front around us, but I also know how hard it is for a mother to be separated from her child."

Hannah recalled the conversation she'd had with Garrett on their way to the ranch. "I'm sure you were worried sick when Jackson was injured so badly."

"I was," she agreed. "But I was referring to a more permanent separation. My boys had a little sister," she explained. "Her name was Mari and she was the light of our lives. But the good Lord called her home when she was only six years old. Meningitis," she said, a slight catch in her voice.

"I'm so sorry," Hannah said, her eyes filling with tears. Life was so unpredictable. Even those far too young to die did, leaving behind so much pain and sorrow. How had Emma gotten through the loss of a child, of all things? Austin had only been in her life for a few short days and Hannah knew she would be lost without him.

Garrett's mother set the cup of tea she had prepared for Hannah onto the table in front of her and then placed a comforting hand over hers. "Oh, sweetie. I didn't tell you this to make you sad. I told you because I wanted you to know that I understand how you feel, and that I am here for you if you ever need to talk."

She was so much like her own mother, Hannah thought longingly. So open and caring. Oh, how she missed her mother. "Thank you for sharing what has to be such a heartbreaking part of your life with me. I don't know what I would do if…" She let the words trail off, too afraid to speak them.

"Austin is going to grow into a big, strong young man. Just like my sons," she told her. "Have faith, sweetie."

"I'm trying," she replied with a tired sigh.

"I know you're still recovering from having given birth to that precious little boy of yours, but, if you feel up to it, Grady and I would love to have you join us for Sunday services this morning."

Church. How had she forgotten that it was Sunday?

"We'll be leaving for church at nine o'clock," Emma

continued, "so you have a little over an hour to get ready if you decide to go. The boys and Autumn and Blue will all be there."

Hannah knew that despite the painful losses she had suffered in the past couple of years, she had a lot to give thanks for, and even more to pray for. She didn't understand the Lord's reasons for taking her mother the way He had, and then, so soon after, her sister and Brian. Those losses had shaken her faith, had pushed her into a place of despair and sometimes resentment toward Him. But she had found herself turning to Him during the storm, and God had listened to her prayers, sending Garrett to her rescue. And He had allowed Austin to be safely delivered, even if he wasn't physically ready to face that world yet. And He had brought Garrett into her life and allowed him to remain. If only for a very short while. It was time to make her peace with the Lord and ask for His continuing grace where her newborn son was concerned.

"As soon as I finish my tea, I'll go upstairs and get ready. Thank you for inviting me."

Emma smiled. "Tea alone is not going to help you keep your strength up. You need to eat. I made blueberry waffles for breakfast. It will only take me a second to warm some up for you if you'd like."

Hannah felt an instantaneous pull of grief and looked away, trying to quell the emotion.

"If you don't care for blueberries..." Garrett's mother began, misreading Hannah's response.

"It's not that," she replied, shaking her head. "I love blueberries. My mother used to make Heather and me blueberry pancakes every Sunday morning before we left for church when we were growing up."

The older woman's face filled with worry. "Oh, honey, I'm so sorry. I never meant to stir up sad memories for you. Let's forget the blueberries, even the waffles. I could fry you up a couple of eggs instead. They're fresh from the henhouse."

Hannah shook her head. "There's no need. Waffles will be fine." Emma looked as if she wasn't sure, so Hannah added, "I promise. If I were to avoid all the things that brought back memories of my mom and my sister, I would find myself living in a colorless world." She smiled up at Garrett's mother. "And I would be very, very hungry."

"Your words couldn't be more true," Garrett's mother said, a touch of melancholy filling her eyes. "Especially, the part about living in a colorless world. I've found that memories, both good and bad, tend to be tightly knitted together. If one attempts to tug an unwanted strand free, they risk causing some of the good strands to fall away as well. Therefore, we must learn to live with all the memories of the moments our lives have been made of and trust in God to give us the strength to continue on."

Emma understood the pain of loss. She had lost a daughter. Eyes stinging, Hannah nodded, unable to speak as she fought to hold back the tears that filled her eyes.

"Oh, honey," Emma said, moving to wrap her arms around Hannah in a warm, motherly hug. "Don't cry. You'll get me going, too."

"I'm sorry," Hannah said with a muffled sob. "I'm just feeling a little melancholy this morning."

"What can I do to help lighten your heart?" she asked as she stepped away.

Hannah brushed a single tear from her cheek. "Just having someone to really talk to helps more than you could ever know. I tend to avoid sharing my feelings with my father because he's already struggling to deal with his own emotions. But I miss him. And I really, really miss Mom and Heather."

"Of course, you do," Emma said with an empathetic smile. "There's no need for you to ever apologize for what you're feeling." She hesitated for a moment, before adding, "Hannah, I know that no one can ever replace your mother, but I would like to be there for you while you're here. Any questions you might have about being a new mother, or if you just need to talk, know that you can always come to me."

Her words touched Hannah's heart. "Thank you, Emma," she said with a soft sniffle. "Thank you for everything."

"No," she said. "Thank you. From the bottom of my heart. If you hadn't come into our lives the way you did, I don't know if Garrett would have ever forced himself to face his past and step into that hospital that day. But he did, and that's a step toward healing. I pray that my son will finally begin to move on with his life."

"Mom?" a male voice, one deliberately hushed, called out.

"In here," she called back with a smile.

A second later, Garrett stepped into the kitchen, his attention fixed on his mother who was standing directly across from him. "I know I said I'd meet you at church, but…" His gaze slid in Hannah's direction and a smile formed across his tanned face. "You're awake?"

"I am," she said, pushing her own troubles aside as she returned his smile. *I pray that my son will finally begin to move on with his life.* What had happened in Garrett's life that he needed healing from? Not that his past was any of her business, but she knew what it felt like to bottle up the pain. She hated to think that Garrett's big, beautiful grin masked some sort of long-withheld emotional suffering.

"I'm warming her up a couple of my homemade blueberry waffles, and then Hannah and I are going to go get ready for church. Have you eaten?" she asked him.

"I've had two cups of coffee," he answered.

"So now I have to worry about both you *and* Hannah keeping your strength up?" she said, shaking her head. "Grab some silverware and a couple of napkins for you and Hannah while I fix you both a plate."

He did as she asked and then slid the items, including a bottle of spring water, in front of Hannah as he took the empty seat beside her. "I know you have tea, but I thought you might like some water as well."

She smiled up at him. "Thank you." Her thoughts grabbed on to what his mother had said about having to worry about him keeping his strength up. Did that mean there was no one special in his life to watch over him? How that was even remotely possible was beyond her. Garrett was caring and kind. And so very handsome, she thought, feeling warmth blossom in her cheeks.

His mother turned from the stove where she had warmed several waffles in the microwave just above it, and carried two plates of blueberry waffles over to the table and set them down in front of them. "Toppings are right there." She pointed to the ceramic butter dish and bottle of maple syrup that sat against the wall at the edge of the table.

"They smell delicious," Hannah said as the aroma of warm blueberries drifted upward.

"Believe me," Garrett said, cutting into one of his waffles, "they are."

Emma smiled at his response and then looked to Hannah. "I'm going to go start getting ready for church. I'm so glad you've decided to join us for this morning's services. Now, if there's anything else you need, I'm quite sure Garrett knows where to find it."

When his mother had gone, Garrett turned to Hannah. "So, you're joining us for church this morning."

"Your mother asked, and I told her I would go," she answered with a nod.

Garrett's gaze shifted to the plate in front of him as he sank the side of his fork into a syrup-covered chunk of waffle. "Are you sure you're up for it?"

Hannah said, "If you'd rather I not go, I could stay here and take a leisurely walk. I've been wanting to see more of the ranch anyhow." The last thing she wanted to do was be the cause of his having to revisit something that had caused him emotional pain in his past.

He paused between chews to look at her. Then he swallowed the bite he had taken before saying, "Why would you think I wouldn't want you to go?"

She couldn't really explain her reason, so she settled for another truth. "You've been forced to spend hours on end with me since coming to my rescue. It only stands to reason that you might prefer to spend some time alone with your family for a change."

He lowered his fork as he looked her way. "Hannah, no one is forcing me to do anything. I spend hours with you because…" He paused, as if trying to figure out the reason for himself.

"Because you're a good Christian," she finished for him, something she found both admirable and attractive. "And it's the Christian thing to do."

"Well, I like to think I'm a good Christian, and that I'd help anyone in need. But that's not the only reason." He let his gaze drop back down to his plate. "I'm doing it because I enjoy spending time with you."

She laughed softly, but inside butterflies were fluttering about in her stomach. She felt the same way about him. "You enjoy having your work schedule all thrown off, spending long hours at the hospital and my using your shoulder to shed my tears on?" Because she had done that more than once while they were there together at the hospital.

"The answer to your question is yes," he told her as he pushed away from the table and stood. He walked over to the refrigerator and grabbed a water bottle from the top shelf.

"Why would anyone—"

"Because it feels good to be needed again," he said, closing the refrigerator door. He stood with his back to her, as if he regretted his words.

Hannah's expression softened. "It feels good to need someone," she admitted. So good. "And to know that I can trust that person to actually be there for me. I haven't trusted another man since my husband walked away from our marriage."

He turned, surprise widening his dark green eyes.

"I was married once," she admitted. "We met at the rehab facility where I worked as a physical therapist. He was an administrator in another part of the building. We dated for nearly a year before getting engaged and married six months after that. I thought we both wanted the same things in life. Especially, a family of our own, when we took our vows before God, but my husband decided not long into our marriage that he wasn't daddy material. Or husband material, as it turned out." She paused to collect herself, because revisiting the past was hard. Not because she still had feelings for her ex; she didn't. It was painful because she had wasted so much precious time trying to build a life with a man who hadn't wanted the same things and hadn't been honest enough with her or himself to realize that before they'd wed.

"Had you tried counseling?" he asked and then shook his head. "Never mind. That's not any of my business."

She didn't mind answering his question. Garrett had been so open with her. "My husband refused to waste his time going to counseling when the lines had already been drawn. I wanted children. He wanted none. To drive that fact home, he took steps medically to make sure that it could never happen, informing me of it after the fact. Then he filed for divorce, citing irreconcilable differences."

"I'm sorry you had to go through that," Garrett said solemnly. "He should have been honest with you about his feelings before marrying you."

She nodded in agreement. "At least I didn't have to go through the divorce alone. I had my parents and Heather and Brian to lean on. After my marriage ended, I moved back home with Mom and Dad, planning to stay there only a few months while I got back on my feet again. But then Mom died unexpectedly of an undiagnosed heart condition and I couldn't bring myself to leave Dad to deal with his grief all alone."

"I'm glad you and your father had each other to lean on through tough times." He searched her face, his expression one of concern. "Do you still have to see your ex at work?"

"No. He took a job elsewhere. And I took a leave after Heather and Brian died, needing time to recoup from yet another loss. Now I'm not sure I want to go back. I failed at marriage. I don't want to fail at being a parent, too."

"From what you tell me, you're not to blame for what happened," Garrett said in all seriousness. "And while I'm not a big fan of divorce, there are times when a future together is just not meant to be. Like Tucker's marriage to Summer. He never intended to marry again, hadn't even sought to put a legal end to his non-existent marriage, but life has a way of making those decisions for you when you least expect it."

"I'm glad he was able to find true happiness," Hannah said. She'd seen Tucker and Autumn together and they were very clearly two people deeply in love with each other. Something she prayed she would find for herself someday. A true and genuine, lasting kind of love. Like her parents had found together. Like Garrett's parents shared.

"You will, too, someday," he said, as if reading her thoughts.

It took her a moment to reply, to separate her thoughts from what he'd actually been responding to. "Garrett," she said with a sigh and a slight shake of her head, "how many men do you think there are out there who are actually willing to date a divorcée who has a newborn to raise?"

"They are out there, Hannah," he said. "I promise. Truth is any man would be blessed to have such a special woman come into his life. And Austin is just an added blessing. Don't ever settle for less than you deserve."

"And that would be?" she heard herself asking.

"A man who will make it his life's goal to keep a smile on your face. One who wants children, just like you. A man willing to love a child that isn't his every bit as deeply as he loves those the Lord sees fit to bless the two of you with. And he definitely has to be a man who likes dogs," he added with a lone-dimpled grin. "Because you come with those, too. Buddy and Bandit if I remember correctly."

She laughed softly. "Yes. My boys." Not only did Garrett have an impressive memory, he always seemed to have a way of lightening her mood when she truly needed it.

"And now you have one more to add to the mix," he said with a smile as he pushed away from the table. "You'd best eat up. I'll be in the doghouse with Mom if I kept you talking so long you didn't have time to get ready for church."

Hannah stabbed at another bite of waffle, while Garrett carried his fork and plate over to the sink. She expected him to set it there and then head out to the barn, but he surprised her by washing his dirty dishes. Something her husband had never done. It might have been nice to have Dave lend her a hand in the kitchen once in a while.

Garrett turned from the sink, drying his hands on a

paper towel. "I'm going to head out to the barn before we leave. If you want, you can ride with me. We can go straight from church for the hospital."

She wanted to jump at his offer, never passing up an opportunity to see her son. But Emma had extended the invitation. "I wouldn't feel right riding to church with you after accepting your mother's invitation to go with them."

He smiled. "Believe me, it's not the method of getting you to church that will make Mom's day, but the fact that you will be joining us for this morning's services. She'll want to introduce you to everyone."

"All the same, I would feel better about it if I were to ask her first."

"If it will set your mind at ease," he said, "run it past my mother. You can let me know when it's time to leave. Now eat."

"Eating," Hannah told him with a laugh as she placed another syrup-covered bite into her mouth. She watched him go, a smile on her face. It was nice, in a way, to have someone looking out for her. In her case, several someones, as the Wades were a very caring family. Her father would like them very much. Lord knows, Garrett had already scored major points with him by saving her life and the baby's.

As she sat alone, finishing her breakfast, Hannah thought about everything that had happened since the flood. She'd given birth to a beautiful baby boy who already owned her heart, and then spent two nights tossing and turning in her hospital bed because Austin was so small and frail, and fighting to breathe. And then she'd learned that he needed even more specialized care because of the jaundice that had set in. In those three days, Garrett had so selflessly taken time away from his own life to run her back and forth to the hospital to look in on her and Austin. Who would have thought it could get any harder? But it had, the moment she'd left the hospital without the baby she'd carried with her for so long. Not even two whole days and it felt like she'd been away from Austin a lifetime.

How many more days would she be without the precious child she'd brought into this world? How many more days would she be dependent on Garrett and his family? Not that they'd ever, not even for one second, made her feel like she was an imposition. If anything, she'd found herself enveloped in the caring warmth of Garrett's family. They treated her as if she were one of their own, which touched her deeply.

And Blue, with her adorable curiosity and sweet nature, had stolen Hannah's heart from that very first moment. Her unexpected questions and adorable comments had not only put a smile on her face, it had helped put Hannah at ease as she was welcomed into Emma and Grady Wade's home.

For all the bad that had come her way the past couple of years, Hannah still couldn't help but feel blessed. Blessed to have had the Wades come into her life. Blessed to have made a special connection with Emma and Autumn that she hoped would carry on once she'd returned to Steamboat Springs. And blessed to have Garrett as her anchor during the stormy weather that was her life.

Chapter Six

Hannah stood beside Garrett on the front sidewalk just outside of the church, smiling politely as Emma Wade introduced her to several of her close friends following that morning's service. Everyone had been so warm and welcoming to her, with several of the women offering advice on caring for a newborn that Hannah appreciated more than they would ever know. Once she went back to Steamboat Springs, she was going to be on her own with the raising of her son.

A man in a lawman's uniform came over to them. "Tucker," he greeted with a nod before turning to Hannah. "You must be Miss Sanders," he said, removing his cowboy hat.

She nodded and then looked to Garrett.

"Hannah, this is Sheriff Dawson."

"Justin," he corrected. "Since I'm not here on official business. I was just passing by on my way back from a one-car accident I got called out to on the outskirts of town. Figured I would stop and say a quick hello."

"Speaking of getting called out," Garrett said, pulling his phone out of the front pocket of his dress pants.

"I forgot to turn my ringer back on after church." As he did so, he glanced at the screen with a frown.

"Something wrong?" Hannah asked.

"Probably not," he said, his attention fixed on the phone. "But it appears that I missed a call while we were attending this morning's service."

"If you need to return the call, I don't mind waiting," Hannah assured him with a smile. "Truth is, I'd feel better if I knew that I wasn't keeping you from your work completely."

He looked to Hannah apologetically. "I won't be long."

"Take however long you need," she told him, meaning it. He had done so much for her, setting a large part of his own life aside. He'd been more attentive to her feelings and her needs than her husband had ever been. Why couldn't she have met Garrett first, when her life was simpler? Happier. Hannah quickly pushed thoughts of Garrett aside. She was going through an emotional time and he was being kind to her like the good Christian man he was. Nothing more.

"No need to worry, Garrett," the sheriff said. "I'll keep her entertained until you get back. I've got all kinds of stories to tell her about you and your brothers while we wait."

She didn't miss the playful grin Garrett's friend aimed in his direction. "This sounds like it could get interesting," Hannah said, unable to resist joining in on the fun.

Garrett shot a warning glance in his friend's direction and then his gaze shifted back to Hannah. "I really do need to see what this call was about. Don't believe a word he has to say about me. None of it's true."

She laughed. "I'll be sure to keep that in mind."

"I won't be long," he told her. Then, bringing the phone to his ear, he stepped into the parking lot, away from the chattering church crowd.

"So, if we go by your not believing a word I have to say, I should begin with telling you what a nice guy Garrett Wade is."

Hannah couldn't help herself, she laughed, drawing a few glances their way, Garrett's included as he paced an empty section of the parking lot.

"In all seriousness, though," Justin said, "Garrett Wade is one of the best men I know, but I suppose I don't have to convince you of that. Not after he put his own life in harm's way to save yours."

"And my son's," she said, finally getting a little more comfortable with referring to Heather's little boy as her own. "And you're right. I need no convincing where Garrett is concerned. He's gone above and beyond what most people would have done to help me out. I'm truly blessed to have had him come into my life. Even if it's only for a short while."

"Speaking of your son," the sheriff said, "how is he doing? Garrett told me they were going to keep him in their care until he's a little stronger."

She forced a cheery smile. "He's holding his own and getting stronger every day." Her smile was merely a front for the fear she felt when she allowed all the what-ifs to creep into her thoughts. And, despite all the extra prayers she had sent heavenward while sitting in church that morning, Hannah knew she wouldn't feel completely at ease until she had Austin home with her for good. Visits to the hospital, which she made every day, thanks to Garrett, weren't the same as having her baby home where she could watch him sleep, could hold him anytime she felt the need. It was a constant reminder that he wasn't strong enough, healthy enough, to be in her life the way she longed for him to be.

"I'm glad to hear it," he said and then reached into the front pocket of his uniform shirt and withdrew a card. "As soon as you're feeling up to it, I'd like to get together with you to finish the report I started on your accident. For my records and for insurance purposes. There are parts of it that you have to supply answers for."

A frown overtook her smile. "I'm sorry to have held your paperwork up. I never even gave that any thought."

"It's not like your mind hasn't been focused elsewhere."

She nodded. "True. But you have a job to do."

"Another day or two won't make a bit of difference." He handed her the card he'd pulled out of his pocket. "My number is on there. Just give me a call when it's convenient, and I'll run out to the ranch to get your information."

"I'll call you tomorrow to set up a time. I'm already keeping Garrett from his normal work schedule. I won't be responsible for keeping you from doing your job, too."

"Garrett is self-employed," he told her. "He's free to adjust his vet and ranching schedules as need be."

She was grateful that he was a close friend of the Wades, and that it was a small town, otherwise she might have been answering his questions from her hospital bed. Lord knew she'd had enough on her mind in the hospital without having had to relive her near-death experience on top of it.

"Sounds good."

"Justin," Garrett's sister-in-law greeted in that sweet Southern twang of hers as she came over to join them. "We missed you at church this morning." Having witnessed the ease with which Autumn interacted with others at Sunday services that morning, Hannah found it hard to remember that she had only been a part of the Bent Creek community for a short while.

"I took the morning shift, so Wyatt and Lloyd could join their families at church."

"From what I've heard, and from more than one Wade brother mind you, all you do is work," Autumn said with a disapproving frown. "How are you ever gonna have a family of your own to attend church with if you're working all the time?"

He chuckled. "Maybe you ought to be giving this scolding to Jackson. As far as I know he's not married yet either. Besides, someone's got to protect this town. In fact, I was on my way back to the office after getting called out to a single-car accident when I saw that church had let out. I figured I would stop and say a quick hello."

"No one was injured, I pray," Hannah said.

"No," he said with a shake of his head. "The car sustained a small dent in its fender, and the runaway cow it crossed paths with sustained an even bigger dent to its pride."

"It's so nice to live in a place where the only real crime is an occasional yard-break by a cantankerous animal," Autumn said with a smile.

Justin chuckled, nodding in agreement. "Our town is

definitely blessed with truly good people." He glanced toward Garrett who was pacing the other end of the parking lot, and then turned back to Hannah. "Garrett looks to be pretty wrapped up in something. I need to get going. Can you tell him I'll catch up with him this week sometime?"

"I'll tell him," she said with a smile. "It was nice to meet you."

"The pleasure was all mine," he replied, and then, with a tip of his cowboy hat, he walked away.

"He's so nice, but like Garrett," Autumn began as they watched the sheriff walk away, "he can't get past the heartache to find love again."

Hannah looked to Autumn. "Garrett had his heart broken?" Even as she asked the question, she had to wonder how any woman could walk away from a man as good and giving as Garrett was. Poor Garrett. Her heart went out to him, knowing all too well how it felt to have one's heart trampled over. No wonder he'd been so sympathetic to her own failed relationship.

"He doesn't talk about it," his sister-in-law explained, "but Garrett was head over heels for a girl he dated when he was in high school. Chances are they would have gone on to get married, but she got sick and was diagnosed with leukemia. He spent hours on end with her at the hospital as she went through aggressive treatments, but it wasn't enough. I think Garrett's dreams died right along with Grace."

Hannah gasped, her eyes welling with tears. "How awful for Garrett and that girl's family."

"Please don't say anything to him about her," Autumn pleaded. "It's not something he talks about. I only know because Tucker and his momma told me what happened when I was teasing Garrett about needing to find him and Jackson women to make their lives complete. Garrett walked away without a word, later apologizing for it, but I knew then why he had reacted the way he had."

Her heart ached for Garrett and the emotional pain he had suffered, to have loved and lost so young. And he must have cared very deeply for Grace to have shut his heart off the way he had in the years since. Would he ever get to a place where he could move on and open his heart up to love again? Garrett deserved to find happiness after what he'd gone through with Grace. Something came to her at that moment. "Autumn, was Grace at the same hospital Austin is at?"

"Yes."

She had no idea how Garrett had been able to deal with being there again. Especially for hours on end, which he had done while Hannah had been in the hospital.

"Which is why we were surprised when he insisted on being the one to take you to the hospital that day," Autumn remarked. "If he hadn't been able to bring himself to step through those doors to check in on his brother during Jackson's stay there, what if he couldn't do it for you once he got you to the hospital? That's why Tucker and Jackson followed the two of you there as soon as they'd put the fence back together."

"They were at the hospital, too? I had no idea."

"Neither did Garrett," she replied. "They waited outside long enough to know you'd have somebody there for you, just in case Garrett needed them to take over."

But Garrett had seen things through, despite the pain it must have caused him to do so. The more she learned about Garrett, the more deeply he weaved his way into her heart. "I had no idea. That was so thoughtful of them. But I feel awful that Garrett had to do something so painful to him because of me."

"Don't feel bad," Autumn told her. "He chose to be there for you. And we are all thanking the good Lord for bringing you into our lives, most especially into Garrett's, because your being here has forced him to push past some of that pain he's held in for so long. In fact, I think as hard as it has been, it's been healing for him."

Hannah had no chance to reply as Garrett returned to where he'd left them standing on the sidewalk. She looked up into his handsome face, noting the lines of worry knitting his brows. It was clear that the lengthy call had been anything but an uplifting one. "Everything okay?" she asked.

"I'm afraid not," he said with a troubled sigh.

"What happened?" Autumn asked, her expression every bit as serious as Garrett's.

"One of Brad Wilson's cows got out of its pasture, a young calf, actually, and got struck by a car."

Hannah looked to Autumn. "That must be the single-car accident Justin told us about."

"The good news is that the injury appears to be below the calf's knee, so there's a good chance she won't have to be put down. Bad news is I'm not going to be able to run you to the hospital like we'd planned. I have to head out to the Wilson farm and tend to the calf's leg. You can ride home with Mom and Dad, and I will run you to the hospital later."

"Of course, you need to go see to that poor cow," Hannah said without hesitation. "I know Austin is in good hands. Jessica will be there with him this morning and part of the afternoon."

"Jessica?" Autumn said, looking to Hannah.

"One of the nurses in the neonatal care unit Hannah's gotten to know pretty well," Garrett explained.

"There's no need for Hannah to go back to the ranch," Autumn said. "Tucker has to see to a few things at the main barn after we get home. Hannah can ride with us to our place, and then she and I can go to the hospital together in my car."

Hannah was about to tell her that she could wait until later when Garrett got home, but then she recalled the conversation she'd had with Autumn while he was on the phone. If she could get to the hospital without his having to take her, then she would. "If you're sure."

Autumn waved a hand, shooing that thought away. "Nonsense. I'm gonna be sitting at home twiddling my thumbs while Tucker is down at the barn. I'd much rather be spending the afternoon with you and seeing that sweet little boy of yours."

"Thanks, Autumn," Garrett said with a grateful smile. He looked to Hannah. "I'll see you later."

She watched as he walked away in long, hurried strides.

"I'll go get Tucker," Autumn said, starting back toward the church.

Emma came over to join Hannah. "Garrett's leaving without you?"

"He got called out to tend to an injured cow. Autumn's going to take me to see Austin today."

"I see. You know I'd really like to see that little one of yours again," Emma said. "If I took you a day or two a week it would give Garrett a chance to work on ranching business, and me a chance to spend some time with that sweet baby of yours."

"I'd like that," Hannah replied, realizing at that moment that Austin would grow up without the warm love of a grandmother. One he could spend Sunday afternoons with. Bake cookies with. There would be no aunts or uncles. But he would have a grandfather who would adore him, she thought, trying to focus on what she did have.

"Then we'll arrange it," Emma said.

Hannah couldn't help but wonder if Emma was offering because she really did want to spend time with the little boy she had helped to bring into this world, or if it was more a mother's attempt to keep her son from having to do something Hannah now knew was an emotional hardship for him. Either way, it was what needed to be done, because Hannah would do anything to keep him from spending more time than necessary in a place that held such sad memories for him. Even if it meant her spending less time with Garrett, a man she'd grown surprisingly fond of in the short time she'd known him. A man she'd come to care very deeply about. And because of that, she would do whatever it took to keep him from having to face the pain of his past, something he did every time he took her to see Austin.

"I have to say that my dress looks much better on you than it ever did on me," Autumn said with a smile as they walked out to her car.

Hannah glanced down at the high-waisted, wispy skirted dress. "It definitely helps to hide my post-baby belly."

Autumn snorted. "What belly? If I hadn't been there for the delivery, I would never guess that you gave birth only days ago. I was referring to the color. Green is so much better suited to your hair color. And it matches, or at least nearly matches, your green eyes."

They settled into the front seats of Autumn's car.

"You can have that dress if you like," Autumn said as she buckled her seat belt. "I will be too big for it anyway very soon." She looked to Hannah. "Which is another reason I wanted to drive you to the hospital. To talk about having babies."

Hannah's eyes widened. "You're pregnant?"

The smile on Autumn's face doubled in size. "Yes. But no one knows yet. We wanted to wait until I get a little further along in my pregnancy before making the announcement. But I have so many questions. And who better to talk to about what to expect than you?"

"Your mother?" Hannah suggested. That's what she would have done if she'd had the opportunity to do so. And she was certainly no expert on the matter. She hadn't even gone through a complete pregnancy with Austin.

Autumn's smiled faded slightly. "She wasn't in my life much when I was growing up. Summer and I were raised by our grandma who is no longer with us."

"I'm sorry. I lost my mother a little over a year ago." Hannah was discovering so many things they had in common. But she still wished Autumn would turn to someone more knowledgeable about having babies. Someone who'd had more practice. Although it meant a lot that Autumn had felt comfortable enough to confide in her. Like a true friend. "What about Emma?

She's given birth many times. I've only done it once, and even that didn't go quite as expected."

"Tucker's momma had her babies decades ago," Autumn said matter-of-factly. "So, while she knows all about raising little ones, she's not as up on the current recommended pregnancy dos and don'ts as you are."

She supposed Autumn had a point. A lot of things had changed since Emma had given birth to her sons. "I'd be happy to answer any questions you might have," she told her. "As long as I have the answers for them." How could she refuse?

Autumn's smile returned. "I would really appreciate it. And I promise not to overwhelm you with too many questions. I know you're still recovering from having your own baby."

Hannah laughed softly. "I highly doubt a few questions are going to tax my strength."

Autumn glanced her way. "Seriously, though," she said, "if I get too carried away with baby talk, feel free to redirect our conversation elsewhere. It's just that I know I've already been talking Tucker's ears off with my endless chatter about our baby and we've only just found out we're expecting. Not that my husband isn't every bit as excited as I am. He's just a lot calmer about it. But then I guess, if you spent years riding horses and bulls bareback, having a baby must seem like a walk in the park."

"That's only because Tucker doesn't have to do any of the carrying part," Hannah pointed out.

Autumn nodded. "True. He only had to hang on for eight seconds. I'll be hanging on for another seven or so months. But I can handle that, I think, as long as he or she is healthy."

Hannah prayed Autumn's pregnancy went full term. She would never wish what she was going through with her own son on any mother. The separation. The waking every morning feeling fearful that things might have taken a turn for the worse and, if they had, that she wouldn't be there to say goodbye. Funny, but she found herself thinking at that moment that Garrett would never allow anything bad to happen. To Austin or her. That, with him by her side, she could face anything. If only she could keep him by her side forever.

"Hannah?" Autumn said worriedly.

She snapped out of her thoughts and looked to Autumn.

"I'm so sorry for being so unthinking when I spoke, with that precious little boy of yours dealing with health issues brought about by his coming too early. I never meant to be insensitive."

"Of course, you didn't," Hannah said with a reassuring smile. "It's only natural for a mother-to-be to hope her child is born free of any health complications. Heather had prayed for that same thing when we found out the invitro fertilization had worked, because all she had known with her pregnancies was loss. I prayed for the Lord to allow me to keep my sister's baby safe." She looked to Autumn. "I never thought to pray to Him to keep her and Brian safe. If only…" She sighed, feeling the tears well up in her eyes.

"It was their time to go, Hannah," Autumn said, compassion in her voice. "Just like with my sister. There were times I wondered why her and not me. Summer had a little girl to raise. I didn't have anyone. I've learned that questions don't always have answers. We just have to learn to accept God's will and live our lives as fully as He will allow us to during our time here on earth. Focus on our blessings, so to speak. And be the best second mother to Blue as I can be."

"Second mother," Hannah repeated in thought. "I have been so torn over having Austin call me Aunt Hannah or Mommy, something he should have been calling my sister."

"But she is gone, and *you* will be raising Austin," Autumn told her. "With Blue, she had been raised by her momma for several years before losing her. I was fine with her continuing to call me Aunt Autumn. But recently she's been slipping a Momma in here and there instead. I think it makes sense to her because Tucker is her daddy and we're a family now. In your case, you are the only momma your son is ever gonna know. I think your sister would understand your becoming her son's mother. She trusted you with his life from the very beginning, and I'm sure she's watching down over the both of you, grateful that Austin has you in his life."

Tears blurred Hannah's vision as she looked at her new friend. Even if they'd only known each other for just a very short time. In a way, Autumn helped to fill a void left in her heart after Heather had died. She'd missed those sisterly talks, that special bond she'd shared with her sister so very much.

"I'm sorry," Hannah said, turning to look out the passenger side window as she brushed a lone tear from her cheek. "Crying seems to be my thing right now," she said with a forced laugh. "Just ask Garrett. I've cried on his shoulder more than I've ever cried in my life. The poor man."

"I'm sure Tucker can relate," Autumn said with a gentle smile. "My emotions are all over the place these days. But from what I've read it's normal during pregnancy and after giving birth, until a woman's body has a chance to return to its normal state."

Hannah nodded with a soft sniffle.

"And you probably still have a lot of grief you haven't dealt with," Autumn said knowingly.

"You're probably right," Hannah said. "I couldn't grieve, wouldn't grieve, around my father. I didn't want to be the cause of any more pain for him."

"Well, maybe you can do some emotional healing while you're in Bent Creek. It took my bringing Blue here to meet her daddy to force my own grief over Summer's dying to the surface. The town, the people, are all so kind and giving. And Tucker's family," she said, shaking her head, "they are the best. I came here determined to prove him an unfit daddy so I could raise Blue myself in Cheyenne, but they welcomed me with open arms. I wasn't their enemy. I was a part of their family because I was family to Blue." This time it was Autumn who was tearing up. "See what you started," she said on choked laughter.

Hannah couldn't help but smile.

"I will tell you," Autumn said, "it was a healing thing to let all that built-up pain go. For both my heart and soul. Just as it will be for you when you are ready to let it go."

"I want to get to that point," Hannah admitted. "But, right now, all I can focus on is my *son* and how unprepared I am for what comes next. I was more than ready to carry a child for my sister, having read all the books on pregnancy I could get my hands onto. But I never thought about what came after giving birth. That was for Heather and Brian to prepare for. And then they died, and I was too overcome by shock and grief to think beyond the gaping hole their deaths had left in my life to focus on what I would need once their son was born. I don't have anything but a crib, which my sister and Brian bought as soon as they found out they were expecting."

"Didn't any of your friends have a baby shower for you?"

She shook her head. "Most of my friends from high school moved away, just as I did after I got married. After moving back home following my divorce, I spent most of my time with my family. Heather was my best friend. I was supposed to have thrown her a baby shower," Hannah said, her voice catching. "Not have someone throw one for me."

Autumn reached over to give Hannah's hand a squeeze. "We'll just have to go baby shopping while you're here. Besides, showers are overrated," she added with a flutter of her hand. "You have to play all those silly games."

"Silly games?" Hannah asked. "I've never actually been to one, so I honestly have no idea what goes on." She had just assumed that it was a cake and some pretzel and chips with dip, followed by the opening of gifts.

"Well, you aren't missing anything," Autumn said a little too nonchalantly, and Hannah knew she was just saying that for her benefit. "No, I take that back. The food is great. Some sort of sandwiches, veggie trays, fruit, chips and dip, and, of course, cake. But there are usually two or three games played during the shower. One of them involves the guests cutting off a piece of string to a length they think will fit around the expectant momma's belly. Whoever's string is closest to the real thing wins a prize of some sort."

Hannah studied Autumn's face for a moment, trying to determine if she was teasing her or not. She seemed serious enough. "They really do that?" She was suddenly grateful she hadn't had anyone to throw her a baby shower, because she had gotten quite round with Austin.

"They do," Autumn insisted. "Believe me. I've played it at several showers. Now that I'm pregnant, I'm rethinking the humor I once found in playing that particular game. I mean, come on, what woman really wants people guessing their baby-expanded waist size? Why don't people just bring pumpkins to the shower and the one that looks closest to the size of the pregnant woman's belly wins the prize?"

Hannah laughed. "Maybe because that would only go over well in the fall."

Autumn's laughter filled the car.

"Autumn," Hannah said, growing serious, "had Garrett planned to have a family with Grace?"

"I couldn't say for sure," she replied. "I only know what Tucker's told me. But if he loved Grace as deeply as I think he did, then I would think he had hoped to have a family with her someday. Why?"

She wanted so badly to confess her growing feelings for Garrett to Autumn. To ask if she felt there was any chance he might open up his heart again. Only she couldn't bring herself to do so. "Because he deserves to find happiness again. Even in the short time I've known him, I can tell he'd be a devoted and loving husband. And I've seen him with Blue. He'd make such a wonderful father."

"I couldn't agree more. If only you lived closer. I think you would be good for Garrett. And we could easily become the best of friends."

Oh, how she wished she did, too. Not only for the friendship Autumn could offer her, but for the unexpected connection she and Garrett had made. Maybe he was just being kind because that was who he was, or felt duty bound, as a faithful Christian, to keep her company during her brief stay there, but it felt like more than that to her. All she could do was enjoy every moment spent with Garrett during her stay there, knowing it would all come to an end in a few short weeks, because her life was in Steamboat Springs, watching over her father and raising her sister's son.

"Not back yet, huh?"

Garrett turned to find Tucker leaning against the open barn door. He shook his head. No sense trying to pretend he was doing anything other than watching for Hannah and Autumn's return. "I should have gone straight to the hospital after I finished up at the Wilson ranch." But his brothers had convinced him to take a step back and give Autumn and Hannah a chance to spend some time together. He might not have given in to their suggestion if their mother hadn't put in her two cents, telling him that sometimes a woman just needed another woman to talk to. Especially, after going through something as life changing as having a baby. So he'd gone home, washed up, and then had driven out to the main ranch to wait for his sister-in-law and Hannah's return with news of her son.

"You did the right thing," his brother told him.

Then why didn't the "right thing" not feel so right

to him? "They've been gone a long while. What if there was a problem with her baby? An emergency," he added worriedly.

"Autumn would have called to let me know, and she hasn't. So stop watching the second-hand sweep by on your watch and find something useful to do."

Tucker was right. Hannah was in good hands, and there was always something that could be done at the ranch. But it was hard to wrap his head around anything other than Hannah. Thoughts of her smile. Her soft laughter. Her willingness to use his shoulder to lean on, to cry on. Her son. Reining in his wandering mind, Garrett said, "I'll go check on the horses we'll be taking on the road." They had been separated out from the other horses so they could be fed a little extra, and so they would be easier to round up when the time came to load them onto one of the tractor trailers they used to transport their stock to the rodeo.

"Garrett…" his brother said, pushing away from the barn door to follow Garrett to his truck.

He glanced over at his youngest brother, his expression no longer filled with humor.

"I know I was just a kid when Grace died, but I saw how hard it was on you." Tucker hadn't even started high school at the time.

"Tucker," he said with a frown, not wanting to go there.

"Even talking about her isn't easy for you," his brother went on. "We all know that. And Jackson and I both said we would have done the same thing if we were in your shoes."

But they hadn't been. He'd been the one who had

lost the only woman, girl actually, that he'd ever loved. "I didn't do anything."

"That's my point," Tucker said. "You shut down emotionally for a long time after Grace's death and I found myself missing the brother I once looked up to. You were closed off, determined to keep everyone at arm's length. At least, emotionally."

"At first, I couldn't feel," Garrett confessed with a sigh. "I was numb inside. And then when my emotions started to thaw, I felt guilt. How could I even consider moving on, when Grace should have been the one I was moving on with? It was easier to sit back and do nothing. Feel nothing."

"We figured as much. I have to admit that it's been hard watching you in your self-imposed isolation where any real relationships were concerned, knowing where it stemmed from, but wanting so much more for you. I gave thanks to God for bringing Blue into our lives for so many reasons, one of them being the change it made in you. You smile more now. Laugh more. It's like you finally gave yourself permission to live life again." His brother looked down, digging the toe of his boot in the dirt, before looking up again. "What I'm trying to say is that you deserve to be happy. Grace would have wanted you to move on, to find someone who makes you feel that happiness again."

Garrett's first thought when his brother spoke of happiness was of Hannah, and then that all-too-familiar feeling of guilt threatened to surface. "If you're thinking about setting me up with someone…"

"Not a chance," his brother replied. "I think you're perfectly capable of finding someone on your own who can make you every bit as happy as you deserve to be. In fact, maybe you already have." Turning, Tucker strode back into the barn, chuckling as he went.

Maybe you already have.

Garrett stood pondering his brother's parting words. Had he? His heart took off in a gallop at the thought and his immediate reaction was to find some way to regain control of that runaway horse.

Autumn's car came rolling up the drive at that moment, saving him from his thoughts. He cut across the yard toward the house to greet them.

Hannah waved to him with a bright smile as she stepped from the car, sending that horse careening right out of his emotional gate once again. Then she bent into the car to retrieve several shopping bags from the backseat.

Autumn closed the driver's side door and looked to Hannah. "I look forward to doing this again soon."

"Me, too," Hannah replied.

Autumn turned and set off for the barn, passing Garrett on the way. "She's all yours."

All mine. That thought set a little too comfortably with him. Garrett looked to Hannah as he moved toward her. She wasn't his. He wasn't even looking for someone to be "his." But if he were, Hannah would be the kind of woman he would look for.

Garrett reached for the packages. "Let me get those for you."

"Thank you."

He glanced down at the numerous bags and then back to Hannah as they made their way to the house. "They put a mall in the hospital I wasn't aware of?"

She laughed softly. "No. Autumn and I stopped by

the mall on our way back to the ranch to pick up a few baby things."

He lifted the weighty bags. "A few?"

"I might have gotten carried away," Hannah said, flushing. "And I picked up some post-baby clothes for me."

"Your taking time to shop tells me Austin is doing well," he said knowingly. Hannah wouldn't have done so if that weren't the case.

Her bright smile widened even further. "He's doing very well," she told him. "Jessica said they expect to be able to remove the bilirubin lights within a day or two. And his lungs are strengthening."

Garrett grinned at the news. "I told you he was a fighter."

"He is," she said proudly. "And I think he's starting to know the sound of my voice."

"Of course, he does," he said. "He's listened to it for the past seven or so months."

"You know what I mean," she said, laughing once again.

The sound of her laughter wrapped around him, did something to him. *Maybe you already have.* Tucker's earlier words came rushing back to him and Garrett went into immediate denial. He couldn't have found the woman meant to make him happy, because he wasn't looking. He was only watching over Hannah and her son until her father was well enough to come to Bent Creek to take over the duty himself.

Garrett stole another glance at Hannah, whose pretty face radiated her joy at the news she'd received regarding her son's improving health. Watching over her felt like the farthest thing from a duty to him, but he had to force himself to think of it that way. Hannah and her son would be leaving, and if Austin continued to improve as steadily as he had been, as they had all prayed he would, that day would come very soon. But he was also well-aware that setbacks happened. If Austin ended up having to remain in the hospital longer than expected, it would tear Hannah up inside. Him, too. Even if bringing Austin home meant letting Hannah go.

"Would you like to take a drive?" Garrett asked as they stepped up onto his parents' front porch. He reached for the door. "I could give you a tour of the place."

"As much as I would love to, I'm going to have to ask for a rain check on your offer," Hannah replied. "It's been such a full day with church, and then the hospital, and then shopping with Autumn. I can barely keep my eyes open."

"Of course," he said, doing his best not to show his disappointment. He really had missed spending time with her that afternoon. But he understood. "Maybe one day this week we'll take that drive. Weather permitting." Storms were expected to be moving into the area over the next several days.

"I look forward to it," she said, smiling up at him.

He looked down into her thickly lashed, pale green eyes and returned her smile. "Me, too."

She looked up at him. "I missed visiting with you today."

There went that funny feeling again. Ignoring it, Garrett said, "I wish I could have been there with you."

"I know you would have been if you could have,"

she told him. "Speaking of which, how is Mr. Wilson's cow?"

"She'll live," he said. "Hopefully, she learned a valuable lesson today. That the grass isn't always greener on the other side. Especially, when the 'other side' consists of a well-traveled road."

Once again, her lilting laughter rose up around him. "A very good lesson to remember. I'm glad she's going to be all right. But then, with you watching over her, how could she be anything but?"

His being there hadn't helped Grace.

"Hannah," his mother said in greeting as she stepped from the kitchen.

"Hello, Emma."

"How's that darling little one of yours doing?"

"Better than expected," Hannah answered. "Thus the shopping bags Garrett offered to carry in for me. Autumn and I stopped by the mall after seeing Austin."

"Ah, good," his mother said. "Nothing more therapeutic than a girls' day out shopping."

"It was nice," Hannah agreed. "But I didn't go as much for me as I did for Austin. When I told Autumn that I didn't have any baby things bought yet, she suggested we stop and pick up a few things. Because, with God's good grace, my son will be coming home from the hospital very soon."

"Amen to that," his mother said.

"You didn't have *any* baby items bought?" Garrett said in surprise.

"Not until today," she admitted. "Now I at least have a few of the essentials I'll be needing, along with a half dozen or so sleepers. Oh, and I do have a crib. Heather and Brian bought one less than a week after they found out they were finally going to be parents. As for anything else, well, I thought I would have more time to prepare for Austin's arrival."

"Our children do like to surprise us on occasion," Emma said.

"With grandchildren, to give one example," Garrett muttered.

"One grandchild," his mother corrected. "And Blue was the best surprise I have ever received."

Me, too, Garrett thought. His niece was the light of his life. Tucker was beyond blessed to have her. He'd never allowed himself to consider what it might be like to have a child of his own to love and to raise after losing Grace, but from the moment he'd first held Austin in his arms, those thoughts had begun nudging at him. But it had been the talk he'd had with his brother that had forced him to rethink the way he'd been living his life. Maybe someday he could have the family he had once dreamed of.

Hannah turned to face him. "I'll take my packages now. Thank you for carrying them in for me," she said as he handed them over to her.

"Anytime," he said.

"I'm on my way upstairs to fold a basket of laundry I carried up to my room a short while ago," his mother told Hannah. "Let me take a couple of those bags for you."

"You don't have to do that," Hannah tried to protest, but Emma was already relieving her of two of her purchases. Then she started up the stairs with them.

"I'll leave these on your bed," she called back over her shoulder. "See you at dinner this evening, Garrett."

"I'll be there," he replied, and then found himself

searching for some other small piece of conversation to throw out there to stall their having to part ways. But there wasn't really anything he could say that wouldn't sound exactly like what it was meant to be—an attempt to stall his departure. So he steeled himself, tipped his hat to her and then headed back out to the barn to find something to keep his thoughts on anything other than his parents' beautiful houseguest.

Chapter Seven

That whole week, storms rolled in and out of Bent Creek, postponing their tour of the ranch. Garrett looked to the window, thanking heaven above that the rain had finally passed. Nothing but clear skies stretched over the distant mountains. That meant he would finally be able to give Hannah the tour of the ranch he had promised her. He'd found himself eagerly looking forward to sharing that part of his life with her. Something beyond the limited view of the ranch that she'd seen from the road as they traveled back and forth to the hospital to see her son.

Her son. His namesake. The child Garrett had found himself bonding with more and more with each passing day when he accompanied Hannah to the hospital to see him. He turned from the window and looked to the specialized crib Austin had spent most of his time in since coming into the world. Then his gaze came to rest on Hannah, who sat next to it in one of the neonatal unit's rocking chairs. She was holding her son, her love-filled gaze fixed on the tiny infant she cradled in her arms.

If one's heart could melt, Garrett was certain his would have. It was a memory he knew would remain in his thoughts long after they went back to the life that awaited them in Steamboat Springs. He had started off bringing her to the hospital because she had no one else to take her there. Because he felt a certain responsibility to do so. But as the days went on, he found himself looking forward to their time, watching Hannah with her son, whom she was now able to hold for short periods, and of getting to hold Austin himself.

While holding her son made him long for something he would never have, it was also a reminder of how precious life really was. That he needed to appreciate the time the good Lord chose to grant him and live it to its fullest. Something he hadn't done after losing Grace. But that had changed with Hannah's unexpected arrival in his life. It had happened slowly. Emotional baby steps so to speak. But he was ready to admit he no longer wanted to be alone. He wanted what Tucker had, a family to love and to love him.

Hannah looked up and graced him with one of her pretty smiles, which she did on occasion, perhaps wanting him to know she hadn't forgotten he was there. Or maybe she just wanted to pass on the joy she felt as she held her son. Either way, her smile was always a welcome thing. He'd been there for Hannah those times she had, fearing for her too-small son, given in to the tears. He'd been there when she'd struggled to keep her eyes open, exhausted by everything she'd been through. And he'd been there when she'd needed to talk. Sometimes about her past. Sometimes about simple things.

There were so many things about Grace he no longer remembered, or maybe he'd blocked them from his mind because it had always hurt his heart to think about her. He'd done more thinking and talking about Grace since Hannah had come into his life than he had for the past seventeen years. Doing so had been surprisingly cathartic.

It was Hannah who had been first and foremost on his mind since coming into his life. He knew her favorite color was red. The one place she longed to travel to was anywhere she'd be able to see the Northern Lights, where their brilliant colors reached far up into the heavens. And her favorite movie was *P.S. I Love You*, because it was about two people who loved each other beyond measure, and the willingness to let love in again after one's first true love was lost.

At least, that's what he'd garnered from the online search he'd done afterward to see what the movie was about. When Hannah had absently mentioned it, she'd quickly changed the subject, but he'd found himself wanting to know more about this movie that had resonated so deeply. Then he knew why she'd tried to redirect the conversation. It had been to protect his feelings. That kind gesture meant more than she could ever know, but like the main character in that movie he knew it was time to move on.

"Would you like to hold him?" she asked with a warm smile. "You haven't held him since that stormy afternoon at Jackson's."

That's because it had felt too right, holding Austin in his arms that day. Like he was meant to be there. "If you don't mind giving him up for a bit," he replied with a widening grin as he eyed the infant asleep in her arms. That day he'd run from the rightness of it.

Today he was ready to open himself up to new feelings. To possibilities.

"I don't mind sharing him with you," Hannah replied, tenderness in her eyes as she handed her son over to him. They'd already washed their hands when they'd first stepped into the neonatal care room. She pushed up from the rocking chair and stepped aside so Garrett could settle himself into it.

"He's growing more and more every day," Garrett said as he began to rock in a slow, easy movement. "In fact, I think that's a whisker I see sprouting from his chin," he teased, making light when the moment felt anything but. Emotion had knotted thick in his throat.

Hannah laughed softly as she leaned over them, admiring her son. "Won't be long before he's asking for a cowboy hat and boots."

"He'll have them. I'll make sure of it."

Her questioning gaze lifted to meet his.

"I want to be a part of his life," he said, looking up into her pretty green eyes. *Of* your *life*, he couldn't quite bring himself to say. "Distance isn't going to change that. He's my namesake. He should have boots and a cowboy hat."

"And apparently a razor," she said, making Garrett chuckle. Then her expression grew serious. "You are going to make a wonderful father someday."

Reaching up, he caressed her cheek. "And you have given that little boy of yours the most loving mother a child could ever ask for."

"Garrett," she said, their gazes locking. Then the baby stirred and let out a soft coo. Hannah straightened. "I… I can't wait for your entire family to meet him."

He wasn't sure what had just happened there, but it was clear Hannah had felt it, too. "They already have," he said. "The very first day he came into this world."

"That was different," she replied, her gaze lifting to meet his. "And not all of your family was there the day Austin was born."

No, they hadn't been. His father had been home watching over Blue during all the excitement. "Be forewarned," he said. "Blue is beyond excited to meet Austin. She's already planning the tea parties they can have together, and even asked Tucker to hang a baby swing from the tree next to hers so they can swing together."

A worried frown settled over Hannah's face. "Doesn't she know Austin and I will be leaving soon?"

"Blue knows what is supposed to happen," he said. "But she's hoping Austin will change his mind about leaving once he sees all the horses at the ranch."

"Oh, dear."

"It's not just Blue wanting you to stay," he said with a grin. He thought back to the nightly family dinners his mother had prepared instead of the usual once or twice a week gathering. He guessed it had been done for Hannah's sake, his mother wanted her to feel included, as well as supported, having none of her own family there for her during her stay. His brothers constantly brought up all of Hannah's wonderful qualities, as if he hadn't seen them for himself. And Autumn, well, she adored Hannah. He adored Hannah for that matter. Admired her. Wanted to kiss her.

"No?" she said, looking up at him.

It took a moment to be certain he hadn't stated his last thought aloud and wasn't rejecting him. "Uh, no.

My family isn't going to want to let you leave when the time comes either. They've grown quite fond of you."

She lowered her gaze, but not before he saw a hint of disappointment in her eyes. "I've grown quite fond of your family as well. They've been so good to me during my stay."

While Garrett had enjoyed those dinners with everyone gathered around the family table, laughing and sharing bits and pieces of their day, he looked forward most to the time he was able to spend alone with Hannah during their drives back and forth to the hospital. Hours spent bonding with her son, and then sharing small talk when they'd taken breaks to grab something from the cafeteria or walked the halls.

"I'll miss having you around," he admitted.

Hannah looked up, a smile softening her face. "I'll miss you, too."

"I'm sorry to interrupt," Jessica said as she came up to stand next to Hannah, "but it's time for me to return Austin to his crib. I need to check his vitals and then we need to run a few tests."

"Tests?" Hannah said worriedly. "Is something wrong?"

Garrett wondered the same thing. No one had said anything to them about new medical concerns where Hannah's son was concerned, and they'd been there all morning.

"Nothing's wrong," the young nurse quickly assured them.

"Thank the Lord," Hannah breathed in relief.

"The tests show us how much your son has progressed. They will also show us where Austin's lung function is and give us a better idea of when his oxygen tube can be removed. If your son continues to progress the way he is, he could be ready to go home in another couple of weeks or less."

A couple of weeks or less. A clock ticked loudly in the back of Garrett's mind. Time was running out. He needed more, but not when that could only happen if Austin's health required it.

Hannah's face lit with the news and her spring-green eyes filled with tears. She looked to Garrett. "We had better leave Jessica to her work, so they can run their tests and we'll pray for good news."

"I'll continue to keep Austin in my prayers as well," Jessica told her. "I know how hard it is to be without your baby."

"Thank you," Hannah said, the words catching in her throat.

"Yes, thank you," Garrett said, nodding. "Not only for remembering Austin in your prayers, but for watching over him when you're here and we're not."

"It's my job to see to his care," Jessica said humbly.

"It's more than that," Garrett told her. "You've been a great source of support for Hannah during this time, over and above the nursing duties you're required to perform as part of your job."

"I know I'm not supposed to get emotionally involved," she said with a hint of a frown, "but it's hard not to. I've been where Hannah is. I know the mountain she's about to climb alone as a single mother. Any words of advice I can offer her, I will gladly do so. She has my number."

"You are my inspiration," Hannah told her. "And when times get tough, which I have no doubt they will on occasion, I'll think of you."

This time it was Jessica's eyes tearing up. "Don't get me crying," she said as she reached out to take Austin from Hannah, carefully maneuvering the tubes and wires so they wouldn't catch on anything as she did so. "I can't have my vision all tear-blurred while I'm working."

Hannah stood and bent to place a tender kiss on the smattering of strawberry blonde hair covering her son's head. "Mommy will see you tomorrow." With a sigh of resignation, she stepped back.

Garrett moved in, running the side of a finger along the baby's soft cheek. "See you tomorrow, little man. Be good for your nurse."

Jessica smiled. "He always is."

Placing a hand at the small of Hannah's back, they made their way out of the neonatal intensive care unit. "Austin really is filling out," Garrett commented as they walked down the long, sterile hospital corridor.

"He is," Hannah replied happily. "It won't be long before we can finally take him home."

Before we can finally take him home. While that was not what she had meant, Garrett had images of Hannah and her son coming home to his house. Of what it might be like if the three of them truly were a family. His family. He shook his head, pushing the thought away.

They walked in companionable silence the remainder of the way through the hospital. When they reached the oversize revolving doors at the building's entrance, Garrett motioned for Hannah to step in first, and then followed her inside as it turned.

"Favorite flower," Hannah said as they stepped out onto the sidewalk.

Garrett snapped out of his reverie to find Hannah glancing over at him with a grin. "What?"

"Think fast," she said, smiling. It was a game they had begun playing to help fill the long hours they spent at the hospital. Throwing out random questions when the other wasn't expecting it. She repeated herself, and then added, "Which is your favorite? Or maybe you don't know the names of any flowers, your being a rugged cowboy and all."

His lifted a brow, and not because of the question she had asked. She clearly assumed that a cowboy-like him wouldn't be able to answer that particular impromptu question. "I'll have you know I'm pretty knowledgeable when it comes to flowers."

Surprise lit her features. "You are?"

"Blue is big on going flower picking," he admitted with a grin as they crossed the parking lot. "As her uncle, it's my job to know which flowers are which."

Hannah lifted a slender brow. "I have to admit I'm impressed."

"And to answer your question," he said as they neared his truck, "A marigold."

She looked up at him. "A marigold?"

Reaching out, he opened the passenger door and helped Hannah up inside. "Yep." His grin widened. "Seems I'm a bit partial to flowers that remind me of you. Dark red marigolds that have shades of yellows and golds mixed in make me think of your hair when you're standing outside, surrounded by sunshine," he said as he closed the passenger side door and walked away with a grin.

Garrett strode from the barn, peeling off his work gloves as he went. It had been nearly a week since he'd told Hannah he liked marigolds, because they reminded him of her. The memory of it made him smile. And while the past couple of weeks had been challenging, fitting in trips to the hospital with Hannah, scheduled vet visits and tasks he needed to see to at the ranch, he was making it work—for her. Even if it meant dropping into bed dog-tired each night. Hannah would be leaving soon, and he wanted to spend as much time with her as possible before that happened. And it had nothing to do with her sunset-colored hair or her big, beautiful green eyes. Well, not completely. He liked her. All of her—from the inside out.

"Perfect timing."

He glanced up to find the woman filling his thoughts walking toward him. Garrett smiled. "Did you rest up like you were supposed to?"

"Yes," she answered with a smile. "Did you get done whatever it was you needed to do while I rested?"

"I did. I've finished with preparations for tomorrow's vaccinations."

Hannah's gaze drifted past him to the corral beside the barn.

Garrett knew without looking what had drawn her attention in that direction. He'd just left Tucker, who was in the midst of breaking in another horse.

"What's he doing?" Hannah asked.

He cast a glance back over his shoulder, his gaze coming to rest on his youngest brother, who stood in the middle of the corral, coaxing the gelding circling the outer edge of the corral to speed up.

"Breaking in a green horse," he explained.

"Green horse?"

"A horse that isn't ready to saddle up and ride yet.

That little filly he's working with right now is young and a pretty feisty yet."

"It looks dangerous," she said worriedly.

"My brother knows what he's doing," he said. "He'll get the job done and come out of it all in one piece. I promise." He inclined his head. "Now come on, let's take that ride I promised you last week."

Once they were seated inside, Garrett started the engine and turned to Hannah. "Windows up or down? There's a bit of a chill in the air this afternoon."

"Down," she answered. "I want to take in the fresh air and the sounds around us."

With a nod, he lowered all the windows, and then slid open the sunroof. "You let me know if the air coming in gets to be too much."

"I will," she said as they pulled away from the house. Hannah glanced around at the outbuildings and various pastures. "So, this is all part of the family business?"

"For the most part," Garrett replied. "The ranch belonged to my father, but he added our names to the deed when we went into rodeo stock contracting. That way we could insure our business, protecting our investments from unexpected loss, such as fire, infectious diseases, natural disasters."

"Like a flood," she said.

"Like a flood."

"Dad also signed over several acres of the ranch property to each of us to build our own homes on."

"That was so generous of him," Hannah said.

"He's always been very giving, wanting the best for all of us."

"I've seen that of him," Hannah said. "Of your whole family, for that matter. Your father reminds me so much of mine. It makes me realize how blessed I was not to have children with my ex-husband. He could never be the kind of father mine was, the kind I know you could be."

Garrett looked her way. "Thank you for that. It means a lot to me." Hannah believed in him. Given the chance, he would prove her right. Having noted the sadness in her tone when she spoke about father, he said, "I know you're missing your father. I'm sorry he hasn't been able to be with you through all of this."

"It's hard," she admitted. "But we talk on the phone every night. Every day he sounds so much better. Hopefully, his doctor agrees when Dad sees him this week." Her father hadn't been responding to the antibiotics treating his bronchitis and had needed to change to a stronger one, delaying his arrival even more. It was tearing Hannah up not to be there to help care for him, but she couldn't leave Austin. Thankfully, her father had several good friends looking in on him and providing him with meals, so he wouldn't have to spend his energy cooking. And he'd sounded better the last couple of times they'd spoken, which surely was a sign of his good health finally returning. "He's praying he gets the go ahead to drive up here this coming weekend. Your mother and father have invited him to stay at the ranch whenever he gets here."

"I'll pray he gets good news this week," Garrett told her, wanting Hannah to have her family, at least what she had left of it, there with her—and her there with him.

"I'm sure Dad would appreciate that."

They drove only a short distance down the road before Garrett slowed and turned onto a pull-off. Up ahead, beyond that pasture's fencing, were the horses that had been retired from the Triple W's rodeo roster. He shut off the engine and looked to Hannah. "I want you to meet some of our veteran horses. They've retired from the rodeo life and will live the remainder of their lives out here on the ranch, eating well and spending their days in leisure."

"Sounds like a pretty nice life to have," she said with a smile. Her gaze rested on the horses gathered just beyond the fence line, grazing contentedly. "They're so beautiful."

So are you was at the tip of his tongue. Thankfully, Garrett managed to hold on tight to those words. He was supposed to be giving her a tour of the ranch, not sweet-talking her with flowery compliments. Even if they were true. She was one of the prettiest, most genuine women he'd ever had the pleasure of knowing. "Come on," he said, opening his door. "Let's go have a closer look." Garrett stepped out of the truck and then made his way around in long, hurried strides to help Hannah down. Then they walked together up to the fence.

Two of the horses stopped their idle grazing to come over and greet them, sticking their heads over the top of the fence where Garrett stood. They nosed at the front of his shirt, nearly knocking him off balance with their enthusiastic greeting.

"What are they doing?" Hannah asked with a giggle.

"Begging," he said with a chuckle.

"For what?" she asked, watching their antics.

He reached into his shirt pocket and pulled out several small cubes. "Sugar. These boys have a sweet tooth like you've never seen."

"A lot like their owners, from what I've heard," Hannah said, smiling.

"We do at that," he agreed. He reached out to run his hand along the side of one of the broncs' necks. "Jackson, Tucker and I grew up surrounded by these majestic creatures. We rode before we could walk. At least, that's how Dad tells it. Mom says otherwise."

"I love listening to your father tell stories at dinner," she told him.

"You mean you love listening to him embellish the truth," Garrett corrected with a grin.

Her smile widened. "He could tell us a story about mowing the grass and make it sound exciting."

"It's not," Garrett told her. "Believe me. I'd much rather be spending time with these horses."

"I can tell," Hannah said, looking up at the mare with a smile. Sighing softly, she said, "If I hadn't just had a baby, I'd ask you to take me for a ride. I've never been on a horse before and I'd trust you to keep me safe."

He'd like to keep her, not only safe, but in his life for good. He could teach her to ride, and she could teach him to enjoy the little things in life a little more. "Someday, I will. Austin, too." Promise made, he inclined his head toward his truck. "We'd best move on. There's a lot to see."

They returned to the truck and headed farther down the road. "How did you get into contracting horses to rodeos?"

He answered, eyes still fixed on the road ahead. "After talking our thoughts over with Dad, my brothers and I decided it was what we wanted to invest our time and money into. It gave us a way to stay connected to the rodeo after we had all finally stopped competing in it. We started out contracting to supply stock to smaller, local rodeos, and, as the number in our herd grew, so did the opportunities for us to contract with even bigger rodeos. The only thing holding us back from supplying stock to the largest rodeos was the fact that we couldn't offer bulls in addition to our broncs."

"Why would you have to do that? You're horse ranchers."

"To provide for most associations, a stock contracting firm has to buy a membership and there are a lot of requirements we have to meet," he explained.

"That's a lot of hoops to jump through," she noted.

"Hoops we're more than willing to jump through," he said.

"But I thought this was a horse ranch," she said, glancing around. "I haven't seen a single bull since I've been staying here."

"It is," he said with a nod. "And you wouldn't have. We don't own any bulls. But Kade Owens does. To meet the mandatory requirements, we formed a partnership with him."

"Who is Kade Owens?"

"A good friend from our rodeo days," he explained. "Kade and Jackson competed against each other in the bull riding events before an injury ended my brother's rodeo career."

"Is that the reason for Jackson's limp?" she asked as she stood looking out over the pasture.

Garrett looked to her in surprise. "You noticed that?"

"I'm a physical therapist," she reminded him, something they had touched upon a few times during their many hospital talks. That she had taken a leave of absence after her sister and brother-in-law's passing and planned to follow that up with the allowed maternity leave after the baby was born. Her sister and Brian's will, drawn up well before Hannah had agreed to carry their child for them, had left everything to her, so she was blessed with the financially stability to stay home with Austin for a while if she chose to. And right now there was no other option. Her son needed her, and she needed him.

"I suppose that means you would be able to pick up on things others might overlook, or not give much thought to. Where Tucker and I rode mostly horses in rodeo competitions, Jackson rode bulls. The bigger the bull, the meaner the bull, the more eager he was to climb on top of it and make the ride."

"That had to be so scary."

"The rush of adrenaline that comes with taking on a sixteen or seventeen-hundred-pound bull tends to push any rational fear aside for those few short seconds. When it's man against beast. Will against will. Sometimes the bull wins," he told her. "Like it did the day Little Shamrock, who was anything but little, won, and Jackson took a loss he couldn't come back from."

"What happened?" she asked almost hesitantly.

"A little over eight years ago, my brother was competing in the National Finals Rodeo in Las Vegas. He was riding the best he'd ever done. Made his way up to the top ten. But when the next day's competition came, Jackson seemed to be out of sorts. I'm not sure what happened to make him lose his mental focus to that extent, but it cost him, not only a lot of money, it nearly cost him his life when he was thrown by the bull he'd drawn to ride."

Hannah gasped, her hand flying up to cover her mouth.

"He landed hard and was too dazed to react before Little Shamrock trampled him."

"I thought they had clowns to chase the bull away when a rider falls," she said.

"Rodeo clowns do their best to keep the fallen riders safe, but sometimes there isn't enough time to get to the rider and to distract the bull before the damage is done. Jackson's leg sustained most of the damage, requiring a good bit of hardware to put it back together."

She groaned, as if imagining his brother's pain. "And therapy, I would imagine, with a break that severe."

"And therapy," he acknowledged with a nod.

"Your poor brother. That had to be such a hard recovery for him."

"More than we ever imagined it would be. It was as if something inside of him was broken, too, and we didn't know how to fix it." He shrugged. "Maybe it was his having been forced to accept the probability that he would never compete again. Or if he did, knowing it wouldn't be at the level he had been."

An empathetic frown pulled at her lips. "That would have to play not only on his heart, but on his mind and his pride as well."

"It did. He was angry a lot of the time in the beginning, convinced he would never be the man he was because of that almost nonexistent limp."

"Nearly nonexistent to you and me," she said, "but in Jackson's mind it's what people notice first, maybe even judge him by. I know because I've provided physical therapy for a few rodeo cowboys who also sustained rather substantial injuries."

"It changes everything for them. Even the slightest impairment can throw off a rider's ability to hold on during the ride. Depending on the kind of injury they sustained, it could affect their grip strength, balance, even the rider's ease of motion during a rough ride, as it had Jackson."

She nodded. "That makes sense. Thank the Lord he wasn't injured worse in that fall."

"I do," he admitted. "Every day. Running this business has brought us even closer than we were before. I don't know what I would do without my brothers." The thought was out before he'd processed what his words might do to Hannah, who had lost her only sibling. "I'm sorry. That was thoughtless of me."

"Don't apologize," she said with a forgiving smile. "You should feel that way. And I pray you never have to find out. At least, not for a very, very long time."

He prayed for the same thing.

"I'm glad you were the one to find me that day," Hannah said, looking up at him with an expression he couldn't quite read.

"So am I."

As if finding herself caught up in something she wasn't prepared for, a feeling he could relate to, Hannah looked away.

They drove a short distance down the road before he turned onto the dirt and gravel drive that led to his place. He'd meant what he'd told her. While he wished that Hannah had never had to go through that terrifying ordeal with the flood, and then unexpected arrival of her baby, he truly was glad that he had been the one the good Lord chose to save her. To save them. To have the honor of caring for them in their time of need.

"Your place?" she asked as they neared the house.

He nodded. "I want to show you my veterinary clinic. Not that I use it much. Except for storing medications and supplies, most of my work is done out in fields and barns, since I deal mainly in the care of large animals. Horse, cows, etcetera."

"What about smaller animals like cats and dogs?"

"There's a vet in town who handles domesticated animals," he explained. "We fill in for each other when needed."

He pulled up in front of the building that served as his clinic and cut the engine. "Now sit tight until I come around to help you down."

"Garrett, I'm perfectly capable of getting out of your truck on my own," Hannah said, reaching for the door handle.

"I prefer to help you down because this truck is higher up than most," he explained. "And if you were to fall getting out, my mother would have my head. The rest of my family probably would as well. I happen to like my head where it sits, atop my shoulders, so please just sit there until I come around."

Hannah laughed softly. "Well, when you put it that way."

After helping her down, Garrett walked her to the office entrance. He unlocked the door and then eased it open. "After you," he said.

She stepped inside, her gaze moving slowly about the room. "It looks almost like a doctor's office," she noted. "Except for the skeletal posters of animals hanging on the wall behind the examination bed."

Before Garrett could respond, his cell phone rang. "I'm sorry," he said, apologizing for the interruption. He pulled out his phone and glanced down at the screen, then back up at Hannah. "Work call. Do you mind if I step outside and take this?"

"Take your call," she said. "I'll be fine."

With a nod, he left and closed the door behind him.

Hannah turned to find the wall opposite to the one with all the posters on it filled with framed pictures. Most of them were of horses. Probably, if she had to guess, horses Garrett had either owned, still owned or had ridden in competition. It made her smile. The room was filled with the things that made him the happiest: his family and his horses.

She walked over to take a closer look at the photos. There were several of Garrett and his brothers, which looked to have been taken at various rodeos. A much larger family portrait hung in the center of the wall, one that looked to have been taken maybe ten years or so earlier. Emma had no streaks of silver in her coppery hair, and her sons had smooth, whisker-free faces with youthful grins, the spitting images of their father, who stood, beaming with pride, alongside his family.

A lone frame, one much smaller than the ones on the wall sat next to a mission-style lamp atop a table by the window. Hannah walked over, thinking it to be Autumn because of the woman's lighter hair. But when she drew close enough to see the fine details of the photograph, she saw that it wasn't a woman, but a girl probably about sixteen or so, with long, blond hair and a sweet smile.

Lifting the framed photo, she studied it closer. The

girl was too old to be the daughter Emma and Grady had lost years before. It took only a moment longer for the realization to strike her. This was Grace. The girl Garrett had given his whole heart to.

A mix of emotions washed over her at that moment. Sadness for the beautiful, young girl who'd fought so hard to live and hadn't. And shame, for feeling even the slightest bit of envy toward Grace because she had been so loved by Garrett. The depth of which Hannah had never known from her husband during their brief marriage.

The office door opened, and Hannah fumbled to return the picture to its place on the table. Then she spun around with a forced smile. "All done with your call?"

Garrett stood silent in the doorway, his gaze moving past her to the picture no longer sitting where it had been. Hannah felt as if she'd been caught doing something she shouldn't have. But it wasn't anger that filled his eyes as he crossed the room to stand beside her. It was pain. "Her name was Grace," he said, looking down at the photo.

"I know," she said softly.

His gaze snapped up to meet hers. "How? Did one of my brothers say something to you about her? Because it wasn't their place to do so."

"Autumn told me," she admitted.

"Autumn?" he said. "I suppose I shouldn't be surprised that she knew about Grace. There are no secrets between my brother and his wife. As it should be," he conceded. "But why would she feel the need to share my past with you?"

"Please don't be angry with her," Hannah said, regret knotting up in her stomach. She hadn't wanted to betray her new friend, but she couldn't lie to Garrett either. "Autumn wants you and Jackson to find the same kind of happiness she and Tucker have found."

"And that's going to happen by her bringing up my past?" he asked stiffly.

"I don't think she would have said anything about it if I hadn't pressed her for the reason you and Jackson are so guarded with your hearts. I, for one, couldn't imagine any woman wanting to break your heart. You're one of the best men I've ever known. I had no idea the loss you had experienced had been so final." A love he had carried with him all those years. Hannah couldn't help but wonder what it would be like to be loved so deeply by a man. By Garrett.

When no response came, Hannah went on, "I know I shouldn't have asked. It wasn't any of my business. But I care about you, Garrett. I want more than anything for you to be happy."

"I can't promise that I'll ever open myself up to the kind of happiness you and Autumn want for me. And I'm good with that. It's better than loving and… It's just better," he said, his voice raspy with emotion.

Her eyes filled with tears as Hannah reached up to tenderly place a hand on his tanned cheek. "Oh, Garrett," she said sadly. "What it must have cost you to step foot into that hospital with me on that rainy day, and all the days since…" Her words trailed off.

"To be honest," he said, his hand covering the one she had place against his cheek, "my past wasn't what was front and foremost in my mind the second I stepped into the emergency room with you and your newborn son. All I knew was that I would not lose you, too, either of you, after promising you that everything would be all right."

"Is that what happened with Grace?"

He looked to Grace's picture. "Yes. That's why I keep her picture there. As a reminder."

"As a reminder of what?" she asked, searching his face.

He closed his eyes. "Of the lie I told her. Her father had taken me aside to tell me that she was dying, and to ask me to pray for her to find peace from her suffering. I couldn't bring myself to pray. I was too angry at God for wanting to take Grace from us. Instead, I went into her hospital room to see her and told her that she was going to be okay. And then she died."

"You didn't lie to her," Hannah told him, her heart aching for all that he had gone through. Watching his first love fade away, day by day, as the life slipped from her weakened body, knowing Grace had no more strength left in her to fight, and he would be there for her until the end.

Garrett opened his eyes to reveal the moisture that had gathered there. "I told her everything would be okay. *She* would be okay."

"And she is," Hannah said. "She is in a far better place than any of us. She's no longer suffering. If you did anything, you gave Grace comfort when she needed it most. Because that's the kind of man you are. I should know."

To her surprise, Garrett drew her to him, hugging her tight. "Thank you, Hannah. You have been one of the biggest blessings in my life."

She hugged him back, a tear slipping out to run down her cheek. "As you have been for me."

Chapter Eight

Hannah's heart skittered, as it always seemed to do whenever Garrett appeared. She watched as he rode toward the house the next day. The man sat as if he'd been born in the saddle, which, she supposed, he pretty much had been.

"Morning," she greeted as he drew back on the reins, stopping next to the porch where Hannah was enjoying a cup of warm cider.

"Morning," he replied, giving his cowboy hat a nudge. "I was on my way to help Jackson and Tucker clear away some of the storm debris that's plugging up part of the creek and noticed you sitting out here on the porch. Figured I'd swing by and say hello."

"I'm glad you did." She found herself imagining what it would be like to be married to Garrett, waiting on their own porch to welcome her husband home every day. The image seemed so clear in her mind, unlike something her wishful thinking might have conjured up.

He looked toward the house. "Mom and Dad up yet?"

"I don't think so," she said, shaking her head.

"Ah, the benefits of retirement." He rounded the

porch and ascended the steps. "You're up earlier than usual, aren't you?"

"A little. I wanted to see the sunrise," she admitted with a smile. "And I have to say it didn't disappoint. The warm, vibrant shades of red and gold the rising sun casts across the land and distant mountains are beyond breathtaking."

"You should see it in the deep of winter," he told her. "When the colors of dawn glisten off the freshly fallen snow." He raised up in the saddle and then swung his leg over the back of his horse, before dropping to the ground below. "So is that the only reason you're up this early?" he asked as he wrapped his horse's reins around the railing and then stepped up onto the porch.

She smiled up at him from the chair she was seated in. "Are you implying that I was sitting out here watching for you?" And how close to the truth that would be.

"Can't blame a man for doing a little wishful thinking," he replied with a teasing grin as he settled into the white wicker porch chair next to hers.

Hannah looked out across the yard. "I might have been hoping for a glimpse of you riding up to the barn." She didn't have to see Garrett's face to know that his smile widened with her admission. "Or," she continued, shifting her attention back to the cowboy beside her, "I might have been hoping to catch a glimpse of that very handsome horse of yours."

"Something tells me I'm not going to find out which it is."

She laughed. "You're probably right."

"Maybe I can weaken your resolve by using my cowboy charm on you," he said with a playful wriggle of his brows.

Hannah laughed softly, despite the butterflies his words had set to fluttering in her stomach. "Now you're not fighting fair." She leaned her head back against the wicker chair. "What I'd really like is to know more about you and your family."

He stretched out his long, denim-clad legs as he eased back in the chair next to hers and tucked his hands behind his head. "Ask away."

She liked that about Garrett. He was always so honest and open with her. "Jackson left the rodeo because of his injury," she began.

Garrett nodded.

"Was it the same for you and Tucker? Injuries forcing you out?"

"No," he said, shaking his head. "He and I left on our own terms. Truth is, Tucker sort of lost his spark for competing on the circuit after his marriage to Autumn's sister fell apart. Not that anyone realized why at the time since he kept his marriage from us. But looking back, knowing what we do now, it all makes sense. I think his focus was consumed by questions he had no answers to, and a loss of focus when riding can be dangerous for both the rider and the animal."

"I can only imagine."

"Would you mind my asking about your sister? That is, unless it's too hard for you to talk about her."

"I don't mind," she told him. She didn't want to set her memories of her sister aside. Being able to talk about them, even though it could be hard emotionally, kept her sister alive in her heart. "Heather was older than me, but only by two years, so we were pretty close. She was the athlete in our family, running track, even in college. I was more gifted on the academic side. Not that I didn't like sports. I played tennis and I liked to swim, just not competitively."

"Unlike my brothers and myself, who lived for the competition," he said with a grin.

"There are times I find myself reaching for the phone to call her," she admitted with a frown.

"I'm sure you do," he said. "She hasn't been gone that long."

Not long, but far too long. "What about you? What made you decide to retire from riding," she asked, her gazed now fixed on him.

"My career," he answered. "I didn't ride at the same competitive level my brothers did, entering only local rodeos while pursuing my degree in veterinary medicine. After graduation, when I opened my own practice, I gave it up altogether."

"Too busy with work?"

"Too concerned I might not be able to work," he told her. "The possibility of getting bucked and breaking an arm wasn't a risk I was willing to take. I'd worked too long, and too hard, to get my degree to throw it all away. I was done. Or so I'd thought. But then I ended up following the rodeo circuit anyway when my brothers and I went into the rodeo stock contracting business, Tucker and Jackson training the horses, and me seeing to any medical issues that might arise with the horses here at the ranch or when we are attending scheduled rodeos."

"I'd imagine it's a big plus to have an on-site vet."

"It definitely saves us money," he agreed.

"Your parents have to be so proud of what you and your brothers have accomplished," Hannah said with a soft smile.

"They are," Garrett said, his parents having told them as much more times than he could count. "I still wish we could've talked Dad into joining us in our venture, but he wanted to spend his golden years focusing on Mom and their life together."

"That's so romantic," she sighed, wondering if she would ever be so blessed as to have the kind of life, the kind of love, that her parents and Garrett's parents had shared. Would Garrett ever want that for himself?

He chuckled. "I suppose so."

"It is," she insisted, laughing softly.

"I'm not sure romance had anything to do with it," Garrett said. "I think it was more Dad's way of doing the right thing. Mom stood by him during all the years he rode rodeo, supporting him completely. When he retired, he decided it was his turn to do for her. Not that he doesn't lend a hand when we need it. For example, he'll be going on the road this rodeo season to cover for Tucker who will be staying in Bent Creek to care for Blue and oversee things here at the ranch."

"And your mom's okay with his leaving?"

"She'll be going with him," Garrett explained. "My parents recently purchased an RV to take trips in, so they'll be able to travel together while lending Jackson and myself a hand at the different rodeos we've contracted for this coming season. Mom can't wait to hit the road again. The only thing giving her hesitation is the thought of being away from Blue for so long, but Tucker and Autumn are going to try to bring Blue to a rodeo or two, which helped ease Mom's guilt over leaving her new granddaughter for most of the summer."

"Who will see to the ranch when everyone's gone?"

"We have part-time ranch hands who we trust to

see to things while we're all away." He looked to her in surprise. "You know, I have to admit I never expected to be having this conversation with you."

"Why ever not?"

"You said yourself that you had never been to a rodeo," he explained. "I didn't think the aspects of my family's business would really interest you."

"I may never have been to any shows," she said, "but that doesn't mean I wouldn't want to go to one. The opportunity just never arose for me to do so."

Her words took him by surprise. "You'd like to go to a rodeo?"

"Yes. Not that it's going to happen anytime in the near future," Hannah said, looking off toward the distant mountains. "But after hearing so much about it from you and your family, my interest is most definitely piqued. Maybe when Austin is older we can go to one."

"I'm sure he'll like that," he said, hating the thought of her having to go it alone when it came to raising her son. "My brothers and I grew up going to rodeos. Dad competed in them until I was twelve or so, so we'd go to watch him."

"That had to be so exciting."

He nodded with a grin as he recalled the special times he'd shared with his family. Times that he as a young boy had taken for granted.

"It was," Garrett replied. "My brothers and I used to love watching Dad ride. We couldn't wait until we were old enough to sit atop a bucking horse ourselves, or in Jackson's case a bucking bull, and compete. Not that Dad didn't get us involved in other activities when we were growing up, like fishing and camping."

Hannah looked his way, something bordering on panic etched in her pretty face. "Garrett, I don't know how to fish or build a campfire. Or any of those things dads usually do with their sons."

"There is no set rule saying all boys have to know how to fish or set up camp," he told her, wanting to ease some of Hannah's worry. She had enough on her mind as it was.

"But most boys do," she argued, fretting her lower lip.

Most did where he was from, but that was the norm in the area he had grown up in. "I could teach him." The offer was out before he considered the impossibility of it. They would be living in two different states.

"You?" she said, some of that sparkle coming back into those beautiful green eyes of hers.

He should have rescinded his offer with an apology for getting her hopes up, reminding her of their geographical differences. He should have suggested that Austin wouldn't be ready for fishing or camping for several more years yet, and that by then she would probably have someone special in her life. A man who would appreciate the wonderful, loving woman she was. A man willing to step in for the father Austin had so tragically lost and give Hannah more children. The ones she'd been denied in her first marriage.

"If you'd like," he said instead, promptly shoving aside any thought of the man Hannah would someday give her heart to. And her smile. And her precious son. The boy she'd so trustingly placed in his arms right after he'd come into this world. It shouldn't bother him, Garrett thought, guilt jabbing at his gut. If anything, he should pray for the Lord to grant her the happiness she deserved. But the problem was *he* wanted to be the man to give her that happiness.

"I can't think of anyone I feel more comfortable with than you when it comes to being there for my son. But I can't ask that of you."

His smile sagged. "Why not?"

"Because that time is years away," she explained. "You'll be busy with a family of your own by the time Austin is ready to learn all of those things."

He shook his head. "Marriage isn't in my future."

She reached out, covering his hand with hers, saying softly, "Because of Grace?"

"That's part of it," he said, his gaze on their joined hands.

"You don't want children?" she asked, her expression troubled.

He hesitated a long moment before answering. "I'm not able to have children," he admitted. "That's pretty much what marriages are for."

"Garrett," Hannah gasped, her hand tightening over his. "I'm so sorry. I had no idea."

"You wouldn't," he said soberly. "It's not something I've felt the need to share with others."

"But you're telling me."

He cleared his throat, which suddenly felt constricted. "I'm telling you because you've shared so many confidences with me." And because he trusted her. "I hope it will help you will understand a little better why marriage isn't in my future."

"Marriage isn't only about creating a family," she told him with a frown. "It's about finding that one special person to love and be loved by. It's about supporting each other through the good and the bad. It's about trust and commitment. It's about sharing a faith and allowing that faith to guide you through your lives together."

"How can you feel so strongly about marriage?" he asked her. "After what happened with your first."

"Because forever is a very long time to spend alone."

"You'll have Austin."

She nodded. "I will. But I pray for the Lord to bring someone into my life to complete our family."

"You deserve that," he said solemnly.

"Garrett…" she asked hesitantly "…are you certain you can't have children?"

"According to the doctors who treated me following the bronc riding injury that sent me to the emergency room in Missouri the year before I gave up competitive riding for good, I am. And I only have myself to blame for it."

"You were a competitive bronc rider," she told him. "That meant risking possible injury each and every time you rode. But accidents can happen in any line of work. You shouldn't blame yourself for what happened."

"It could have been prevented," came his muttered admission.

She looked up at him. "What do you mean?"

"My sterility could have been prevented." His frown deepened. "I put off going to the ER after my ride, even though I was in a great deal of pain, because of my aversion to hospitals after losing Grace. If I had sought medical attention right away, sterility would probably not have been an issue." He laughed, the sound almost brittle. "The rodeo left its mark on all of us. Jackson with his lame leg. Tucker's broken marriage. And my infertility. The funny thing is, despite all of that, we still love being a part of the rodeo circuit."

Moisture filled her eyes as she sat looking up at him.

"Hannah, please don't cry."

"I can't help it," she said as her tears swelled in her eyes. "When I think of all my coming here has cost you emotionally. Having you hold Austin so I could rest after giving birth to him. That had to be so hard for you. If I had known…"

"I would have held him anyway," he told her with a tender smile. "You needed to get some sleep. And I promise my thoughts weren't on anything but the un-expected little blessing I was holding in my arms at that moment."

"But then you drove Austin and me to the hospital. To the place that holds your last memories of Grace. Painful memories. And it didn't end there. You spent hours on end on a floor filled with newborns when you can't…" She didn't finish what she'd been about to say.

It had cost him emotionally. He couldn't deny it. But it was nothing compared to what it had gained him. "That first day," he began, "when I brought you and Austin in through those emergency room doors, my main focus was on getting you and your son the medical help you both needed." His gaze locked with hers. "I wasn't going to lose you. Either of you. And while I'll admit it's been hard, I found myself wanting to be there for you in the days following Austin's birth more than I wanted to avoid memories from my past."

"Garrett," she said with a tender, teary-eyed smile.

"It's true," he said. "You've given me new memories where that hospital is concerned. So if anyone should be doing the thanking, it should be me. You've helped me to let go of some of the past that I should have let go of a long time ago."

Tears spilled out onto her cheeks. "How can I ever thank you for the emotional sacrifice you've made for us? Are still making," she added with a soft sob.

Garrett turned his hand over, threading his fingers through hers. "By being happy."

Nodding, she brushed a tear from her cheek with a soft sniffle. "I want the same for you. And whether or not you can father a child makes you no less lovable. Plenty of couples adopt."

He frowned. "Maybe so, but I would always wonder if any woman I would marry would start to resent having to raise someone else's child when they could have had one of their own."

"If you were my husband, would you feel that way about raising Austin?" she asked, making him take a mental step back. "Because he's my sister's son, not mine. Just as he won't be a physical part of any man I might marry. Should I avoid ever marrying again because my husband might resent, if not me, then the child I will be raising as my son?"

The last thing he wanted to think about was the man who would be part of Hannah's future. But her bringing it up made him rethink his thoughts on the matter. "No," he muttered. "*If* I were your husband, I would love you even more for opening your heart and giving a motherless child a special place in your heart. And I would love Austin. I can't imagine any man not wanting to be a father to your son." But to be that meant that man would be more than just a father to Austin. He'd be Hannah's husband and all the things Garrett found himself wanting, despite knowing they were just out of reach.

"I pray you're right," she said with a soft sigh. Looking his way, she asked, "Do you have time to go for a short walk? I'd like to stretch my legs a bit."

He managed a smile. "For you? Always." Reaching out, he took hold of her hand.

Hannah glanced down at their joined hands, her heart dancing happily as he walked her across the porch. She felt like a young girl on a first date, rather than a grown woman simply spending time with a friend. Because that's what Garrett was to her—a very dear friend. Someone she could share her innermost feelings with, with the exception of those she held for him. Something that had been missing from her life since losing her sister.

"Will you tell me a little more about the ranch and your rodeo business?"

"What would you like to know?" he asked as they walked along.

"How big is your ranch?"

"Eight thousand acres in total," he replied.

"That's huge." She looked around, her gaze coming to rest on the herd of broncs grazing in the distance. "But then you probably need that much land for all the horses you have."

"They're our livelihood," he explained. "They need room to roam."

"How many horses live on your ranch?"

He followed the line of her gaze. "We have 110 rodeo-ready horses, foals that have yet to come into their own, about a dozen or so retired broncs. That's not counting our own personal saddle horses." He pointed to the barn. "We store supplies and feed for our stock horses in the main barn."

They moved past the barn to where a pair of double-decker semitrucks were parked next to one of the galvanized grain bins. "Horse trailers?" Hannah inquired as she took in the sight of them. They looked newer and had fancy, scrolled detailing around their doors, a saddle painted on each side of the elongated horse trailers with Triple W Rodeo Ranch arched over the top.

Garrett nodded. "We use these for equine transport to the various rodeos. They are top-of-the-line with every safety measure and comfort taken into consideration. We want to be certain our horses make it to their contracted destinations safely, experiencing as little stress as possible."

"Wow. So much goes into operating a stock contracting company," Hannah said in awe. "This," she said, motioning to everything around her, "is all so impressive, Garrett. And to think I had only pictured a rodeo consisting of a fenced-in riding area with a gate for riders to come in and out of, and a bunch of horse trailers. But there is so much more to it."

Garrett chuckled. "A lot more than in your imaginings from the sounds of it. You really need to experience the real thing."

"I know," she said with a wistful sigh as she stared off toward the herd galloping across the pasture beyond the barn.

"How about this evening?"

She looked his way, her questioning gaze meeting his. "What?"

"There's a local rodeo this evening over in Shanter," he said of the town thirty-five minutes away from

Bent Creek, even closer from the hospital they drove to every day. "It's an indoor competition, one that's a somewhat scaled-down version of the rodeos our company normally contracts for, but it's a rodeo all the same. I was thinking that if you are feeling up to it after visiting with Austin today, we can take a ride over and check it out."

Her face lit up instantly at his suggestion, snagging yet another piece of Garrett's heart.

"We can even grab some dinner there if you're good with burgers."

"You already had me sold on the idea, but burgers totally sealed the deal."

"It's a date then," Garrett said without thinking. Then frowned at his words. "Well, not a date exactly. You know what I mean."

Her smile sagged ever so slightly. And then she laughed, sounding forced. "Of course. I've just had a baby. Not what most men are looking for when it comes to dating."

His brows drew together. "It has nothing to do with your son. If things were different," he told her, regret filling him, "I would ask you out in a heartbeat. I like you, Hannah. I like you a lot. But you deserve a man who can give you children. A man who can give Austin brothers and sisters." He looked around, feeling uneasy with the direction their conversation had taken. The last thing he wanted to do was lay his heart out there on the line when doing so wouldn't change anything. "I should be going. I'm supposed to help Tucker and Jackson clean some of the storm debris out of the creek before it damns up."

"Thank you for taking the time to walk with me this morning."

He nodded. "I'll be back to pick you up around three." Walking over to his horse, Garrett unwound the reins from where he'd secured them to the porch railing, and then swung up into the saddle.

"Garrett…" Hannah said as he turned his horse to leave. "You never did ask what my favorite flower is."

He cast a curious glance her way.

"A while ago, I asked what yours was," she explained. "You told me a marigold. I thought you might want to know what my favorite is." She waited patiently for him to ask.

Unable to help himself, Garrett smiled. He'd wanted a change in conversation. This was definitely it. "All right, Hannah, what is your favorite flower?"

Her lips drew up into a bright smile. "That's easy. A sunflower."

As her reply settled in, Hannah moved up onto the porch.

"A sunflower, huh?" he repeated. "Not a perfectly bloomed rose or brightly colored tulip,"

"Nope. Definitely a sunflower," she replied. Reaching for the screen door, she glanced back at him over her slender shoulder. "They're tall and I like tall. And strong. Always tipping their faces upward to soak in the warmth of the sun. Mostly because they remind me of you," she said with a playful wink. "See you after work."

The screen door swung shut behind her, leaving Garrett to process her admission. It didn't matter that she'd compared him to a flower. What mattered was that he was *her* kind of flower. Hope, as irrational as it was, stirred inside him as he rode away.

"The burgers were awesome, but these are the best fries ever," Hannah said, looking up at him with a happy grin as they made their way to their seats in the front row of the rodeo arena.

They had grabbed a couple of burgers and fries when they'd gotten to the rodeo. Garrett had finished all his, but Hannah was still enjoying the last bit of her fries. "Mine were good," he replied. "But that's because they weren't all smothered in ketchup and vinegar, like some people's." He followed that up with an exaggerated cringe.

Laughing, she held the cone-shaped paper cup out to him. "Don't knock it until you try it, cowboy."

He eyed the cup's contents warily. "Thanks, but I'm a plain fry kind of guy."

"Don't tell me a man who used to climb onto a bronc, risking life and limb, is afraid to try a little, tiny, flavor-induced French fry."

"You don't play fair," he said with a grin as he reached out to pluck a couple of fries from the cup. Then he popped them into his mouth, prepared to force them down just to prove to Hannah that he was still the fearless cowboy he'd once been. But Garrett discovered, much to his surprise, that fries were actually very tasty with ketchup and vinegar added to them. "Mmm…" he moaned.

Her smile widened. "Good, right?"

"Best fries ever," he agreed, helping himself to another one as they headed toward the arena to take their seats. There had been so many firsts for him since

Hannah came into his life. First time he'd ever rescued someone. First time he'd ever held a newborn. First time he'd ever thought about how empty his life, a life filled with work and family, still was.

"Garrett?"

Garrett stopped and turned, catching sight of two men he used to compete against when he was riding the circuit. "Huck," he greeted with a nod. "Ben."

"You thinking about coming out of retirement?" Ben asked with a grin. "Here to check out the competition?"

"Not a chance." He looked to Hannah. "I'm just here with a friend."

"Well, if I had the choice of sitting atop a bronc or beside this pretty lady here, I'd definitely stay retired." Ben's words made Hannah blush.

Huck nodded in agreement.

"Hannah Wade, meet Huck Salyers and Ben Freeman," Garrett said.

Both men tipped their cowboy hats, murmuring their greetings.

"It's my first rodeo," Hannah told them. "I'm so excited to see this part of Garrett's life."

Both men slid questioning glances his way.

Not wanting to have to make explanations to soothe their curiosity, Garrett said, "I hate to cut this short, but we really need to get to our seats. The bareback bronc event is getting ready to start."

The men nodded.

"It was good seeing you," Huck said.

"Enjoy the rodeo," Ben told Hannah.

"I'm sure I will," she replied with a smile.

Garrett felt a stirring of something akin to jealousy as he stood listening to his friend make small talk with

Hannah. Maybe it was because they were on the receiving end of her pretty smile. One he'd prefer to have aimed solely at him. He should have introduced Hannah as his girl, because that's what he wanted her to be—his girl. It was high time he stopped fighting it. He turned to her as the two men walked away, intending to tell her just that, but the rodeo announcer came on the speakers to announce the bareback bronc event was about to begin.

"We're going to miss the start," she fretted.

"Not if we hurry," he said, taking her hand as he led her through the thinning crowd.

She tossed her empty fry container into a nearly trash barrel as they hurried toward the bleachers that wrapped around the dirt-packed arena.

"Why are there other riders here?" she asked, sounding almost breathless with anticipation as they made their way up the steps and along the front row of bleacher seats.

"Those are the pickup men," he explained as they located their seats and settled onto them. "Their job is to see to the safety of whichever cowboy's competing at that time. At the end of the ride, or even during if there appears to be trouble, they come in and help him safely to the ground. Then they herd the horse out of the arena."

"That's comforting to know," she replied as she eyed the two men on horseback.

The rodeo announcer's voice boomed out of the overhead speakers, "This is Give Him a Shake, seeing if he can do just that to Brock Lemley from Utah." Music began to play. A second later, the chute opened.

From that moment on, Hannah was riveted, at the edge of her seat as she watched the competition.

Despite the action going on inside the arena as rider after rider came out, each one trying to bring in the top score of the night, Garrett's attention kept drifting to Hannah, who was leaning forward, both hands curled tightly around the railing in front of her.

Her gaze stuck like glue to the bronc rider currently making his ride in the arena. Her wide-eyed expression, and soft, worried gasps as the bronc bucked with increased determination had Garrett wondering if Hannah was going to last the entire rodeo. The night was only beginning.

The buzzer sounded, signaling the end of the required ride, but the bronc wasn't ready to quit. Another violent buck, followed by a sharp cut to the right, sent the rider airborne.

Hannah let out a terrified shriek as the rodeo cowboy hit the ground about twenty feet away from where they sat watching, hard enough to send up a small cloud of dust. "Garrett—" her hand shot out, frantically grabbing for his "—is he okay?"

He eyed the fallen cowboy, praying that he hadn't brought Hannah to a rodeo only to have a serious injury happen right there in front of them. Thankfully, the man pushed upright, shook his head as if trying to clear the cobwebs from it, and then scrambled to his feet.

"A little dazed," Garrett supposed as he watched the rider break into a jog toward the fence, slapping his dust-covered cowboy hat against his leg as he went. "But medical will check him out."

Nodding, she watched in silence as the young rider

made his way out of the arena, her hand still clutching Garrett's like a lifeline.

He liked being the one she turned to when she was afraid. Giving her hand a squeeze, he said, "You okay?"

"A little shaken," she admitted. "Are those horses always so…rough? Yours always seem so calm."

"That's because they don't have riders on them," he told her. "But these horses are bred to buck hard. That's how those cowboys want it. The rougher the ride, the better the score, as long as the rider holds on for the mandatory eight seconds. Getting bucked is a part of this sport."

"Do riders get disqualified when they're thrown?"

"Not if they're still on their bronc when the buzzer sounds," Garrett explained. "That last rider made it the eight seconds before he was thrown, and it was a hard ride. All in all, it was a pretty good one."

"Good that he didn't break his neck when he fell," Hannah muttered. "I can't believe you used to do this."

"It looks worse than it actually is," he said, wanting to set her mind at ease. "Most riders are experienced enough to know how to fall to prevent any real serious injury. Not that accidents don't happen on occasion." He and Jackson were living proof of that. "And most riders opt to wear protective vests and chaps, which help to cushion falls as well as offer an extra layer of protection between the skin and the flailing hooves of a bucking horse. Helmets and face guards have also become more commonplace with riders."

She appeared to relax with his explanation. "That's reassuring." Her gaze returned to the arena as the next rider shot out of the chute. The bronc bucked hard, with a sidestepping hop into the fence. Pain registered on the cowboy's face as he struggled to regain his balance. The second the pickup men knew the rider was in trouble, they moved in to help get him safely off the horse.

Hannah gave a quick prayer of thanks that the man had come away with little more than a limp. She turned to Garrett. "I can't believe you used to do this."

"I did," he acknowledged.

"Weren't you terrified when you climbed onto whatever horse you had to ride?"

He shrugged. "It was more of an adrenaline rush, combined with the determination to make each ride better than my last. But then I grew up around the rodeo, not to mention having two very competitive brothers who were both happy to give me a push whenever I needed it."

She bit at her bottom lip as the next rider came out of the gate.

"If this is too much for you, we can go," he told Hannah worriedly.

"We can't leave yet," she said, looking up at him. "This is the most exciting thing I've ever done, and all I'm doing is sitting here."

Her response made him smile.

"I'm glad you're enjoying yourself."

"I am," she said happily. "More than you could ever know."

If it was anywhere close to the way he felt about the time they had spent together that evening, then he did know.

Still holding hands, they watched the rodeo, Hannah never hesitating in asking questions whenever one came to mind. Her interest was genuine, and Garrett was touched that she truly wanted to learn about the world he'd grown up in. A world his life was now built around. The women he'd come across during his years on the circuit, the ones seeking to strike up something with a rodeo cowboy, the ones he hadn't been inclined to take interest in, hadn't really cared about who he was. It was all about what he was—a fairly successful rodeo cowboy. With Hannah, the connection was more genuine.

The ride back to his parents' place was filled with Hannah's excited chatter.

Garrett pulled up in front of his childhood home and shut off the engine. "I'll walk you to the door."

"You don't have to," she told him. "I know it's late and you have to get up at the crack of dawn."

"I want to." He made his way around to the passenger side where he helped Hannah down and then walked her to the porch.

Stopping at the door, she turned to look up at him. "I had so much fun this evening."

He smiled down at her. "I'm glad."

"I just wish I could've gone to a rodeo with you back when you were competing."

He found himself wishing she had been a part of his life back then, too. He liked having Hannah around. Their conversations. Her laughter. Her smiles. "You would have seen pretty much what you saw there today."

"Only it would have been *you* out there, making my heart pound," she replied.

"And here I thought it was just being with me that made women's hearts pound," he said with a teasing grin. "Looks like I'm going to have to work on my cowboy charm."

Hannah laughed softly and reached up to give the brim of his hat a playful tug. "I think between this cowboy hat, this adorable dimple," she said, her finger jabbing lightly at the divot in his cheek, "and your big heart, you have more than perfected the charm."

"Enough to convince you to go on a date with me again?" he teased.

"I thought this wasn't a real date," she said, her eyes searching his.

Garrett took a mental step back, his grin flattening. "I'm sorry, Hannah. I'm not real sure what this is." He hadn't dated since high school.

Her smile sagged, and she immediately averted her gaze elsewhere. "Don't apologize. Your inability to call it that is answer enough."

He hated that he'd hurt her feelings with his thoughtless words. "If I could be the man you deserve, which we both know I will never be, then this would have been a real date, as far as I'm concerned. The best I've ever been on," he admitted.

"It was for me, too," she said softly. "My ex-husband and I didn't go out much. He was more of a homebody. Tonight showed me what I've been missing all these years."

He reached out, cupped her chin and turned her head until she was looking up at him once more. "I'm sorry your marriage didn't work out the way you'd hoped it would."

"It wasn't meant to be," she told him. "And the Lord blessed me with the chance to carry a child. Not my own, but I was able to experience the feeling of a life growing inside of me, something I had longed for. It was wondrous. And then it was scary, having nearly lost Austin. I'm not sure I want to ever go through that again."

He let his hand fall away, his brows drawing together in surprise. "I thought you wanted a big family." They'd talked about her desire to have several children more than once during those long days spent at the hospital.

"I would very much like to have a big family someday. But there are other ways. Other children are in need of someone willing to raise and love them like they were their own. Of course, that would depend on whoever the Lord has in mind for me, and if adoption is something my husband would consider."

It was hard for Garrett to process that. But he supposed Austin's early arrival and the complications that followed had been traumatic enough to have Hannah considering adoption for her future family. Then it struck him, his sterility wouldn't come into play if Hannah preferred adoption instead of giving birth to her own children. Hope flared to life inside him.

"Hannah..." he said, trying to get a grip on all the emotions that had suddenly stirred up inside him. Happiness. Excitement. A little fear. Because this moment could change everything he had always envisioned for his future.

"Yes?"

"I think we should call this a date."

She gave a regretful shake of her head. "If things were different," she said, "and I'm not referring to having children, I would love to. But it would be too hard to start something, fall for you even more than I already have, and then have to say goodbye in a week or so, maybe less."

More than I already have. His heart began thudding against his chest with her admission. "Then don't say goodbye. Move here to Bent Creek. Give this connection between us a chance to grow." *Let me love you.* "There are plenty of hospitals and rehab facilities, even nursing homes, where you could seek employment if you decide you want to go back to work."

Her smile slid away. "If only it were that simple."

"It is," he said, despite knowing better than most that nothing in life was simple.

Hannah shook her head. "If it were only me, I'd give it some serious consideration. It's hard to live in a place where I am constantly surrounded by memories. Of Mom. Of Heather and Brian. Of the happy, loving family I once had."

He nodded in understanding, having gone through that himself after losing Grace. So many memories. Memories he suddenly realized had grown hazy since Hannah's unexpected arrival in his life.

Before he had a chance to respond, she went on, "But I have my father to think about. He needs me right now. And he needs his grandson. We're all he has left in this world. I can't take that from him, no matter how tempting the thought of building a new life in a place like Bent Creek might be." Hannah rose up on her toes and then leaned in to place a sweet kiss on his cheek. "If things were different, I would choose to stay here with you." Stepping back, she opened the door, her suddenly teary gaze meeting his. "Thank you for tonight, Garrett. It's a memory I will hold dear forever." Then she was gone, the door easing shut behind her.

Chapter Nine

"Thank you again for the omelet," Hannah said as she stood from the table to carry her plate and fork over to the sink. "It was delicious."

"I'd like to say they're my specialty," Garrett replied as he followed her with his own breakfast dishes, "but I only make omelets because I can't flip an egg without breaking its yoke."

She laughed. "Good for me you're a poor egg-flipper. I much prefer an omelet over a no-frills egg."

Garrett chuckled, despite the growing sense of panic in his gut. They had been informed the afternoon before, while visiting her son in the hospital, that they expected to release Austin that coming Tuesday. That meant he had two, maybe three days left to spend with Hannah before she walked out of his life forever.

"You wash, I'll dry," Garrett said, pulling a tea towel from the kitchen drawer.

"Sounds like a plan," Hannah said, setting their dirty dishes down into the still-sudsy water his mother had left in the sink before rushing off to church that morning.

His parents had told Hannah they had to leave early that morning to meet with a few of their church parishioners. It wasn't a lie, because they were joining his brothers, Autumn and a few of his mother's friends, all members of their church, at Garrett's place where they were setting up for the surprise baby shower Autumn and his mother were throwing for Hannah.

Garrett was in charge of taking her to church and then coming up with a reason to delay his taking her home to give everyone time to get to his place before her. He couldn't wait to see the look on her face when she realized the party was for her. But he was even more anxious to see her response when she saw the surprise he had for her.

He watched as she rinsed off a plate, handing it to him to dry with a cheery smile. Neither of them had brought up the talk they'd had the night they'd come home from the rodeo. What more was there to say? She wasn't at a point where she felt comfortable moving to Bent Creek with her son and leaving her father in Steamboat Springs all alone. And Garrett couldn't just pick up and leave his brothers to run the business without him. He'd prayed about it, but no amount of praying was going to change those facts. Nor would her leaving change the feelings he'd come to have for her. Just as he'd had to do with Grace, he would lock those feelings away, and go on with his life as he'd been living it before Hannah had come into it. Emotionally alone.

Clearing his throat, before emotion got the better of him, Garrett cast a quick glance at the LED clock display on the stove's panel. "We'd best get a move on."

"Almost done," Hannah said as she rinsed the remaining suds off the two forks she held in her hand. Then she turned, handing them over to him. "Here you go. While you dry those and put them away, I'll go grab my purse."

Nodding, Garrett placed the forks in a dish towel and began to dry them.

Hannah paused, looking up at him with a tender smile, the sight of which had the beat of his heart kicking up a notch or two. Clearly the uncooperative organ forgot that it was Sunday, a day for relaxation, not for skittering about wildly just because Hannah had blessed him with one of her sweet smiles. "I really am going to miss being here," she said, her green eyes misting over. "Thank you for being my friend."

He wanted to be so much more. "Always," he said, determined to make her last few days there ones she would always remember, starting with the surprise he had for her that afternoon.

"Surprise!" The word rose up around Hannah in multitude, and from all around her, the second she and Garrett stepped into his house.

Hannah looked past the opening that led into the living room to see Garrett's family standing in front of the fireplace, smiles on their faces. Blue and white crepe paper was draped across the thick wood mantel, while a dozen or so matching balloons swayed to and fro on each side of the fireplace.

She looked to Garrett. "It's your birthday?" Why hadn't he said something? Thankfully, he'd needed to drop off the bread and milk he'd picked up after church before leaving for the hospital, or he would have been a no-show for this wonderful surprise birthday party his family had planned for him.

"This party isn't for me," Garrett replied, his green eyes twinkling. "It's for you."

"What?" It wasn't her birthday.

"Mom and Autumn wanted to throw you a surprise baby shower before you went back to Colorado," he explained.

"And me!" Blue exclaimed from where she stood holding Tucker's hand.

"And Blue," Garrett said with a chuckle.

Hannah's gaze shifted back to the gathering of grinning Wades in the adjoining room. The blue streamers and balloons that surrounded them had been meant for her. Tears filled her eyes as Emma and Autumn stepped forward to greet her.

"Well, I'm certainly surprised," Autumn said, the words catching on the emotion building in her throat as Garrett's mother leaned in to give her a hug. "But you shouldn't have gone to all this trouble. You've done more than enough for me already."

"It was no trouble," Autumn assured her as she stepped in for her turn to give Hannah a hug.

"Not at all," Emma said in agreement. "We had so much fun planning this baby shower."

"They weren't about to send you home without one," Garrett told her.

"Not a chance," Autumn acknowledged with a bright smile. "You're gonna have your hands full with a newborn once you get home. We didn't want you to have to worry about running out to pick up the essentials you're gonna be needing."

"We got you lots of presents!" Blue piped in, her tiny voice carrying across the room.

Hannah felt the sting of tears in her eyes. "Thank you."

Emma Wade smiled warmly. "No tears. This is a happy occasion. Now come on in and greet your guests."

She followed Garrett's mother into the living room, intending to thank Garrett's father and brothers for joining in on that afternoon's festivities, but stopped short as her gaze was drawn to the occupied folding chairs that had been placed along the wall to her left on each side of the sofa table that sat below the front window. Her guests, women Hannah had met through Emma at Sunday services, smiled back at her, uttering words of greeting and congratulations.

"Thank you all for being part of this," Hannah said. "I feel so blessed."

"You are," a familiar voice said. "With a very special little boy."

She turned to find Jessica grinning up at her from the sofa on the opposite side of the room.

"Agreed," Autumn said as she moved to take a seat at the other end of the sofa.

"Jessica?" Hannah muttered, pleasantly surprised, yet shocked to see her there.

Her friend gave a small wave. "Surprise!"

"I thought you might like having her be a part of your special day," Garrett said behind her.

Like Autumn and Emma, Jessica had become a good friend. "Yes," Hannah replied. "Thank you so much for including her." Her gaze traveled about the room and her vision blurred with tears. "I'll never forget all the kindness I've been shown during my stay here in Bent Creek."

"We should get started," Emma said, stepping back into the living room.

Jackson pushed away from where he'd been leaning back against the fireplace. "Guess that means it's time for us men to go do 'man' things while you ladies do whatever it is you all do at baby showers."

Tucker and Grady were right on Jackson's heels, clearly anxious to take their leave from the room filled with women.

"You coming?" Tucker asked Garrett on his way past his brother.

"Not until Hannah opens his gift," their mother said.

"You got me something?" she said, looking up at him, not having expected that. But then she hadn't expected any of this, the party, the kindhearted women who had come to celebrate her son's birth.

"Just a little something I thought Austin might like." His gaze shifted toward the window and then back to her. "I had something else I had hoped to surprise you with, but it's going to have to wait."

"Garrett," she chided, "you didn't have to get me anything."

He smiled. "I wanted to."

"Hannah, honey," Garrett's mother said, "why don't you go ahead and have a seat on the sofa to open your gifts? Afterward, we'll have finger sandwiches and cake."

"Your homemade cranberry-walnut-chicken salad sandwiches?" Garrett asked his mother.

His mother smiled. "That and egg salad sandwiches which Autumn and Blue made."

"We put it inside half-moon sandwiches," Blue informed him.

He looked to Autumn who laughed softly. "Croissants," she explained with a grin. "Thus the 'half-moon.'"

He nodded in understanding. "Of course," he said, looking to Blue. "Those are my favorite."

"Mine, too," Hannah said with a smile as she settled onto the sofa between Jessica and Autumn. She turned to give Jessica a quick hug. "Thank you for coming," she said softly.

"I wouldn't have missed it for the world," her friend replied, reaching out to give Hannah's hand a squeeze.

Garrett crossed the room to a gift-laden table, one Hannah had failed to notice when she'd first entered. Then again, her attention had been drawn to all the people gathered there. She watched as he picked up a large, misshapen package from the floor by the table, one that had been wrapped in a bright red, oversize gift bag, and carried it over to where she sat waiting.

"Little something?" she repeated as she eyed the not-so-little package he had just placed on the floor in front of her.

"It could have been a real one," he said with a grin as she opened the bag.

"Garrett," she said as she pushed the plastic covering away to reveal an old wooden rocking horse. One with such fine detail and craftsmanship that Hannah had to assume it had been handmade.

"There wasn't time to order a new rocking horse," Garrett hurried to explain, "so I thought I would give Austin mine."

She ran her fingers appreciatively over the horse's braided rope mane. "This belonged to you?" It was hard to imagine a man Garrett's size ever being small enough to ride the wooden horse. She was about to tell him he needed to keep something that special for his own child, but then remembered he would never have a child of his own.

"It most certainly did," his mother said, drawing everyone's attention her way. "My son nearly rocked a hole right through his bedroom floor when he was little, he loved that thing so much. Born to ride, he was."

"You don't have to keep it," he said, sounding almost anxious about the gift he'd given her. "We can order Austin a new one and have it sent to Steamboat Springs. I just thought he ought to have a horse of some sort, seeing as how he was born on a horse ranch."

Hannah smiled up at him. "It means so much more to me that this horse belonged to you. If it weren't for you, I might not be sitting here today. And my son…" She let the words trail off, unable to even speak them.

"I'm glad you like it," he said.

Hannah nodded, her smile returning. "I do. And thank you for choosing to go with a wooden horse as opposed to a real live flesh-and-blood one. Taking care of a newborn is going to keep me busy enough."

A warm chuckle passed through his lips. "You're welcome."

"My turn!" Blue announced as she skipped over to the present table.

"She's in charge of bringing you your gifts to unwrap," Autumn explained.

"I can't think of a better present-helper to have than Blue," Hannah said, earning a toothy grin from her little helper.

"Time for me to make my exit," Garrett said. "You ladies enjoy the party."

The second he stepped from the room, Hannah's

gaze shifted over to Blue who was lifting, with great effort, a neatly wrapped present topped with curling strands of multicolored ribbon.

Blue turned, wobbling slightly as she carried the elongated box over to Hannah. "I picked this out all by myself," Blue told her.

"Then I'm sure it's going to be very special," Hannah replied, taking the offered gift. The weight of it surprised her. "Whatever could this be?" she said, enjoying the delight on Blue's face as she worked the ribbons off one end of the wrapped box. "A real horse, perhaps?"

Blue giggled. "A horse can't fit in a box."

"No," Hannah said, "I suppose not. Well, let's see then…" She peeled the paper away. "A swing," she announced, holding it up for the other women in the room to see.

"It's just like mine," Blue said excitedly.

Autumn nodded. "Just like her uncle Garrett loved his rocking horse, Blue loves her swing."

"You gotta tie it to a tree," Blue explained, her gaze fixed on the gift in Hannah's lap.

"I will have to find the perfect tree to hang it from," Hannah said as Blue hurried over to get her another gift to unwrap.

Once the gift opening was done and the delightful luncheon Autumn and Emma had prepared for the shower all eaten, Hannah went around personally thanking her guests. When the door closed behind the last of the ladies from the church who had come that afternoon, Hannah hurried over to help Emma and Autumn with the cleanup.

"Thank you both for the surprise shower," she told them as she gathered up empty paper cups.

Autumn smiled. "We're glad you enjoyed yourself."

The sound of the front door opening drew Hannah's gaze that way. A second later, Garrett appeared in the living room entryway, grinning like she had never seen him grin.

She looked at him questioningly.

"Remember that other gift I mentioned?"

"Yes," she said with a nod.

"They've arrived."

Her brows drew together. "They?"

He inclined his head in the direction from which he'd just come. "Come see."

Hannah set the stack of cups she'd collected down onto a nearby end table and then followed him from the room.

Garrett lifted Hannah's spring jacket from the hall tree by the door and helped her into it. Then, with his grin still intact, turned to open the front door, motioning her outside.

She'd barely taken two steps out onto the porch when a bark sounded, followed immediately by another. Barks she knew. With a gasp, Hannah spun around, her gaze landing on her father who stood smiling at her from the yard, a leash held securely in each hand. At the end of those leashes, her beloved dogs jumped and tugged at the nylon straps, barking excitedly.

"Daddy!" she exclaimed.

"Hello, baby girl," he called back. "Sorry we missed the party. It took longer than I thought to get here."

Tears streaming down her cheeks, Hannah started across the porch in quickened steps. Garrett's steadying hand close around her arm as she reached the edge of the porch.

"They're not going anywhere," he assured her as he helped her down the steps, something Hannah was grateful for as her legs suddenly felt as wobbly as Jell-O. "No need to risk taking a tumble down the steps."

Her father moved toward the house, the energetic, young golden retrievers eagerly towing him.

There was no way she was going to get to hug her father until she'd acknowledged her whimpering pups. "Buddy," she said as she bent to receive a wet kiss. She gave him a loving scratch behind his long, floppy ears and then turned to acknowledge Bandit, giving him a quick hug. "I've missed you boys so much," she said, her voice catching.

"What about me?" her father teased.

She straightened, her dogs still vying for her attention.

"I've got them," Garrett said, taking the leashes from her father who immediately gathered Hannah in his arms.

Tears rolled down her cheeks as she hugged him back. "I've missed you so much. I'm so happy to see you."

"I've missed you, too, baby girl," her father replied, his voice cracking ever so slightly. "I wish I could have been here sooner."

"You were sick," she said with an empathetic smile. "I'm just thankful you're finally over that awful virus."

"That makes two of us," he agreed. "When Garrett called to see how I was feeling, as he's done several times since you arrived in Bent Creek, he asked me if there was any chance I could make it to the surprise baby shower they were having for you after church today. I knew I couldn't miss it."

She looked to Garrett in surprise. "You've been talking to my father?" How could he have kept that from her?

"A few times a week, and I called him first," her father clarified. "You gave me Garrett's number in case I couldn't reach you on your phone. I wanted to make sure you weren't keeping things from me. Especially, since I haven't been able to get here to see how you and my grandson are doing for myself."

"I've told you everything there is to know," she said in her own defense, and then realized she hadn't told him *everything*. She hadn't mentioned anything to her father about her feelings for Garrett. Hadn't even told Garrett how much she cared for him. That she was falling in love with him. But that was for the best, seeing as how they would soon be living miles apart from each other.

"Honey, you and I both know you tend to sugarcoat things nowadays where I'm concerned. But I'm a lot stronger than you think I am."

"I think we're both stronger than either of us realize," Hannah admitted.

Her father nodded.

"I wasn't trying to go behind your back," Garrett said, drawing her attention his way. A troubled frown pulled at his mouth. "Just trying to assure your father that you and Austin were both doing well, which is the truth. Then our conversations would go to everyday things, including sharing a little bit about each of our lives."

How could she hold it against Garrett that he'd kept this from her? When the secret she withheld from him, the fact that she had fallen in love with him, could be far more life altering. "I'm not upset with you. Just surprised."

"Understandable," her father said. "But know that I am beyond grateful for the conversations Garrett and I have had. The house has been far too quiet. At least, it is when the dogs are outside playing. More important, our talks gave me the chance to get to know him better, and his family through him. They were caring for my baby girl after all."

"Oh, Dad," Hannah said with a sad smile. "I'm sorry you've had to be alone."

"It's not like you had a choice in the matter," he told her with an affectionate smile. "I'm just thankful the good Lord has more planned for you and my grandson in this life."

She nodded, saying softly, "So am I."

"It's been tearing me apart," he went on, his expression pained, "knowing I was finally well enough to come to Bent Creek to be with you and my grandson, but unable to find a kennel to take Buddy and Bandit until the end of next week."

"If I had known that was what was keeping your father from coming here, I would have said something earlier," Garrett said, shaking his head. "He never made mention of it until I called to see if he was able to come sooner than you expected him to be here."

"Garrett insisted I bring Buddy and Bandit with me. That you were missing not only me, but your boys as well." Her father looked to Garrett with a grateful smile. "And here we are."

Garrett looked her way. "If you had told me that was why your father hadn't been able to come after having been cleared by his doctor to travel, I would have told you the same thing."

"I didn't want to burden you any more than I already have," she told him.

"Hannah," Garrett said, his tone lightly scolding, "you are not, nor have you ever been, a burden to me. And this is a ranch. A dog or two added to the rest of our animal menagerie of horses, chickens and cats is no big deal. Your happiness is."

Hannah felt her father watching her, but couldn't look his way, knowing that if she did he'd see the truth of her feelings for Garrett written on her face. "Thank you for that," she said, kneeling to give more attention to her pups. "Having my boys here, having my father here, makes me beyond happy." She lifted her gaze, finding Garrett's warm smile. "Thank you for making this day even more special than it already was. I'll never forget everything you've done for me." And she would never forget him. Ever.

"I can't wait for you to meet your grandson," Hannah said as she and her father stepped away from the desk where they had signed him in and moved toward the NICU doors. Garrett had driven them there as soon as they'd gotten her dogs settled in at his place. Not that it had taken much effort. Buddy and Bandit had made themselves right at home on the rug in front of Garrett's fireplace and were napping within minutes.

"I can't wait to meet him," her father replied with a grin as he placed the sterile mask over his nose and mouth and drew the elastic string back over his head.

"Your doctor cleared you to see Austin," Hannah said. "You don't have to wear that."

"I'm not taking any chances," he replied.

Nodding in understanding, she led him to the room that housed the babies needing more specialized care. "Austin is the only baby in here right now."

"I'd say that's a blessing," he replied. "And he gets to come home within the next few days."

They were greeted by the nurse assigned to watch over Austin that afternoon. After introductions were made, Hannah led her father over to the incubator that held his grandson. "Austin, look who I brought to see you. Your grandpa."

Her father placed a flattened hand against the glass, and then cleared his throat before speaking. "I've been waiting for what feels like forever to be able to meet you," he said, his voice cracking. He looked to Hannah, concern knitting his graying brows. "He's so small."

Her smile softened. "Not as small as he was. He's filled out quite a bit since he was first born."

Thick tears looming in his eyes, he looked back to his grandson. "To think what might have happened to the both of you…"

"But it didn't," she said. "That's all that matters."

"I owe Garrett Wade more than I could ever repay him in this lifetime."

"Garrett would never accept any type of repayment for what he's done," she said, knowing that without a doubt. "He risked his life for us because that's the kind of man he is. Brave and caring. And it doesn't end there. He's kind and dependable, and a man of his word." She looked over to find her father studying her.

"You've grown quite attached to this young man," he noted. "And something tells me the sentiment goes both ways."

Garrett had gone from being a stranger to being someone she could confide in. A man she had come to care about. Probably too much if she were being honest with herself. But she couldn't bring herself to admit her feelings aloud. "I've grown attached to the entire Wade family. They've all been so good to me." She looked to her son. "To us."

"I'd like to take a moment to say a prayer of thanks," her father announced, bowing his head.

Hannah closed her eyes and lowered her head as well.

"Thank You, Lord," he began, "for blessing us with this child, a piece of Heather for us to love and to always remember her by. Thank You for bringing Garrett Wade and his family into my daughter's life to watch over Hannah and my grandson when I wasn't physically able to do so. And thank You for allowing Austin's fragile little body to grow and strengthen with each passing day. Amen."

"Amen," Hannah repeated, tears stinging her eyes.

Josie, the nurse on shift, one who had been assigned to Austin when Jessica wasn't there, walked over to join them. "He's doing well," she told them. "No more fussing when it comes to his feedings."

"He's eating already?" her father said in disbelief.

She smiled. "Not actual food. I was referring to his taking the bottle, something he struggled with at first. But he's come around, taking his formula like the growing little boy he is."

"I wasn't able to nurse him," Hannah admitted, feeling as if she had failed her son. The nurses had stressed to her that this can happen when the mother is overly stressed, which she had been, between the loss of her mother and sister, the flood, and then Austin's early arrival.

"Your mother wasn't able to nurse you or your sister either, and you both turned out okay," her father said with a warm smile.

"I never knew that," Hannah admitted, wondering if it wasn't stress that had affected her milk flow, but something genetic. She knew that if her mother were still alive, she would have shared those sorts of things with her daughters when the time called for it.

"Would you like me to get him out for you so you can hold him?" her son's nurse asked.

Hannah nodded. "Yes, please." She looked to her father. "You can go first. But we have to wash our hands before we can hold him."

"Understandable," her father replied as he followed her over to the sink.

After they had both washed their hands, she led her father to the rocker that sat next to her son's crib.

Once her father was settled comfortably, Josie removed Austin from the incubator, carefully adjusting his remaining tubes and wires as she settled the baby into his grandfather's outstretched arms. "He just finished eating a little while ago, so he's a little sleepy right now." Her gaze shifted to Hannah. "Let me know when you're ready to change places with your father."

"I will," Hannah said. "Thank you." She turned her attention back to her father who was looking down at his grandson, a mixture of both adoration and grief etched into the lines around his eyes. A feeling Hannah understood all too well. Overwhelming love for her sister's child, and, yet, a deep pain for the knowledge that her sister would never have the chance to be the mother she had always longed to be.

"He has your sister's eyes," her father muttered as the infant stared up at him, his sleepy eyes drifting open and closed.

Hannah looked down with a sad smile. "Yes, he does."

Her father sniffled, clearly overcome by emotion.

She placed her hand on his shoulder. "I miss her, too, Dad. But our focus right now needs to be on getting Austin home, and giving him the happy childhood Heather would have wanted for him."

He looked up at her. "Are you ready for this?"

"I have to be," she answered honestly. "I just pray that I can be the kind of mother Austin deserves."

"You will be every bit the mother your sister would have been," he replied, his gaze dropping down to the babe in his arms. "How could you not be? You were both raised by an incredible woman who exemplified what a mother should be."

Hannah nodded. "She was the best."

"That she was."

Hannah watched her father as he held his grandson, his eyes filled with such love. Rocking slowly, he examined Austin's tiny fingers and toes. Then he smoothed the side of his finger along the infant's baby-soft cheek. "Your grandpa can't wait to have you home with him." He glanced up at Hannah, adding with a tender smile, "Both of you."

Garrett looked up from the magazine he'd been skimming through as Hannah's father stepped into the waiting room that sat just outside of the NICU's doors.

The older man made his way over to Garrett who was rising to his feet to greet him. "Your turn."

"My turn?" He'd driven them to the hospital but hadn't counted on getting to visit Austin with only two visitors being allowed.

"I thought you might want to go in and see Austin. Hannah tells me you've formed a special bond with my grandson."

Garrett couldn't deny that he felt a deep emotional connection to Hannah's son. With Hannah, too. They'd been through so much together in the weeks since the flood. "I can't answer for Austin, but I can tell you that he's definitely touched a big part of my heart." Just as his mother had.

"Then why don't you go on in and see him?" James Sanders suggested.

"I wouldn't feel right taking time away from your seeing him," Garrett said honestly.

Hannah's father smiled. "I have a lifetime to spend with my grandson after we take him home. I think I can share a little time with you while we're here."

Garrett glanced in the direction of the NICU doors. While he'd known Hannah would be leaving and taking her son with her, hearing her father talk about it really made it hit home.

"Garrett," her father said, drawing his gaze back his way. "I know I've already expressed my gratitude for everything you've done for Hannah and my grandson when you called to tell me about the shower, but words don't seem to be enough. Not for all that you've done."

"I'm just grateful the good Lord set me on the path I was on that day the flood struck," Garrett replied.

"Be that as it may," Hannah's father said, "you are

the one who risked his life to save my daughter and her unborn child. You are the one who got them safely to the hospital when the storm rendered the main road impassable. And you are the one who has given Hannah emotional support when I wasn't here to do so. I don't know what I would have done if I'd lost them, too," he said, his voice cracking. "So, if there's ever anything I can do for you, all you have to do is ask."

Garrett hesitated, his heart pushing him to open up to James. To at least try to work something out before the woman he loved drove away with not only his heart, but with the child he'd grown so very fond of. He cleared his throat, gathering up his nerve. "There is something," he told the older man. "I'm just not sure how to approach this."

James Sanders motioned to the empty waiting room seats. "Have a seat, son. Then you can approach whatever it is you have to say the same way you live your life. With honesty, and good measure of faith thrown in."

Garrett sank down onto one of the padded chairs and waited until Hannah's father had taken the seat beside his before saying, "I love your daughter."

"Well, that's getting right to the point," James teased. "But it's nothing I haven't already figured out."

"You knew?" Garrett said, shocked by the older man's response.

"Son, I knew something was building between you and my daughter by our third phone call. And you aren't the only one who wore their feelings on their sleeve when I talked to them. My daughter is quite taken by you to say the least."

"I'd like to ask Hannah to marry me," he announced, his heart pounding. "And I'd like to ask for your blessing."

James studied him for a moment before saying, "The two of you haven't known each other for very long. Are you sure about this?"

"I've never been more certain of anything in my life," Garrett replied. "And I can't blame you for questioning my feelings for your daughter. I would do the same thing if I were in your shoes. But what I feel for Hannah is beyond anything I've ever felt before. And we've spent hours, days, weeks, getting to know each other. I know what her hopes and dreams are, and I know her fears. We share the same faith and family values."

When James said nothing, just stood there watching him, the knot of anxiety in Garrett's gut grew, but he went on, needing Hannah's father to understand how very much he had come to love his daughter. "I've seen how incredibly brave and strong your daughter can be in the face of adversity. I've watched her with her son, knowing without any doubt that she was put on this earth to be a mother. When I think about Hannah going back to Colorado, I know without a doubt that she'll be taking my heart with her." A heart he never thought would feel again after losing Grace.

"I don't like to speak ill of people," James began, making Garrett wonder what he was about to say, "but I don't think Hannah's first husband ever fully appreciated those qualities in my daughter."

"He gave up someone truly special," Garrett said.

"She reminds me so much of her mother."

His heart went out to the man for the loss of his wife, the woman James had spent so many years loving, had raised a family with, had given his heart to. It had been hard enough for Garrett when he'd lost Grace, and they had barely begun to share all of life's experiences together. He just prayed that if Hannah agreed to marry him they would be blessed with a long, happy, marriage, just as their parents had been. "I'm sorry I never had the chance to meet Hannah's mother. I would like to have asked for her blessing, too."

The older man glanced heavenward and then back to Garrett. "Something tells me she would have happily given it to you. Your love for my daughter is evident, son. I could hear it in your voice every time you called to give me an update on Hannah and my grandson. I see it on your face whenever the two of you are together. Her face as well," he said, emotion thick in his voice. "My daughter deserves the happiness she was denied in her first marriage, and, after getting to know you over the past several weeks, I believe in my heart that she can have that with you. But Hannah wouldn't be bringing just herself into any long-term relationship. She'll be bringing Austin."

"Your grandson snagged a huge piece of my heart from the first moment I held him in my arms. I would feel blessed to be able to raise that little boy as my son. And, just so you know, I'm going to ask Hannah to marry me, but I don't intend to rush her into setting a wedding date. I know there are some things we need to work out first, but I'm more than willing to wait until the time is right for her. And for you. Because you are a very big part of what I hope will be our future."

"I would be proud to have a man like you as my son-in-law," James said with a smile, "so I'm giving you my blessing. But the decision is Hannah's to make."

"That means a lot to me," Garrett said with the utmost sincerity, because Hannah's father could one day be his father, too, if everything worked out as he prayed that it would.

Chapter Ten

The entire family had gathered on Garrett's parents' front porch to welcome Hannah home with her newborn son. Or, at least, welcome her to what had been her temporary home during her stay there. A stay that ended with Austin's release from the hospital. Hannah and her father were leaving to go back to Steamboat Springs the following morning. But not for good if Garrett had his way.

He helped Hannah down from the backseat of his truck where she had been seated next to her son, who was tucked securely inside his brand-new car seat. The one his mother and father had bought for the baby. Her father was already on his way to the house, carrying the bag of baby items they'd brought home from the hospital, including the stuffed bear with the bright blue ribbon his brothers had bought for the baby right after Austin was born.

"I'm sorry about this," he said, inclining his head toward the house. "I should have thought to tell them to give you a little bit of breathing room when we got home."

"I don't mind," Hannah replied as she turned to get

her son from the car seat. Other than a few coos to Austin during their drive home, they were the first words she'd spoken since leaving the hospital.

"Let me," Garrett told her. "It's a bit of a reach for you from where you're standing."

Stepping aside, she waited as Garrett leaned in to unlatch the safety belt that held her son in, and then gently lifted him from the car seat.

"Everything okay?" he asked as he turned to place the tiny, sleeping bundle into Hannah's outstretched arms.

She smiled, but Garrett could tell it was forced, and he found himself hoping that she was as troubled by her leaving as he was. "A little anxious," she replied. "I'm about to be someone's mother all by myself."

"You won't be alone," he told her as he closed the truck door. Then, wrapping a supportive arm around her waist, they started across the yard. "You'll have your father. And you'll have us."

"I know," she said with a sigh. "And I'm so grateful to have you all in my life. But knowing that this precious child will be dependent on me now for his every need, to give him guidance, to assure his happiness, and to do things I don't even know I'm supposed to be doing as a mother, is a little daunting."

Her silence on the way home made much more sense to him now that she had told him what was troubling her. He smiled down at her. "You are and will continue to be an incredible mother, Hannah Sanders. Don't you doubt that for even a second."

"The baby's here! The baby's here!" Blue squealed as she bounced down the porch steps and hurried across the yard to meet them.

Garrett chuckled. "Ready to face your welcome committee?"

Hannah nodded, this time with a genuine smile. "As ready as I'll ever be."

Tucker jogged after his daughter, catching up to her not quite halfway across the yard, and swept Blue up into his arms. Then he turned and waited for Autumn who was trailing after them.

"But I wanna see the baby," Blue whined as she peered at the bundle in Hannah's arm from over top her father's shoulder.

"We will," Autumn said. "But we have to wait for Grandma and Grandpa, and Uncle Jackson, so we can meet Austin together."

His parents caught up to them with Jackson moving in unhurried strides behind them.

Garrett's family formed a human circle around Hannah and him, effectively blocking out the chilly breeze. James Sanders stood a few feet away, grinning as he watched the excitement his grandson was causing.

"I can't see him," Blue muttered with a frustrated frown as she looked down at the bundle from her perch in her father's arms.

Smiling, Hannah peeled the blanket away from her son's face, just enough to give everyone a peek at her son without exposing him fully to the crisp fall air.

Blue let out a little gasp. "He looks like a baby doll."

"Give him a few months," Garrett said with a chuckle.

"Oh, my," his mother sighed, a hand going to her heart. "He's beyond precious."

Garrett's father leaned in for a closer look. With a nod, his gaze lifted to Hannah's. "Looks like you have yourself a fine, strapping son."

Her smile widened. "Hopefully, he will grow up to be as strapping and kindhearted as your sons."

"He's named after one of them," his father replied. "How can he grow up to be anything but?"

Autumn, who stood next to Hannah, reached out to run a fingertip along the baby's cheek. "He's so perfect," she said, her eyes misting over. "And seeing you holding your son makes me wish that I were already holding our baby in my arms." Her softly spoken words of longing immediately drew everyone's gaze her way.

"Baby?" Jackson repeated, looking to Tucker.

"Baby?" his mother repeated, her face lighting up.

Their little brother looked to his wife, one lone brow lifting.

Autumn giggled and, with a shrug of her slender shoulders, said, "Oops."

Grinning, Tucker shook his head. "It appears the cat's out of the bag. Autumn and I were going to wait until Thanksgiving to tell everyone our good news."

"Why did you put a cat in a bag, Daddy?" Blue asked as she stood looking up at him.

Jackson snorted. "I was wondering the same thing myself."

Tucker shot him a warning glance. "Just wait until the shoe is on the other foot."

"Never going to happen," their brother said, some of the humor leaving his face.

"Never say never," their father muttered, no doubt having taken stances in his life that he hadn't been able to hold firm to.

Garrett had done the same himself, vowing to never love again after losing Grace. But here he was, head-over-cowboy-boots in love with Hannah.

Blue's brows creased in confusion. "Why would Uncle Jackson wear his shoes on the wrong feet? That would hurt."

Garrett's mother laughed. "I think we need to take this conversation inside, so Hannah can get her son settled in." She looked to Autumn with a delighted smile. "And you can tell us all about your exciting news."

The circle his family had formed around them disbanded as everyone moved into the house. A bassinet had been set up against the wall where the living room opened up to the dining room. That way Hannah could keep an eye on her son during dinner and then afterward when they moved to the living room to share some lighthearted conversation.

"Hannah…" Garrett said when there was a lull in the conversation going on around him.

She looked his way with a soft smile.

"Would you mind taking a walk with me?"

Her gaze automatically went to the bassinet where her son slept.

"He's sound asleep," her father assured her. "Go on and enjoy your walk. I think you have plenty of backup should my grandson awaken before you get back." He looked to Garrett with a nod, and Garrett knew that it was time to lay his heart on the line in hopes of convincing Hannah to place her own heart into his safekeeping.

"It's colder out than I thought," Garrett stated with a frown as they stepped out into the starlit night, the decorative, battery-operated lantern his mother had given him dangling from his hand.

Hannah snuggled deeper into her coat, her long,

coppery hair whipping about in the breeze. "It's the start of spring," she reminded him as they stepped down from the porch, knowing that during that time of year the weather could go from decently warm to raining, or even snowing that same day. And, at that moment, it felt cold enough to snow.

He paused at the base of the steps, looking about with a troubled frown.

"Garrett?"

"Let's go to the barn," he said. "It'll be warm enough there."

"I thought we were going for a walk."

He looked down at her. "We need to talk, and I don't want you standing outside in the cold. Not with the wind kicking up the way it is."

"Garrett, please don't make this any harder than it already is," Hannah pleaded. Ever since he'd admitted to having feelings for her, asking her to give them a chance, and she'd had no choice but to turn him down, her heart had been aching.

"I don't intend to," he said. "But there is something I need to say, and I'd rather do so where it's somewhat warm."

"The house was warm," she said, thinking it might have been best not to have accepted Garrett's invitation for a walk that evening.

"But not private," he replied.

With a nod, she conceded, and then started for the barn, her heart pounding. She didn't want to talk about her leaving. Or about feelings neither of them would ever be able to act upon. And she didn't want to cry, but even now her eyes were tearing up. She could blame it on the brisk breeze, but her heart knew better. She loved Garrett. And she was going to leave him. Not in the same way Grace had, but it tore at Hannah all the same. She didn't want to be the cause of his closing himself off to love again. Garrett deserved to be happy, even if it couldn't be with her. *Lord, please help me to be strong. And please help guide Garrett down a path that allows him to find the happiness he deserves.*

When they entered the barn, Garrett closed the large door and then turned to face her, his gaze meeting hers. "I had planned to have this discussion out under the stars with the mountains in the backdrop gently lit by the light of the moon. I hadn't counted on a cold front moving in."

A discussion under the stars? And with moonlight on the mountains. That sounded far too romantic a setting for a goodbye. Before she had a chance to dwell on it any further, Garrett closed the distance between them in three long strides and took her hands in his.

"Hannah Sanders," he began, the sound of her name on his lips making her heart race, "you came into my life so unexpectedly. So vulnerable, yet so very strong. From that very first moment when your fearful gaze met mine through that rain-splattered car window, I knew God had placed me there for a reason. What I hadn't realized then was that it was to do more than rescue you from the storm. It was to save me from myself and the emotional isolation I had placed my heart in when it came to ever loving someone again. You made me feel again."

"Garrett," she said with a panicked groan. She couldn't do this. They'd already discussed the reasons why. Tears filled her eyes.

"Hannah, please hear me out," he said tenderly. "The

more I came to care for you and Austin, the more I wanted to throw a lasso over time to keep it from moving forward. But that wasn't an option. Telling you that I've fallen in love with you is. I want to marry you and take that trip to see the northern lights you've longed to go on for our honeymoon. And if you want more children, I'm willing to adopt. We can have that large family you've always dreamed of."

A small sob escaped her lips. "Oh, Garrett…"

"I'm not ready to let you walk out of my life without fighting for you," he told her. "Fighting for us."

She shook her head. "We've already been through this. Neither of us is free to move at this point in our lives, and I can't do a long-distance relationship."

He reached for her hands. "What if you don't have to?"

"Garrett, you can't leave the business you've built here with your brothers for me," she told him, despite her heart wishing otherwise.

"If that's what it takes," he said.

He would do that for her? Tears blurred her vision. "I would never let you do that."

"Then we'll make the long-distance thing work until you feel your father can manage on his own," he told her. "I'm willing to wait as long as it takes if it means you'll be a part of my future. Or have him move to Bent Creek with you and Austin. He's retired, so you wouldn't be asking him to leave his job."

"But I would be asking my father to give up the life he's built in Steamboat Springs, the friends he's made, for me. I can't do that. And I can't take his grandson away from him. Not this soon after losing Mom and Heather," she said, eyes tearing up. "And it wouldn't only be me moving here if I accepted your offer. I have a son that I'll be raising."

"I know that. I want the entire package, you and Austin. How do you feel about raising children and horses?" he countered with a casual shrug, flashing her that charming cowboy grin she'd come to adore.

"Garrett, be serious," Hannah said. Only Garrett could make her want to cry and laugh at the same time.

"I am," he replied, meeting her tear-filled eyes. "And I hope someday to be the man helping you raise your son. I love you, Hannah Sanders, and, at the risk of sounding a little too self-assured, I think you feel the same way about me."

It would be best to put that notion to rest, to tell him that she was grateful for all he had done for her, but nothing more. Only that would be a lie, something she couldn't bring herself to do. "I do love you," she admitted softly. "With all my heart."

His smile widened. A second later, Garrett was kneeling before her, her hand still in his as his free hand slid into the front pocket of his jeans, pulling out a small black box. "Your father has given me his blessing."

Hannah placed her hand over his before he could open the box, tears rolling down her cheeks. "I love you, Garrett Wade. I always will. But I can't accept your proposal. You deserve to find happiness with someone who is free to be with you here in Bent Creek. As much as I want to be that woman, I can't leave my father to deal with his grief alone. And I have no idea how long it will be before I feel comfortable doing so."

Garrett searched her face for a long moment, as if trying to commit it to memory. Then, with a nod of surrender, he stood and released her hand, tucked the ring box back into his jeans pocket. "We'd best get back to the house. I've kept you out here in the cold long enough." He turned, opened the barn door and then reached for the lantern.

Hannah wanted so desperately to throw her arms around Garrett and tell him she was sorry. That she wanted more than anything to be his wife. But life didn't always work out the way one hoped it would. She knew that better than most. Brushing the tears from her cheeks, Hannah stepped out into the night, her heart breaking.

They walked back to the porch in silence. But when they reached his parent's front door, Garrett turned to her. "Just so you know. There will never be another woman for me." That said, he opened the door, the cold wind whipping in behind her, forcing Hannah to step inside before she could respond.

"Back already?" Tucker said when they entered the living room.

"A cold front moved in," Garrett muttered, not meeting Hannah's gaze. He was closing himself off again. She could feel it. And it was all her fault.

"Take off your jackets and warm up by the fire," his mother suggested.

"I have to get going," Garrett announced.

"Already?" Autumn asked in surprise.

"I have a few things I need to do at home yet this evening," he told them.

"Will we see you in the morning?" Hannah asked, not wanting this to be the way they parted ways. With Garrett hurting and her regretting.

He finally looked her way. "I'll be here." With a nod, he bid everyone good-night and then walked out.

Hannah shrugged out of her jacket and draped it over her arm. "I think I'll turn in early tonight."

"Is everything all right, dear?" Emma Wade asked with a worried frown.

"It's been a long day," she told her, forcing a smile. "I'm tired and should try and get some rest before I have to get up through the night for feedings."

Her father pushed out of the chair he'd been sitting in. "You get Austin. I'll carry the bassinet upstairs for you."

Nodding, Hannah walked over to where her son lay sleeping and eased her hands beneath his tiny, blanket-bundled form, gently lifting him. Then she turned and thanked Garrett's family for all they had done for her and her son during their stay there.

"We'll be here to see you off tomorrow," Autumn said. "So, I'm going to save my goodbyes for then."

The others nodded in agreement.

Tears pooled in her eyes. "Good night then." Hannah carried her son up the stairs, her father, carrying the bassinet, followed behind her.

"What happened between you and Garrett?" he asked, the moment they entered the guest bedroom where Hannah had been staying.

"I don't know what you mean," she said, unable to look her father in the eye. He knew her too well. He would see her pain.

He placed the bassinet beside the bed and then turned to her. "I was expecting you and Garrett to come back to the house with an announcement. Not part ways like neither of you could bear to look at one another."

"I told Garrett no," she replied, a tear rolling down her cheek.

Her father's brows drew together in confusion. "Why? That young man's heart is overflowing with love for you. I thought you felt the same way about him. Was I mistaken?"

"No," she said with a sniffle. "You weren't."

"So you do you love him?"

She nodded. "Yes."

"Then why did you turn his proposal down? Is this about what happened with Dave?" he asked with a frown. "Because Garrett isn't anything like your ex."

Lifting her gaze, she said sadly, "No, it has nothing to do with Dave."

"I know your relationship with Garrett happened faster than most do, but I believe it's real."

She walked over to place her sleeping son into the bassinet. "It's not just about Garrett and me. There are others to consider. He can't just up and leave his brothers and the business they run together. Although, he offered to give it all up for me. And there's you."

"Me?" he said with a lift of his slightly graying brows.

"Dad, I can't leave you alone in Steamboat Springs," she admitted. "Not now."

"You gave up your chance at happiness with Garrett so I wouldn't be alone?"

Tears ran down her cheeks. "You've lost so much already. I won't take your grandson away from you."

He walked over and drew her into his arms for a comforting hug, resting his chin on the top of her head.

"Honey, all I want is for you to be happy, something you won't be back in Steamboat Springs. Not only because Garrett won't be there, but because our home isn't really home anymore. Not without your mother there."

She lifted her head to look up at him questioningly.

"What would you say if I told you that I'd like a fresh start somewhere else?" he asked as he released her and took a step back.

"You would leave Steamboat Springs?" she asked in disbelief. "Where would you go?"

"I was kind of thinking Bent Creek would be a nice place to begin anew," he said with a smile. "Especially, since my daughter and grandson will be living here."

"But you'd be leaving the home you and Mom made so many memories in."

"Memories can be taken with you anywhere," he said with a wistful smile. "I'd like to find a smaller place with a little bit of land, maybe even get a dog, because Bandit and Buddy will be moving out when you do, and start making new memories for myself. More important," he said, "I want you to find the same happiness I found with your mother. And for that to happen you need to follow your heart."

Her father's words were the answer to her prayers. She would no longer be forced to choose between the two men she loved most in the world. She could follow her heart, knowing right where it would lead her—to the kind, loving cowboy who had come to her rescue and had shown her what true love really was.

Garrett pulled up to his parents' house, his gaze immediately drawn to Hannah who was sitting alone on the front porch. She wore a sweater and a denim jacket, but the way she was hugging herself told him Hannah was still chilled.

Cutting the engine, he stepped out of his truck and strode toward the porch. "It's a little cold to be sitting outside," he remarked.

"I was waiting for you," she said, a hint of uneasiness in her voice. She stood and made her way down the porch steps until she stood in front of him on the walkway. "I thought we could take a walk."

A frown tugged at his mouth. He knew what the walk she wanted to take was about. She wanted to tell him goodbye in private. Maybe so he wouldn't cause a scene like he had the night before when he'd left so abruptly. "About last night," he said. "I'm sorry I left the way I did."

"I'm sorry I hurt you," she replied. "I tried to call you last night, but I couldn't reach you. Not that I blame you for not picking up the phone."

"It wasn't on purpose," he told her. "I set my cell phone on the kitchen counter last night after I got home, and then went outside to sit and think for a while. I didn't see that I had missed your call until this morning. My first thought was that something was wrong with Austin. But my brothers would have come to get me if that were the case. Not sure what else there is for you and I to say this morning other than goodbye." It hurt even speaking the words. He didn't want her to leave—ever.

"Let's take that walk," she said with a smile that made his heart yearn.

He had to be the man his mother had raised him to be and tuck his hurt and frustration away. With a nod, they started away from the porch. "At least, the wind isn't whipping about today."

"It wouldn't matter," she told him. "We're going to the barn."

The pain dug a little deeper. The last place he wanted to be with her was the place where Hannah had put an end to his hopes and dreams of a future together with her. "Okay," he conceded in silent suffering.

They crossed the yard and stepped into the barn, only this time it was Hannah who closed the door behind them. Then she turned to look up at him. "I have to leave this morning," she told him.

He nodded knowingly, his mouth pressed into a firm line.

"But only to go back and give notice to my job and help my father get the house ready to put up for sale."

It took a long moment for her words to settle in. "You what?"

"Garrett Wade," she said, her nervous smile softening, her beautiful green eyes searching his, "you are everything I could ever want in a husband. You're compassionate, strong of faith and a devoted family man—one I'd love to raise my son with. So, if your offer of marriage still stands, and you don't mind my father moving to Bent Creek to be near us, then my answer is yes. I would love nothing more than to marry you."

He had spent all night preparing himself for their goodbye, praying to the Lord to watch over Hannah and her son. Now it seemed he might have the privilege of watching over them himself for the rest of their lives together. Joy filled his heart and spread through him.

"If you've changed your mind, I understand," she said, worry replacing her confident smile.

The softly spoken words had him drawing her to him. Looking down at the woman he held in his arms, Garrett smiled. "Not a chance. You are the woman I want to spend the rest of my life with. As your husband, and as the father of your son."

"And you're okay with my father moving here?"

"More than okay," he told her. "I suppose we should go inside and share our good news."

"My father already knows," she admitted. "And I have a feeling your family knows now, too."

He chuckled. "You're probably right."

She leaned into him. "I love you, Garrett Wade."

"I love you, too, Hannah Wade," he replied, his heart filled with it.

Laughing softly, she said, "My name's not Wade yet."

"Just testing it out," he said with a grin.

"It sounds perfect to me," she sighed happily.

"No, you are," he told her. "The perfect woman for me. Thank you for giving me the family I never thought I'd have."

"Thank you for making my family complete," she replied, tears in her eyes.

Emotion welling up inside him, Garrett lowered his mouth to hers in a tender kiss, one that promised a lifetime of love and devotion.

* * * * *

THE COWBOY'S
UNEXPECTED BABY

Stephanie Dees

For all the mamas and daddies
who open their hearts and homes to unexpected
babies, who freely offer their love while expecting
nothing in return and who know down to their soul
that every child deserves a family.

Have not I commanded thee?
Be strong and of a good courage; be not afraid,
neither be thou dismayed: for the Lord thy God
is with thee whithersoever thou goest.
—*Joshua* 1:9

Chapter One

Garrett Cole stumbled into the kitchen where he'd set the coffee to brew exactly seven minutes before his alarm went off. The last of the water sputtered through the filter as he pulled the coffeepot out and reached for a mug that wasn't there.

He heard a mewling sound and froze. It sounded like a cat. Or a kitten. He thought about investigating, but no—coffee first, then strange sounds. Opening the cabinet, he pulled out a mug and, still half-asleep, went through the coffee ritual. One spoonful of sugar, a splash of vanilla almond milk, stir. Drink. *Yes.*

As the first jolt of caffeine hit his system, he started running the day's schedule in his mind. Juvenile court at ten o'clock. Mrs. Bledsoe at three o'clock to final-ize her latest will. The new social worker Wynn hired was dropping by today or tomor—he stopped, tilted his head and listened.

Was it a cat?

At least one single cat would be easier to deal with than the dog who'd had nine puppies under his porch a few months ago. Puppies everywhere. Puppies galore.

He and his brothers and new sister-in-law had chased those little rascals all over the ranch and called in every last favor they were owed to find those pups a home.

He took another swig of coffee and listened. Silence.

In Garrett's mind, he had three things going for him: his passion for his work, his dedication to family and his willingness to risk everything for a lost cause. And, boy, did those lost causes find him. Puppies under the house. Parents on their last chance to prove their sobriety. And now, apparently, kittens.

Garrett pulled open the door and stepped outside, stopping short when he heard the small cry again.

He spun slowly to the left.

It wasn't a cat.

Garrett blinked, his mind refusing to process what he saw. There was an actual *baby* on his front porch. He took a step closer and closed his eyes. It had been a rough week—lots of late hours prepping for the last court case. Maybe he wasn't as awake as he thought he was. But when he opened his eyes, it was still there—a very tiny baby in a pink outfit, rocking gently on the porch swing in its car seat.

He spun around, peering into the woods, sure his brothers were about to jump out laughing at how good they'd gotten him. But he saw nothing, heard nothing— only the sound of the wind rustling through the dried stalks of the cornfield yet to be cut and the rooster crowing in the distance.

In the car seat, the baby was starting to squirm.

Garrett stabbed his fingers through hair that was forever in need of a cut, the same two questions on repeat in his mind. Who left a baby on his porch? And what was he supposed to do with her?

The tiny face was getting redder, the grunts and whimpers coming more often. Garrett had almost no experience with babies, but he was pretty sure that wasn't a good sign.

Picking up the seat and the diaper bag sitting next to it, he carried her—pink clothes, so it had to be a girl, right?—into the house. By the time he set her down again on the coffee table, the fussing had turned to full-out wailing, her color going from red to blotchy purple.

Garrett stared at her for a second, indecision paralyzing him. He had no idea what to do. Fingers shaking, he opened the diaper bag and tried to remember what he knew about babies, the sum total of knowledge coming from the few hours he'd spent with his brother Devin's four-month-old twins.

"If they're crying, there are three reasons," Devin had said, ticking them off on his fingers. "Diaper. Dairy. Daddy."

Garrett had rolled his eyes at his brother's alliterative description. Now he wished he'd paid more attention. What did that even mean? He grabbed his phone from the coffee table and shot a text to Devin. Need you. Now.

Okay, three *D*s. Diaper, that one was easy. The baby could be wet or need a change. And yes, there were diapers in the bag!

But dairy? He chewed his lip as he dug through the bag. That had to be milk.

"Oh, you're hungry!" He grinned at her like he'd made a breakthrough scientific discovery. She was unimpressed, the crying ratcheting up to a decibel he had no idea a child could reach.

Frantic now, he went back to the bag, searching the pockets in desperation. *Nothing*. He looked inside.

There were a couple of little outfits, but he didn't see a bottle. With a frustrated grumble, he picked up the bag and shook the contents onto the couch cushion.

Finally, he found two small prefilled bottles, the kind Devin's twins had when they first left the hospital. He picked up another small package with the nipple, screwed it on to the top of the bottle and set it on the coffee table.

He unlatched the buckles, freed her arms from the straps of the car seat and gingerly lifted her out. One hand under her backside and the other behind her head, he held her like a bomb that could explode any second. Come to think of it, he was pretty sure he'd be less freaked out holding a bomb than he was holding this screaming baby. A baby he'd just found on his front porch.

Going on pure instinct and vague memory, he moved her into the crook of his elbow and picked up the bottle. As soon as he touched her mouth with the nipple, she latched on and began to drink, her distraught cries subsiding except for a few lingering shuddery breaths.

She looked up at him with bottomless blue eyes, tears still pooling in the corners.

"I'm sorry," he whispered. He eased into a chair and stared, shell-shocked, at the wall across from him.

Whose baby was this? He ran through his list of clients in his mind. Would one of them be so desperate that they would leave a baby on his doorstep?

His head jerked up as the front door swung open.

"I need coffee. What's so important that…" His brother Devin limped into the room, his voice trailing off as he spotted the bundle in Garrett's arms. "Uh, that's a baby."

"Brilliant deduction."

Devin shot him a look and continued to the kitchen. He took a mug out of the cabinet and filled it with coffee before he came back to the living room and sat down in the chair across from Garrett. "Yours?"

"What? No! I walked outside and she was there, on the porch." His voice sounded panicky, even to his own ears, but that was probably because he *was* panicking.

"Why's all that stuff on the couch?"

"She was screaming and I couldn't find the bottles so I dumped everything out."

"I get it, trust me. But it looks like you've got it under control now." Devin reached over and picked a white envelope up from the floor. "What's this? Want me to open it?"

"Yeah, go ahead." The baby sucked the last little bit of milk from the bottle. Her eyes were closed now, her little body finally relaxed. "Wait. She finished the bottle. Am I supposed to burp her now?"

"Just put her on your shoulder and pat her back." Devin didn't look up from the papers. "The baby's name is Charlotte. She's two weeks old. Wow. Two weeks?"

"Who thought it was a good idea to leave a two-week-old baby with me?" Garrett's voice rose in alarm as he patted the back of the tiny little girl.

"Well, there are some legal papers here that look like someone thought it was a good idea to leave a baby with you forever. You're listed as Charlotte's legal guardian." His brother laughed. "Well…this will put a damper on your merry-go-round of girlfriends."

Garrett scowled.

"You know I haven't been out with anyone si—" His mouth dropped open. *"Guardian?"*

His mind would not process this. Finally, he said, "The mother's name?"

"Brooklyn Brady. Do you know her?"

Garrett slumped back in the seat, one hand holding the baby in place on his chest. "I know her. I was her law guardian until she aged out of foster care. I didn't even know she was pregnant."

Garrett's eyes stung. Brooklyn had been his client for as long as he'd been doing family law. She'd grown up in foster care with her own mother dropping in and out just often enough to keep the courts from terminating parental rights. Brooklyn had finally been freed for adoption, but by that time she was an angry fifteen-year-old and no one wanted to adopt her.

"There's a letter here for you." Devin looked up from the papers in his hand. "How old is this girl?"

"Eighteen." Garrett's emotions had been on a roller coaster—no, roller coaster wasn't descriptive enough. This morning had been more like one of those slingshot rides that shot you into the sky and bounced you around on rubber bands until you got sick.

Mostly now, he just felt sad. Sick, but sad.

"She says she can't give Charlotte a stable life. She can't give herself one. So she's leaving Charlotte with you because…" His brother cleared his throat. "…because you're the only person who ever made her feel like she wasn't damaged goods. Like she was worth caring about. That's why she left the baby with you."

Garrett had tried to do his best for Brooklyn, but he felt like he'd failed her. She'd aged out without a family, without anyone to guide her and be her support system. She'd kept in touch with him for a while but when she'd stopped calling, he hadn't tried very hard to find out why.

"What are you going to do?"

Garrett *wanted* to settle down. He wanted to know that when he came home from work, someone would be there waiting for him. He hadn't found the right person yet—not for lack of trying—a fact his brothers teased him about incessantly. But he was tired of being alone.

He wanted a family. He just hadn't expected it to happen like this. "If the paperwork holds up?"

"Yeah."

Garrett tucked a sleeping Charlotte into the crook of his arm. She barely stretched from his elbow to his wrist. So tiny and so dependent. He blew out a shaky breath and looked up at his brother. "Guess I'll have to learn how to change a diaper."

Abby Scott strolled down the main street of Red Hill Springs, Alabama, getting her first look at the little town where she'd taken a temporary grant-funded job as the town social worker. Her golden retriever Elvis walked calmly beside her. He was on a leash, but didn't need to be. He wouldn't budge from her side unless she asked him to.

Together, she and Elvis had traveled almost constantly for the last eight years, providing animal-assisted therapy in disaster areas. She was the expert in mental health, but Elvis was her partner, the one who really made the kids she worked with feel better.

Compared to the places she usually stayed, the small house she'd rented in Red Hill Springs had seemed positively luxurious when she'd stopped by this morning to drop off her stuff.

The town was charming with the carefully curated storefronts and restaurants. There was even a pediatrician's office on this street. For a moment, she wondered if he saw a lot of childhood trauma in his practice and then shoved that thought right out of her head. She'd find out soon enough.

The call from Mayor Wynn Grant asking her to set up a program in their town to make sure no kids slipped through the cracks had come at a perfect time. She was on leave from her job at the disaster relief organization, making her own mental health a priority for a few months.

Her last assignment had been hard. She needed a reset. Brain. Heart. Body. Faith.

A car door closed behind her and she turned around to see her old friend Wynn, hair flying, heels clacking, arms stretched out to sweep her into a whirling hug.

Abby stepped back, laughing. "You haven't changed a bit since our days on Capitol Hill, Mayor Grant."

"Ha! I've seen the bags under my eyes in the mirror. I know that's not true." Wynn locked arms with Abby and drew her down the street. "Come on. My office—*your* new office—is just a few doors down. You might need to pick up a few things before you start next week."

"I can't wait to see it. You're happy? You look happy."

Wynn smiled as she pushed open a door next to a small brass sign that said Cole & Grant, and underneath, in smaller letters, Attorneys at Law. "I am. I'll tell you all about it. But we have plenty of time to talk while you're here. I'm so excited!"

Abby really didn't have to ask. She could see the happiness and peace radiating from her friend's face. A knot formed in Abby's stomach, the same knot she'd been pushing down, pushing away, for months. She hadn't felt at peace in a long time and a part of her was afraid she would never find it again. She'd seen so much, experienced so much. Her hand inadvertently went to her side, where the scar from the bullet wound that had been her ticket home still ached.

Her job as a social worker on a disaster relief team wasn't made up of predictable pieces. It was random and exhausting, but also meaningful. Her decision to go on a training mission to a refugee camp near the Syrian border had seemed like more of the same. She'd never worried much about her own safety. Danger to herself had always seemed sort of abstract.

Until it wasn't.

Wynn's voice dragged her back to the present. "So this is it. Nothing extravagant. But we have Bess—the best executive assistant in the southeast. Bess, this is my friend Abby. She's joining our staff here for a few months—unless we can convince her to stay."

"Nice to meet you." Bess was young and pretty, and from the looks of her spotless desk, frighteningly efficient. She picked her bag up from a hook on the back of the chair. "Wynn, I have a dentist appointment this morning, but I'll be back as soon as possible."

"Garrett should be in any minute. We've got it covered." Wynn turned to Abby. "I have a few minutes for coffee, if you do, Abs."

"Of course." Abby followed Wynn to the coffeepot against the back wall and leaned against the counter while her friend filled two mugs. "I love this. I love all of it. The town, the office, your happy face. I'm so glad I'll get to be here for a few months to enjoy it."

"Me, too." Wynn handed her a cup of coffee with a speculative look Abby recognized. "So tell me why you really had six months to give me for this project. I'm thrilled, believe me. But I thought you were planning to go back to your job when your doctor gave you the all clear."

"I was." Abby hesitated. She wanted to go back to work. She found it fulfilling in a way that nothing else in her life ever had been. But being wounded in Syria had changed things, left her feeling helpless in a way she never wanted to feel again. She needed time.

She took a deep breath, about to say just that, as the front door slammed open.

A man struggled through the opening with an infant car seat over one arm. On the other, he'd strung a diaper bag and a half-dozen plastic bags from a discount store.

He was dressed in a suit, but he'd missed a couple buttons on his shirt, which was only tucked in on one side. She narrowed her eyes, glancing over at Wynn. "Client?"

Wynn's eyebrows shot up. "Ah...no. My partner, Garrett. Who doesn't have any kids and is usually fully dressed when he comes to work."

Abby watched as Garrett strong-armed his load onto a conference table. His dark hair was in haphazard disarray. Behind dark-rimmed glasses, his deep brown eyes were expressive and desperate.

"Garrett, what in the world?" Wynn reached him in time to help him untangle himself from the line of plastic bags. A pink plastic baby bottle tumbled out of the bag and bounced off the concrete floor.

Abby crossed to the table and picked up the bottle, holding it out to Wynn's partner.

He took it from her hand and then looked up, shoulders squaring as he realized he didn't know her. His gaze shot to Wynn, who grinned.

"Garrett, my best friend Abby, our new town social worker. Abby, this is Garrett. And I have no idea who this baby belongs to."

"That would be me. For now. Apparently." Garrett shoved his fingers through longish dark hair, making it stand on end. "I'm her guardian."

"I'm sure there's a story there and I definitely want to hear it," Wynn said. "But right now, I have a date with Judge Morrison."

"You're in court this morning? I was hoping you could watch Charlotte. I have court, too. I'd ask for a continuance, but it's a permanency hearing."

Wynn shrugged into her suit jacket and picked up her briefcase. "I'm sorry, Garrett. I'm cutting it close as it is."

She wrapped her free arm around Abby and cinched her in for a sideways hug. "I'm so glad you're here for a while. It's been too long. I wish I didn't have to go."

"Go do your job. We have time to catch up before I start work next week."

As Wynn blew out the door, an uncomfortable silence stretched. Abby shot Garrett an awkward smile.

"I'm usually a little more together than this." Garrett smiled sheepishly, rubbing the stubble on his chin. "I usually shave."

He was obviously in over his head and since she

could understand that, Abby gave him an empathetic smile. "It sounds like you've had quite a morning. Most of the time Elvis and I work in places where there's no running water, so there's a decent chance I wouldn't have noticed anyway."

He looked around the office. "Bess?"

"At the dentist."

His head dropped. He muttered, "Family emergency justifies a continuance and this is most definitely a family emergency."

Was he talking to her?

A second later, he dug his cell phone out of his pocket and snapped off a text. He didn't look up again until he'd shoved the phone back into place in his pocket. His eyes widened when he saw her, like he'd forgotten she was there.

He rubbed his forehead. "Sorry. This morning really threw me. I have no idea what I'm doing."

Abby told herself this wasn't her problem. She told herself not to get involved. She even told herself to think about that long nap she'd promised herself this afternoon. "I could stay. I guess?"

His eyes snapped to hers. "Are you sure?"

The hope in his brown eyes made her glad she'd made the impulsive offer. "Sure. I like babies."

"Do you know how to change a diaper?" His grin was lightning fast as he turned to unbuckle the baby from the car seat. "Oh, no, I left the diapers in the car."

Abby let out a stunned laugh as he handed her the baby and sprinted out the door. She touched the baby's dimpled chin with one tentative finger. "Hey, little girl."

The baby blinked up at her, a fleeting smile crossing the small face. Just like that, Abby was charmed.

She glanced down at her golden retriever, who waited patiently beside her. His blond eyebrows seemed a little skeptical, even as his tail thumped on the floor. "Oh, come on, she's cute, but we're just helping out for a little while." His expression didn't change. "I mean it. We're not getting sucked into anything, I promise."

Chapter Two

A few minutes later, Garrett kicked open the front door of the office and dragged in the box with the porta-crib. Under his other arm was a box of diapers. "Got 'em."

"Wow. You bought a crib."

"Yeah, I didn't have time to do research this morning. I just bought everything. Too much?"

"I've been out of the country for a while. I think I've forgotten what it's like to have choices and everything available right when you need it." Her voice was soft, her eyes on the baby.

Garrett snuck a glance at her. Short dark brown hair prone to wave, long black eyelashes, pretty hazel eyes that looked just a bit wary. He flipped through the information in his mind that Wynn had shared with him about Abby. Licensed clinical social worker. Disaster relief overseas. Old friends. Wait—she got shot. That's right. She was working in a Syrian refugee camp and somehow got shot.

He gave her a rueful smile. "I'm not usually so impulsive. Or maybe I am, I don't know. Either way, I just remembered you got shot. I'm sorry. That must've been horrible."

Abby made an attempt at a smile. "Yeah, it was pretty bad. I know all the things to do for people who experience traumatic events, but education only goes so far when you're the one with the trauma."

"I was pretty young when my parents were killed in a car accident, but I still remember what it was like to have that safety net pulled out from under me. If you ever want to talk, I'm a good listener."

She nodded but didn't say anything, just looked away.

Okay, then. *Way to go, champ. Batting a thousand.* "So what's next? Maybe I should set up the porta-crib?"

Abby wrinkled her nose. "Actually, I think now might be a good time for Diaper Changing 101."

Gingerly, he leaned forward and sniffed. "Oh, yeah. So what do I do first?"

"I laid out the changing pad and the wipes on the conference table." Abby walked over to the table and, with her hand supporting Charlotte's neck, laid the baby gently onto the mat. "Make sure you hold her head up if you're not cradling her against you."

"Support the neck. Got it." Oh, surely he hadn't been letting Charlotte's head flop around all morning?

Abby stepped to the side and said, "The first thing you do is take off enough clothes so you can change her."

"I think this is a see-one-do-one learning experience. I'll just watch you this time." Garrett mentally crossed his fingers.

"Sure, but you have to take her home with you tonight whether you know how to change a diaper or not."

"You're not nice."

A laugh sputtered out. "Tactfully put. But I get it, it's cool. You'll probably be fine on your own."

"Wait…that came out wrong. You're obviously *very* nice." He shot a grin at Abby and stepped up to the edge of the table. Beads of sweat formed across his forehead as he looked down at the baby, who stared at him with her fist in her mouth. Charlotte's legs were no bigger than his thumb.

"You just have to go for it. She won't break, I promise you."

He could do this, no problem. He'd raised newborn goats and they'd survived. How different could it be? He tucked his fingers under the elastic band at Charlotte's waist, and after a few minutes of wrangling, he managed to get the baby partially undressed. "Now what?"

"Slide the fresh diaper underneath but keep the dirty one under her until…" Abby's voice trailed off as he pulled the soiled diaper out and got the clean one dirty.

"Oh. Oh, no."

She didn't say anything, just handed him another clean diaper. This time, he slid the clean one under and took the wipe she held out.

"Take two. No worries, Charlotte. We got this." He held her feet up, took a swipe and gagged.

Beside him, Abby tried—and failed—to hide the fact that she was laughing at him.

"Hey, feel free to get in here and—" He made another pass at the mess. "Oh, this is awful. She's so wiggly. Stop laughing, Abby."

She held out another wipe. "Here, but be quick about it, or…"

He sighed, and without a word held out his hand for another diaper.

The giggle from Abby started him chuckling and before he knew it, he was laughing, but he got the diaper around the baby and fastened the tabs. When he looked up, he caught a glimpse of Abby's smile and it stopped him in his tracks, made him want to dig deeper and find out what really made her tick.

As if his life wasn't complicated enough.

So that was a big fat no. He was full up on lost causes. He'd tried to help Brooklyn—all that time spent as her law guardian and for what? He was caring for an abandoned baby—*her baby*—and she was nowhere to be found.

He was on lost cause number umpteen thousand forty-two. He didn't have time for any more. Even one with pretty hazel eyes and a sharp sense of humor.

Brushing his fingers across the peach fuzz on Charlotte's head, he picked her up. And the diaper he'd struggled to put on her slid halfway down her legs. "Umm…help?"

"Easy fix." Abby laid the baby back down on the mat and deftly released and refastened the tabs before slipping the leggings back on bird-thin baby legs. "You did great. You just have to make the diaper tighter than you think."

Garrett shook his head. "Not as easy as it looks. How'd you learn to do that?"

"I put myself through college being a nanny." She lifted Charlotte and handed her back to Garrett. "Good to go. You'll be a pro in no time."

He cradled Charlotte in his arms and looked down at her little face. She was precious, with that dusting of strawberry-blond hair on her head and long blond eyelashes. And that whole ugly diaper business faded from his mind.

His heart squeezed.

Was he really going to be able to do this?

Abby picked up the diaper-changing paraphernalia and tucked it into the diaper bag, trying to ignore the warm feeling in her chest as she watched Garrett's face soften. "So how does one end up being surprise guardian to an infant?"

He glanced up. "She was left on my doorstep this morning."

"What?" Abby gaped at him. It sounded like something from the plot of a TV movie. "Do you know who left her there?"

He swayed back and forth as Charlotte's eyelids fluttered closed. "Her mom is a former client. I was her law guardian when she was in foster care."

"Maybe this is an obvious question, but how'd she know where you live? I'd guess that's not something you share with your clients on a regular basis."

"No. My brothers and I own a ranch and we have some horses and goats and cows. Last spring, we invited a bunch of foster families out for a picnic. Brooklyn was one of those." He shrugged. "It seemed like such a small thing at the time."

"It's a nice thing. I wouldn't second-guess it now." She put her hand on his arm and his dark brown eyes darted up to meet hers. She swallowed hard. "So, um… she just left the baby on your porch?"

"She also left signed papers giving me custody— technically a delegation of parental authority—but I have no idea if that will stand up to scrutiny. To make matters more complicated, I'm a mandatory reporter. I can't just pretend that a baby didn't appear on my front porch. I have to report this to family services."

His eyes were steady behind the lenses of his dark-rimmed glasses and Abby realized that momentary flash of attraction hadn't gone away. Instead, she found herself drawn to find out more about him. His laugh lines told her he was a man who smiled often, his gentleness with the baby revealing a kind heart.

Oh, girl, get a grip on that wild imagination. She had no space in her life right now for any kind of entanglement, romantic or otherwise, even if she did that kind of thing. Which she didn't. She had to focus on rebuilding her life. Or building a new life?

Whatever—she had to focus. "Do you know how to reach the mother?"

"I tried calling her. Or at least the last number I had for her, but I didn't get an answer."

"Tough situation." Abby paused a moment, not sure if she should even ask the next question. "Do you... want to be her legal guardian?"

He looked down into Charlotte's guileless face, raised one shoulder and let it drop with another sigh. "I don't know what I want. I want to make this better—for everyone."

Abby nodded slowly. "I'm familiar with that feeling. If I can help, let me know."

"Thanks." With Charlotte firmly asleep, he laid her gently into her car seat and eased himself free. "Come on, I'll give you the grand tour."

The office space was open, industrial almost, with three small offices and the receptionist's desk on one side of the room. The walls of the offices were glass panels which, now that she considered it, was a thoughtful choice. Enough privacy for confidentiality but enough visibility for everyone's safety. Something she could appreciate these days.

"Before Wynn joined the practice, the whole space was open. It was just a few chairs and a desk."

By the front door, there was a cozy seating area. Behind that a conference table and, in the very back of the room, a small kitchenette. The overall effect was warmth from the exposed brick and reclaimed wood, but with enough polish that it would give clients a sense they were in good hands. "It's really a remarkable space. I can see that you both had a hand in designing it."

"Thanks. I like it."

A quick look at the baby reassured Abby that Charlotte was still sleeping, so she followed him across the room for a closer look at the individual offices. Elvis lifted his head to track her movement.

"This one is Wynn's, if you couldn't tell from the desk. Her husband Latham made it."

Like Wynn herself, the small office managed to convey chic and approachable at the same time. The desk was a smooth concrete surface over reclaimed wood supports. It was bare except for a closed laptop and a small bird's nest with four hand-carved eggs. "I love it. It looks just like her."

Garrett's office was next to Wynn's. In contrast to Wynn's pristine office, his space was…lived in.

"I like a creative organization system, as you can see." Garrett grinned.

A long wood counter stretched the length of the wall behind his desk. His filing system seemed to be a series of labeled boxes stacked three deep. She snorted a laugh as she noted the huge black cat stretching in the corner, underneath a signed poster of Michael Jordan dunking a basketball.

"Barney Fife came with the place. No idea how old he is, but I'm guessing at least fifteen."

She smiled. "I didn't know you had an office cat."

"Will your dog be okay having a cat around?"

"Elvis likes cats. Worst-case scenario, he just ignores Barney. Best case, they'll be BFFs."

The cat turned one sleepy yellow eye toward her before going back to his nap.

From the door, Garrett said, "He's very demanding."

She laughed again. "I can see that."

"So this one is yours. The desk came out of the historic school. I rescued it before they tore the place down. It's probably at least a hundred years old."

"I like it. It has personality." The two leather chairs were generic but in good shape. She made a mental note to buy a plant and some art for the walls. Maybe a throw rug. Here she had time to make the place—the job—her own. It was a shift in thinking, but a much-needed one. "Oh, there's a dog bed."

"Wynn wanted to make sure that Elvis would feel comfortable here, too. She's really excited about this project. I am too, to be honest. If we can identify ways to help people before they need a lawyer, maybe we can really make a difference in people's lives."

"I agree. I can't wait to get started." Their tour ended back at the conference table. She started picking up the stuff Garrett had bought for the baby earlier this morning. She found two packages of bottles, a can of formula, three different kinds of pacifiers, some baby socks and, even though he wouldn't need it for some time, a baby-proofing kit.

Abby was still staring at the assortment of stuff when a woman carrying a diaper bag and a large translucent plastic tub came in through the front door. Garrett sprang into action and met her at the door, taking the big storage tub out of her hands.

"Thanks, Garrett." The woman's blond hair was piled on top of her head and, despite circles under her eyes, she sent Abby a bright smile. "You must be Abby. I'm Wynn's sister, Jules. It's great to finally meet you."

"Nice to meet my landlord in person." Abby smiled. "I dropped my stuff off at the cottage this morning and came straight into town to meet Wynn. I didn't even have a chance to look around."

"And I got an SOS call from Wynn about Garrett's surprise baby, so I packed up a few things just to get him through." As she spoke, Jules walked to the table and looked into the baby carrier. "Oh, she's precious, Garrett."

Garrett seemed to have things under control now, so Abby picked up her purse. She used a hand motion to call Elvis, who was by her side in an instant. "I guess I need to get going."

He looked up in alarm. "You're leaving? But I haven't learned how to make a bottle yet."

"I think I've got you covered there." Jules unzipped the large diaper bag. "There are some benefits to having a pediatrician for a brother and one of them is free samples. I stopped by his office across the street and filled this bag with little bottles of ready-made formula. They should last a few days, at least."

"Oh, wow, Jules, thank you. I hadn't even thought

about the pediatrician. I guess I need to make an appointment for Charlotte."

"You have a lot to learn, but you'll figure it out. We all do, eventually." Jules glanced at the smartwatch on her wrist. "I've got to run, too—I'm due to meet with the restaurant staff—but if you need anything, let me know. Abby, I hope we can get to know each other better while you're here, especially since we're neighbors now."

"Thanks so much, Jules."

With a grin shot back over her shoulder and a quick wave, her new neighbor hustled out the door and down the sidewalk. And as the door swung shut, Abby heard the first whimper from baby Charlotte.

"I think that's my cue."

"Wait." Panic laced Garrett's voice. "Can you get her while I fix the bottle?"

The bottle was easy to prepare thanks to Jules's thoughtful delivery. A quick shake and he was ready to go. He was holding his hands out to take Charlotte to feed her when the phone rang.

"Do you mind giving her the bottle? I'll grab the phone."

Abby hesitated, but took the bottle from his hand and sat down in a chair she toed out from the table. A few seconds later, Charlotte was eating like a champ, her dark blue eyes focused on Abby's face.

After all that Abby had been through, all that she had seen, she would've sworn that her heart was a piece of granite in her chest. She had to be able to stay calm to help the children she counseled, no matter the circumstances.

She'd closed herself off, willed the feelings to go

away. And she'd been successful at it until she'd been hit by a bullet. All those walls she'd spent years shoring up had come crashing down, leaving her grieving and exposed. Hyperaware.

Hypersensitive.

Looking into baby Charlotte's tiny, trusting eyes made her want to make promises. But that was one thing she just couldn't do. She'd made a promise to a child once and she would never get over the guilt of not being able to keep it.

Elvis laid his big head on her knee, his deep brown eyes looking into hers as if he knew what she was feeling. He probably did. She was the counselor, but Elvis? He was the magic maker. Even traumatized children relaxed when stroking his silky golden retriever fur. She smiled at him, despite the pain she still grappled with. "I'm okay, don't worry."

Her dog grumbled, turned a few circles and settled, laying his head on her feet. Elvis worked as hard as she did. In fact, it was his willingness to push through his exhaustion and keep working that had convinced Abby she needed to take a break. They *both* needed a rest.

So Abby had written a resignation letter—which her boss had refused to accept, instead sliding it into a desk drawer. She'd then promised she would accept it at the end of six months if Abby was still absolutely certain she wanted to quit. Abby had gone from one natural disaster to another for years, never knowing where she would be from one month to the next. So why did six months seem like such a long time to wait for closure?

Looking back at the baby, Abby realized that Charlotte's eyes had closed again, the bottle slipping out of her mouth. Setting it on the table beside her, she lifted

Charlotte to her shoulder. This baby was so new that her legs didn't even unfold when Abby picked her up. But as Abby patted her back, she let out a soft burp and melted into Abby's shoulder.

Abby sighed, too. It felt good to be able to solve Charlotte's immediate problem with a bottle and a burp. So she took advantage of the sweet baby-holding feeling and let it sink in—the muted hum of the HVAC overhead, Elvis's soft snores and the comforting weight of the baby on her chest.

Her eyes popped open as the sound of the phone hanging up interrupted her almost nap. Garrett grinned as he caught sight of her in the chair with the baby. His long legs ate up the distance across the room.

Leaning forward, he peeked over her shoulder at the sleeping baby. Elvis lifted his head, suspicious of this man getting so close to her, his eyes unerringly following Garrett's movements.

"Do you want to hold her?"

Garrett's smile vanished, replaced by a wary look that she instantly knew wasn't a feeling that Garrett Cole was very comfortable with.

"Come on, no turning back now."

She switched Charlotte to a cradling position and stood, placing the tiny bundle in Garrett's arms. His expression gentled as he watched Charlotte sleep, and Abby's heart gave a painful thump. She stepped back, away from him. "No."

"Pardon?" He looked up, his eyes crinkling as his smile returned.

"Nothing." She let out a shaky laugh and picked up her bag. "I've got to go."

These couple of hours with Garrett had been fun.

He was smart and compassionate and… She was here to heal. To get a family preservation program off the ground.

Not to try to date her best friend's partner—no matter how adorably befuddled he was.

Chapter Three

Three days later, thanks to Abby's expert tutelage, Garrett had the diaper changing down. He could change a diaper like a champ, he thought. It was the rest of his life that was going down the tubes.

This week had been the longest of his life and it was only Thursday afternoon. Rather than go home to his tiny empty cabin, he'd gone to the home where he'd grown up, where his brothers still lived, hoping a visit would take his mind off of all the unknowns.

He stuffed Charlotte's legs back into the leg holes of her sleeper and zipped it. Sliding one hand under her head and the other under her bum, he lifted her up. "Time!"

Devin's head jerked up from where he was snapping the twins into their pajamas. "What? Not possible. You're still an amateur."

Garrett's sister-in-law Lacey looked up from the book she was reading. "I think he has an advantage since he only has one baby, honey."

With a laugh, Garrett plopped Charlotte into one of the bouncy seats Lacey and Devin had for the twins and turned on the vibrating gizmo. "The zippered out-fits that Jules gave me were a game changer."

"Zippers?" Devin narrowed his eyes. "Mine are wearing pants!"

Garrett raised his eyebrows and made a zipping sound as he reached for his mug.

"Don't encourage him, Garrett, because the next thing that happens is he'll be headed into town to get new clothes for Phoebe and Eli so he can beat your time." Lacey closed her book as Phoebe started to fuss, but she paused to drop a kiss on Devin's head. "I'll get the bottles."

"She does know me well." Devin buckled Eli into the other seat, lifted Phoebe to his shoulder and stood, bouncing. "Well, you seem to be taking all this in stride."

Garrett nearly spit his cold coffee out. "Really? Because I feel like I'm slowly sinking in quicksand while the rest of my world is falling apart and struggling is only dragging me in deeper."

"That seems kind of dramatic." Devin took the bottle Lacey handed him and settled on the sofa with Phoebe as Lacey picked Eli up to feed him. "Like what?"

"Like, I need to talk to Charlotte's mom and I can't get her to respond to my texts or calls. Like, just about the time I open a file and really start working, it's time for feeding or diapering or bouncing or she needs her pacifier."

His voice was climbing. "She only sleeps in thirty-minute snatches. I have her seventy-two-hour hearing tomorrow in family court—when the judge will decide if she needs to be in foster care—and the most efficient assistant in history is one more poop explosion away from quitting. And if she quits, Wynn will kill me and I can't let that happen because I have a baby now." He ran out of breath about the time he ran out of words and at the exact time that he realized his brother and Lacey were both staring at him, eyes wide.

He sighed and stabbed his fingers into his hair as he muttered, "Sorry."

"Don't be sorry, Garrett. We're your family. Who else are you going to tell?" Lacey, beside Devin on the sofa, elbowed her husband, who cleared his throat.

"Yeah, babies are hard. What can we do to help?"

Garrett let his head fall back against the leather seat of the recliner. "You guys have your hands full with your own kids. I've seen Lacey making cookies in the middle of the night to sell at the farm stand and I know how slim your margin is. I'll figure it out."

"There's always day care, right? Where does Wynn take A.J.?" Devin asked.

"To Community Church, but they have to be six weeks old to go there. And who knows if I'll have her then, or if they'll even have a space for Charlotte when the time comes."

Lacey lifted a sleeping Eli to her shoulder and stood. "Give yourself some grace, Garrett. Even people who have time to plan are overwhelmed with the reality of what it's like to have a baby."

He nodded, his gaze going to Charlotte asleep in the bouncy seat. She was so little, the size of one of his hands, and just so dependent on him for everything.

Yeah. *Overwhelming* was a good word for it.

His brother Devin said, "I bet one of the church ladies would be willing to babysit."

"Normally, yes, but they're all in Branson, Missouri for ten days. Some kind of quilting conference and then they're hitting a bunch of shows. Their timing is terrible." Garrett heard the words he'd just said and wanted to gobble them back. "That was a joke."

Eli's pacifier popped out and Lacey bent her knees and snagged it before it could hit the floor. "Ooh, I know—what about the new social worker, the one who kept Charlotte a couple of days ago while you were in court? Has she started her job yet?"

"You mean Abby?" A smile started at the corner of his mouth. She'd saved his skin that first day and he'd thought of her often since then. She didn't even know him, but her quick humor and totally unfounded confidence in his ability had made Garrett feel more in control.

"See? Right there. There's the look I was telling you about." Devin pointed at Garrett. "He makes that face every time she comes up in conversation."

Lacey studied Garrett's expression with a squinty eye. "Hmm. I see what you mean. Very curious."

"You guys are hilarious." Garrett started tossing stuff back into Charlotte's diaper bag. "I'm leaving."

Lacey smiled, clearly amused, but her voice was kind. "Garrett, you're always the first one to step in and help when we need it—when anyone needs it. It's all right to ask for help yourself."

He much preferred being the one doing the helping, but maybe Lacey was right. In any case, he didn't have much choice. He was desperate to find a sitter for tomorrow afternoon. "Okay, I'll text her."

Abby's shiny dark hair and pretty hazel eyes came to mind. She was the silver lining to this absurd situation if there was one. And if he had to ask for help, at least he'd get to see her again.

Abby stirred sugar into her coffee, the very act seeming like a luxury. She'd had instant coffee in the refugee camp, and she could almost always find a way to boil some water, but it wasn't the same as freshly brewed. Not even close.

A knock at the door startled her and she glanced at the clock on the oven. Ten thirty! She'd expected it to be seven o'clock. Maybe it was a good thing she was starting work on Monday.

The knock came again. She glanced down at her yoga pants. Old, but the holes were all in discreet locations. Her feet were bare, toenails in the screaming pink neon polish that had been an impulse when Wynn had dragged her to the salon for a much-needed pedicure the day before.

With a quick fluff of her bedhead, she wrapped her fuzzy gray sweater around herself and took a quick peek through the peephole in the door. Garrett stood on her doorstep, his collar turned up against the wind, the handle of the baby carrier gripped in one hand.

She tugged the belt on her sweater a little tighter and pulled the door open just as he was turning away. "Hi."

Garrett turned around, his beaming smile fading just a bit as his eyes traveled from her disheveled hair to her bare toes. "I think maybe… I came at a bad time. I texted you."

"Not a bad time. This is just me, not working, and I turned my phone off because my former boss keeps asking me to come back to work." Tucking a piece of hair behind her ear, she shivered. "I thought winter was supposed to be mild in Alabama. It's freezing out there. Come in, please."

He followed her into the living room and she saw him take note of the dishes in the sink, the pillow and blanket on the couch. Inwardly, she might have cringed a little, but what was the point? "Sorry for the mess. I'm making up for lost sleep. Like four years' worth. So what can I do for you? Or is this a social call?"

Garrett placed the baby carrier on the kitchen table and took a deep breath as he folded back the cover. "Not exactly."

She leaned forward to sneak a peek at Charlotte before she leaned back against the counter and crossed one ankle over the other. "Okay?"

He rubbed one thumb across his lips. "Wow, this is more awkward than I thought it would be. I need help. I've asked all the church ladies and pretty much everyone else I know and I can't find a babysitter for Charlotte. I know it's not fair to ask, but is there any way you could help me out this afternoon?"

"You talk so fast." Abby crossed to the table and unbuckled the car seat straps. She lifted Charlotte into her arms, smiling down at her. "Hi, baby girl."

"Yeah, sorry. Hazard of the job. Judges never give you enough time to say what you need to say." Garrett sat down in one of the chairs at the kitchen table. His cheeks were ruddy with cold, or maybe a little chagrin at having to ask for help.

Abby swayed back and forth as Charlotte's eyelids drooped closed. Garrett was clearly overloaded and Charlotte was just sweetness. "I can watch her. I don't mind."

Garrett closed his eyes for a second and she wondered if he was praying. When he opened them, he said, "You're sure? It's just for the afternoon."

"Truthfully, I've been in a lot of situations where I wished there was something I could do. If this actually helps you, I'm glad to do it."

"The seventy-two-hour dependency hearing for her is at two o'clock."

"That's fine. I don't have anything else to do. And I'm well rested." Abby's lips twitched, but she kept patting Charlotte, not sure the baby was firmly asleep yet. "What happens at the hearing?"

"A social worker from the Department of Human Resources will tell the judge what happened and make a recommendation to the court. I think they'll recommend that she be officially placed with me." He nudged his glasses farther up his nose and stabbed his fingers into his hair in a motion that she realized telegraphed his stress. "Then the judge will make a decision. He could leave Charlotte with me since we have the papers from her mom. Or he could decide that Charlotte would be better off with foster parents. I really have no idea. This situation isn't one I've come across before."

"Do you want to keep her?"

The question echoed the one she'd asked him the first day and again Garrett paused. His eyes lingered on Charlotte's little face and his eyes softened before he nodded. "Yeah. I want to keep her. I may be the strangest choice for a guardian anyone's ever made, but she's safe with me."

"Good. I can see why her mom chose you."

Garrett blinked and then he grinned. When he smiled, it wasn't just his lips. His smile broke through the winter gloom, brightening the whole room.

"Thanks, Abby. I appreciate that. I've got to run. I'll be back as soon as I can."

"Just text me when you're done and I'll bring her to your office. I need to get out of the house anyway."

"Perfect. I'll leave the car seat base on the front porch." He took a moment to brush his fingers across Charlotte's forehead and then was gone, leaving her staring at the closed door.

Okay, so he was really attractive. It had been a long time since she'd been around anyone other than fellow disaster relief workers and they had been as exhausted and careworn as she was.

That didn't mean a flirtation was a good idea. In fact, it was a very bad idea. His smile might warm a room, but everyone knew that getting too close to the sun would burn you.

Garrett leaned on the counter where Bess worked, talking into the phone she handed him while he texted on his cell phone. He heard the door open and turned to see Abby coming in the office door. He quickly ended the conversation, hung up the phone and crossed to her, lifting the heavy infant seat from her hand. "Everything go okay?"

Abby grimaced. "I think maybe she's hungry. She cried all the way here."

Little hiccups could still be heard coming from underneath the stretch cover over the car seat. Garrett pulled the cover back to peek inside. "Aw, Charlotte. What's the matter?"

As soon as she heard Garrett's voice, a thin wail rose from the infant car seat.

"She really isn't happy, is she?" Garrett shifted the

seat to his elbow and carried her to the conference table. "Are you ready for a bottle?"

When Charlotte responded with increased volume, Garrett laughed and began the process of unbuckling her. "I think that's a yes."

"Thankfully, I made one before I left the house. I had a hunch we might need it."

He lifted Charlotte out of the seat. "Did Miss Abby try to starve you?"

Abby swatted his arm. "Not funny."

Garrett settled into one oversized leather chair in his office, while Abby perched on the arm of the other one, digging the bottle out of the side pocket of the diaper bag.

He gave it a little shake and then let Charlotte have it. She really did eat like she was starving.

"I fed her three hours ago, I promise!" Abby's dark brown hair was pulled back in a low ponytail with little tendrils curling around her face.

She seemed as casually friendly as usual, but that neon pink toenail polish he'd spied this morning seemed to hint that there were facets to Abby's personality he hadn't yet seen. It made him want to poke and dig and figure her out.

Her eyes lingered on Charlotte, the expression on her face thoughtful.

"What are you thinking?"

Her cheeks colored, a dimple at the corner of her mouth appearing and disappearing. "Just that Charlotte's blessed. Not all kids who go through a childhood trauma have someone who cares as much as you do to take care of them."

He wasn't sure how to feel—flattered that she

thought he was caring, or concerned that she thought Charlotte could be traumatized. "Do you think I should be worried about Charlotte?"

"Babies recognize their parents from the first moments they're born—their smell, the way their voice sounds. So she's had a loss. But it helps that she has you."

"Is that your professional opinion?" He shifted in the chair, a little uncomfortable with the intensity of her study.

"My experienced opinion. You haven't said… How did things go in court?"

"Okay. Child Protective Services recommended that Charlotte be placed with me, I think partly because of the mother's request. Partly because they know me."

"That's good." Abby frowned. "Right?"

His head bobbed back and forth—not a yes, not a no. "The judge wasn't happy. Technically, Brooklyn abandoned her baby, and while it's understandable that she picked me to leave her with, in a weird way, the judge wants to make sure that she wasn't coerced."

Abby narrowed her eyes. "So, you have to find Brooklyn?"

"Someone does." He tipped the bottle up so Charlotte could drink the last ounce.

"But it seems like she doesn't want to be found."

"Therein lies the problem."

"From a legal standpoint, I guess I can see the judge's point. The situation *is* weird, but… Charlotte's staying with you, right?"

"The judge said CPS could leave her in my care as a kinship provider, but he's given me until the next hearing to come up with proof that Brooklyn made the choice to leave Charlotte voluntarily. And then there's the issue of the dad."

"Who's the dad?"

"Exactly. We have nowhere to start." Garrett made a face. "So that has to be addressed at the adjudicatory hearing as well."

"Which is when?"

"Supposed to be within thirty days or the earliest practical date, which in this case happens to be a little over six weeks from now if it doesn't get continued."

"How do you feel about that?"

His eyes were on Charlotte as she slowly took the last little bit from the bottle. How he felt was as complicated as the case. "I feel guilty that I couldn't just leave it alone, that the mandatory reporter thing took that decision out of my hands. I feel relieved that Charlotte won't be dragged into another foster home with someone she doesn't know. And at the same time, I wonder if I'm making the best choice for her because I don't have any clue what to do with a baby."

Abby's lips curved into a soft smile. "You're doing fine, but all of those feelings seem perfectly valid to me. Any thoughts on where Brooklyn might be?"

"Not a clue."

"I'll think about it. There's got to be some way to find her. In the meantime, I'm gonna get going. I've got to run to the grocery store before I head home." She walked toward the door and turned back to hand him the burp cloth. "Oh—you might need this."

As if on cue, Charlotte burped and Garrett smiled. "Good call. Thanks for keeping her today. I owe you dinner."

"You're welcome. See you Monday."

As Abby walked away, Garrett's eyes followed. She was beautiful and complicated and a part of him wanted to figure out what was really under that shell of serenity.

He shook his head, chuckling under his breath. His brothers teased him about his idealistic streak. He fell in love about as often as other guys washed their clothes. Any other time in his life, he wouldn't have hesitated to ask Abby out. Now?

Even if he did lose his mind and consider it, he had no idea if she was even planning to stay in Red Hill Springs. It was a nonstarter.

They were working together. And maybe...friends?

And that was all he could let it be.

Chapter Four

Abby's first few days at work were spent brainstorming with Wynn—what specifics the program would focus on, how she would get referrals, and people she needed to contact once she had all the pieces in place to begin the actual work.

Most referrals would probably come from teachers and police officers, but family court attorneys like Wynn and Garrett could request appointments for their clients. There were resources out there for all kinds of obstacles people faced. The problem was connecting the resources with the people who needed them and that's where she came in.

It had been a while since she'd felt anything but helpless, but somewhere down inside, there was a bubble of hope. Putting a program like this in place was a bold move for a small town, but one that could really impact the lives of the residents. She was excited to get started.

Her experience working in the refugee camp along the border of Jordan had broken her, for lack of a better word. She hadn't realized how broken she was until she'd finally gotten to her apartment in Atlanta. She'd barely recognized her own home.

She'd been exhausted but she couldn't sleep. Too thin, but food hadn't appealed to her. In the middle of the third sleepless night, when she'd been mindlessly scrolling through social media, she'd seen Wynn's message, asking if she knew any social workers who might be interested in a job like this. She'd called the next morning and two hours later, she'd talked to her boss, (tried to) quit her job and packed her suitcase.

It had been the right decision. After a week in Red Hill Springs—sleeping at night, eating at the café— she was starting to feel not quite so fragile, like the pieces of herself were slowly knitting back together.

"Knock, knock." Garrett opened the door to her office. He was holding two white paper bags, which he placed on her desk.

She leaned toward him. "You know that's not actually the same as knocking, right?"

"Yes, but I brought goodies from the Hilltop Café. Doughnut or cupcake?"

"Which one has frosting?"

"Oh, please. Who do you think I am? Both."

She found herself smiling, another sign that she was reentering the land of the living, and a not-uncommon occurrence around Garrett. "In that case, please do come in. I'll have the doughnut."

"Good choice." He handed her the doughnut still in the wrap and pulled out the cupcake, vanilla with white frosting, before dropping into the chair opposite her. Peeling back the paper, he took a gigantic bite.

With her doughnut halfway to her mouth, she stopped to watch.

In two more bites, he'd finished it off and caught her watching him as he licked frosting off his thumb. He laughed, wiped his mouth with the back of his hand and brushed the crumbs off his coat. "Two brothers. I had to learn to be fast when there were treats around. Do you have any siblings?"

"In a way, I do. I have some half siblings that are a lot younger. And I grew up with my cousins. My mom and I lost our house to a tornado when I was five. I lived with my grandma for a while, and then with my aunt and uncle." She took a bite of the doughnut and pointed at it with the other hand. "Mmm, really good."

His eyebrows drew together. "I have so many questions. Were you in the house at the time?"

"Yes. We were in the bathroom under the stairs. It was the only part of the house that survived."

He let out a low whistle. "That's extreme. You didn't go back to live with your mom?"

"No. My mom got married the next year." Elvis nosed her hand and leaned into her leg. She took another bite of the light-as-air doughnut and sighed in appreciation.

"So?"

She put the rest of the doughnut down and brushed the sugar off her hands. "So, nothing. You asked if I had siblings. And the answer is, kind of. We're not that close, though. My life up to this point has been pretty different than most people's."

"You could say that. You gonna eat that?" When she shook her head, he picked up the other half of her doughnut and scarfed it down. "Where was your dad?"

"He was military. Killed in a training accident when I was just a baby." She realized Elvis was standing beside her and wondered if her voice had betrayed some tension that she hadn't even realized she was feeling. Her dog was sensitive to every nuanced emotion, which was what made him so good at his job.

She sent him back to his bed with a hand signal.

Because she was fine. A lot of kids had chaotic childhoods. It wasn't like she hadn't had food to eat or a roof over her head. Garrett opened his mouth, she could only assume to ask another question, and she didn't want to answer any more questions. "So what's up with you?"

"Oh, right. Why I came to find you. I have a client coming in today. Melanie. I'd love it if you could talk to her while I play with her little boy for a few minutes. She doesn't get a break very often."

She picked up the bakery bag and tossed it into the trash can under her desk. "Sure, I'd love to. What's the story?"

"You know how sometimes the deck is so stacked against you to start with that no matter how much you want to, you can't get ahead?"

Abby looked up. "Yes. Is that what happened to Melanie?"

"Yeah. She's on a safety plan with Child Services. She made some questionable life choices, but she wants to do right by her kids. You're gonna love Nash. He's four and he has cerebral palsy but it hasn't slowed him down much. He's a little carrottop with a pistol-ball personality to match."

"So basically, you want me to find out what needs she still has and connect her with the resources?"

"Exactly." In the other room, Charlotte started to cry. "Oops, that's my cue."

He was gone with as little fanfare as he'd arrived, but she realized she felt good, like she could breathe. And she knew it wasn't just gaining distance from all she'd been through. It was a job where she knew she could make a difference. It was doughnuts and laughter and baby snuggles and…it was Garrett.

For some reason, it was Garrett. In the back of her mind, she heard an alarm bell go off that said this is different, *he* is different. But she wasn't going to listen to it, not right now. Right now, she was going to take Elvis outside for a quick walk and wait for her first client to arrive.

Garrett met Melanie at the door as she tried to maneuver a very small wheelchair. Nash was bouncing in the seat.

"Garrett!"

"Hey, buddy." He held out a fist and Nash smashed it.

"He's been so excited to get to come to your office." Nash's mom looked like a teenager with her hair pulled back in a ponytail.

"Glad you could make it." He'd been her court-appointed attorney for the past year and she was doing good. Trying. But trying didn't mean succeeding. He was here to make sure she had everything she needed to succeed.

Abby opened the door to her office and she and Elvis started toward them. The golden retriever's tail was wagging a mile a minute.

Nash's face lit up as he saw the dog. "Doggie. Mama, doggie!"

"I see, Nash. He's a pretty doggie." To Garrett, she said, "He's been begging for a dog, so his day is made."

"This is Elvis. He loves to play with boys." Abby gave Elvis a hand signal. As he laid his head in Nash's lap, the little boy squealed with excitement. To Melanie, she said, "Hi, I'm Abby. I work with Garrett."

"Melanie. And this is Nash. He's a little excited to meet your dog."

"Elvis loves to meet new people, so I think he's pretty excited, too."

Garrett leaned over and stage-whispered, "Nash, Elvis is so soft, you could use him as a blanket!"

Nash squinted up at Garrett, clearly thinking that through before he giggled. "Uh-uh. Doggies can't be blankets!"

Abby shook her head at Garrett, but she had a twinkle in her eye, so he'd count that as a win on two fronts. He clasped his hands together. "I have a surprise for you guys."

He'd worked for weeks trying to scrape together funding for a specially made stroller for Nash, one that would accommodate his baby sister as well. He brought it out of his office into the open space near the conference table.

Melanie's eyes widened. "Garrett, what is that?"

"Hopefully, the solution to your problems."

"Seriously?" Her eyes filled with tears and she put a hand out. "Garrett, you know I can't pay for this."

"Don't worry about that. Let's see how it works." In one quick motion, Garrett popped open the stroller and locked the seat into place.

The sound caught Nash's attention and he looked up. "What's that?"

"A new stroller. Try turning it around, Melanie."

She turned it with one hand and looked up in wonder. "Oh, it just glides."

Garrett grinned as he reached for a couple of levers near the back wheels and folded a smaller seat into place. He had a new appreciation these days for baby products that were so idiotproof even he could work them. "And this is the sibling seat. Little sister gets to sit here."

Melanie's face crumpled, her eyes filling with tears.

"Melanie?" Garrett's smile faded.

"I don't know how you did this..." She sniffed, visibly struggling for control. "It will change everything. No more missed appointments."

"Wanna ride. Garrett, I wanna ride." Nash untangled his fingers from Elvis's fur and held his arms up.

Melanie laughed. "Hang on, little man. I got you."

After Nash was unbuckled, Garrett reached down and lifted Nash, placing him in the seat.

"Awesome!" The little boy let out a delighted laugh. "Go, Garrett. Ride."

Garrett looked at Abby. "I could take him for a quick spin around the block, to try it out."

"I think that might be necessary." She laughed as Nash bounced up and down in the seat. Garrett caught him as he launched himself into midair.

"Dude. You have to sit still while I buckle you!" While his fingers were busy with the buckles, Garrett looked up at Melanie. "Abby's the new social worker in our office. If it's okay with you, I asked Abby if she had time to talk to you this morning."

The smile on the young mom's face faded. "Sure, I guess."

Abby put her hand on Melanie's arm. "Don't worry. It's just a casual visit. Would you like a cup of coffee?"

"Sure, thanks." She followed Abby to the kitchenette but looked back toward the door where her little boy was rocking back and forth in the new stroller.

"We won't be long." Garrett double-checked the buckles holding Nash into the seat. "No more trying to pretend you're an astronaut, hear me?"

Nash giggled. "Three, two, one..."

"Blast off!" Garrett blew through the front door, pulling it closed behind him as they raced down the sidewalk. The ecstatic laugh from the four-year-old in the seat told him he'd definitely made the right decision on the stroller.

He gave a quick glance back at the office. He knew Abby was a pro and together she and Elvis were a formidable team, but it was his first time trusting one of his clients with her. Melanie's confidence was still a little shaky. He hoped he was doing the right thing.

Abby handed Melanie a mug of coffee. "Sit down with me? I bet you don't have much time to rest with Nash around, not to mention your little girl. How old is she?"

"Nova's almost six months old. She's with a neighbor right now." Melanie followed Abby into her office, pausing to look at the pictures Abby had hung on the wall the day before.

Abby sat in one of the chairs that she'd moved into a conversational grouping. Elvis sat beside her, his attention glued to her face. "Those are photos of people I've met at some of the disaster areas I've worked in over the years."

"I can see the destruction in the background, but they look so... I don't know, strong?"

"Some of the people in those photos lost everything, but despite that, they were still standing. It's a powerful statement."

"I can so relate to that." Melanie sat in the chair next to Abby, the wariness gone from her face. She was young, early twenties maybe, but the way she carried herself made her seem much older.

With a barely perceptible motion of her hand, Abby released Elvis to go to work. He sat in front of the young mom and tilted his head. Melanie smiled at him. "Hi, buddy."

He nosed her hand and when Melanie reached out to scratch him, Abby knew the connection had been made.

A smile played across Melanie's face as she rubbed one of Elvis's ears. She kept her eyes down, but she said, "I don't know what Garrett told you..."

"He didn't tell me much. Truly."

"I'm on a safety plan with the social services people, and Garrett's my attorney. When we went to court, he fought for me to get to keep my kids with a caseworker checking in on us every month."

"I don't want to be nosy, but if you want to talk about it, I'm a good listener."

The young mom blew her thin bangs out of her eyes and shook her head as if she wanted to negate the memory itself. "My fiancé got high with his friends and came to the hospital when Nova was born. He got a night in jail and I got a caseworker. I had to choose between keeping my children or keeping him. Getting rid of him was the easiest choice I ever had to make."

Melanie had one hand deep in Elvis's fur now, the other one smoothing the small hairs on his forehead. "What was hard was that our car was in my fiancé's name. Without a car, I missed some of Nova's well-baby checkups and that brought the caseworker back to my house."

"Oh, wow. That must be so scary."

"It is—was. The safety plan says I have to take the kids to the doctor and to their therapy appointments on time. The caseworker comes to visit. And we have to go back to court in six months."

"And where does the stroller fit in?"

There was silence for a moment, the struggle to rein in her emotions once again visible on Melanie's face. Finally, she looked up with a small shrug. "I couldn't get on the bus with both kids because I couldn't push Nash's wheelchair and a stroller at the same time. And I couldn't lift the wheelchair if I had Nova in a carrier. I just—I couldn't do it. Someone at church let me borrow a double stroller, but Nash needs more support than a normal stroller can give him."

"What a rough time for all of you. Anyone would be reeling after all that."

"You think so?" Melanie's shoulders slumped, but hope flared in her eyes. "Do you know how much that stroller was? Ten thousand dollars. I could never have bought that for him. And I guess I just worry how I can be a good mom if I can't provide what my kids need."

"Melanie," Abby said gently, "your kids need you, not what you can buy for them."

Melanie's sigh turned into a sob. Elvis nuzzled her chin with his nose, eliciting a strangled laugh.

A squeal of joy reached them from just outside the

office. Melanie immediately straightened, swiped tears from her face and smoothed her shirt into place. "I don't want Nash to think I'm worried."

As the boys came in the front door, Abby held out a business card to Melanie. "Write down everything you need to really feel like you have a handle on life. Then call and make another appointment with me. There are resources out there and my job is to connect you with them."

Hope flared in the young mom's eyes. "You're serious?"

"One hundred percent." She paused, looked back at the photos on the wall. "The people in those photos? You're strong, just like they are. Things have happened that you need to take care of, but you're still standing."

Nash shouted from the front door. "Mama! Come see!"

Melanie tucked Abby's card into her back pocket, swallowing hard before looking up. "Thank you."

Abby heard her laughing at the engine sounds Nash made as she walked back to meet him. She hoped Melanie would take her up on the offer. Their family, who because of circumstances mostly beyond their control needed help to get back on their feet, was exactly the kind Abby had been brought in to help.

As Garrett walked Nash and Melanie to the door, Abby heard Charlotte waking up in the porta-crib in Garrett's office and went to check on her. The baby girl had a decidedly crabby look on her face.

"Hi, Charlotte. I bet you need a clean diaper after such a long nap, don't you?" She reached into the crib and picked Charlotte up. The change was easy with Garrett's office nursery setup, but clearly, a dry diaper was not what Charlotte wanted. Her cries were getting progressively louder and more annoyed.

Abby picked her up again and tried the pacifier. Charlotte sucked it for a few seconds before spitting it out. "Oh, baby girl, you are mad, aren't you?"

From the door, Garrett held out a bottle. "She's probably ready for this."

"I'd say so." She took it from Garrett and offered it to the hungry baby.

Over the bottle, Charlotte scowled as if she couldn't possibly understand what took Abby so long to get it right. Abby laughed. "Hey, I'm not the one in charge of the bottles."

"She's opinionated." Garrett dropped into the chair behind his desk. "Wow. Nash wore me out. Did you and Melanie have a good conversation?"

"I think so. Elvis is kind of a genius at getting people to talk." She studied Garrett's face, so handsome with that quick smile that went all the way to his eyes.

"I'm sure it's all Elvis."

"Melanie's doing her best to take care of her kids. That's gonna be a lot easier with that fancy stroller you got her. How'd you pull that off?"

"It's just a stroller." He picked a file up from his desk and spun around to put it away.

"A ten-thousand-dollar stroller?"

He glanced back at her. "Where did you get that idea?"

"Melanie."

"Oh." He shrugged. "It wasn't a big deal. I called in some favors. Asked for some donations. Got a small grant. It was a little legwork, but the end result is that Melanie can get her kids where they need to go."

"A car would've been cheaper."

"Yeah, but then it would've been for Melanie and she probably wouldn't have accepted it. A gift for Nash and Nova is a little harder to turn down."

"Smart *and* thoughtful."

"It's all part of the service. Plus, you're gonna get her the rest of the way. We make a great team." He shot her a nonchalant grin.

He wasn't fooling her, though. There was nothing nonchalant about him. He was a full-out idealist and she could feel herself getting sucked into his life, bit by bit. How could she not? He genuinely cared about people and wanted to help. If anyone could understand that, she could.

Garrett was a great guy. A sweet guy. She liked him, but she had to be careful. Because if she wasn't, he would pull her into his windmill-tilting plans and she'd been down that path. Had the bullet wound to prove it.

And that was the last thing she needed right now.

Chapter Five

Garrett got out of his SUV at the ranch, where he was supposed to be meeting his brothers for a look at the current finances. After a scare the year before, when the ranch almost got foreclosed on by the bank, the brothers had solidified their pact that they were in this together. Brotherly competition and ribbing aside, nothing happened on this ranch that didn't get run by all three of them first.

He popped the baby carrier out of its base. Charlotte was out like a light. Frantic bleats sounded from the goat pasture. His first goats, Thelma and Louise, had been joined by siblings and they had a good little crew going. He loved those ornery little rabble-rousers. The first two had been a gift from a client, but the other four he'd adopted just because he got a kick out of them. He scratched Mason's head and pushed Dixon back with a laugh when the persistent goat tried to get into Garrett's pants pockets. "Sorry, guys, no treats today."

And when all of them turned away, he shook his head. "I know you only love me for food, but you could at least pretend."

Brushing his hand off on his pant leg, Garrett crossed the drive, taking the porch steps two at a time. By the number of cars in the yard, he was pretty sure he'd stumbled unwittingly into Lacey's Bible study night. In fact, he thought he'd spotted Abby's car in the mix. He paused to glance back. And Wynn's?

The door flew open. Devin stood in the doorway, with a baby on one hip, the other strapped to his chest and his cane in the other hand. "Well, are you coming in or not?"

"Wow, I think someone missed their afternoon nap and it wasn't the babies." Garrett strolled into the house, slowly stumbling to a halt as he realized the entire place was decorated in a sickening shade of pink. Balloons, streamers… His eyes lingered on a lace-edged banner hanging above the kitchen door. Slowly, he turned back to face his brother. "Surprise?"

With that, people came pouring out of the farm office, the kitchen and the hall, yelling, "Surprise!"

He staggered backward, his right hand grabbing his heart. Abruptly woken from her nap, Charlotte let out a wail. With an apologetic smile, Abby reached for the carrier. "I'll take her."

His sister-in-law Lacey appeared in the kitchen door with a big plate of pink frosted cookies, followed by Jules Quinn carrying a tower of pastel confections.

"I think I'm starting to sense there's a theme to this gathering." Garrett laughed, shaking his head.

"It's a baby shower." A big laundry basket full of gifts wrapped in pink and white landed in the center of the living room, dumped there by his older brother Tanner.

"I gathered." When Garrett looked up, he caught a

glimpse of Abby standing against the wall, about as far as she could get from the hullabaloo and still be in the room, calmly unbuckling his screaming baby from the car seat. Bless her. She wasn't used to this bunch of rowdies. She looked so pretty, an island of calm in this sea of chaos. He took a step toward her.

Wynn appeared in front of him, holding a shiny pink metallic crown with giant faux jewels glued to the points.

"Whoa." He put up a hand to stop her. "I will never get the glitter out of my hair if you put that thing on me."

His partner shrugged, unconcerned. "Suck it up, cowboy. Penny made it for you. You have to wear it."

He searched out Wynn's eight-year-old daughter Penny. "You made this crown for me?"

The little girl's eyes shone, her blond curls bobbing as she nodded her head.

"It's quite lovely," Garrett said, in a British accent, which elicited giggles from his buddy. And since he had no choice, he bent down to let Wynn attach the atrocious thing to his head.

Someone pushed him into the big chair and someone else tossed a gift in his lap. A pink plastic cup filled with some kind of frothy liquid appeared on the table beside him. He sought out Abby again, his eyes meeting hers. He mouthed, "Help?"

A wail went up from one of the many babies in the room. Instantly, attention was diverted from Garrett as all the parents searched out their kids.

"Mine! No worries—happens all the time." Wynn scooped up her toddler, who'd somehow gotten caught underneath the coffee table. She slid into a seat and motioned for Abby to join her, waving a hand at the chair between her and Garrett.

He was pretty sure that the last place Abby wanted to be was at this raucous excuse for a baby shower, much less this close to the center. She gamely joined the group, though, laughing as one of his brothers shouted from across the room, "Just open the presents already."

"Okay, okay," he grumbled. "Nothing like a little de-stressing with a surprise baby shower for your surprise baby after a long day of lawyering."

He wasn't sure but he thought he heard a little snort from Abby.

Ripping into the first package—from Devin—Garrett pulled out a hot pink T-shirt. He read the slogan out loud. "Tea Parties and Tiaras."

He laughed and a shower of glitter landed on his face and shoulders. "Well, Dev, I've got this crown and I think I have a stash of Earl Grey somewhere in my house, so if anyone wants to join in, it's BYOT. Bring your own tiara."

"All that pink glitter is definitely you," his brother Tanner said dryly as he handed over the next package. "This one's from Wynn."

Garrett tore open the box to reveal a necktie covered in pink pacifiers. "Wow! Thanks, partner. The other lawyers are going to be shaking in their boots when they realize I'm man enough to wear this tie."

Beside him, Abby giggled. He glanced over at her, raising an eyebrow. "Did you know about this?"

Her eyes widened, cheeks staining pink. "Nope."

"Why don't I believe that?"

The next gift, from his pal and pediatrician Ash

Sheehan, revealed a set of tools with pink rubber handles. He couldn't help but laugh. "I see how this is going to go."

From Abby, Lacey and Ash's wife Jordan came the basic necessities: pink bottles. Pink pacifiers. Pink blankets and baby onesies.

So. Much. Pink.

Finally, Wynn's husband Latham handed Garrett a card. Inside was a photograph of a beautiful crib. He glanced up. "You made her a crib?"

Latham shrugged. "Least I could do. Everyone pitched in for the materials."

"Also," Ash spoke up. "You shouldn't be surprised if you find a truckload of diapers on your front porch when you get home. My mom told the Ladies' Auxiliary about the baby and they asked what you needed."

"And you said Cubs tickets but they decided on diapers anyway?"

Ash laughed. "Very funny. You need the diapers more. Trust me."

For the next few minutes, he was inundated with questions and well wishes. It was fun and he was touched, but he hadn't slept in over a week and the noise in here was making his head ache. He was desperate to sneak out the front door for a few minutes of silence.

He looked around for Abby to see if she wanted to join him, but she—and Charlotte—were gone.

Abby rocked the porch swing idly with her toes as Charlotte took her bottle. The quiet was a relief after the hubbub inside. She was healing, but the crowd and the noise inside had made her feel claustrophobic and more than a little desperate to escape. A few random raindrops tapped on the tin roof above her head.

It was peaceful here, the rhythmic squeak of the swing and the sounds of the animals drifting on the misty breeze. She could see why Garrett chose to live on the ranch with his brothers instead of in town.

The front door opened and Garrett stepped out, closing the door quickly behind him. From the look on his face, he'd felt the need to escape as keenly as she did. His eyes searched the dim porch and she could see him smile when he spotted her in the swing.

He sat down, stretching his arm out behind her. "Little too rowdy in there?"

"I don't get out much."

He barked a laugh. "Neither do they. It's why they're so loud. Plus they have a lot of kids."

"A *lot* of kids," Abby agreed. "She's ready for a burp."

As Abby handed Charlotte to Garrett, he brought her to his chest, kissed her little head and whispered something Abby couldn't hear.

The sweetness of the gesture made her throat ache and she looked away, instead watching the glimmer of raindrops in the circle from the pole light by the barn.

Patting Charlotte's back, Garrett said, "It was nice of you to come tonight."

Abby leaned back against the seat and brought one knee up to her chest, wrapping her arms around it. "Wynn made me come. She said you celebrate everything in this town."

"Yeah." His chuckle made her smile. "A lot of my friends, like Wynn, are either foster parents or have adopted kids. When they started fostering, they realized that no one really celebrated foster babies the way they do biological babies. So they decided to make it a thing."

"It's really sweet. Every baby should be celebrated."

"I agree."

They sat in silence for a few seconds, the rhythmic squeaking of the swing and the rain on the roof making Abby feel relaxed and sleepy. "Did you always know you wanted to come back to Red Hill Springs to practice law?"

He glanced over at her with a smile. "I guess I did. Devin left home at eighteen and competed on the rodeo circuit. I went away to school, thanks to some scholarships, but I never seriously considered living anywhere else. My roots are here."

The stab of longing surprised Abby. She had no roots, not really, and there was a part of her that wondered what it would be like, what kind of deep confidence that kind of belonging would inspire.

"I sold my house in town last year. First, because we needed the money so we could hang on to the ranch and then... I guess it's not really true what they say about never going home again. My cabin was a ramshackle dump, but it felt more like home than my place in town ever had."

"You guys manage the ranch together?"

"Yep. Lacey and Devin run the farm stand, which has been way more successful than we ever thought it would be. Tanner's the one who got the farming gene." Charlotte started to fuss and Garrett shifted her to his arm.

"And you?"

"I mostly manage the finances...and raise the goats." He sent her a sideways glance, the perpetual amusement that was so much a part of him twinkling in his eyes.

"What?" She laughed softly. "I never pictured you as a goatherd."

"Oh, there's no herding involved. All I have to do is walk into the field with a box of raisins in my pocket and they'll do my bidding."

"That's hilarious. I had no idea the depth of your talents. I've eaten goat but I can't say that I've ever had any as pets," Abby mused.

He gave an exaggerated look over his shoulder. "Shh—they'll hear you."

She laughed again. "My apologies to your goats."

"They accept."

With the baby drifting back to sleep in the crook of his arm, he stretched the other one out behind her again. His fingers played with the ends of her hair, sending shivers down her back.

The rain was coming down harder now and she sighed. "I think it's settling in for the night and I've got to get back and let Elvis out. I'd love to bring him out to the farm sometime though. It's good for him to be exposed to new sights and sounds. Keeps him from being spooked when we're in the field."

"Sure. If the rain clears tomorrow, bring him over. He can chase chickens." He looked down at her as she shook her head. "I mean, no, he definitely can't chase chickens because that would be...wrong."

She chuckled. "He has to completely ignore them and keep doing his job."

"Which is?"

"Making people feel safe, giving unconditional love

and acceptance. And he does that with my cues, so he can't get distracted or he'll miss them."

"I saw the hand signal you gave him when Nash came in the office. Was that how he knew to go to him and lay his head on Nash's lap?"

"Yes, along with the verbal cue to 'go say hello.'"

"So, if you mostly do mental health work with kids during disaster relief, how did you and Elvis end up working in a refugee camp?" Garrett's question was innocent but it sent her edgy nerves into overdrive, her pulse skyrocketing.

She took a deep breath and tried to ground herself here, in this moment. Rain on the roof. Cool breeze against her skin. "Some people in Syria have been displaced by violence over and over again. Children are suffering. When one of the agencies I worked with in the past asked me if I'd take Elvis and do some training with their counselors there, I couldn't say no."

She waited, tension knotting between her shoulders. She was afraid of what he would ask next. Not that she was secretive, but the memories were still so raw and so painful. What if the floodgates opened and she couldn't get them closed again?

"I can't imagine how hard that must've been."

"It was very different. Even though disaster relief is hard, usually by the time I leave, I can see small signs of recovery and I know that things will continue to get better. In the refugee camp where I worked, it was harder to find things to be hopeful about. And I was there for a long time."

"How long?"

"Eight months. I was supposed to stay for a year, but after I was injured, I got sent home."

"I'm sorry." His hand dropped on her shoulder as he rocked the swing gently, but that was it. She knew he had to have questions, but he didn't pry, didn't even make her feel bad about not sharing more.

Abby jerked upright as the front door slammed open. Latham backed out the door with a sleeping A.J. draped over his shoulder, calling back into the house. "It's pouring out here. If you'll come get her, I'll bring the car up."

Charlotte woke and started to fuss. Latham turned toward the sound and winced. "Oops, sorry, guys."

A few seconds later, Wynn came out of the open front door, followed by Penny. "Oh, there you are, Abby. Thanks for coming tonight. You're a big part of Project Help Garrett Survive."

"I don't know about that, but it was fun."

Latham handed A.J. to Wynn. "Be right back with the car. Congratulations, Garrett."

"Thanks, man."

Abby dug her keys out of her pocket, following Garrett to the top of the stairs. "I've really got to go, too."

"I'll touch base with you in the morning about bringing Elvis over," Garrett called to her as she started down the steps into the rain.

Abby tossed a wave in his general direction and ran through the downpour for her car, beeping the door locks open as she ran.

She slid into the car and slammed the door, shaking water off her hair. The conversation about her work in the refugee camp had unnerved her. She fought the urge to look in the backseat. She was safe here.

Latham pulled his car around to the porch. Abby watched as he jumped out to open the door for Penny while Wynn ducked through the rain to buckle the baby into her seat. They worked together as a unit and Abby couldn't help but feel a little envious. The family she'd had as a kid hadn't exactly prepared her for a relationship, not the kind Wynn had, anyway.

Garrett was still on the porch with Charlotte, swaying a little as he tried to get her back to sleep. His friends and family had been poking fun at him tonight, and he'd handled it in his easygoing way.

If she allowed herself a minute to wonder what it would be like if she and Garrett and Charlotte were a family, it was just normal curiosity. More than ever, she was at a crossroads in her life. Goals had to be set. Decisions made.

Her phone buzzed in the seat beside her. She picked it up. The message was from her former boss, who didn't seem to be able to accept no for an answer. In the past, Abby had willingly given up vacation, Sundays, holidays. Disasters happened without regard to what day of the week or year it was. But this time, she couldn't.

She wasn't saying never, but she was definitely saying *not right now*. She had to rebuild her resilience, and Red Hill Springs was a part of that, giving her something positive to focus on.

She'd told the truth when she said good-night to Wynn. Tonight had been a fun reprieve. But as good as it was, now that the party was over, she only felt more alone. She'd never felt like she belonged, not like that.

She was a bystander at best. This was their life.

But maybe for a little while, she would let herself pretend that it could be hers, too.

Chapter Six

The next afternoon, Garrett held Charlotte nestled in the crook of his arm. Her cheeks were rosy, her little mouth primping. She was sleeping but he didn't want to let go of her. "She had a bottle at noon, so when she wakes up she'll be hungry. I fixed a three-ounce bottle but sometimes she wants an extra ounce."

"I got it. The twins aren't so old that I don't remember the newborn stage." Lacey held out her arms for the baby.

He still didn't give her up. "She's been spitting up a little bit so I try to sit her up after she eats."

"Yep."

"There's this one rattle she likes that lights up. It's in the bag. Her favorite blanket is in there, too."

"She has a favorite blanket? She's a month…" Lacey's voice trailed off as she caught his warning look. "Favorite blanket. Got it. Garrett, you have to actually leave her if I'm going to babysit while you show Abby around the farm."

A knock on the door emphasized her words and

Garrett reluctantly handed the baby over to his sister-in-law. "Are you sure you don't mind?"

"Pish. What's one more? Besides, the twins will be napping most of the time. And you'll be within shouting distance if I need you."

"I know, I know." He opened the front door to greet Abby, then stooped down to give Elvis a scratch. "You ready for a tour?"

"Definitely." After the rain, the weather had turned warmer and Abby was dressed in jeans, cheerful yellow rubber boots and a heather gray T-shirt. Her dark hair was a riot of curls with the humidity.

He smiled at her. "You look nice."

"You mean the circles under my eyes have faded from black and purple to a mere lavender?"

"No." He made a quizzical face. "I don't think that's what I meant."

"Oh, I didn't know you guys had a dog! Hello, girl." Abby's normally alto voice rose as she knelt down to greet Sadie, Tanner's rottweiler-shepherd mix. She held her hand out for a sniff before she scratched Sadie's big black head. She looked up at Garrett. "She's gorgeous. Farm dog?"

Garrett laughed. "More of a lie-by-the-fire dog. But she's smart and completely unflappable, so sometimes Devin uses her to help calm a spooky horse."

Sadie was curious about Elvis, who waited patiently as the big black dog sniffed him from nose to tail. And when Abby straightened, Sadie nudged her hand, greedy for more attention. Abby laughed and obliged her with another good scratch as she looked across the driveway to where Devin patiently circled his latest equine client. "What's going on over there?"

"Devin's gotten kind of a reputation for being able to work with problem horses, so these days we almost always have an extra boarder in the barn. He has a knack with them, probably because he was such a problem child."

"Oh, I can't believe that." Abby laughed as they walked, Sadie running ahead. She gave Elvis a hand signal which apparently gave him the freedom to leave her side because he took off, joining Sadie to romp in the wet grass along the side of the dirt road.

"His attention is always on you. Does everyone train therapy dogs like you have?"

"No, Elvis is different. He's trained to do animal-assisted therapy. His superpower is making people feel comfortable enough to talk." She stopped as they rounded a bend and a field of multicolored wildflowers stretched out as far as they could see. She breathed out an awestruck sigh. "Oh, Garrett. These are beautiful."

"We raise them to sell, but we get to enjoy them for a while first."

"They're so pretty." Abby walked into the field, letting her hands skim the tops of the flowers. She turned back, laughter in her eyes. "I'm probably not allowed to do this, but I don't care. I love how happy they are."

He pulled a folded knife from his pocket and sliced the stems of a handful of the colorful, bright blooms.

She left the field, oblivious to the mud coating her rubber boots, eyes lighting up in delight as he handed her the small bouquet. "Thank you."

"My pleasure." As she brought the fragrant blooms to her face, he caught himself wishing for simpler times. That their lives weren't so complicated, that they were just two ordinary people who met at church or at the diner and struck up a conversation.

Deliberately, he folded his knife and slid it into his pocket before looking up again. "So, since we're here so Elvis can get some exposure to farm life, I'm curious about how you got started doing…what you do."

The sun was weak but welcome as it dappled the ground in front of them. She walked a few steps beside him down the gravel road. "My master's is in trauma and crisis counseling. I started out on a volunteer team while I was doing my training and eventually transitioned into full time."

"That easy, huh?"

"Yep. I guess you could say I stumbled into my calling."

Garrett stopped next to the pasture fence. Elvis loped toward them, circled Abby and then ran back to join Sadie. "How long have you had Elvis?"

"Five years. He was a game changer. Kids love him and maybe they don't want to tell some strange lady something, but they'll tell Elvis."

"I saw him with Nash. He's amazing."

"He's a natural." Abby gave a low whistle and, even though Elvis was roughhousing with Sadie, his head came up immediately. He trotted back to her side and dropped into place. She discreetly slipped him a treat. "Regardless of what's going on, he has to stay calm and obedient."

"Like when there are strange dogs or loud roosters or goats?"

"Exactly." She laughed. "It's funny, but it really helps."

He paused at the end of the lane, where the path

forked. "To the left is the pond. It's spring fed, so it's around fifty-four degrees even in the middle of the summer. It was great when we were kids. My dad would make us work in the fields and barn and we would sweat and complain. But then late in the afternoon, we'd go swimming in the pond. My mom would bring us frozen pops and sit in the chair with her book, trying not to get wet."

A smile curved her lips. "It sounds like fun."

"It was." At least until his mom died and everything fell apart. And then it hadn't been fun at all. He took a deep breath. "My cabin's just over the hill to the right."

"Oh, wow." Her voice was pensive. "Charlotte's mom had to walk a long way to drop her off. I wonder what she was thinking. If she was scared. How desperate she must've felt, but also maybe, how hopeful."

He glanced over at her. Her eyes were a little misty and he could tell she was thinking about Brooklyn and what she must've been going through to make the choice to leave her baby behind. Most people would judge, but Abby didn't. "How do you do that?"

"What?"

"See things from the other person's point of view so easily? Most people are horrified that Brooklyn abandoned her baby."

"That's valid, too. But people do things for all kinds of reasons that we don't understand if we haven't been in their shoes. And we really have no idea what she was thinking and feeling."

"I've been texting her a photo every day. So far no response, though." He turned back toward the barn and the house and the dogs followed, bounding around them.

"Have you asked her to contact you again?" Abby tapped her hip and Elvis fell into step beside her.

"Not yet." He shrugged. "I want her to feel like her wishes have been respected, I guess. I don't know. I'm honestly flying blind here."

"It seems like your instincts are good. I wish I'd met her."

"I wish she'd had the chance to talk to you. Maybe she will one day." As they made their way back toward the house, he stopped in the middle of the lane. "What next? We have a new litter of kittens in the barn."

She held both hands up. "Uh-uh. I can't resist fluffy baby kitties with their tiny pink noses and scratchy little tongues."

Garrett stifled a laugh. "Yeah, that's how I got Thelma and Louise. They were each the size of a big puppy when I got them, and so feisty and cute. Irresistible. The kittens aren't ready to leave their mom yet if that makes you feel any better."

"It totally does. I'm dying to see them." She looked up at him, eyes sparkling under her dark lashes. "No matter what I say, promise me you won't let me get a kitten."

She disappeared into the barn.

Garrett stood, feet rooted, in the middle of the drive.

He was no stranger to trauma. He'd been through it himself. He'd seen it in countless clients—adults and children—that he'd worked with over the years. He recognized it in Abby, too.

But today, he was seeing glimpses of who she was without it, and she was stunning. He pressed his fingers into his forehead. His timing could not be worse. "Get it together, Garrett."

Abby poked her head back out the barn door. "Did you say something?"

"Nope. Not a thing." He shook his head and followed her into the barn.

Abby stopped in the doorway to let her eyes adjust to the dim space. She stood in a shotgun building with doors at either end of a long hall. The floor was dirt and the walls full of cracks, but it smelled of fresh hay and farm animals.

Garrett appeared at her elbow, his voice low. "We've got plans to build a new barn so Devin can expand his horse business."

She looked up at him. "I like this one."

"Me, too." He pointed to the stall in the back of the barn that was next to the partially open doors leading to the round pen where Devin had been working the horse earlier.

At the back of the stall, tucked into a corner, was a gray striped kitty with four little kittens—one gray tabby, two orange and one calico—in tumbled disarray around her. Abby melted. "Oh, they're so sweet. Is it okay if I get closer?"

"Sure."

She dropped to her knees and got a sleepy stare from the mama kitty, but no other signs of alarm. "When did their eyes open?"

"Just yesterday. A couple of them have started exploring but they don't get far before they fall over and have to take a nap."

Abby picked up the calico baby and gently rubbed its tiny forehead as she cupped the kitten in her hands. She laughed. "This was such a mistake. I love this one."

The mother cat had shaken herself loose, literally, from the babies and rubbed her head against the leg of Garrett's jeans. He rubbed her head. "Mrs. Smith is the best barn cat we've ever had. She runs a tight ship around here."

Abby smiled. "You have working animals around this farm. Sadie helps Devin with training. Mrs. Smith keeps the barn tidy."

"Devin's horse Reggie is one of the best cow horses in the country."

She lifted a shoulder. "There you go. The idea of animals having jobs that help humans is nothing new around here."

"Point taken. It's not so weird to have a partner that's a dog after all."

The cat, who'd been the picture of feline adoration, stretched her paws up Garrett's legs and stabbed him with her claws. He yelped.

"That is why you're not allowed in the house." He scowled at Mrs. Smith, who primly made her way back to her kittens and flopped down.

Elvis nosed his way into the barn. Abby smiled. "Hey fella, you having fun?"

He stuck his nose into the curve of her neck where she cuddled the kitten, and snorted. She obliged him with a good long sniff of the strange-smelling thing she was holding.

"Wish my life was in a spot where I could adopt her. She's so cute. I would name her Frances Perkins after the first woman who was on a president's cabinet. She was a social worker."

"Well, Frances it is, then."

Abby kissed the kitten on the nose and reluctantly returned her to her mom. Maybe one day.

She stood and brushed the hay from her pants, putting her hand on a ladder as she stepped out into the breezeway again. "What's up there?"

"I'll show you if you're feeling adventurous."

"Am I going to fall through the floor?"

His laugh filled the barn, as well as some of the dark spaces in her that hadn't heard laughter in a long time. She crossed her arms. "I'm guessing that's why this is an adventure? Because my life might be in danger?"

His eyes, dark and a little serious, met hers. "I wouldn't let anything happen to you, Abby."

Because she believed him and because her heart seemed to suddenly be beating erratically, she motioned for Elvis to stay and took the first step onto the ladder.

At the top, Garrett reached around her and threw open a small window. From this vantage point, she could see for miles. What had seemed like flat farmland was really a series of rolling hills. Streams and creeks were dark slashes in shades of green. The spring-fed ponds that the area was known for gleamed in the distance.

"It's breathtaking, Garrett. I had no idea."

He sat down against a post. Warm afternoon light speared into the space, making the dust seem like tiny sparkling fairies. "When my dad was alive, he always seemed to be surrounded by a halo of dust. Dusty boots, dusty hat. He'd appear in the door of the barn in the late afternoon and he'd just be a silhouette."

Abby sat beside him, looking up at the square of blue sky that showed in the window he'd opened. "He must've been an amazing man to raise three sons who turned out like you and Devin and Tanner."

He snorted. "We've all had our moments, believe me, but he was amazing. He wasn't a big talker—Tanner takes after him, I think—but he was always teaching us. How to take care of the land. How to be a man. How to love a woman. He loved my mom so much."

She swallowed hard but he didn't notice. His eyes were on the beams of sunlight.

"My mom, on the other hand, always seemed to be bathed in sunlight. She'd come out onto the porch in the evening and hold her hand up to shade her eyes. When I think about her, she always seems golden."

"You miss them."

"I'd gotten used to not thinking about them but then, I'm sitting there holding this baby, trying to figure out how to be a dad…" His voice trailed off. The corner of his mouth tipped up. "After my mom died, I used to come up here in the afternoon and watch those beams of light walk across the floor. They'd slide across my skin and I'd pretend it was a message from my mom, that she was touching me from up in the sky."

Her throat ached, thinking about him as a young boy, needing his parents, missing them.

"How old were you?" Her voice, though it was quiet, seemed loud in the space.

He looked at her then, the smile lines crinkling around his eyes. "Fourteen. Devin was twelve and he needed parenting. Tanner had lost his wife and baby, but he did his best to be there for Devin."

"Who was there for you?" She could feel the ache in his words and she was afraid she knew the answer.

"Everyone was grieving so hard." He held his hand

out, letting the sunlight filter through his fingers. "I just kept my head down and tried not to make any trouble. Devin made enough for both of us."

The smile was back.

She said, "Oh, Garrett."

"When Mom and Dad died, I felt like I might never be put back together. But I kept coming up here and looking at those beams. I didn't even know why. But then one day I realized that without all the cracks in the walls, the light wouldn't be able to get in. The beauty of the sunlight comes from the cracks."

His hand brushed hers, sending electric shocks up her arm. Tension stretched but it was like a tight string between the two of them. It scared her a little how much she wanted to reach for him, comfort him.

In the distance, a screen door slammed and a thin wail rose. Garrett stood with a laugh and held his hand out to her. "Wow, I brought you up here to show you the view, not to tell you all my adolescent secrets."

Grasping his hand, she let him pull her to her feet, wincing as the healing wound in her side stretched. She followed him down the ladder, pausing almost imperceptibly when his hands gripped her waist to steady her as she stepped off the last rung.

On solid ground, she looked up. His face was inches away, his eyes warm on hers. He whispered, "Abby."

She knew he was about to kiss her. As if a breath of air nudged her, she moved closer.

Garrett reached up and brushed a piece of hair away from her face, his touch achingly gentle.

Elvis bumped her leg, grounding her in reality. Abby took a step back, one hand moving in a hidden hand gesture to Elvis, who wedged his way between them, creating space.

"Were you wondering where she went, boy?" Garrett laughed and gave Elvis a good scratch, the moment gone so quickly Abby almost wondered if she'd imagined it.

As they stepped out of the barn, fat raindrops started to fall, splattering on the ground. Garrett squinted up at the sky. "I guess that's the end of our sunny day. Want to come in for something to drink?"

Dark clouds were gathering in the west. It was tempting to extend the time she'd spent with him today. It was easy to be with him, easy to feel close to him. But for him, doing that was just part of who he was— he gave his best to everyone.

For her, it was starting to feel a little too personal. Too important.

So Abby shook her head. "Thanks, but I need to be getting back."

"It was fun showing you around. Next time, you'll have to meet the goats and we'll ride if you want to."

He lifted his hat and ran his fingers through his hair, looking down at his dusty boots, and she wavered. But she knew there probably wouldn't be a next time. There was a good chance she wouldn't be here much longer. This attraction she felt to Garrett was just that, a temporary attachment. To believe anything else would be setting herself up for heartache.

And she had enough of that already.

Chapter Seven

"Hey, is Garrett in yet?" Abby stopped at Bess's desk on her way to her office. "I think I was supposed to watch Charlotte this morning."

"Nope." Bess looked up with a smile, her light brown hair in one long braid over her shoulder, fingers pausing on the keyboard. "Haven't heard from him but he's got court in less than an hour."

"Do you think I should text him?"

"Already did. I'll let you know if I hear from him." The executive assistant's eyes were back on her screen.

"Thanks, Bess." Abby walked back to her office. She pulled her cell phone out of her purse but there was no message from Garrett.

Sitting down at her desk, she opened her laptop, glanced at the time on the screen and back at the empty office. She'd caught a glimpse of Garrett at church yesterday but he had to leave early and she didn't get a chance to talk to him. She couldn't stop thinking about that moment in the barn Saturday afternoon. Had she imagined the connection between them?

Was she the only one who felt it?

Was thinking about this a total waste of her time? Yeah, she knew the answer to that question.

Abby blinked her eyes and forced them to focus on the computer screen. She'd had a very promising meeting with the counselors from the local schools early this morning. They'd been excited by the possibility of referring families to her for counseling and support, so she wanted to send them a follow-up email while the meeting was fresh in their minds.

The front door opened. Finally. She listened for Garrett's voice, but all she could hear was Charlotte screaming. Oh, boy. She closed her laptop and walked to the door of her office, swallowing a gasp as she took in his appearance.

He looked awful—eyes red-rimmed, skin tinged with gray, hair standing on end. "What's going on? Are you okay?"

"Were you at church yesterday?"

"Yeah. I saw you get the nursery SOS." She reached for the infant carrier and placed it on her desk. Charlotte's face was red, eyes squinched shut, her tiny lips trembling with each new cry.

"She's barely stopped since. The only time she slows down is if I'm holding her *while* I'm standing up." He rubbed his eyes and blinked at Abby wearily. "She can be dead asleep and if I sit down, she starts up again."

"No wonder you look tired."

"I have a court appearance—" he flipped his wrist over to glance at his watch "—right now, and then a couple of meetings, but I'll be back as soon as I can. Sorry to leave you with her like this."

"It's okay." Abby had to raise her voice to hear her

own words over Charlotte's loud wails. "Did you call Ash?"

"Texted. He said sometimes babies cry and if she starts running a fever or gets lethargic to bring her in. In other words, not helpful at all." He had his keys in hand as he backed toward the door. "She had her last bottle an hour ago."

"Got it." Abby rocked the seat back and forth, but Charlotte's cries never wavered. "Don't worry, we'll be fine."

Garrett looked skeptical but he grabbed his briefcase from his office and walked out the door, clipping the door frame with his shoulder on the way out. Oh, man. She said a quick prayer that he made it to his appointments in one piece.

Charlotte, all ten pounds of her, was trembling and sweaty and mad as a hornet. Abby unbuckled her and lifted her out, holding the tiny body gently as she bounced up and down. "Oh my goodness, little girl. You're all worked up."

The question in Abby's mind was *why*? She ran through a mental checklist of things that could be bothering Charlotte. Hungry? No, Garrett said she'd eaten an hour earlier. Wet? Maybe.

Abby grabbed the diaper bag and carried Charlotte into the bathroom and laid her on the changing table, trying not to wince as the crying intensified. "Hang on, Charlotte, let's just see what's up."

She started with baby's head and closely examined every inch to make sure Charlotte didn't have an insect bite or scratchy clothing tag or something bothering her, but she saw nothing. Not even a little diaper rash.

Was it possible she was itchy? Allergic to the detergent Garrett used to wash her clothes?

Iffy, considering she'd had no reaction before, but Abby pulled a thin muslin blanket from the drawer of clothes Garrett kept here for emergencies. Placing Charlotte in the center of it, she tucked the blanket around the baby until she was completely swaddled.

For the next forty-five minutes, Abby walked in circles around her office. Charlotte would take the pacifier and act like she was sleepy, only to spit it out and start fussing again moments later.

Abby tried holding her in different positions. She tried walking outside. She even tried laying Charlotte down in the porta-crib in Garrett's office and letting her be. Nothing seemed to appease the normally easygoing infant.

Wynn opened the office door. "*What* is going on? I could hear her screaming when I came in the front door."

"According to Garrett, she's been crying like this since he picked her up from the nursery at church yesterday."

Wynn shrugged. "I don't know. Have you tried feeding her? Could be a growth spurt."

Abby's phone buzzed on the desk: a phone call from Garrett. She looked down at Charlotte. "It's your dad. You're gonna need to be quiet for a second."

Charlotte didn't look convinced. She didn't sound convinced either, letting out another loud cry.

"Let me have her while you answer the phone." Wynn took Charlotte and Abby ducked out of the office, closing the door behind her.

"Hello?"

"Hey, I was just calling to check and see if she was any better, but I can hear her."

Abby glanced back to where Wynn was swaying back and forth with Charlotte. "Yeah, she's still not happy. I've tried everything I can think of. It's a little early, but I was about to give her a bottle."

"I wonder if we should just take her to the doctor."

We? "How about this? I saw the thermometer in her bag. I'll take her temperature and if she's running a fever, I'll call and make an appointment. If not, I'll just give her a bottle and we'll go from there."

"Did I put a thermometer in her diaper bag?"

"Yep. It's in the same little zipper pouch as the infant acetaminophen."

"Okay, good plan. Oh, hang on." She heard rustling and muffled voices and then Garrett's voice came back. "They're calling our case. I'll get back there as soon as I can. Thanks, Abby."

The phone went silent.

When she opened the door to the office, Wynn handed Charlotte back. "She definitely doesn't want me. Should I fix her a bottle?"

"That would be great." As she spoke, Abby realized she could hear herself. She looked down. Charlotte had gone silent and was staring intently at her face, more alert than Abby had ever seen her.

Then the little bottom lip poked out and Abby's eyes went wide. "No, don't do that. No, no, no. Aunt Wynn is getting the bottle, I promise."

A few minutes later, Abby settled in the chair with Charlotte and the bottle, which seemed—fingers crossed—to be doing the trick.

Abby wedged the bottle between her chin and the

baby and picked up the thermometer. Thankfully, she just had to run it over Charlotte's forehead to check her temperature. The screen flashed green. Ninety-nine.

So no fever to speak of. Charlotte's eyes were closed and she didn't notice when Abby removed the bottle. Easing a limp-noodle newborn into position on her shoulder without waking her up was easier said than done, but she did it. She leaned back against the seat with a sigh of relief as she patted the little back.

Wow. That hour had been intense, and poor Garrett had experienced nearly twenty-four hours of that. No wonder he looked shell-shocked.

Wynn paused outside the closed door and gave Abby a thumbs-up.

Abby returned a wan smile and let her head drop back against the seat. She picked it up as her phone buzzed again. Expecting Garrett, she was surprised to see her boss's name pop up on the home screen. Her thumb hesitated over the notification. There'd been a time when she would've been excited to see the name, ready to grab her go-bag and head for the airport at a moment's notice. Her work was important and she'd loved it.

Five years later, she'd been tired, but still, she'd believed in the difference she made with kids who'd lost everything. She'd believed until her time in the refugee camp. Rationally, she knew that she'd helped in a small way, that the children she and Elvis worked with knew someone cared about what they had gone through.

Her heart—that was a different story. Her heart said the hours she spent with the kids couldn't stack up when it came to what those little people had been through. It wasn't just losing their homes, or losing their families. Or the abuse that happened in so many forms. It wasn't the absence of the familiar. Or a life-changing injury.

In some cases, it was *all* of that combined. She'd given them everything she had. She'd almost given her life and still, she didn't feel like it was enough.

With a quick flick of her thumb across the screen, Abby opened the phone and read the text from Greta. I know we said six months…

Abby wanted to laugh because her vacations, such as they were, always ended early. But this time, she couldn't make that happen. She'd stepped away from a precipice when she'd given her notice. And this time it wasn't as simple as canceling hotel reservations.

She had responsibilities here.

In her arms, Charlotte gave a quivering sigh. Abby rubbed the tiny back and put her phone aside. So many things were up in the air for her right now, but she'd always been a person who'd given her best to every moment of her day. And right now, that meant being here for Charlotte.

Garrett stepped into the office, stopping with his hand on the doorknob, phone to his ear. "No, I'm not happy with status quo. I don't want a continuance. This family deserves permanence and I don't want to wait three more months to give it to them."

Somewhere in the back, he heard the baby start to cry. He closed his eyes. "I have to go."

Garrett's head was pounding. His feet felt like they weighed two tons and he just wanted to lie down somewhere. But he had other responsibilities now. He pushed the door closed and turned around to find Bess with noise-canceling headphones on. Smart.

In his office, he found Abby pacing the floor with Charlotte. "Still at it, I see."

"Well, she was sleeping until you started shouting as you came in the door."

"I wasn't shouting. I was getting my point across." He scowled at Abby. "Why doesn't she have any clothes on? She's probably crying because she's cold."

"She's not cold. It's seventy-two degrees in here, thank you."

Garrett pressed the fingers of both hands against his temples. "No one's getting any work done anyway. I'll just take her home."

"Hey, guys." The voice startled both of them and the pitch of Charlotte's cries grew louder.

How was that even possible?

Ash Sheehan stepped into Garrett's office. "My sister told me if Charlotte was still fussy that I should stop by on my way back to the office from the hospital."

Garrett said, "She's still fussy."

"She slept for about forty-five minutes, until Garrett got here. Now she's crying again." Abby followed Ash into the main office with Charlotte in her arms.

Ash set his bag on the conference table and walked to Abby, with his hands out. "May I?"

Crooning softly, the pediatrician held Charlotte face down, folding her arms against her body. As her arms stopped flailing, her frantic cries tapered off.

Garrett stared at Ash. "What kind of mind control am I seeing here?"

"Nothing like that. Just experience." When Ash wiggled her legs a little bit with his other hand, Charlotte's breath hitched, but she stopped crying. Ash looked at Garrett. "How old is she?"

He blanked. "Uh…"

"Five weeks." Abby didn't even glance at Garrett as she answered. And he deserved it. He'd been a jerk.

"I learned this trick from one of my pediatric attendings. I don't know why it works, but it always does." Ash moved from the leg jiggle to a slow, rolling bounce. Charlotte's eyes were open, her mottled color returning to normal baby pink. He held Charlotte out to Garrett. "You try."

After an awkward transfer, Garrett copied the hand position and movement he'd seen Ash do and it worked for him, too. The supersecret-pediatrician baby hold wouldn't help the not-sleeping situation, but at least maybe he'd be able to calm her down.

Ash nodded his approval. "Good, you got it. Okay, so here's what you need to know. Five weeks is one of those times when you can get a double whammy with newborns. They're growing so fast that sometimes they need extra feedings or to have the amount of formula increased."

Abby nodded. "I gave her an extra bottle this morning and it seemed to help."

"The second thing is what some call Wonder Weeks. You might notice that she's holding eye contact better. She may get more control of her head. Stretch out her sleeping time at night. Stuff like that. New parents call us all the time saying their easygoing baby is inconsolable. A few days later, that baby will roll over or start crawling or say their first words. And then they're like, *oh*…"

Abby shrugged and met Garrett's eyes. "I did notice she was very alert this morning. Maybe there's something to this."

"There is something to it, trust me." Ash reached in his bag and pulled out an instrument that Garrett recognized as the thing doctors use to look in ears. The doctor checked Charlotte's ears, took the cover off and used the light to check her throat and then asked Garrett to lay her down. After he listened to her heart and felt her belly, he draped his stethoscope around his neck. "I don't think there's anything to worry about, but you can always bring her in if things don't get better."

Abby scooped Charlotte up. "I'll change her diaper."

Garrett walked Ash to the door. "I appreciate you coming by. I know it's not normally part of the service."

Ash raised one smooth brow. "You need to take a nap. Charlotte's fine but you look like day-old stew someone left out all night."

"Yeah. I'm aware."

"All right then, see you Saturday at the Winter Carnival?"

"Sure." Garrett closed the door behind Ash. If he was actually able to break away for the carnival, he'd probably end up napping on a blanket while the party went on around him. This newborn thing wasn't for the weak. He sighed.

For now, though, he had a more pressing duty. Turning to Abby, he noted that she had put clothes on Charlotte, which made him feel worse. "I'm sorry I was a jerk."

With the baby on her shoulder, she shoved a few ibuprofen across the surface of the table. "I'm going to drive you home so you can take a nap. Get rid of your headache and then we can talk."

He wanted to argue but he felt so horrible that he just did what she said. He took the ibuprofen. He let Abby drive him home. He pulled his tie off and dropped it on the floor before falling face-first onto his bed, asleep before he even closed his eyes.

Two hours later, he woke up with a start, not sure where he was. He squinted at the window. The sun was low in the sky, sending stripes of light through the blinds. He took stock of himself.

Headache down to a dull roar.

Body aches almost gone.

Court case still a nightmare.

Baby girl…quiet?

He smoothed the cover of the bed into place before walking out to the family room. Abby was in his over-sized chair, her feet propped on the ottoman, with the sleeping baby on her chest. It was a punch in the gut to see her there, comforting the baby that he'd some-how claimed as his own.

Abby was beautiful, but it wasn't her beauty that drew him. It was her generosity, even after he'd showed his worst side. She had her eyes closed and at first, he thought she was asleep, but every once in a while, her hand moved on Charlotte's back. She was tired too, fighting emotional and physical exhaustion, the very reason she was in Red Hill Springs to begin with.

She opened her eyes and looked straight at him.

He smiled, despite the nagging feeling of guilt. "How long has she been out?"

"Almost as long as you have. But she's going to need a bottle soon."

"I'll make it." He crossed to the kitchen counter. "Thanks for letting me sleep. I feel almost human."

"What happened today?" she asked softly.

"One of the lawyers didn't show up for court, so instead of my client getting her kids back, they have to wait three more months. Three more months of the kids being in foster care when they could be with their parents. It's maddening." He went through the motions of making the bottle, everything second nature to him now. At least this one thing was easy.

"I'm sorry, Garrett."

"I'll never stop getting mad about stuff like this, but usually I handle it better than I did today. I think the situation with Charlotte and not being able to find her mom is stressing me out more than I thought it was."

"That's understandable. Have you heard from her?"

"Brooklyn? No. Every day I text her and hope this will be the day she responds. And every day I'm disappointed."

He looked at Charlotte, who was still completely tuckered out. "I'll take her. I'm sure you're ready to go home. You can drive my car back to the office. I'll get Devin to chauffeur me to work tomorrow."

Abby didn't say anything, just handed the baby to him. Charlotte squirmed, but her eyes stayed firmly shut. Probably saving up her energy to keep him awake tonight.

He touched Abby's arm. "I really am sorry. I was a jerk about the clothes. I guess all new parents get cranky with each other."

Her eyes went wide and he realized—and immediately regretted—that he'd made it sound like *they* were the parents.

"It's fine, Garrett. I know you've had a rough couple of days." She stayed at arm's length, but gave him a too-bright smile as she opened the door. "Okay, hope you two have a better night. Just shoot me a text if you need a ride in the morning."

He stopped. "Abby..."

"I'll see you tomorrow." She closed the door, leaving him standing there staring at it, more confused than ever about what to do next. What happened to the effortless communication they'd seemed to have in the barn?

His brothers teased him about how easily he fell in love, but what he'd felt on Saturday wasn't just attraction or infatuation. It had seemed real and deep. And he wondered if she felt the same way.

Maybe it was just him.

By the time he'd finished feeding Charlotte her bottle, he'd decided the best—and only—course of action was to pretend the awkward conversation never happened.

Chapter Eight

Abby didn't hear from Garrett the next day or the next, other than a quick text to let her know that he was working at home. She had an uneasy feeling that the "new parent" comment had messed up the easy relationship they'd built. Surely he hadn't meant to imply anything except that other people with babies probably dealt with conflict. Crying babies were stressful.

Ugh. It had been so awkward.

Worse, she missed him. *Them.* She missed *them*.

Yesterday after work, she'd ended up walking up and down the aisles of the drugstore in bored desperation and had spent her evening trying various colored face masks, which she was completely convinced were overrated. Her skin was not glowing and poreless, thank you very much.

She'd tried reading but couldn't concentrate, all of which made her wonder if maybe she should consider her boss's offer to come back to work. So when Wynn asked if Abby wanted to meet up at the park for a walk Thursday morning, she'd jumped on the offer.

Unfortunately, she'd forgotten how out of shape she was.

"What is bugging you? You've barely said two words to me since we got here." Beside her, Wynn was walking at a brisk pace, elbows pumping, ponytail swinging.

Abby wasn't sure she could breathe, much less talk, but she tried. "I'm fine. Why aren't you working today?"

"Most of the time, I only take the cases I really want to take and the rest of the time, I work as the mayor. I'll be in the office to meet with clients this afternoon. Then tomorrow I'll be helping to get things ready for the Winter Carnival on Saturday. The vendors start setting up at daylight."

"What's the Winter Carnival?" Abby wheezed out the words. Her lungs were burning. She couldn't feel her legs anymore.

Wynn shot her a sideways glance and slowed the pace—marginally. "You'll love it. We have all kinds of food trucks and craft sellers and bouncy houses for the kids. Bands playing all day. It's really fun...as long as it doesn't rain."

"Is it supposed to?"

"As of an hour ago, there was a forty percent chance, but I don't even want to think about that. Let's talk about you and Garrett instead."

Despite years of practice at keeping a noncommittal expression, Abby was sure her inner feelings were broadcast over her face. She stopped walking, hands on her hips as she sucked in air. "There is no me and Garrett. He's already...oh, never mind. I'm helping with the baby just like everyone else, and that's all."

Wynn slowed to a stop and paced back to Abby, concern in her blue eyes. "I touched a nerve. I'm sorry.

I blunder in sometimes without thinking first. But, honey, you know you can talk to me about anything. I care about you."

Abby sighed, turned Wynn back to the path and started walking beside her. Slowly. "I'm sorry, too. I'm just on edge. I am worried that I might've messed things up with Garrett. And on top of that, my boss keeps pressuring me to come back."

Wynn walked in silence for a few seconds. "Let's table the Garrett discussion and talk about that last thing. Are you going to?"

"Go back? No. I made the decision that was best for me." Abby paused, trying to think how to put into words what she was feeling. "There's a point when you've been dealing with trauma for so long that all the intense emotions start to feel normal. Your body can't live in a heightened state for months or years on end—it's just not possible."

"And that's what happened in Syria?"

Their path wound past the playground. Little kids were playing tag and squealing with laughter. A couple of moms pushed their babies in the swings. And across the green field, there was a group of people doing yoga in the park.

It was peaceful. Happy. What normal *should* be like. "In a way. I lost my sense of fear and went into an area I shouldn't have been in. Trusted someone I shouldn't have trusted." She shook her head and sighed again. It all still felt so heavy. "I have to find my baseline again."

"You're welcome to stay, you know that." Wynn's expression was hopeful as she sent Abby a sideways glance.

A laugh, the release of the pent-up tension, burst out. "You really are relentless, aren't you?"

"I might have heard that a time or two." Wynn shrugged with a laugh. "But listen, this is important. Any decision you make doesn't have to be an either-or thing. You can still make a difference even if you don't go back to traveling the world."

Abby's eyes filled and she looked away, across the park. The words felt like what she'd been waiting to hear, which seemed silly. She was an adult and didn't need anyone's permission to make decisions.

Still.

Wynn's voice softened. "I know a little bit about this battle. Changing the world doesn't have to be on a large scale. Because with every single thing you do, you have the power to change one person's world."

"I guess I feel like I'm giving up. Running away."

Wynn stopped walking and faced her. "Don't take this the wrong way, okay?"

Abby crossed her arms with a sigh. "When someone says, 'Don't get offended,' that's usually a sign you're about to be offended."

"Okay, you're right." Wynn laughed. "But seriously. Is it possible you've *been* running all this time and now it's time to stop? I know from experience that children right here in my hometown need people willing to wade into trauma with them. People who can help them see there's more to life than just survival. You and Elvis could do that."

Despite her vow to not get offended, Abby felt the words hit home. She stepped off the path to let a jog-ger pass them, and took a calming breath. "That's definitely something to consider. Thank you for being honest with me."

"I'm sorry." Wynn put her arm around Abby and steered them both back to the path. "I know it's hard. Believe me."

It was hard. Hard to think about giving up the thing that she'd felt defined her for so many years, but maybe Wynn was right. Maybe work, with its emotional demands and need for constant travel, had given her a convenient excuse to not build ties.

She'd known from an early age that it hurt when bonds with people were broken. It didn't take a genius to figure out that her mother's rejection had created a deep mistrust within her. So maybe Wynn was right that she'd used work to keep other people at a distance. Maybe even to escape conversations like the one she needed to have with Garrett.

Helping other people through their pain and fear came easily for her.

Facing her own fear?

Not so easy at all.

With Charlotte asleep in the swing beside him, Garrett studied the plan he'd put together for the case he was trying on Monday. The witness list was complete. His line of questions for each of his witnesses and each of the witnesses from the other side made sense.

He heard a little sigh from Charlotte, but when he glanced over, she was still sleeping soundly. The growth spurt—or whatever it had been—seemed to be over, at least this time around. And taking these few days to really get her on a solid schedule was the best thing he could've done for his sanity.

Unfortunately, it did nothing for the fact that he missed seeing Abby. Which was weird, in itself. In just a month, she'd become a part of his life that he *missed*. If he didn't know better, he'd think he was actually falling for her. Was it possible that just when he'd stopped looking, the woman he'd been looking for walked into his life?

Even if it was, the panicked look on her face when he'd said they were "new parents" indicated she probably wasn't feeling the same way.

Garrett dragged his thoughts back to work. His strategy was strong. He just needed to go through the files one more time over the weekend to make sure he had all the moving pieces straight in his mind before he headed into court. Well, that, and pray everyone showed up, which seemed to be as big a problem in family court as anything else.

As he was putting his files back into the accordion folder he took to court, he heard a soft knock at the front door. He glanced at his watch. He wasn't expecting anyone.

He took a peek at Charlotte, who was still sleeping, and crossed to the door. When he pulled it open, he saw Abby heading down the stairs, back toward the farmhouse. "Hey, where are you going?"

"Oh, you're here." She stopped and slowly turned around, a blush rising on her cheeks. "I dropped by because I wanted to make sure we were okay, but then I figured if you wanted to see me, you would've."

A bright turquoise umbrella formed a halo around her head. She had on some kind of flowy floral shirt with her jeans and those bright yellow rain boots. She looked like sunshine.

"Come on in. I've got some coffee on." He held the door open. "I should warn you, it's kind of a mess in here."

Abby folded her umbrella and set it beside the door, but when she caught sight of his paper-strewn dining room table, she faltered to a stop. "You're working. I really should go."

"You're here. Please stay for coffee?"

She slid her hands down the front of her jeans, a nervous gesture that seemed so out of place with her normally serene personality. "Water, please?"

"I have water." In the kitchen, he pulled a clean glass out of the dishwasher and filled it with ice, while she stopped to steal a look at Charlotte, who was still asleep. "So what's up? How's your day been?"

"Fine. I went for a walk in the park with Wynn. Red Hill Springs is so pretty. I understand why you guys like living here."

"It's a nice place to live. I appreciate it more now that I'm older. Everyone knowing my business doesn't bother me as much." He added water to the glass from his filter system and slid it across the counter to her.

She took a sip and wandered the room. It didn't take long. "I like the flowered couch. It's you."

He smirked at her. "It was free. Also my mom's. When we were kids, it was in her sitting room where we boys were never allowed to barge in. I get a kick out of thinking how mad she would be that I put my feet on her coffee table and drink juice while I'm sitting on her yellow couch."

"I'm sure she'd be happy you're using it." Abby stopped beside him, placed her glass on the island countertop and drew in a deep breath. "I'm sorry about the other afternoon. I was bossy and we were both stressed about Charlotte crying."

"No, I'm sorry about what I said. Like we were Mom and Dad or something…"

"It's fine. I just don't want there to be something weird hanging between us. I don't have many people in my life that I care about, but I do care about you. And Charlotte, of course." Her cheeks were pink again, words tumbling out in awkward succession.

Garrett looked into her pretty hazel eyes, so full of consternation. Later he could wonder why he'd been so bold. Why he didn't just tell her it was no big deal and move on. But right now he wasn't thinking. Instead, he put his hands on her waist, tugged her forward into his arms and settled his mouth on hers, stopping the words with his lips.

Tension trembled through her before she relaxed, her lips curving under his, her eyes drifting closed. He banded one arm around her waist, sliding the other hand into the hair at the nape of her neck.

Her lips were soft and warm and, as she melted into him, his only thought was: Why had he waited so long to kiss her?

She pulled back, blinked a few times and raised an eyebrow. "You didn't have to kiss me to make me feel better."

Her subtle humor slayed him. She could easily have chosen to smack him instead. "You really have no idea how beautiful you are, do you?"

"What? No." She stepped back. "Stop that, Garrett. You're about to make things weird again."

He leaned back against the island and crossed his arms to keep from pulling her back into his embrace.

"Probably. But I like you and I feel good when I'm with you, like things are going to be okay. It was unfortunate phrasing the other day, but I can't say I haven't been thinking what it would be like between us if we were more than just friends."

"Really? I haven't done this—" She made a vague motion toward the two of them. "I *don't* do this. When I didn't hear from you, I don't know… I guess I thought I'd been mistaken about what I was feeling." She shoved a hand into her hair. "Ugh, this is so awkward."

He was an idiot and he needed to fix this. "Abby, I like you. I don't know what this is either, but I'd like to follow through and see. If that's okay with you."

"It's okay." A hint of a smile deepened the dimple at the corner of her mouth and he wanted to kiss her again. Somehow, though, that seemed like it would be crossing a line that he didn't know how to get back from. He'd already done the two-step on that line as it was.

"I should've called you. After you left, I decided that if I'm going to survive this, Charlotte needs to be on a schedule."

"Did it work?" Her eyes were twinkling now.

"Ah, yes and no. She's eating on a schedule. Sleeping, not so much."

"I should go and let you get back to your work while she's napping. Let me know if there's anything I can do."

Garrett walked with her to the door and picked up her umbrella to hand it to her. "Go to the Winter Festival with us on Saturday? There's music and the food is amazing. It'll be fun if the rain holds off."

She nodded. "I'd love that. See you Saturday."

He closed the door gently behind her and let his forehead drop against it. What had he been thinking? Neither one of them was the type for casual kissing. Abby seemed tough, but she'd been through a lot. The last thing he wanted to do was add to her pain.

His watch buzzed on his wrist, the reminder to make Charlotte's bottle for the upcoming feeding. In the kitchen, he pulled the formula can down from the cabinet and scooped the chalky powder into the bottle.

Garrett sighed. He did like her a lot, but her assignment here was temporary. And suddenly, he wasn't worried so much about breaking her heart.

Maybe he needed to keep an eye on his own.

Chapter Nine

Garrett walked alongside the stroller as Abby pushed Charlotte. There was a throng of people around them but he was hyperaware of Abby's presence, his mind reliving the moment in his kitchen when they kissed.

She, at least, seemed to be enjoying the Winter Carnival. She'd already bought goat's milk soap that smelled like lavender and vanilla, a print of the main street in Red Hill Springs and a piece of pound cake, and they'd only been here an hour.

Garrett squinted up at the sky. Its heavy gray color looked a little ominous, but so far the rain was holding off.

The band was playing country music covers and Abby sang along as they walked. He scowled, half-convinced she was driving him crazy on purpose. He followed her toward the next booth, where Lacey and Devin had set up a tiny version of their farm stand. They'd brought a variety of root vegetables, the first of the lettuce and asparagus and buckets of the wildflowers they'd grown in the field at the farm.

"Looks like y'all have had a lot of customers today." Garrett held up a hand to high-five his brother.

"We're about to close up shop, I think. We sold out of Lacey's cookies in the first few hours. Have you seen the weather report lately?" Devin turned his phone around to show Garrett. "Two hours from now, this place is gonna be a swamp. I also heard on the news this morning there was a strong possibility of some flooding along the river north of here."

Garrett frowned. "I knew it had been raining a lot, but I didn't know that."

Someone handed Devin a five and pointed to the flowers. Devin handed over a bouquet. "Thanks, man. Enjoy."

"What's Tanner think? Is he worried?" Tanner was the oldest by seven years. Garrett and Devin both depended on his quiet leadership when it came to the farm.

Devin glanced at Lacey, who was engrossed in conversation with her order pad out, and back to Garrett. "Yeah. He is. We've gotten a lot of rain, but from here to Nashville, they've had nonstop downpours for days. All that water's gotta go somewhere."

"Tanner's worried that the farm will flood?" Abby asked.

Devin shrugged. "It hasn't happened in our lifetime, but yeah, I think he's worried."

Garrett squinted at the heavy clouds, which suddenly seemed a lot more than a little ominous. He put his hand over Abby's on the stroller handle. "Want something to eat?"

"Sure. See you guys."

Before Garrett moved to join her, he leaned in to

speak quietly to Devin. "Keep me posted. I'll be home as soon as I can."

Devin nodded. "You got it."

Garrett caught up with Abby. "How about some shrimp tacos? You ever had them?"

"I've seen them on menus, does that count?"

He rolled his eyes. "Absolutely not. Come with me."

Abby's face was skeptical as he ordered them for her, complete with cabbage slaw and spicy mango salsa, but he saw that expression change when she took her first bite. "Well?"

She made him wait while she finished the first taco and delicately wiped her mouth, before she said, "I still think they're more like a shrimp salad in a tortilla than an actual taco…"

"Oh, come on." He laughed. "Your eyes were rolling back in your head, it was so good."

"You're not wrong." With a chuckle, Abby picked up her second taco and took a bite. Her next words were muffled. "It's so good."

Charlotte started to squirm and fuss in the stroller, so Garrett pulled a bottle out of the bag and set it on the table. He unbuckled the baby, tucked her into position and started to feed her before he noticed Abby's eyes on him. "What?"

"You've come a long way since the first day with Charlotte. Now you barely have to think about it."

He raised his eyebrows. That first day, he'd seriously wondered if he was up for the challenge. "I guess getting thrown into the deep end will do that for you."

She giggled. "You had your shirt buttoned wrong."

He deadpanned her. "It wasn't funny."

She laughed harder. "And your hair was sticking straight up like Albert Einstein."

"It was not." A twitch started at the corner of his mouth because he knew it had been.

"Did you even have socks on with your dress shoes?"

"No," he admitted, and he started to laugh, too. "I couldn't find any. I picked up the first tie I saw on the chair by my bed and draped it around my neck. I have no idea if it matched or not."

"It didn't." She tried to stop, wiping tears from under her eyes, but giggles were still escaping. "I'm sorry. It's funny now thinking back. I bet you were scared out of your mind."

"That's the understatement of the year." Garrett looked down at Charlotte. He may be an unexpected daddy, but he tried to be a good one. He loved her and that had to count for something.

"I think I might have found something that could help you with your search for Charlotte's mom." Abby rubbed a spot of salsa off her cheek with a napkin and pulled her phone out. "I've been reading through Brooklyn's Facebook posts."

"She hasn't posted since she left town." Garrett looked down at the bottle, tipping it so he could see how many ounces were left.

"No, she hasn't. It doesn't look like she's been in contact with her friends either if this post on her page is any indication." Abby tapped on the screen, scrolled for a second and then turned her phone so Garrett could see it.

He leaned forward to read the post she pointed to.

"'Girl, answer your phone. Where you been? We need ta party.' Charming."

"Yeah, well, you knew she wasn't hanging out with the best crowd. But when you read further down, like way down, there are some posts about how she wants to go to cosmetology school. I'm wondering if Brooklyn decided to actually do something about it."

"Maybe, but why leave Charlotte? Couldn't she go to cosmetology school here?"

Abby shrugged. "Maybe not if she wanted to steer clear of friends who were trying to get her to party instead."

"That makes the most sense of anything I've heard so far. Unfortunately, we still have to find her. There have to be hundreds of those schools around." Garrett sighed, put the bottle on the table and lifted Charlotte to his shoulder.

"Yeah. I'll keep looking. Maybe there's a clue buried in the comments somewhere."

"Remind me on Monday and I'll take another look at my files. Maybe she said something about her dream place to live in one of my interviews with her. Sometimes I write stuff like that down."

A fat raindrop hit Abby in the forehead. She squinted up at the sky. "I think it's time for us to go."

Garrett nodded. "Yeah, it looks like the bottom's about to fall out."

As they started packing up, the band was doing the same and a few minutes later, Mayor Wynn took the stage.

She cleared her throat. "Hey everyone, as most of you know, I'm Wynn Grant, the mayor here in Red Hill Springs. I'm sorry to say that we're going to close up early this year, for everyone's safety. Thanks so much for coming and y'all be safe going home."

Wynn's brother Joe, the police chief, bounded up the stairs. He said something to Wynn that Abby couldn't hear and then took the mic. "I'm Joe Sheehan, the police chief here in Red Hill Springs. Everyone listen up for an announcement: the bridge over Red Hill Creek is washed out on Highway 43. There are multiple reports of flooding in Triple Creek. If you're headed north, please be careful. Do *not* drive through water that's covering the road, even if you think it isn't deep."

Abby turned to Garrett, eyes dark with concern. "Triple Creek? That's just north of your farm, right?"

His face was serious. "Pretty close. I need to call Tanner."

As Garrett reached for his phone, it buzzed. Around him, he saw his friends reaching for their phones and kissing their wives. He knew what that meant. And it wasn't good.

Garrett checked his message and stood. "I've got to go. I'm on the volunteer fire department and they're calling me in."

Abby didn't hesitate, just held her arms out for the baby. "Take my car. I'll take yours with the car seat and you can pick Charlotte up later."

"Are you sure?"

"Of course." Abby paused in the middle of buckling Charlotte back into the infant seat.

From across the park, he heard someone yell his name and he took a step in that direction. "Be careful, okay? It's going to be dark soon and no one knows how fast the water will rise."

"I'll take care of her, I promise. But Garrett?"

With her keys in his hand, he stopped. "Yeah?"

"Promise me you'll take care of you."

Abby threw a blanket over the stroller and ran for Garrett's SUV—as fast as she could with a crowd of people also hurrying to get out of the park. When she finally made it, she popped the infant seat off the stroller and locked it into place on its base.

"Hey, Abs, got a second?"

Abby peered through the rain and saw Wynn jogging toward her. She thunked the stroller into the back of Garrett's SUV. "If you get in while we talk."

She slammed the rear door shut and slid into the driver's seat, squeezing the rainwater out of her hair. Ugh. The clouds that had been threatening all day hadn't been bluffing.

A second later, Wynn slid into the passenger seat and pushed the hood of her raincoat away from her face.

"Hey, you really know how to throw a party." Abby started the car and pressed the defrost button as the windows started to fog.

"You know it." Wynn groaned, shaking her head. "We'll be trying to regrow the grass for the next four months."

"So, what's up?"

"Tomorrow morning, we'll start sending out teams to check houses. If we need it, the church will open up as a shelter for evacuees from the storm. If that happens, it's going to be all hands on deck. I know you didn't sign up for this, but we'll need you—and Elvis, too."

"Tell me where you need me to go and I'll be there."

If people were in need, she couldn't turn away. She looked out at the dark stew of clouds. "Garrett's out there in this."

"I know." Wynn put her hand over Abby's. "But our volunteer fire department is well trained. And he's been doing this a long time. He'll be okay."

"He also goes to extremes if he thinks he can help."

Wynn smiled. "He does. A lot like someone else I know. I've got to run. Be safe. I'll see you tomorrow."

Abby took a second for a deep breath and a whispered prayer for the first responders' safety. Traffic eased so she put the car in Reverse, slamming the brakes when a knock at the window startled her. She rolled the window down to find Wynn standing there. "What's going on?"

"I just got word there's a child trapped by the floodwaters and the firefighters can't get her to budge. Are you up to getting Elvis and heading out with the next group?"

"Of course, but I have Charlotte."

"I forgot about that." Wynn squeezed her eyes shut, thinking. "Okay, this could work. I'll call Jules and see if she can meet you at your house. You'd have to pick Elvis up, anyway."

"Sounds good."

"Yes? Good. I'll send you more information as I get it." Wynn drew her finger in a circle in the air and behind Abby, flashing blue lights came on. Apparently, Abby was getting a police escort. She sucked in a breath, nerves skittering in her stomach.

It wouldn't be her first trip out with first responders—she'd participated in rescues before—but with unpredictable floodwaters, it would certainly be the most dangerous.

It didn't matter.

There was a little girl out there who was scared and alone with the water rising around her.

Garrett shielded his face against the pelting rain. He and his partner had gotten a call that there was a child stuck on the roof of a mobile home. In rising water like this there were no landmarks, no visible street signs. That they found the mobile home at all was their first break.

That the child was still on the roof? That was a gift from God.

His partner Jackson Andrews steered their small inflatable raft closer to a large oak tree and Garrett tossed a line over one of the larger branches. Anything to give them a little more stability to maintain their position in the fast-moving water.

Another crew was on the other side of the mobile home. At this point, whichever team had the leverage would get the child off the roof.

His boat bumped the side of the mobile home and from a gaping hole in the roof, another small head poked out. There were two?

Jackson apparently realized the same thing because he shouted, "There are two of them!"

The child tried to climb on the roof, wobbled and tumbled backward into the hole. On the other side of the roof, the other child was being helped into a life jacket.

Garrett wasn't sure the roof was going to hold him, but it didn't look like he had much choice. He yelled to Jackson, "Get as close as you can. I'm going over."

In response, Jackson steered the boat closer. He fought against the current to stay as close to the home as possible. Garrett waited for the firefighters on the other side to help the older girl into the boat. Then he took a deep breath and leaped across the water, landing on the roof.

The mobile home rocked with the force of his weight and from inside he heard a weak scream of fear. Unwilling to rock the unsteady trailer any more, he lay down on his stomach and belly crawled over to the jagged opening. Down below, he saw a little boy, around five or six, standing on a kitchen cabinet. Water lapped at the cabinets, at least twelve inches deep and rising.

"I'm Garrett. I'm a firefighter. What's your name?" Garrett looked around the mobile home, checking for any hidden dangers.

"Toby."

"Okay, Toby, I'm gonna get you out of there." The little boy's lips were blue with cold, his skin like marble. Garrett pulled straps off of his utility belt and made a loop that he could drop through the ragged opening. "How old are you, Toby?"

"F-f-five."

"You're a very brave five-year-old." Garrett hung as far into the space as he could without falling in and draped the strap around Toby. The little boy was quick, grabbing on to it with each hand.

"Her is free."

Garrett stopped midmotion. "Your sister is free? The one who got in the boat?"

Toby shook his head vehemently. "No. Her."

He pointed into the bedroom. Garrett couldn't see anything. He grabbed his flashlight and shone it as far into the murky space as he could, eyes roaming over every inch.

With the water still rising, he'd decided to haul Toby out and go back to check, when his flashlight fell on the corner of the dresser. And he could see five tiny fingers with chipped pink polish gripping the edge.

He lifted his head. "We've got another one in here!"

To Toby, he said, "Come on, buddy, let's get you out of there."

In one heaving motion, he swung Toby off the countertop and dragged him onto the roof, so fast that the little boy almost didn't have time to be scared. When his feet grabbed purchase, Toby locked his scrawny little arms around Garrett's neck, burying his face in Garrett's shirt.

Garrett managed to half crawl, half slide to the edge where he unclenched Toby's arms and stuffed them into the life jacket that Jackson tossed him. A few minutes later, with Toby safely curled up on the bottom of the inflatable raft wrapped in a space blanket, Garrett said, "I've got to go back."

"I heard on the radio that they've got another crew on the way. The big sister told Gary and Max that the little one wouldn't come out. She's apparently terrified of men. They asked the sister if the little one could talk and she said no. May have autism. They weren't sure." Jackson managed to keep the boat close, but with the water rising, the current was getting stronger.

At least the rain had slacked off. For now.

"That complicates things a little bit." Garrett started back across the roof as the whine of another motor sounded across the water. He glanced up, looked away and then back again. Was that… No. It couldn't be…

"Abby?"

Chapter Ten

As their very small boat zipped across the water toward a red dot on a GPS screen, Abby kept a firm grip on Elvis's collar and a constant stream of silent prayers going up.

More information had been trickling out from the firefighters who'd rescued the trapped child's sister. According to her driver, a firefighter named Jed, the little girl's name was Maya—three years old, nonverbal and terrified of men.

Abby hoped she liked dogs.

The light was dimming, daylight fading. They weren't going to have long.

She heard the motor throttle back and looked up. The mobile home was directly in front of them, tilted at an angle, like it had been pushed off its blocks by the rushing water. One of the volunteer firefighters lay on his belly near a gash in the roof.

Jed dropped the motor speed even more, easing up to the side of the mobile home at idle speed. And now that they were closer, she realized the water was over the steps by at least a few feet, maybe more. There was no way that Elvis would be able to get in there. But she could.

"Abby?"

Her head jerked up as she heard her name. Garrett was the firefighter on the roof of the trailer. His face was blank with shock. "What are you doing here?"

"I'm here to help." The rain had slacked to a sprinkle, but dark clouds billowed in the west. They weren't going to have long between the sun going down and the next round of storms. To Jed, she said, "If you can pull up next to the roof and cut power, I'll be ready to go."

Abby crouched in the boat, keeping her center of gravity low, until they were just close enough. Standing now, Garrett gripped her hand and swung her onto the roof. The whole thing careened under them, shifting with her added weight. She dropped down, mimicking Garrett's position, and army crawled closer.

"Abby, how—where's Charlotte?"

"Jules is watching her. Wynn asked me to come since the little girl likely has autism. I have search-and-rescue experience. Not a ton, but this isn't my first time coaxing someone out of debris. Is this gonna be a problem for you?"

He looked directly into her eyes. "Not at all. She's in the bedroom, on top of a chest of drawers against the wall."

"Does she look injured?"

He gave a slight shake of the head. "Not that I can tell, but every time I try to get a better look, she starts screaming."

Abby followed the beam of light from his flashlight down into the mobile home. It was dark in there. The water was murky and brown, lapping at the edges of the countertops in the kitchen. And at the very farthest reach of the flashlight, she could see the little girl's white-knuckle grip on the edge of the chest of drawers. *Oh, sweet girl.*

With one last quick prayer for the right words, Abby shimmied closer. "Maya? My name's Abby. If you can hear me, can you wiggle your fingers?"

For a moment, there was no response, then a hair of a second when the grip loosened and the fingers moved.

"Good job! That's really good. We're here to help you stay safe in the water. Can you peek your head around so I can see your pretty eyes?"

Again the seconds ticked by.

"We can't wait much longer, Abby. It's getting dark." Garrett swung his feet around and got one booted leg through the opening before the little girl started screaming. Terrified, hysterical screams.

"Stop! Garrett, stop." Abby drew in a slow, patient breath. They were all stressed. It was fine. She said quietly, "You trust me with Charlotte. Trust me now. Give me a few minutes to work and if I can't get her out safely, then we'll do what we have to, okay?"

She held her hand out for the flashlight and, with his eyes on hers, he placed it in her hand. "How much daylight do we have?"

"Ten minutes, maybe fifteen. Then it gets too dangerous for anyone to be out in this mess."

"Got it." She leaned forward so Maya could hear her voice. "Hey, Maya, he's gone. It's just me. Can I see your sweet face now?"

The seconds ticked by, turning into a minute and Abby wondered if Maya was too scared to cooperate or maybe she just didn't understand. But then, a curly mop of blond curls appeared along with a set of big blue eyes. "There you are! Can you see me, too?"

Maya nodded, the curls bouncing on her head. Abby smiled. "Good. I need to ask you a couple of questions."

Another nod.

"Can you swim?"

A negative shake of the head.

"Yes?" Garrett asked.

"No." Abby locked her gaze on his, stifling a scream as the mobile home shifted. Garrett grabbed her arm as she started to slide and hauled her back to the edge of the opening in the roof.

"We can't wait any longer, which means I'm gonna have to go in after her."

For a second, she thought he would argue, but instead, he gave her a firm nod. "We do this together. I've got your back. Whatever you need."

"Thanks, Garrett." Abby leaned forward. "Maya?"

The little girl peered around the corner again.

"Do you like dogs?"

A single nod in answer.

"Me too! My dog is in the boat out here. I bet he'd like to meet you. Would you like that?"

Another single nod.

"I'm coming down. There'll be a big splash and a second later, I'll be right there beside you, okay?"

Before she could rethink her decision, Abby dropped through the opening in the roof into the kitchen of the mobile home. One foot landed on the floor, the other on something unseen in the water, her ankle twisting underneath her. She sucked in a breath.

Garrett's voice came from above. "Abby?"

"It's okay. I'm okay." She held her breath and counted. *One, two, three, four.* Eased out the breath as the pain started to lessen. "I'm good. I'm going to the bedroom."

With the flashlight shining in front of her, she could see Maya squatting on top of the chest of drawers, dressed in only an oversized T-shirt. The tiny lips were purple, the little girl's whole body trembling. Abby smiled. "Well, hello there. You must be Maya. Very nice to meet you."

That silly bit of politeness elicited a scant smile.

"You ready to get out of here?"

A vehement shake of the head.

"No?"

Maya pointed across the room.

"Is there something you need from over there?"

More nodding. Abby fought the desire to grab the little girl and sprint out of that murky, disgusting water as fast as she could. But a few seconds spent here could save them a lot more in the long run. She sludged a few steps further into the bedroom and heard Garrett's warning tone. "Abby…"

Maya let out a keening cry.

"It's okay, Maya." She started humming "Jesus Loves Me" while shining the flashlight around the room. Finally, she caught sight of a stuffed dog wedged between the headboard and the wall. Maybe? She plucked it out. "Is this little guy what you were looking for?"

Maya reached with one hand for the stuffed dog and Abby edged closer. "You think you can come and get him?"

Abby opened her arms and Maya jumped into them,

scrambling up Abby's body to get as far away from the water as she could. Keeping her voice as calm and steady as she could, Abby said, "Good girl, Maya. You're doing so good."

In the kitchen, she glanced up at the space above, where she'd dropped in. If she had to get out that way, she could, but it would be difficult, but maybe… She sloshed a few more feet through water nearly up to her waist and tugged on the door. It cracked a couple of inches.

She called upward. "Garrett, can you get Jed to pull up close to the door? I think I can get it open."

Garrett relayed her message and she heard the boat's motor pick up. It was hard to get enough leverage while holding Maya, but she put one foot on the frame and tugged as hard as she could on the doorknob. "I can't get it to budge. It's stuck on something."

A split second later, she heard a splash outside and Garrett wrenched the door open. One more obstacle down.

Now to get Maya on the boat. "Elvis, watch me. Look, Maya. There's my dog. He's waiting for you to come and give him a big hug, just like you do with your little dog. Do you think you can do that? I know you can. You've been so brave."

With all her strength, Abby lifted Maya onto the edge of the boat, ignoring the sudden tearing pain in her side. Through gritted teeth, she said, "Elvis, give hugs."

Elvis leaned forward, resting his nose on Maya's shoulder. The terrified little girl wrapped her arms around him and buried her face in his soft fur.

Abby breathed a sigh of relief. The hardest part was

over, and now that they were out, the fire rescue team worked quickly—and quietly, obviously trying not to scare Maya more.

"They have an ambulance waiting just outside the flooded area to take the two of you to the hospital to meet her siblings." Garrett touched her arm. "You were amazing, Abby."

"We make a good team. Thanks for the muscle."

He grinned. "Anytime."

Above them, the ruined trailer groaned and shifted. Garrett shouted. Jed reached a hand out and heaved Abby into the boat. She was dripping, soaked to the skin, shivering and exhausted. But they had all three kids safely out of that mobile home and on their way to being reunited.

She sat next to Maya against the side of the boat. The little girl kept her face hidden, but she scooched closer, bringing Elvis with her. Abby put her arm around them both, sucking in a breath as she pressed on her side with the other one.

"We'll have y'all on dry land just as fast as we can. Hang on." Jed turned the boat away from the ruined trailer and toward safety.

An hour and a half later, Garrett strode through the glass door leading into the ER. He'd only stopped long enough to shower off the mud and get into dry clothes. After a quick call to Jules to make sure Charlotte was still okay, he'd come straight to the hospital.

Almost everyone had gotten out in time, loading their cars with their belongings and driving out, but in total, he and his team had rescued one elderly couple and two families—including the children in the mobile home and one couple with a day-old baby—who'd been trapped by the rising water.

A handful of dogs, a couple of cats and a parrot named Bert had also been boated out by various first responders and taken to the local vet for boarding until their owners were safely able to return home.

Garrett heard from the paramedics that Abby was in the ER and he couldn't rest until he knew she was okay. He found her in one of the small rooms, scrolling through her phone. It looked like she'd managed a shower too, because her hair was damp and she was wearing an oversized green hospital gown.

He cleared his throat. "They'll just give anyone an exam room these days."

"Ha ha, very funny." Abby smirked up at him and the coil of tension he'd been carrying since she sped away on the boat unwound just a bit.

But she had an IV hooked into her arm and when he stepped closer, she pulled the blanket up self-consciously.

"What's going on here? Did something happen that I don't know about?"

Her cheeks colored. "It seems that I reopened a wound when I was 'traipsing around in the flood,' as the ER doctor put it."

He dragged a chair up to the side of the bed and sat. "Are you okay?"

"I'm fine. Nothing a few more stitches and a whopping dose of antibiotics won't fix. Apparently floodwater really is as disgusting as it looks." She rolled her eyes. "Please stop making that face. I'm going to be fine. How's Charlotte?"

"Apparently, she's loving life with the Quinns. Jules said she is fascinated by all the kids and the older ones are fighting over who gets to hold her, so she is in hog heaven."

"I'm sure." Abby laughed. "Did you get in touch with Tanner and Devin?"

"Yep. Talked to Tanner just now. They're dry at the moment. The flooding is supposed to crest tomorrow afternoon and then start receding. We're at a higher elevation than the neighborhoods that flooded today, but tomorrow morning we're going to move as many of the livestock as we can to higher ground."

"It's never flooded before?"

"We've had high water in the swampy areas, but the water never reached the fields and pastures, much less the house. This time? The amount of rain dumped upstream… I think the weather people on the news are calling it *unprecedented*. We won't know if we're out of the woods until tomorrow night."

"You can use the barn at my house if you need it."

"That's a good idea. I'll let Tanner and Devin know."

"Good. And I'll keep the babies tomorrow so you can help move everyone to high ground."

"Okay. That sounds like a plan." Garrett reached for her hand, gently sliding it into his. "I was so worried when I saw you coming in on that boat. But I didn't need to be. You're a pro, Abby."

"I appreciate that. Both the concern and the compliment." Then, "Have you heard anything more about the kids?"

"They were reunited with each other here at the hospital. They got checked out by a doctor and they got away with minor cuts and bruises. The oldest—who is ten—said her mom was at work, but she couldn't remember where." He rubbed her fingers gently with his thumb.

"What will happen to them?"

"My guess is they'll go to an emergency foster home until Monday, so a caseworker can do a little digging. It's not ideal, but they're safe and together. It's something."

"You're right. It's a lot, actually."

Her eyes had dark smudges underneath them. When she yawned, he wondered if he needed to leave so she could rest. "Do you want me to let you sleep?"

"No. I tried. I just keep replaying the rescue over and over again in my mind." The admission slipped out, revealing that this afternoon's adventure hadn't been the walk in the park for her that she wanted him to believe.

"How about this? Scoot over." He slipped out of his shoes, nudged her over and climbed into the bed beside her, snugging her into the curve of his arm. "I've been saving these videos for when I had time to watch them. It's Abbott and Costello. Have you seen them?"

"Not that I know of."

Garrett tsked. "Your education is sorely lacking. You're going to love them."

Holding his phone where she could see it, he started the *Who's on First* episode. Within two minutes, she was giggling, and by four minutes in, she was wiping tears from under her eyes. He'd seen this episode at least twenty times, but seeing it through Abby's eyes made it even better.

He was content. Today had been incredibly stressful

and he was tired, but he needed this. Holding her, laughing with her—there was nowhere else he'd rather be.

Somewhere in the back of his mind that thought set off alarm bells, but he shut them off without a thought.

Chapter Eleven

Abby blew hair off her forehead and looked around at her living room. It was completely trashed. There were bouncy seats and toys, burp cloths and baby bottles littering the floor from one end to the other.

Next time there was a flood, she was not going to volunteer to keep all the Triple Creek Ranch babies. Moving cows and angry pigs had to be easier than this. She had baby cereal stuck to her hair and spit-up on her shirt, three cribs lined up in the guest room and a newborn goat in the bathroom.

Two of the babies were asleep. The third one, Eli, she could see on the video monitor with his thumb in his mouth. He was "singing" himself to sleep. Jules's youngest was in the playpen in the living room, playing with some toys.

Jules dropped into a chair. "I'm not even kidding when I say if someone offered me a free spa day, I would tell them I'm too tired."

"I think you're delirious." Abby picked up her mug of tea, which she'd just warmed in the microwave for the fourth time, and limped over to her chair. She just wanted to sit down for five minutes. Every muscle in her body ached after her adventures fighting the flood yesterday.

The watch on her wrist buzzed and she thought she might cry. It was time to feed Garrett's baby goat who, as the runt of the litter of triplets, was improbably named Hercules and was currently in her guest bathroom because he couldn't keep his body temp up.

Any other time, she'd be thrilled to feed a baby goat. He was the size of a toy poodle and adorable. But her feet were so tired, she couldn't feel them anymore. Three infants plus goat were no joke.

Not to mention, the antibiotics she was on after her dip into the floodwaters were making her sick to her stomach. Super fun.

"Time to feed the goat." She hauled herself to her feet. The other two newborn kids were in one stall in the barn with their mother. The rest of the goats were in stall number two. Lacey and Garrett were on their way with a couple of horses to stay in stalls number three and four. The rest of the animals had either been moved to pasture on higher ground or were staying with other people.

The rattle of a horse trailer on the gravel driveway alerted her to Garrett's arrival. She peeked out the window as he parked in the lit area of the yard and slid out of the farm truck. In his cowboy hat and jeans, Garrett fully looked the part of a rancher today.

Jules stopped at the window beside her and hummed appreciatively. "I love a good cowboy hat."

Abby laughed. "Get out of here and back to your children. It looks like reinforcements have arrived."

"If you're sure, I'll grab Micah and head home. The

other kids are going to be hungry and as good as my oldest is with the kids, he is a terrible cook." Jules slung a diaper bag over her shoulder and reached into the play area for Micah, stopping on her way to the door to give Abby a hug. "I'm so glad you're here. Thanks for letting me hang out with you today."

"I couldn't have managed without you." Abby heard a thin bleat from the bathroom. "And I better get in there before he wakes up the human babies. See you tomorrow."

When Abby opened the door to the bathroom, Hercules bounded out. She scooped him up into her arms. He was black and white and fluffy and nuzzled her face with his nose. "Poor Hercules, you have no idea where you are, do you?"

As she talked, his little tail was going ninety miles an hour. He was pretty new in general, so bottle feeding wasn't second nature for him yet. She eased down onto the floor of the bathroom and pulled a towel over her lap. With the fingers of one hand, she opened his mouth and when she stuck the bottle in, he grabbed hold. "That's the way, bud. You got it. Oh, you're hungry, aren't you?"

He stopped for a little breather, bumping her face with his forehead.

She laughed and repositioned the bottle for him. "It's over here."

By the time she finished giving him the bottle, nearly nodding off herself, she was pretty convinced that she had as much milk on her as he had in his tummy. He was calm and sleepy, so she took a moment to enjoy a little snuggle before tucking him into his box.

Finally. All the babies were in bed.

She reached up for the counter to haul herself off the floor and nearly screamed as she grabbed a firm hand instead.

Garrett grinned as he pulled her to her feet. "I'm impressed. All the kids are fed and asleep and I met the pizza delivery guy outside which makes me *so* incredibly happy. Lacey's already stuffing her face."

"I heard that, Garrett." Lacey appeared in the door to the hall with a piece of supreme pizza in her hand. Her dark hair was in a messy bun on top of her head and she had a streak of mud on her cheek. "Also, it's true. It's the best thing I've ever eaten in my entire life."

Garrett leaned over and scratched the goat's tiny head. "Hercules seems to be holding his own. Tomorrow we'll put him in with the others so he can learn to be a goat. How are you holding up?"

"No problems." She wavered on her feet, contradicting her own statement. "Yeah, wow, I'm tired."

"Come get some pizza. I'm feeling better by the minute." Lacey waved Abby into the kitchen. "You've had a busy day. The twins are a handful by themselves. No wonder you're tired."

"Sit." Garrett shoved Abby into a chair at the kitchen table as she protested.

"You guys have been working all day, too. And I had help. Tell me what's going on now." Despite her protest, she took a bite of the pepperoni pizza Garrett put in front of her. A few seconds later, he set a fizzing cola by the plate.

"We sandbagged a couple of areas that we thought might flood." Lacey took another bite of pizza. "Garrett, Devin and Tanner moved most of the animals, except for the two we just put in the barn. We were working them pretty hard. The other horses are in the pasture at Red Hill Farm. Jordan's going to board them with her horses."

"The cows are on high ground. The pigs are with Mr. Haney on his farm, but let me tell you, those pigs were not happy." Garrett finished his first piece of pizza and refilled his cup from a can of soda. "The animals will be safe. We may have some work—a lot of work—to do to rebuild the lower pasture areas, but I don't think the water's going to get up to the house or barn."

"Hey, guys." Devin opened the back door and stood in the opening while he toed off his muddy boots. "Is that pizza? I'm starving."

Abby frowned. "Where's Tanner?"

"Staying at the house. He won't leave. We didn't even try to argue." Garrett reached for another piece.

"Garrett, what about the kittens?"

"No worries. We put them inside in one of the upstairs bathrooms. They'll be safely out of harm's way." He cut his eyes at her. "Unless you want me to bring them over here?"

"Uh, no. We have enough babies in this house, thank you very much. Tanner can take care of the kittens."

"Tanner might want to run away by the time the mama cat stops her caterwauling." Devin grinned. "Get it, *cat*erwauling?"

"Ugh. That was terrible." Garrett shook his head. "I'm just thankful the puppy incident is behind us."

"The puppy incident?" Abby asked with a mouthful of pizza.

"You haven't heard about that?" With a piece of pizza in one hand, his soda in the other and a wide grin on his face, Devin sat back. "Someone left a litter of barely weaned, starving puppies in the alleyway behind the main street shops. Garrett the Noble took them home and fed them every couple of hours for two weeks. He hauled those puppies everywhere, trying to fatten them up."

"Oh my goodness, the poor little things. Did they make it?" Abby's face was stricken.

Garrett laughed and put his arm around her shoulders, the unconscious gesture making her feel like she was a part of their group. "They're fine."

Devin scoffed. "Of course they made it. Those were the fattest puppies you've ever seen."

"Hang on, I've got a pic." Lacey was flipping through her phone. "Here it is."

Garrett was seated on the ground with nine pudgy black and white puppies crawling all over him. His head was thrown back in a laugh.

"They're precious. What happened to them?"

Lacey rolled her eyes. "We begged and pleaded and called in all the favors from everyone we knew until finally they were all adopted."

"You saved their little lives, Garrett."

He slung his arm around her chair and thumped his chest with his fist. "Yep. Heart of gold."

Puppies. Baby. Special stroller for a little boy who needed one. Not to mention how he looked in jeans and a cowboy hat. Was it any wonder she was head over heels for him?

Wait—*was* she falling for him?

That didn't seem like something she would do.

But Garrett wasn't like anyone else she'd ever met.

Oh, boy, she had a feeling that, floodwaters or no floodwaters, she was about to be in over her head.

Heart of gold? Garrett wasn't even sure where that came from except that it sounded ridiculous. He was definitely more tired than he thought he was.

"Hang on." Devin raised a cynical eyebrow. "You haven't heard the best part, Abby. Word got around about what Garrett did for the puppies and people started dropping all kinds of animals off at the end of our lane. Kittens and puppies galore. One person even tied a donkey to the fence and drove off."

"What? That's not cool."

Garrett finished off his pizza and brushed the crumbs off his fingers. "Well, he is a pretty great donkey."

"He is, that's true. We named him Sheriff and put him in the field with the cows. And now he's a watchdog. Watch-donkey?" Lacey laughed. "I have no idea. But I know I'm exhausted and this is pathetic, but the babies will be up in a couple of hours for a bottle and I've got to take a shower and get at least a few hours' sleep before we're back at it tomorrow."

"Good idea." Devin picked up the paper plates on the table, reached for his cane with the other hand and limped to the trash can. "I'm going to my Narcotics Anonymous meeting and then I'll be back to hit the sack myself. I have a feeling we're going to have more long days in the future before things get back to normal at the ranch."

"Yeah, we all need to hit the hay early." Garrett gathered up the pizza boxes and drink cups that were scattered on the table. "I'll be right back."

Garrett walked outside and dumped the trash in the big trash can. When he turned around, he was facing the pasture behind Abby's rental house. The grass glowed with a blue-green hue and the moon coming up on the horizon was spectacular. The storms had passed and he could see every star in the Milky Way. He stuck his head in the back door. "Hey, Abs, come here for a minute."

She joined him at the porch rail and, as if it were the most natural thing in the world, his arm slid around her back. "Look at that moon."

With a sigh, she gazed at the huge golden orb slowly rising from the horizon. "It's incredible."

Maybe it was silly and a huge mistake to pull her closer. After all, he didn't know what the next few months would bring for her...or him, for that matter. What he did know was that he felt good when he was with her. With other people, he often felt that he had to always be on. Always meet the expectations of other people. With Abby, he just felt...accepted. And after watching her with that little girl yesterday, he thought the ability to convey caring without judgment might just be her superpower.

He looked down at her. "We couldn't have made it through these last couple of days without you. I couldn't have made it through last month without you."

"This may seem a little out-there, but I feel like God put me in just the right place at the right time. I'm just glad I could help."

"It's not out-there at all. I feel that way, too." He tilted her chin up and kissed her gently, just a soft brush of his lips against hers before he turned back to the moon.

"I'm...not sure where we're going with this, Garrett." Her eyes stayed on the moon, but the question was in her voice.

"I have a habit of bouncing from one thing to another as the spirit moves me. I enjoy my life. Even when I'm suddenly making gruel for nine scrawny puppies at all hours of the night. It's the adventure of it all, I guess." He looked down into her eyes, which looked huge and dark in the shadows of her back porch. "But I like where I am, right at this exact moment."

"Me, too." Her watch buzzed. She stopped the alarm and looked up. "Time to feed Hercules."

"I'll feed him. You get some sleep."

"I *am* tired," she admitted.

The back door opened and a bleary-eyed Lacey stood there in her pajamas and robe, damp hair curling down her back, Charlotte in her arms. "Your baby's hungry, Garrett."

Abby smiled, her face softening as she reached for Charlotte. "I'll get the baby, you get the goat?"

"Sounds like a bad country song." He hummed a few bars as he followed her into the house to fix the bottles, her laughter wrapping around him.

And he smiled because despite all the crazy stuff going on, this at least was right.

Three days after the night spent waiting out the flood at Abby's house, Garrett turned Reggie toward the barn, keeping pace with Devin, who was up on Icarus. Reggie was Devin's horse, but the unvarnished truth was that if Garrett was going to help with the livestock, he needed Reggie. The horse had the talent. Garrett was just along for the ride.

The pond had turned into a lake and the back fields were either underwater or too muddy to use. It was a mess, but the house and barn had survived. They'd survive, too, but it was going to set them back at a time when they were just getting on their feet.

He sighed.

Devin glanced over at him as they kept the horses to a slow walk. "How's Charlotte doing in day care?"

"Oh, *she's* doing fine. I, on the other hand, am a wreck after I drop her off." In all the hubbub, Garrett had almost forgotten that six weeks was the magic age and, if he forfeited Charlotte's spot, she'd be on the waiting list at least another month, maybe more. So, with no other alternative, she'd started on Monday and he'd had a lump in his throat all the way to the office. "Abby asked if she could pick her up a little bit early and bring her home for me."

Devin rolled his eyes toward the finally blue sky. "You two are pitiful."

Garrett made a derisive snort. "As if you're not wrapped around the itty-bitty fingers of your twins."

"No doubt." Devin shook his head. "I never dreamed I'd settle down and be a family man, especially here. But I love it. Wouldn't change a thing."

Garrett knew his brother deserved the contentment he was feeling now. Devin had run from their past for a long time. But Garrett would be lying if he didn't admit, at least to himself, that he envied his brother that domestic bliss.

He rode in silence for a few beats, then perked up as he remembered his favorite moment of the day. "Hey, did you see me and Reggie catch that calf this afternoon? It was epic."

Devin laughed. "Yeah, I saw it, but you're gonna feel it. It's been a long time since Mom packed us a lunch and we rode horses all day every day. You're gonna be sore tomorrow."

"Tomorrow?" Garrett snorted. "I'm gonna need help to get into the house today."

As the horses approached the barn, he saw Abby step out the door in her sock feet with Charlotte in her arms. Her cheerful yellow rain boots were covered in mud and sitting by the mat.

He'd barely seen Abby since the night they'd stayed at her house. They'd crossed paths in the office, but she was busy seeing clients and he, for the most part, had been working from dawn to dusk with his brothers to salvage what they could of the rain-soaked crops in the low areas of their farm.

Garrett guided Reggie closer to the house so he could speak to her. "Hello, ladies."

"Hi. You guys are looking good on horseback. Thanks for letting me pick Charlotte up. I missed her. Hey, Devin," she said.

"Abby." Devin tipped his hat at her and she grinned. Garrett rolled his eyes. His brother, the former rodeo heartthrob.

Abby laughed. "Looks like y'all have had a busy day."

"It's been an interesting week, to say the least. Garrett, I'm gonna get Icarus put away."

As Devin turned away, Reggie pranced sideways toward the barn, wanting to follow, but the big horse was much too much of a gentleman to really press the point. Garrett patted his neck and he settled down. "How was your day?"

"Long." She shrugged a little. "Word's gotten out that I'm seeing people and I'm getting referrals right and left."

"You need anything?"

A small head shake. "I'll be fine after a good night's sleep. No worries."

"Staying for dinner?" Reggie's ear flicked back and Garrett would've sworn he'd heard the word *dinner*.

"I'm not sure. I'm exhausted. I just needed some Charlotte snuggles for a few minutes." Her hair wafted in the breeze as she looked down at Charlotte. The last of the afternoon sunlight speared through the trees, bathing her and the baby in rose gold.

Garrett blinked.

"I'm going to head home soon."

Reggie was restless, dancing in place. Garrett took him in a tight circle and stopped him again in front of Abby. "If you can keep Charlotte a little while longer, I'll get Reggie settled and then I'll be on dad time."

"Of course."

He wanted to slide off and walk Reggie into the barn, but he wasn't sure his legs would hold him, which would be humiliating. So, he waited until he was in the barn and Devin could hold Reggie's head before he tried to get off. He managed to do it without whimpering, so that was something.

"You good?"

Garrett let his head drop against the saddle. "Oh, yeah. Good."

"Your voice is, like, two octaves higher than usual. You need to borrow my cane?"

"Maybe." Garrett laughed. "What I need to do is ride more often. This is embarrassing."

"You can ride anytime." Devin took Reggie's bridle off and gave him a good scratch. "At some point, you're gonna ask Abby out, like on a real date, right? It's getting a little embarrassing, the way you guys look at each other when you think no one is watching."

Garrett unbuckled the girth and lifted the saddle off of Reggie's back, suppressing the groan as his legs protested the movement. He called back to Devin from the tack room. "When exactly am I going to have time to take Abby on a date?"

"How about tomorrow?" Devin hung up the bridle and picked up Reggie's soft halter before sliding it into place.

"It wouldn't be much of a date with Charlotte along. Not complaining, just being realistic. Plus, I think Abby's got something at the elementary school tomorrow."

"Friday, then. Tanner will keep Charlotte."

"Tanner will *what*?" Their oldest brother walked into the barn and hung the keys to the ATV on a nail by the door.

"Babysit Charlotte so Garrett can go on a real date." Devin led Reggie into the stall where his hay was waiting for him. Garrett picked up a brush and started working the mud out of Reggie's coat while Devin cleaned his hooves. They'd been ingrained from an early age to take care of their animals' needs before they took care of their own. Neither of them really even considered doing anything else.

Garrett paused in the brushing and gave Devin a pointed look. "You don't have to do that, Tanner. I can find a babysitter *if* I need one."

Tanner leaned on the doorjamb, lifted his ball cap and rubbed his head before settling the cap back into place. "I can knock off early Friday and keep her. Late afternoon work for you?"

Garrett paused. "Ah, yeah. I guess? I think. I mean, I haven't asked Abby yet. You think I should?"

"Yes!" his brothers said in unison.

"Okay, okay. I guess it's unanimous then."

Devin lifted his fist up for a bump. "Dude. I'm proud of you. Now go ask her before you lose your nerve."

"I'm not gonna lose my—" Garrett stopped. What was he thinking? Devin was offering to finish grooming Reggie. He held out the brush. "Okay, thanks."

In his mind, he jogged toward the house with a plan to ask Abby out on a date. In reality, he moved at a snail's pace, clenching his jaw to keep from groaning out loud because his muscles were screaming at him.

But Devin was right. Abby wasn't just another girl to date. She was special and he had to make a move or she was going to slip away, back to her old life, and she would just be someone he knew once.

Chapter Twelve

Abby dumped the cutting board of chopped bell pepper pieces into the pot of chili and reached for an onion, stopping midmotion as she caught the look on Lacey's face. "What? I never said I knew how to cook."

Lacey laughed and held up her hands. "I'm just joking. No judgment here. My dad was our cook after my mom left us. He was terrible. It was pure self-preservation that I learned to cook."

"Do you see your mom now?" Abby kept her eyes carefully on the onion she was cutting.

"Never. Not even sure she's alive, to be honest. You?"

"No. She calls every once in a while, just often enough to pretend she cares. My dad died when I was a baby in a military training accident."

"I'm sorry. It's tough losing a parent."

"I guess. I wish I'd gotten to know him, but it's hard to miss something you never had, you know?"

Lacey looked skeptical, but didn't say anything. Instead, she asked, "So your dad died when you were a baby. Where did you and your mom live?"

The onions were stinging her eyes and Abby

blinked. "I didn't live with my mom. After our house was destroyed by a tornado when I was five, I went to live with my grandma. She was the best. She'd wrap you in big hugs and she always smelled like rose-scented lotion."

Her grandma had passed away when she was nine, leaving the house to Abby's aunt, who'd grudgingly allowed her to stay with them. She still kept in touch with her cousins from time to time, but it wasn't like having a real family. "I don't have family. Not like this, anyway."

"So are you and Garrett gonna make this a thing or what?"

Abby went still. "Uh…"

Her eyes on the pot of chili she'd gone back to stirring, Lacey said, "All I'm saying is that you should think about it. He's sweet and funny and he really cares about everything."

Thinking carefully, Abby replied, "I like Garrett. I like Red Hill Springs. I love Charlotte. I enjoy being with you guys."

"That's not exactly what I asked." Lacey tasted the chili and added some more cumin to the pot, before turning to Abby with her hand on her hip. "So?"

"Does he know you're talking to me about him?"

"Oh, no. No, no, no." Lacey laughed. "He would die."

Abby rested a hand on her forehead, her eyes on Lacey's. "I went on some dates in college, but I've never had a boyfriend. I don't even have family memories to fall back on. I don't think I'm a very good risk in the love department."

"Oh, honey. Have you met me and Devin? All that stuff is great, but if you don't have it, that's what counseling is for. All I'm saying is, maybe you should go for it." Lacey laughed again. "It's hard. Relationships are hard. Not saying it's not. It's a lot of work, but it's also really worth it."

"I hear you, wise one."

Lacey giggled. "You're the best, you know that? I've loved having you around this last month. It makes me think about what it would be like to have a sister. I've always wanted one."

"Me, too." Emotion—which she usually had so tightly under control—clogged her throat. She hardly ever cried. She prayed instead, giving her tears to the Lord. But at Lacey's words, her eyes filled, threatening to spill over.

Lacey glanced at her face. "Oh my goodness, you have to stop or I'll start crying, too, and we can't have tears in the chili."

From the living room, Abby heard Garrett come in the door. She grabbed Lacey's arm. "Not. Another. Word. I'm serious."

Lacey made a locking motion with her fingers over her lips.

Garrett stuck his head in the kitchen. "Hey Abs, can I talk to you for a minute?"

She followed him into the living room. "Is everything okay?"

He looked at the floor. "Tanner offered to babysit Charlotte Friday night. I was thinking, if you're free, that we might go out, like on a real date. What do you say?"

Butterflies multiplied in her stomach and she forced herself to focus on his handsome, earnest face. He seemed confident, but when he looked up, his eyes gave him away. He was nervous, just like she was.

She thought about the ridiculous conversation with Lacey. Despite the absurdity, maybe Lacey was right. She and Garrett had taken care of Charlotte together. They'd played "house," acted like they were parents.

They'd shared kisses.

And now, he was offering her the chance to see if there was actually something there, something real, not just circumstance.

He cleared his throat. "So, Abby Scott…do you want to go on a date with me?"

She smiled. "Yes. I'd love to go on a date with you."

His face lit up and he wrapped his arms around her, picking her up in a hug, setting her down instantly as he yelped in pain.

"Garrett? What's wrong?"

Waving away her concern, he eased down into Tanner's recliner. "I'm—ah—not used to being in the saddle all day."

She tried not to laugh, covering her mouth with her hand, but his face was so crestfallen, she couldn't help it. A delicate little snort came out.

His head snapped up and he narrowed his eyes. She laughed harder.

"I'm glad my predicament is amusing to you. Hopefully I'll be able to walk tomorrow so we can go on that date."

"I'm sure you'll be fine." She picked up her keys and called into the kitchen. "I'm heading out, Lacey. And Garrett needs some ibuprofen."

His laugh followed her out the door.

Later, curled up in front of the fire with Elvis by

her side, she hoped she'd done the right thing in saying yes to Garrett. Going on a date with him, that wasn't scary. He was fun to be with and she was looking forward to it.

It was the rest of it that scared her. The possibilities. She'd been hurt by people who were supposed to love her—her mom, her aunt. Trusted the wrong people. She wanted to believe that, this time, she could trust that her heart would be safe in someone else's hands, but it was a big leap of faith.

She wasn't sure she was ready.

Her phone buzzed and the sight of her boss's name again sent a jolt of adrenaline through her system. She had a choice. She could go back to her life, go back to traveling and protect her heart from a possible heartache. Or she could take a chance with Garrett, risk it all.

And maybe lose it all, too.

She just hoped she was making the right choice.

Garrett swung through the doors into the law office he shared with Wynn Grant, a tray of coffees in his hand and a bag of doughnuts under his arm. Which on second thought might not be the best idea, since they were likely smushed beyond recognition, but he didn't care.

He whistled a happy melody as he dramatically placed one of the cups of coffee on Bess's desk. His assistant was on the phone and looked up with one suspicious eyebrow raised. The second cup went to Wynn as he switched from whistling to singing.

She laughed. "What is up with you today?"

He did a spin, one of his signature dance moves, remembered his sore legs, and flopped down in one of the office chairs. "You are looking at a man *with a date*."

Wynn's eyes widened over the top of the takeout cup. "Oh, really? With who?"

"None other than the beautiful, mysterious Abby."

"She's not mysterious. She's just… Abby. But wow."

"Exactly. Wow. I don't know why I didn't think of it before." He opened the bag, pulled out a smashed doughnut and took a bite.

"Are those doughnuts? Give me one."

He tossed the bag onto her desk. "I'm going to take her somewhere nice for dinner. Somewhere with no kids menu."

Wynn raised one amused eyebrow. "I see the appeal. So what made you take this momentous step?"

"My brothers threatened me."

She snorted and took a pink frosted doughnut with sprinkles out of the bakery bag.

"I'm joking. They *encouraged* me to ask her out. Tanner's watching the baby." He picked up his coffee and took a sip.

"Wow, he really must want you out of his hair. But all kidding aside, that's a pretty big step for Tanner."

"Yeah. It was Devin's suggestion. I guess he's decided that Tanner needs to rejoin the land of the living. It's been fifteen years, almost."

"I can't imagine that kind of grief just goes away."

Garrett looked down at his cup. "I don't think it does. I think about them every day and they weren't mine, not like they were his."

"That's understandable." She sat back in her chair, her coffee cup in her hand. "So, you're taking my friend out on a date. I have so many questions."

He grinned. "Stop. You're way too quick for your own good."

"She needs some fun in her life. I'm just glad she decided to turn down her boss's request for her to go back to work. It'll be good for her to stick around for a while."

"Her what?" Garrett suddenly didn't feel like whistling anymore. Instead, he felt a knot in the pit of his stomach.

Wynn closed her mouth sharply and he could almost see her mind turning, trying to figure out how to spin what she'd just said.

He sighed. "No, she didn't tell me. And yes, you should feel bad."

She blinked a few more times, clearly scrambling for words, which was very unlike his partner. "Look. I'm sure if it had been important to her she would've mentioned it to you."

"She told you," he pointed out.

"Yes, but only because I forced her to. She's working here in Red Hill Springs for a reason. I'm sure she didn't tell you about her boss's offer because she wasn't intending to take it."

"Yeah, okay. Or maybe she wanted one fun night before she leaves."

Wynn's eyebrows drew together. "That doesn't really sound like Abby."

"You don't think so? She goes from place to place, disaster to disaster. She's never settled down. Maybe she doesn't know how to."

From the look on Wynn's face, he realized he wasn't telling her anything she didn't know.

"Garrett, stop. You're jumping to conclusions. You

don't know what she's thinking. Take her out anyway. Go out and have a good time. You *both* deserve that." She swiped a stray sprinkle off her desk. "And pretend you never heard anything about her boss's offer to go back to work."

"I'll take it under advisement, counselor." He grabbed the bag of doughnuts off her desk and walked back to his office, minus the dance steps. But maybe Wynn was right.

He wanted to spend time with Abby. Maybe they'd go on a date, decide they had nothing in common and it was best to go their separate ways. Unlikely, given their similar passions, but possible.

Also possible, they'd go on a date and she'd realize maybe it was worth a shot. Maybe *they* were worth a shot. Some of the sweetest things in his life were the ones he'd fought the hardest for.

Or maybe he was right and she was just going out with him so she could tell him in person that she was leaving.

He stabbed his fingers into his hair. So far they'd spent more time focused on Charlotte than they'd spent getting to know each other. He'd left her with a goat.

Time to regroup. He cared what happened with Abby. He liked her.

And *maybe* it was time for him to show her.

Abby dragged herself through the door of her house. She was exhausted. Elvis walked straight to his bed by the fireplace and waited for her to turn on the fire, which she did, just before she face-planted on the sofa.

How had she forgotten what school visits were like? And most of the day she'd spent seeing individual kids teachers had identified as needing a little more attention. But, along with the Comfort Dog team, she'd been on the playground and outside the school as the kids were leaving. Her introverted self was not cut out for this kind of day. She was done. Out of words.

Her phone buzzed on the coffee table, mocking her wish to just lie here with her eyes closed. Maybe she could just ignore it. The phone buzzed again, insistent. With a sigh, she rolled over and picked it up, looking at the readout. It was Garrett.

She may be close to death from sheer exhaustion, but not so close that her heart rate didn't pick up a little when she saw his name. She answered the phone. "Hey."

"Hey, you. Don't talk. I know you're tired, but I sent you something. A delivery guy just left it by your back door. He's already gone—you don't have to talk to him, either."

She smiled. *Don't talk.* It was almost as if he knew her.

"I considered flowers. But then, no one really *needs* flowers. Doughnuts, sure."

"Did you send me doughnuts?"

"No, not doughnuts. Are you following this conversation at all?"

"Garrett…" A warning tone with a hint of laughter behind it.

"Sorry, bad joke. You didn't go to the door yet?"

She rolled off the sofa and to her feet. "I'm going. Right now."

"Okay, do that. It won't keep."

Opening the back door, Abby found a box with several takeout containers inside it. She picked it up and carried it to the table, narrating as she opened the boxes. "Sweet tea, chicken potpie, a green salad, fresh yeast rolls. Garrett, you are the best." She pulled a roll from the bag and took a bite. "Comfort food is way better than flowers."

His voice sounded smug as he said, "I thought so."

With a laugh, she said, "Don't let it go to your head."

"I sent you an email, too. You can look at it later."

"Okay." She took the container of potpie, a plastic fork and the tea back to the couch with her. "How was your day?"

"I was in court this afternoon. Nash's mom got full custody of the kids again."

"That's awesome. Really good day." She took a bite. "Wow, this chicken potpie is the best thing I've eaten in decades."

"I'm glad you like it. I didn't make it."

Abby laughed again. "I figured, since there's a sticker on the container that says Hilltop Café."

"Yes, there's a clue. Okay, I'm gonna go. Enjoy your night. Sleep well. Because tomorrow is our date."

"I'll be ready."

"How does four o'clock sound? Too early?"

Four was early, but why not? "It sounds great. I'm looking forward to it."

She *was* looking forward to it. She had fun with Garrett, even if they were just exchanging quips about their day. Flipping on the television, she ate her potpie and rolls while she considered how thoughtful Garrett was. He'd realized she'd be tired and arranged the perfect thing to make her feel better.

Remembering the email, she picked up her phone and pulled it up. It was a link to a playlist. She clicked through and when she realized what it was, she laughed. Every song referred to the moon, the moonlight and stars.

It was hilarious and perfect—a subtle reminder of their kiss on her front porch under the light of that gigantic moon.

She sighed. He was goofy and silly and had the biggest heart for other people. He wasn't perfect, probably, but was he perfect for her?

Nope. She didn't need to think about that. It put too much pressure on both of them. She cared about him. They had fun together and that was good. She'd gone through all the worries in her head when she decided to go on a date in the first place. She'd come to Red Hill Springs to heal, to find the person she was…and maybe the person that she wanted to be. Letting fear get the best of her wasn't the way to do it.

No matter what happened in the future, no matter where she went, she wanted to know that she'd made the most of the time she had here, that she hadn't held herself back.

So far she'd managed to keep that promise to herself. She wasn't going to stop now.

Chapter Thirteen

"Ouch!" Abby shook the fingers she'd just burned on the curling iron that Wynn let her borrow. She needed four hands to do this thing. How was anyone supposed to keep from getting burned when their hands were behind their head?

She hadn't curled her hair in years. Sometimes she was lucky to get to wash it. But tonight seemed special. She wanted to dress up and wear makeup and put waves in her hair. It seemed weird to her that a guy she'd seen with spit-up on his shoulder could still make her feel like a teenager getting ready for prom.

Wynn stepped into the open doorway. "Your hair looks great. It's so shiny. Want me to get the pieces you missed in the back?"

"I missed pieces... Never mind. Yes, please." Abby laughed and handed Wynn the curling iron.

Spring was definitely arriving in Alabama. Redbud trees were bursting with color. Even the grass was greening up a little bit. But since it was chilly still in March, she'd opted to wear a blouse with some lace insets, olive jeans and brown booties that she'd picked up at an end-of-season sale.

Holding out a small bag, Wynn said, "Makeup?"

"I don't even know what to do with that!"

Her friend looked at the screen on her phone and made a face. "Latham can't find Penny's soccer uniform and she has pictures tonight. I'm gonna have to run." She hugged Abby. "Have fun tonight. Be happy. You deserve it."

"It's been so good getting to spend time with you. Who knew when we were roommates in the intern dorm that we'd end up being friends for life?"

"I did." Wynn smiled. "But I'm still grateful God put us together. Call me tomorrow and let me know how it went."

"I will, I promise." Abby unzipped the makeup bag, dumped the contents onto the counter and stared at them for a minute. She picked up a large square compact and opened it. Twenty shades of eyeshadow and a small brush.

She picked the palest pink shadow and brushed it across her eyelids, peering at herself in the mirror. Okay, that made her hazel eyes kind of pop. That was a good thing, right?

Unscrewing the top on the mascara, she brushed a tiny bit on her eyelashes. Wow. Her eyes looked huge. Cool.

The next compact held blush. Her cheeks were warm already, so she dropped that back in the bag and pulled out…lip gloss. She used the wand to smooth some across her lips, took a step back, evaluated. Not bad.

The doorbell rang.

Nerves zinged in her stomach. She put her hand

there and took a deep breath. It was going to be fine—fun. Fun. It was going to be *fun*.

Abby pulled the door open and Garrett stood on the porch. His hair was neatly combed and she had the urge to put her fingers in it and mess it up.

He held a bouquet of yellow wildflowers in his hand. "I rescued these from the flood. You look beautiful."

"I love them. Wait just a minute while I put them in water?"

"Sure." He stuck his hands in his pockets and took a deep breath. "It's a little bit of a drive, where we're headed. Just over an hour."

"Okay." She laid the flowers on the counter and pulled a clear pitcher from the cabinet. While it filled, she put her palms on the granite countertop and gave herself a silent pep talk. It was silly to be nervous. This was Garrett.

She cut the water off, unfolded the paper from around the flowers and put them in the pitcher. From the door, Garrett said, "Ready?"

Abby smoothed down her shirt. "Ready. Also really, really nervous. I know it's silly."

Garrett laughed. "I'm nervous, too. C'mere, I've got an idea."

She walked closer.

He linked his hand with hers with a gleam of humor in his eye. "Thumb war?"

"You're on." She suppressed a grin as she looked into his eyes. They said together, "One, two, three, four. I declare a thumb war."

Thumbs racing in circles, she stared him down until he started laughing, lost his focus and she pinned him.

Garrett's laugh burst out unrestricted. "You distracted me with the death stare. Two out of three?"

"Nope. I know how to quit while I'm ahead. Better luck next time."

"You are brutal." They left the house and walked to his SUV. He pulled open the passenger side door for her and she slid in, laughing a little as she remembered he'd said something similar when she'd made him change Charlotte's diaper the first time.

The game had done the job to dispel the tension. Her nerves were gone. In their place was the feeling that they were escaping for an adventure. That skipping-school-music-loud-windows-down kind of freedom.

She glanced over at Garrett and he flashed a grin at her and turned the music up. On the same wavelength, as usual.

It had been a long time since she felt so good. Since she'd been in Red Hill Springs, she was figuring out that she hadn't let herself find happiness—she'd been afraid of it. If she locked people out and didn't share anything with them, maybe she wouldn't get hurt.

That was no way to live.

The protective shell she'd built around her heart as a kid was slow to crumble, but Garrett's warmth and open heart had given her a reason to learn to trust again.

Garrett caught her pensive look out of the corner of his eye and turned the music down. "You got quiet all of a sudden. What are you thinking about?"

She leaned back, closer to the window. "I don't know, just how weird it is that if you hadn't had a baby left on your doorstep, we probably wouldn't be here right now."

He drove in silence for a moment or two. "We would have met anyway. Your office is right next to mine."

"Sure, but who knows if we would've even gotten beyond pleasantries. I don't know—it's just, I wonder if Charlotte's mom had any idea what she was setting in motion."

"I don't think there's any way she could have. Mostly, I think she was trying to figure out a way to save herself."

"But even that… She wouldn't have known she could trust you unless she'd known you to be trust-worthy as her guardian ad litem." Abby picked at her jeans with her fingers, but looked up with a wry smile. "I think about ripple effects sometimes. You know, I don't get to see what happens after I leave the places I work. I always pray that whatever small difference I make will ripple out in every direction."

"A tiny rock in the middle of the pond causes waves to lap against the shore." He switched lanes as they passed the welcome-to-Florida sign.

"You get the idea." Her eyebrows drew together. "Wait. We just…are those *palm trees*?"

Garrett laughed. "Yep. A friend of mine has a va-cation home on Pensacola Beach and he asked me to check on it while he's out of the country. And since I had to come anyway, I thought it would be a great place to have dinner."

Her head swiveled from side to side as she took in the scenery. "I haven't been to this part of Florida in at least five years, since Hurricane Kate came through here. So much looks different."

. "I wondered if you'd been back since the hurricane. I came a few times with mission teams our church sent over. There wasn't a roof spared in the whole county. On the plus side, I know how to fix a roof now."

"It looks so different. The trees were all bare and leaning over the last time I was here. It's really green now. Oh, this is so good to see."

"So you don't usually go back to the places you do disaster relief?"

"No. There just always seems to be another disaster to go to. My organization is kind of like triage or EMS. We do first aid—stem the bleeding, so to speak—until the long-term assistance organizations have time to get rolling."

He took the turn toward the beach and smiled as, once again, she let out a happy sigh.

"Kate was bad. A strong Category 3. The beach road was completely washed out. The debris, well, we couldn't even get down the roads along the water. You'd see people's clothing in the very tops of pine trees—the ones that hadn't snapped in half. Photographs scattered among the splintered wood. Bare foundations where you knew a life used to be lived."

Her voice grew husky and he reached across the armrest to take her hand. "You don't have to talk about it if you don't want to."

"It's okay. I don't mind. I think what we do has some common threads. We both come into people's lives on their worst day. And we try to make it better." Her chin trembled. "Every disaster is different. Mudslides, fires, hurricanes. But some things are the same. The way people walk around in a daze, wondering how they will overcome something so huge."

"It is huge. Literally everything is harder. So you wade in with kids and tell them…what?"

"They carry a lot of bottled-up fear and grief. So I let them talk. Remind them to look for the changes. One day something will happen… They'll be able to brush their teeth using water from the tap and they'll think today was a little easier." She was on the edge of her seat as they turned onto the beach. "This is amazing, Garrett. Thank you."

"You always see the storm. I thought you might like to see the rainbow." The houses had been rebuilt. Roads were in great condition, landscaping perfect. The beach had been restored. The dunes were slowly returning and the rosy hue of the fading sunlight made them look like they were glowing.

"That's a perfect way to put it. Thank you for bringing me here. What a gift."

He turned into a driveway and pulled to a stop under the house. "You ready?"

The house was right on the beach. He'd been coming here with his friend since he was a little kid. It had been rebuilt after the hurricane, too, and it was gorgeous, with windows across the whole width of the house, a wide porch and stairs leading down to a boardwalk.

They walked up to the porch and Abby stood next to the railing, looking out, while he set up their picnic on a small table between some loungers and started the propane heaters. With music on and string lights crisscrossing over the deck, it was cozy. Romantic. He shivered. "Wow, it's getting cold. You okay?"

She walked toward him, the breeze tossing her hair around her face. "Just awed, I think. The ocean is so peaceful and so powerful at the same time. It's amazing and awful. I've always wondered why people stay in areas like this. Why they rebuild again and again. But I can see why it's worth it."

He took her hand and tugged her closer, into the circle of warmth from the heaters. "Come on, let's sit where it's warm."

They sat cross-legged on the chaise lounges with the food between them. Abby picked up a chocolate-covered strawberry. "What about you? What gives you the ability to persevere in your job? I know it's not easy."

"Unlike you, I do get asked this a lot, like why I didn't go into corporate law, or even become a district attorney or something like that."

"And?"

"You've heard that saying, 'stand in the gap?'"

When she nodded, he said, "I think it goes back to when my parents died. I had a place to live, people who looked out for me. If I needed a place to stay, there were ten people in town I didn't even have to ask. I have a safety net a mile wide. The vast majority of people who become my clients don't have that kind of safety net. They don't have backup."

"So you stand in the gap for them." Her voice was soft.

"It sounds silly and idealistic, but yeah. Everyone needs help sometimes."

The music changed and she brushed crumbs off her fingers and held out her hand. "Come on, let's dance."

He put his hand in hers. "Okay, but I'm warning you, I'm a terrible dancer. You may have to show me."

Abby laughed. "Who, me? I can't dance."

He slid his arm around her waist. For a moment, they swayed a little, feet shuffling in time. He breathed in, letting the peace soak in as they swayed in time to the music, the percussion of the waves pounding on the sand.

Abby looked up at him, her hazel eyes dark in the dim light, full of emotion. "These last few weeks have been the best I can remember. I'm so full inside—and I was so empty when I got to Red Hill Springs. Spending time with Charlotte, soaking up those baby snuggles, and with you. Even the basic things, like going to church and having coffee with a friend. It's helped me heal. I've always known there had to be places like Red Hill Springs. I guess maybe I just thought they weren't for me."

"Is it presumptuous of me to ask if you've thought about staying?"

"I've thought about it. My boss left the option open for me to come back to work. And showing up for people when they're in crisis is important, even if it just lightens the load momentarily."

He leaned back, gave her a speculative look. "But…"

"But I want to belong somewhere." The admission slipped out. And she panicked. "You want to walk for a minute?"

"Sure."

The moon was still almost full and as it rose on the horizon, it sent waves of shimmery light across the surface of the water.

When she reached the bottom of the porch, she slid out of her shoes, stepped off into the sand and hissed. "It's so-so-so cold."

"We can stay on the porch with the nice, warm heaters."

She scoffed. "We could, but two adventurers like

us? What fun would that be? Let's walk to the edge of the water. I just want to stand there for a minute."

"Of course."

It should be dark by now, but it wasn't. The moon reflected off the pure white sand. She ran for the water, hair flying out behind her, her laughter coming back to him on the wind. He chased after her, grabbing her by the waist and spinning her around, both of them laughing like children.

She pulled him toward the water where she held out her arms, letting the wind buffet her. "Wow. This is incredible."

Out of the corner of his eye, he saw something move across the sky. He put one arm around her and pointed with the other. "Look."

It was gone in a split second, that shooting burst of a star, but to Garrett it felt like it had been put there just for the two of them. She shivered and he wrapped her in his arms. She was a warrior. She went into battle for people when they were in their worst moments. But she had scars.

And his greatest desire was to stand for her, too.

Keep her safe.

But right now, her teeth were chattering. He squeezed her close and said, "Let's go. We can come back another time."

Back at the house, Abby packed up the picnic while Garrett closed up the house and locked up, making sure the lights and music and heaters were turned off.

The ride home was more subdued than the ride out, the music a little softer. The conversation, too. Abby's eyes were on the moon as it seemed to follow them along the road.

Garrett's thoughts rambled as he drove. Abby's time in Red Hill Springs was limited. She said she felt at home, that she felt a pull to stay in Red Hill Springs, but that wasn't the same as making plans to stay.

Would they really ever come back to the beach together?

He hesitated to ask, but he really wanted to know. "Did you like your job before your last posting? Were you happy?"

She smiled. "That's such a loaded question. And the answer is I'm not sure. There was a time when I loved it, when I couldn't wait to grab my go-bag and head for the airport. Maybe I just needed some rest, to be at a place where I could rediscover the joy I felt from being with people when they needed help. Or maybe it's time for me to hang up my traveling shoes. I'm not sure yet."

"Wynn said your boss wanted you to cut your leave short and come back to work." As soon as he said it, he wanted to grab the words from the air. He hadn't meant to bring that up.

"She told you that?"

"Accidentally. She thought I knew, but yeah."

Abby made a face. "I've been avoiding my boss's calls. I've told her no twice, but disasters don't take vacations just because I do and there are only so many people like me around."

"People willing to drop their lives in a split second's notice?" He heard the edge come into his voice, a tone he didn't recognize, but one that, for some reason, had been hiding there, tucked away.

She went still and shifted ever so slightly away from

him. "No. People who *live* their lives working with disaster victims."

With her arms crossed, she looked out the window and the rest of the drive was spent in uneasy silence. Garrett could feel the breach between them growing and he wanted to fix it.

When they got back to her house, he pulled into the drive and parked. "Abby, I didn't mean to be disrespectful. I misspoke and I'm sorry."

"It's fine," she said, but her body language said it was anything but.

"It's not fine. I don't think you had no life before you came here. What a presumption that would be. But I hurt you and I'd never do that intentionally."

"It's fine." She opened the door. "I really did have a good time. Thank you for taking me."

He met her on her side of the vehicle and walked her to the door. He wanted to snap his fingers and return them to the way they felt when they were dancing. He leaned forward and gave her a rather unsatisfying kiss—on the cheek, as she turned her head.

He got back in the car and waited for her to close the door before he slammed his hand on the steering wheel. He'd offended Abby. And he was pretty sure he'd blown any chance he had of convincing her to stay in Red Hill Springs.

Chapter Fourteen

Abby found Lacey on her doorstep the next morning. She opened the door and waved her friend inside. "Why am I not surprised to see you here?"

Lacey plopped her purse onto the kitchen table and pulled out one of the chairs while Abby took another mug out of the kitchen cabinet. "Cream?"

"Yes, please."

Setting the mug of coffee and carton of cream on the table in front of Lacey, Abby joined her at the table. "Okay, what's up?"

Lacey tried to give her an innocent look but gave up after about half a second. "Okay, fine. I have to know what happened with you and Garrett last night. He left home like he was on cloud nine, but this morning he just about bit Devin's head off. Abby, I like you, but if you broke Garrett's heart, I'm gonna have to hurt you."

Abby nearly choked on her coffee. She had a feeling she was seeing rodeo Lacey, who had the nerve to barrel race at champion speed. "Glad to know where I stand. We had a great time. It was a beautiful night."

"But?"

"I thought we ended things okay last night, but Garrett hurt my feelings and I guess I showed it."

"You're going to get over it, though?"

That was the million-dollar question, wasn't it? She cared about Garrett, but if he was going to get his back up every time she had to go out of town, they wouldn't be able to take this relationship to the next level.

She sighed. "Honestly, I'm not sure I'm relationship material. Not everyone is like you and Devin."

Lacey laughed. "Thank God for that. We almost got a divorce before the twins were born. If Devin hadn't had the sense to fight for the relationship, we would have."

"Are you joking?" Abby gaped at Lacey. "But he's so—and you're so—"

"He's so good-looking? Charming? Talented? Yeah, he's all those things, but he was—is—also an addict and he did some really awful things, like leaving me the morning after our wedding night."

"I'm floored."

Lacey's revelation was truly shocking, but if the two of them had survived that kind of trouble, maybe there was hope for her and Garrett. Assuming there even *was* a her and Garrett.

"By God's grace, Devin convinced me to give him a second chance. To give *us* a second chance." Lacey picked up her mug and held it between her hands. "Loving someone—truly loving them—isn't easy. Even if you think you've met the perfect person, they're not perfect. Everyone has flaws. If you don't see them, you're just blinded by infatuation. Real love sees the flaws and decides to love anyway."

Abby sat quietly in her chair. She didn't like hearing it, but Lacey was right. "He said he was sorry. I think he knew immediately that he hurt my feelings."

"What did he say?" Lacey asked gently.

"He implied that I didn't have a life because I travel all the time. But I chose to live my life that way." She shook her head. "I know it's a fine distinction, but it's an important one. The thing is, I think what he said hit so close to home because I've wondered the same thing. Have I spent all these years running from job to job because I don't know how to find peace?"

Lacey leaned toward her. "You do something not many people could do. You lend your strength to people who've used theirs all up."

Abby swallowed hard around the lump in her throat. "Thanks."

Lacey reached across the table and gripped Abby's hand. "But it's okay for you to need to borrow some strength when you need it, too."

A tear streaked down Abby's face and she scrubbed it away, horrified. "Sorry. I don't know what's the matter with me."

"Nothing is wrong with you." Lacey's voice was firm. "You have emotions. It happens."

"Not to me." Abby laughed through her tears.

"To you *and* to Garrett. He's steady as a rock. Funny and sweet and would give his last dollar to anyone—literally anyone—who needed it."

"Now I feel a *but* coming on."

A smile flitted across Lacey's face. "The car accident that took their parents and Tanner's wife and baby—no one could survive that and come out unscathed. Garrett has an amazing heart, but I wonder sometimes what he's hiding behind all that generosity."

"You think he's afraid of...really caring?"

"I don't know. You're the professional—I'm just an armchair psychologist—but they lost a lot that day, all three of them."

Abby took a deep breath and used those few seconds to settle herself. "What you're saying makes sense. I need to think about it a little bit more."

Her phone buzzed on the table and she glanced at the screen. Her boss again, but this time, the text just said, 911.

Abby's stomach dropped. That kind of text could only be bad. She excused herself and walked outside to make the call. A few minutes later, she returned to the kitchen.

Lacey looked up. "It's bad news, isn't it?"

"There was an earthquake this morning in California. A school was damaged and children are trapped in the building. Elvis and I have to go."

Elvis's tail thumped on the floor and, though Abby's heart was breaking, she reached down to scratch his head. He was always ready to go. His big heart never got tired.

Lacey hugged Abby. "I'll be praying—for the kids and for you. And I'll see you when you get back."

"Thanks, Lacey." She walked Lacey to the door and pushed it closed behind her, before looking back at Elvis. "Time to pack, buddy. We're on the 3:00 p.m. flight."

A few hours later, Abby stood in the kitchen, running through her mental list. She'd called Wynn, arranged to be away, packed their necessities. She hated to leave, especially leaving things with Garrett the way they were, but she was needed and it was time to go.

Stepping out onto the porch, she let Elvis go through the door before she moved to lock it. When she turned back, Garrett was standing in the driveway, leaning on her car.

Her stomach flipped. He looked miserable. Which, she guessed, was fitting because she felt pretty miserable about how their date ended last night, too.

She stopped about a foot away, facing him. "Hi."

"Lacey told me you got called in for the earthquake in California. I wasn't sure what to do, but I knew I didn't want you to leave without talking to you first." Garrett looked over her shoulder and back again. "I brought you some snacks for the plane."

She couldn't help it—she started to laugh. "You really have a compulsive need to take care of people, don't you?"

"Maybe I need therapy." He smiled, but his eyes, which were usually so full of life, didn't reflect it. "I really don't want you to go. And, trust me, I know how selfish that sounds."

"I wish I didn't have to go, too." She lifted her shoulders. "But it's what I do."

"I know. I'm proud of you for doing it, too, even though it worries me."

The uneasy knot she'd been carrying since last night loosened a little. "Why are you worried?"

"I feel like we're just getting started and I'm not ready to say goodbye."

She wanted to reach out to him, to reassure him that she would always come back, but the truth was she couldn't predict what was going to happen.

Instead, she touched his hand. "I have to come back—I left Elvis's bed here. He'd never forgive me."

"I'll count on it." He smiled then and handed her a gallon-sized plastic bag full of trail mix, candy bars and peanut butter crackers.

"This should get me to Atlanta, at least."

His eyes on hers, he slid his fingers into her hair but he didn't kiss her. She could see the need—she could feel it in herself, too. The connection between them had been there from almost the very beginning.

She leaned forward and pressed her lips to his. "I'll see you in a few days."

Four days passed, then six, as Garrett got moodier and moodier. Devin threatened to punch him more than once. Tanner suggested that maybe he could find a place to live back in town. Charlotte didn't care if he was grumpy. Which is why she was his favorite.

He'd followed the news coverage of the earthquake, even catching a glimpse of Abby in the background of a picture someone had taken of the Comfort Dog team, who was also in California.

Every night at ten o'clock, he sent her a picture of Charlotte—the cutest, sweetest one he could find. And unlike Brooklyn, Abby always texted him back. The first night she'd texted, I know what you're doing and it's totally working. I miss you guys.

He should've guessed that she'd see through him, but he kept sending the pictures because he wanted contact with her. He asked her how she was doing, and she always said tired, but doing good. And he wasn't sure if she meant that she was feeling okay or that she was actually participating in doing good. Either way, she had to be exhausted, so he kept the conversations light and short.

On day eight, he sat in the porch swing on the front porch of the farmhouse, rocking Charlotte. He'd picked her up early because the day care workers said she was fussy and wasn't taking a bottle. She'd taken a couple of ounces from him, but her nose was stuffy and she still wasn't happy.

The door opened and Lacey stuck her head out. "Hey, supper's almost ready. Why don't you come inside?"

"Devin said I couldn't come over anymore."

"When Devin cooks, Devin can decide who comes over for dinner."

Garrett shifted Charlotte to his shoulder and stood. "Sounds logical to me."

He was sitting at the table with Charlotte beside him in her swing when Devin walked in from the back porch. Devin stopped halfway through the door and growled, "All right, but if you moan and groan the whole time you're here, you're gonna have to leave."

Garrett buttered his biscuit calmly. "I promise."

Tanner came in and poured himself a glass of tea. He didn't say anything, just sat down at the table and picked up a biscuit. The twins were in their high chairs. Lacey handed each of them a cold teething ring, sat down at the table and held out her hands. "Let's pray."

All four of them bowed their heads. Their mom had always insisted on saying grace before meals and they'd continued the practice even after her passing. Lacey finished the prayer. Devin said amen. And Charlotte sneezed.

Garrett's head snapped up. "What was that?"

"It was just a little sneeze." Lacey patted his hand and held out a platter. "Pork chop?"

He stabbed one with his fork. "Parenting stinks."

"No. Uh-uh." Devin pointed at the door. "Out. I warned you."

Garrett blinked mildly. "Lacey invited me."

"It's true, I did. Garrett, mind your manners. Abby will be home soon."

Tanner looked up. "For all our sakes, I hope that's true."

"*Et tu*, Tanner?" Garrett took a bite of his pork chop and heard a tiny cough from the swing. He glanced over to check on Charlotte and noticed her cheeks were bright pink. "Uh, Lacey, she doesn't look very good."

Lacey took a good look at the baby and stood up. "I'll go get the thermometer."

Garrett's heart started racing as Charlotte coughed again. This was the part of parenting that he hated. The part where you had no idea what to do and every decision counted.

Lacey ran the thermometer across Charlotte's forehead. The screen flashed red. Garrett didn't know much about sick babies, but flashing red couldn't be good. Lacey looked up, concern on her face. "I think you better call Ash. Her temp is 104."

Devin shoved back from the table. "I'll get the baby fever reducer."

Tanner stood, too. "I'll get a cool washcloth."

Charlotte started to cry, but it ended in a wheezy cough. Garrett lifted her into his arms. Her tiny body was burning up.

He dialed the phone, spoke to Ash and then turned to his brothers. "Can one of y'all get the car? He said he'd meet us at the ER."

* * *

Three hours later, Garrett was still waiting in a tiny cubicle in the ER. Charlotte had been crying for an hour and had finally exhausted herself, falling into a restless sleep. He'd been on pins and needles waiting for word from the doctors about what was going on.

He was worried. On a regular day, he tried to pretend it was normal that his heart was wrapped up in this baby girl's tiny fist, but today, he couldn't do it. He needed to know she would be okay.

The door opened and the emergency room doctor came in, followed by Ash. Dr. Seagar sat on the rolling stool and pulled the computer monitor closer to him. "Okay, so we have some results for you. Charlotte's chest X-ray is normal, which is good. She doesn't have pneumonia. She's a little dehydrated from not taking in very much fluid today, but that's easily treatable. Her flu test was negative."

"She was positive for RSV." Ash pushed off the wall where he'd been leaning, his hands going to the pockets of his white coat and pulling out a brochure and sliding it onto the bed.

"What's RSV?" Garrett looked down into Charlotte's little face. Her cheeks were pink, hair a little sweaty and stuck to her head. Her breathing was fast and raspy.

"Respiratory Syncytial Virus. In adults and older kids, RSV isn't any worse than the common cold, but in small babies, RSV can be dangerous because it can worsen quickly. Charlotte has bronchiolitis and the wheezing and high fever make me a little nervous about sending her home."

"You're going to admit her?" Garrett unconsciously squeezed Charlotte a little tighter.

"Not necessarily. If you're dead set on taking her home—"

"No." Garrett interrupted Ash. "If you think she needs admitting, then admit her. I'm not going to argue about that."

"If she were three months older…" Ash's statement trailed off. He tucked the eartips of his stethoscope into his ears and placed the round part on Charlotte's back, listening for a minute before taking it off and curling it back into his pocket. "As it is, I'd feel better if we keep her overnight, get some fluids in her and support her with oxygen. You agree with that, Dr. Seagar?"

"I do. Breathing treatments will help the wheezing and we can check her again tomorrow for developing pneumonia."

Garrett knew they were talking and he heard them say they wanted to go ahead and admit her, but the words dwindled away, replaced by a roaring sound in his ears.

Seagar left the room. Ash placed a hand on Garrett's shoulder. "Call me if you need anything. I'll check on y'all tomorrow."

"What happens now?" His voice came out hoarse.

Ash leaned against the counter. "They'll send someone from Admission in to go over the paperwork with you. They'll give both you and Charlotte new ID bands. Then they'll send a transporter down to take you upstairs to the room."

"Can I stay with her?" Charlotte stirred in his arms, whimpered and the sound turned into a wheezy cough.

"Yes, of course. There's a chair that folds out into a bed in the room. She's in good hands, Garrett."

A woman wearing a hospital badge came in the door rolling a computer. Ash squeezed his shoulder one final time and left.

When the seemingly endless paperwork was finished, a volunteer walked him and Charlotte up to the second floor and handed them over to the nurse at the desk.

She was an older lady with gray-blond hair pulled into a knot at the back of her head. "I'm Susan. This must be Charlotte. We've got a room ready for you."

The walls of the hall were painted in a jungle theme, with happy monkeys, giraffes, tigers and lions. He personally didn't think children would want to see happy predators when they were in the hospital, but what did he know? He'd been a dad for six weeks now and his baby was in the hospital. He cleared his throat. "She hasn't eaten in a while. She might need a bottle."

In lieu of an answer, the nurse held her hands out for Charlotte. "I'll take her now."

Lawyer that he was, he couldn't hand Charlotte over without comment. "Why?"

"We're going to get her IV started and get her hooked up to the monitors. Trust me, you don't want to be in here for this part."

He kissed Charlotte on her warm little head with its peach-fuzz hair and passed her to the nurse. Charlotte started to cry, which Garrett understood because he was barely holding it together as he stood outside the door to the room. He only had a vague idea of what was going on in the room, but Charlotte was screaming louder and more vehemently than he'd ever heard her, the kind of cry that went straight to his gut.

Maybe he should be in there. Maybe he wasn't cut out to be Charlotte's dad. The thought that something could happen to her shattered him.

A few minutes later, a different nurse in pink scrubs with yellow ducks on the top came out the door, pulling off gloves and a mask. This nurse smiled. "Charlotte's dad?"

"Yes." Where was his baby?

"I'm Lucy. I'm Charlotte's nurse tonight. Don't worry, she's doing fine. We'll have her settled in just a few minutes. There's a family room at the end of the hall. You can get a drink and a snack if you'd like. This would be a good time to call who you need to call to let them know Charlotte will be in the hospital for a few days."

"A few days?"

She paused in the doorway. "Typically, when we have babies admitted for RSV, they stay a few days, but it's just a guess."

The crying had waned. Charlotte's raspy cry didn't sound angry anymore, just pitiful. "I don't want to leave her."

"Get something to drink. Take a breather. She's going to need you to be strong for her." Nurse Lucy went back into the room and he stood there for a moment staring at the door. If the two nurses were playing good cop–bad cop, this one was definitely the good cop. But he took her advice and went down the hall to find a vending machine.

Then he had to call Brooklyn. It was a call he dreaded.

More than anything, he wanted to call Abby. He'd give anything to see her walk through that door, but she was in California and already exhausted. It might make him feel better to talk to her, but it would only make things harder for her.

He needed her calm confidence right now.

He needed her.

The thought knocked him back.

In the space of two months, he'd gone from single bachelor, no kids, to being the dad of a two-month-old he'd give his life for in a hot second. And on top of that, he was in love with…

He staggered against the wall of the hospital and buried his face in his hands. The truth was right there in front of him. He'd fallen in love with Abby.

Everything was spinning out of control. Two months ago, he'd been content with his life, before a tiny baby and a strong-willed woman had shown him just how much he'd been missing. Now, Charlotte was struggling for breath. Abby was gone. And he was facing losing both of them.

Even if he'd never gotten over it, he'd managed to get through the loss of his parents. But the thought of losing Charlotte and Abby rocked him to the core.

And he didn't know how he could possibly live through it.

Chapter Fifteen

Abby rushed in the doors of the hospital and up the stairs to the second floor, Elvis at her side. When her flight arrived at the airport in Mobile, she'd gotten a text message from Wynn that Charlotte was in the hospital and she'd headed straight here.

Her heart was in her throat. Sweet baby girl. Abby couldn't bear the thought of her being sick.

Stopping at the nurse's desk to check in with Elvis, she asked for directions to Charlotte's room. A nurse named Lucy pointed her down the hall.

When she arrived, the door was slightly open. She could see Garrett sitting in a chair, his face in his hands. Softly, she said, "Elvis, go say hello."

Elvis streaked across the room to Garrett, stuck his head between Garrett's arms and nuzzled. Garrett's head shot up as his arms closed around Elvis, his eyes searching for hers.

She smiled even as she felt her eyes prick with tears. Despite the circumstances, she was happy to see him. Glad she could be here for him.

Abby stepped into the room, her gaze going to Charlotte, who was asleep in a crib under the only light in the room. Her arm was wrapped in a splint to protect her IV, her lower leg encircled in a blood pressure cuff. On the opposite big toe was the glowing red light of the pulse oximeter and in her nose, a tiny nasal cannula delivering oxygen so her body didn't have to work so hard.

Abby reached Charlotte's side and brushed her fingers across the downy soft hair. "Oh, baby girl."

Garrett walked to the end of the bed. "She's holding her own. They gave her something to bring her fever down and she's been sleeping."

Resisting the urge to throw herself into his arms and sob, Abby blew out a breath. She'd been at the bedside of literally hundreds of children and never shed a tear because it was her job to hold it together. But Charlotte was hers—even if she wasn't, not really.

"When did she get sick?"

"I noticed she had a stuffy nose yesterday. She didn't sleep well last night. They called me from day care and said she hadn't been eating, so I picked her up early. She started coughing at dinner tonight and her fever was 104."

"Oh, Garrett. How scary."

"We haven't been in the room very long, just long enough for them to get her settled and for me to realize what's at stake here."

"I'm so sorry. Can I hug you?"

The words were barely out of her mouth before he pulled her into his arms, burying his face in her hair. "I missed you. How did you even know to come?"

"I was on a plane already. Wynn texted me and I got it when I landed. I came straight here."

"I'm so thankful." He let her go but kept his arm around her as they stood at the side of Charlotte's crib.

"Can we pray for her? Will you?" He placed his hand on Charlotte's foot while she kept hers on the downy head.

Abby's voice shook with emotion as the words poured out. "Papa God, You are our Father, always watching out for us, caring for us in ways we can't even understand. We know You watch over Charlotte, too. Please lend her Your strength to fight off this illness. Protect her from harm. Be with Garrett. He needs Your peace and Your wisdom right now more than ever. And thank You, God, for never leaving us alone to face our hardships. Amen."

"Amen." Garrett cleared his throat. "I'm glad you came."

"I can stay, but if you'd rather try to sleep while she's sleeping, I'll go."

"Please stay?"

She dragged a visitor's chair across the room so she could sit next to Garrett. "So other than ending up in the hospital, how was your week?"

Unbelievably, he chuckled. "Terrible. Devin threatened to punch me. Tanner wanted to kick me out."

"Oh, no!"

His smile faded. "I missed you. How was yours?"

"It was good to be back at work, but this deployment was intense. All of them are, I guess, but because the children were trapped, this one seemed more so. I guess you saw on the news that they got them all out?"

"I did. And you got to visit with them?"

"Yes. They were really brave and funny. Reminded me of Nash. You would've loved them."

"I would."

"I fell right back in the rhythm of things. Red Hill Springs felt like a weird, wonderful dream."

"I was afraid you'd get back to work and wouldn't want to come back." His eyes were on Charlotte, on the monitors which, though silent, recorded every heartbeat, every breath.

"I needed to come back." She hesitated to say more, not because she didn't understand how he was feeling, but because it wasn't the time to talk about her feelings, not with so much at stake here.

His face was scruffy, eyes tired as he looked back at her. She'd had some time to think in California, but she wasn't ready to talk about it yet. Not until things were certain and definitely not until Charlotte was better.

"I called Brooklyn. She didn't answer so I left a message. Then I texted her. I'm not sure what else to do." Garrett yawned and squinted at his watch. "I'm exhausted. We didn't sleep much last night and I blew through a ton of energy when I realized how sick she was."

"Why don't you sit down and sleep for a while? I'll keep watch."

He held his hand out and she slid hers into it, trying not to make a big deal out of how natural it felt to do so. Their relationship wasn't a given, not by a long shot, but she'd been with Garrett and Charlotte since the beginning and being here felt right.

As his eyes closed, hers were drawn to Charlotte, the rapid rise and fall of her tiny little chest. *Please God, let her be okay.*

Garrett woke with a start, rubbed his gritty eyes and stumbled to his feet. He needed coffee. The agonizingly slow night had finally turned to daylight. He'd tried for hours to comfort Charlotte after the nurses had to suction her nose and mouth around one o'clock in the morning.

He looked over toward the crib. Abby was in the reclining chair, where she'd finally settled millimeter by millimeter with Charlotte on her chest after the baby had fallen into a fitful sleep. Elvis, on the floor beside her, lifted his head to watch Garrett, but didn't move.

None of them had gotten more than an hour or two of rest. The one thing he could say on the positive was that Charlotte seemed to be breathing a little bit easier now that she wasn't dehydrated and was getting supplemental oxygen. The nurse had told him in the middle of the night that Charlotte wouldn't be able to leave the hospital until her fever was gone and she could take a bottle and keep it down.

Garrett slid his feet into his shoes and picked up Elvis's leash from the counter. "Come on, boy, let's go outside."

Elvis's tail thumped but he didn't stir from Abby's side. Garrett shrugged. "Okay, your call."

Pulling open the door to the hall, he stopped short, face-to-face with a young girl with bright pink hair that matched her high-top tennis shoes. The hair stood up on the back of his neck.

Brooklyn. Charlotte's mother.

He physically took a step back, before he closed the door and stepped into the hall, still trying to process her presence. "Wow, hey."

He studied her face. She looked good. Tired, but better than he did, for sure.

Her chin came up. "I'm not using."

"Good. Come on, let's go get a cup of coffee. I'm about to fall over and I want to be back before the doctor comes for rounds."

She glanced wistfully at the door, but followed him. "How is she? I got in the car as soon as I got your text."

"She's not critical, but she's not good."

"I don't know what that means."

"She needs support to get over the virus she has because she's so little. You know, tubes and IVs and monitors and stuff." He stopped walking. "I can't believe I'm just standing here having a conversation with you. Where have you been?"

"I know you have a lot of questions. I'll get to the answers, I promise. Just please, tell me about Charlotte."

"It's serious, but she should be fine. Most babies with this go home in about a week." He repeated what the nurses had told him, trying to infuse the words with more confidence than he felt.

"A week? I'll get kicked out of school if I stay a week."

"You're in school?"

She reached a hand up and self-consciously touched a lock of cotton-candy-colored hair. "Cosmetology school."

He held the door to the cafeteria open for her. "Last time I checked, we had cosmetology school right here."

Technically, he had no idea if that was true. He'd never checked to see if there were cosmetology schools in Alabama. He walked over to the cafeteria line and pointed at a sausage biscuit. "Two, please. Do you want anything?"

"No, thanks."

He paid the cashier for the biscuits and two cups

of coffee, walked to a table and sat down, assuming Brooklyn would follow him. She paid for her own cup of coffee and sat down across from him.

"Why don't you start at the beginning?"

Her eyes were big and round, the same dark blue as Charlotte's. She didn't have the benefit of growing up in a family like his, with the moral compass of his father. And he reminded himself to show her compassion. She deserved that, no matter how bad her decisions had been.

"You know I was hanging out with a rough crowd when I was aging out of foster care."

"I had that idea, yes."

She twisted the foam cup in her hands. "They were—are—pretty hard users. I was, too, when I was with them. But when I found out I was pregnant with Charlotte, I stopped."

"Who's the father?"

Her cheeks colored and she looked away. "I don't know."

"Okay. Go on."

"I couldn't figure out how I could stay clean. Once she came, I couldn't stay at the pregnancy shelter anymore and I knew if I went to any of my so-called friends, I'd be back in the same place I was before I started. I knew I needed to make a clean break."

"Why didn't you ask me for help?"

"That's a question I've asked myself a billion times. And I don't know. I guess I was embarrassed. And desperate. Would you really have said yes to Charlotte if I had asked you?"

She had a point. He wouldn't have. He might have found a place for Charlotte, maybe even for both of them, but he wouldn't have taken her. He took a slow sip of the hot coffee. It tasted terrible.

He took another sip and sighed. "I get why you left. I even understand it. But I don't understand why you couldn't make contact with me after you left."

"I thought you'd be mad or try to convince me to come home." Her eyes were pleading with him to understand. "Garrett, I can't come back here. There's a way for me to make a better life. I'm so close. I know it'll be hard but I need to do this. I won't make it if I stay here."

Garrett was too tired to argue. Too tired to come up with a creative solution. Too tired, period.

He stood and tossed his empty coffee cup into the trash can and picked up his uneaten biscuit and the coffee and biscuit he'd bought for Abby. "All right, let's go."

Brooklyn's footsteps seemed to get slower and heavier the closer they got to the room. "I don't know if I can do this."

"My friend Abby's been helping me with Charlotte. She's in there with her now."

Brooklyn stopped, tears brimming in her eyes. "What if Charlotte hates me?"

He put an arm around her shoulders. "Then you'll really be a parent. You came all this way to check on her—at least come in and see her."

"Hi." Abby looked up as the door opened. Garrett paused halfway through. "Is that coffee? You might be my hero."

She looked down at Charlotte, who squirmed but didn't wake up. "The nurse came in a few minutes ago to check on her and said they'd be coming back to do some blood work."

"Fabulous news."

"They want you to try a bottle with her and see if she'll take it." They'd tried a bottle twice during the night and both times, Charlotte had not been able to keep it down.

"Abby?"

Something in the tone of his voice made her look up again and she realized he wasn't alone. As he stepped into the room, a young girl with pink hair crept in behind him.

"Sorry, I didn't realize we had company. Hi, I'm Abby."

Silence stretched for a long few seconds. Garrett nudged the girl forward.

"I'm Brooklyn. Charlotte's, um, mom."

Only long years of practice schooling her expression enabled Abby to say with a smile, "It's nice to finally meet you in person."

After another nudge from Garrett, Brooklyn muttered her thanks.

Despite trying to give Brooklyn the benefit of the doubt all along, Abby's feelings had ping-ponged from judgment to compassion and back again. When she saw Charlotte's mom in person, though, all those mixed feelings vanished. All she could see was a terrified teen, trying to do the best for her baby in the only way she knew how.

"Take a look, B." Garrett edged her forward. "She won't bite."

"She looks so sick," Brooklyn whispered.

"She *is* sick." Abby found Garrett's eyes with hers

before going back to Brooklyn. "But they're taking really good care of her here. Why don't you wash up at the sink and you can hold her?"

Brooklyn took a step back. "I don't know. She's not used to me. And all those wires and tubes…"

Garrett's eyebrows drew together into a frown. Abby could tell that he was hanging on to decorum by a thin thread. She quickly said, "You came all this way to see her. It would be a shame if you didn't try."

Brooklyn dropped her backpack in a chair, moved to the sink and turned the water on. Garrett mouthed, "Sorry."

Abby lifted a shoulder and shook her head.

Once Brooklyn had used the hand sanitizer and stood awkwardly waving her hands in the air to dry them, Abby eased to a standing position. Garrett helped her untangle herself from the wires recording Charlotte's vital signs.

She sent Brooklyn a reassuring smile. "Come on over. You sit in the chair and I'll put her in your arms. Garrett, you want to hand Brooklyn one of those gowns to put on over her clothes?"

While Brooklyn slid the gown on, Abby had a chance to study her. Hands were steady. Eyes and skin clear, if tired. She really seemed to be free of drugs. Abby silently prayed that God would support this young girl, who just seemed so lost.

With a trembling smile, Brooklyn sat in the chair. "Y'all are sure this is okay? I'm so nervous."

"It's perfectly fine, but if she cries, it's not you. It's because she's not feeling well and she hasn't been very tolerant of being handled." As slowly and gently as she could, Abby moved Charlotte into Brooklyn's arms.

Charlotte let out a small cry that quickly turned into a wheezing cough. Brooklyn's head jerked up, her eyes widening in alarm.

"She's okay. Give it a minute." Garrett's jaw clenched, his features strung tight.

Abby touched her eye. Elvis had already been watching her closely as the tension grew in the room. He rose to a sitting position, his ears perking up. She pointed at Garrett. "Rest."

Elvis trotted across the room and sat as close to Garrett's legs as possible, leaning into them. Garrett's hand dropped to rub the dog's head and he took a deep breath.

Good boy, Elvis.

It was totally natural that Garrett would feel protective of Charlotte, even angry at Brooklyn. She'd taken advantage of a professional relationship, plunging it into the personal the moment she'd left the baby on Garrett's porch. But right now, their focus had to be on Charlotte.

Brooklyn being here was a huge answer to prayer. Maybe Garrett could get all of his questions answered. Maybe all of them could see this through to a resolution that made sense. But it all—every bit of it—hinged on Brooklyn's next steps.

Abby stripped out of the hospital gown she'd been wearing over her own clothes. She stopped next to Garrett. His eyes didn't move from Charlotte.

Tears ran down Brooklyn's face.

It was time for Abby to go. She'd done everything she could to help Garrett and now he and Brooklyn had to work things out. Abby might be a buffer for the tension, but they were going to have to figure out how to talk without her, for Charlotte's sake.

Her purse and Elvis's leash were on the counter and she picked them up. "I need to go home for a while. Elvis needs a break. I'll text you later."

Panic flared in Garrett's eyes but he didn't say anything. She gave him a quick hug with Elvis between them and left the room.

When the door closed behind her, she rubbed a hand across her eyes. Garrett's pain and confusion and worry was hard to handle. She wanted to take it away, to fix it. But that wasn't her job.

Being in California had clarified a few things for her. She loved her job, but she needed roots. She was fine alone, but she needed family—even if it was one she created for herself. And being independent was great, but as much as she'd tried to keep Garrett firmly in the friend column, she'd done the one thing she'd always said she never would.

She'd fallen in love.

And now her heart was in his hands.

Chapter Sixteen

Garrett watched Brooklyn's face soften with love. His jaw clenched tighter. He wasn't even sure how to feel at this point. He wanted to believe she'd do what was best for Charlotte, but how could he know that?

After all of this, if Brooklyn changed her mind and decided to take Charlotte, what choice did he have but to let her? Yes, Charlotte was in his temporary legal custody, but only because Brooklyn had signed it over to him.

He was exhausted. Worried because Charlotte was sick. And more than a little desperate. In one horribly unfair accident, he'd lost his parents, his sister-in-law, his baby niece, and for all practical purposes, his brothers. How could he stand it if he lost Charlotte?

And Abby? With her back doing disaster relief, he wasn't sure Abby wasn't already gone.

His breath hitched out and his lungs refused to draw in another one. Brooklyn glanced up at him. "What's wrong? You look like you're about to have a heart attack."

"Are you planning on taking Charlotte back?" The question was so weighted that it seemed to hang in the air. He couldn't hear a thing over the roaring in his ears as he waited for her answer.

She ducked her head, a lock of candy-colored hair falling into her eyes as she looked down at Charlotte. "Maybe one day I'll be ready to be a mom. I hope so. I love her more than anything. I know that's probably hard to believe, but it's true. The second I saw her..."

Her voice broke and he had to fight hard to squelch the urge to let his questions go. But he needed answers. Charlotte needed answers. "But?"

Brooklyn squirmed under his scrutiny. "I can't take care of anyone else until I can take care of myself. I want you to raise her. She needs a real family. You have the paperwork, right?"

He nodded slowly. "There's one thing you didn't consider. I'm a mandatory reporter. I had to tell Child Services that you left her."

Her mouth gaped open, angry tears instantly in her eyes, her voice a hot whisper. "She's in *foster* care? I trusted you!"

"Calm down and let me finish, please." Somehow he'd ended up as a father figure to this eighteen-year-old girl. She *had* trusted him and maybe what she'd done was unfathomable to the average Joe, but to him—knowing what had happened to her and all that she'd been through—it made a sad kind of sense. "I convinced the judge to let her stay with me. She's been with me all along."

"Okay." Brooklyn closed her eyes and took a deep breath, the word tumbling out again as she let it go. "Okay."

He crossed his arms. "But I need to hear you say what you intend to do now."

She hesitated and in that split second, the door opened.

The daytime nurse, Darla, came in with a perky smile. "Time for vitals. I need to draw some blood and then we're going to try a bottle."

The color drained from Brooklyn's face. "Come get her, Garrett."

"She's doing fine with you."

The color drained from her cheeks. "Garrett, please. Come get her."

Taking pity on her, Garrett crossed the room to the chair where she was sitting by the crib. His hands sure, he lifted Charlotte from Brooklyn's arms. The baby squirmed and her cold-swollen eyes squinted up at him.

He smiled down at her. "Hey, sweet girl."

She opened her mouth and wailed—a raspy cry which brought on a coughing fit. He wished with everything he had that he could take her sickness from her, that he was the one in the hospital instead of her.

The nurse pulled the tray of instruments to a spot within her reach. "She really doesn't like being moved, does she? Okay, Dad, hold her in your lap, with her head against your chest and wrap your arm around, yep, just like that." She looked up at Brooklyn. "Can you grab a toy and try to distract her? We use a tiny little butterfly needle. It won't be bad. She may not even cry."

Brooklyn froze, a deer in the headlights. She blinked a couple of times and then ran from the room.

Garrett sighed. "Sorry. Just go ahead. I've got Charlotte."

Charlotte cried, but Garrett thought it was more that she was mad and hungry and hated being held down than the needle stick. That part was over fast thanks to Nurse Darla with the steady hands.

Darla stuck a cartoon character bandage over Charlotte's boo-boo. "She's good to go. The doctor wants the results before he does rounds, so I'm going to run this down to be processed and I'll be right back with a bottle."

Garrett turned Charlotte toward his chest and held her close, gently patting her back. She was so tiny to be going through such a rough time.

Her hoarse cries broke his heart.

He haltingly began to sing her favorite Beatles song about holding hands and her cries began to lessen. When she finally stopped crying, he eased her onto the bed and kept singing, grabbing a clean diaper from the drawer and changing her as she watched him with her dark blue eyes.

Her little chin wrinkled, the bottom lip poking out as he fastened the last tab and picked her up. "All done. You are such a good girl. And you have good taste in music."

When he turned around, Brooklyn was standing in the door, tears drying on her cheeks. "I'm sorry. I couldn't stand seeing her that way."

"It's okay. I don't like it either."

"But you did it. You're a really great dad." She paused and looked down at her pink tennis shoes. "You asked me if I was planning to take Charlotte back. The answer's no. It's always been no, but if I had any question about it, I don't anymore."

"Brooklyn... I want you to be sure."

She nodded and said, almost too quiet for him to hear, "I wish I had a dad like you."

Her words cut straight to his heart. He'd known her a long time. And he was the one who'd been the most stable influence in her life. He quirked a finger at her. "Come here."

With Charlotte between them, he put his arm around Brooklyn. "You do have me. You're not alone."

She laid her head with her cotton-candy hair on his shoulder and wept. His heart broke for this sweet young woman, who hadn't been loved the way she deserved by the people who were supposed to love her.

When she finally stepped back, he said, "I mean it, Brooklyn. You might've aged out of foster care on your own, but you're not on your own now."

Twin tears tracked down her cheeks. "Why aren't you mad at me?"

He shrugged, but he looked down at Charlotte, the blush of strawberry-blond hair, long blond eyelashes fanning across her cheek—almost invisible unless you looked really close. She'd changed his life for the better in so many ways. "I think you believed you were making the best choice for you and for Charlotte. I may not like how you went about it, but I understand it."

Brooklyn's cheeks puffed out as she blew out a breath. "I'm wrecked. I need to go wash my face and then I really have to get back to Nashville."

"That's where you are? Nashville?"

She nodded. "It's far enough away that I don't know anyone. Close enough that I don't feel like I'm living in a foreign country."

"Before you go, I need you to do something."

The wariness returned to her eyes and he was reminded again that she'd experienced things in her short eighteen years that no person should have to. Her reactions to things were extreme because she'd lived a life of extremes.

"It's not bad, but I need to get sworn testimony from you about your intentions when you left Charlotte with me. The only alternative to doing that would be to come back when we have court."

"I can't come back. I need to get my degree."

"Okay. Let's see if we can get Charlotte to take a bottle while we wait for Abby. I'll call my office and see if I can get someone in to take a sworn statement and one of the caseworkers from the Department of Human Resources to witness it, so they can testify in court." He tugged his phone out of his pocket and texted Abby to see where she was.

When he looked up, Brooklyn's eyes were intent on his. "I'm glad I came today."

"Me, too."

"Did you mean what you said about me having family now?" She looked down at her hands, twisting together in a fruitless, anxious knot.

"Yep. Holidays. Birthdays. Pretty much anytime anyone has a big deal going on, you'll have to be there. It's required."

"That sounds like a pain." She spoke softly, but her lips curved into a trembling smile.

"Yeah, I'm getting pretty good at this dad stuff. So, you know, if you need advice or anything…" He laughed. "I'm just kidding. But seriously, go take a nap, young lady. You were driving all night and if you insist on going back tonight, you need some sleep."

She rolled her eyes, but as she turned away, she was smiling.

Garrett swayed back and forth with Charlotte. His

mom used to say they were a family who believed in do-overs—because God gave them the biggest do-over. It was called grace.

Brooklyn needed a do-over. He could give her one by sharing his family with her. This, at least, made sense.

His feelings for Abby...less sense. That uneasy feeling settled in the pit of his stomach. This experience with Charlotte had shown him that he wasn't cut out to be worried all the time.

Abby's work was risky—obviously—she'd been shot on assignment. There was always going to be a need for her somewhere in the world. And just like she did last week, she would go.

Could he really get used to watching her walk out the door not knowing if or when she'd come back to him?

He pressed his thumb and finger against his eyes at the bridge of his nose, but tears welled up anyway. He loved her. He just wasn't sure he could deal with the threat of losing her.

When this was all over and Charlotte was out of the woods, he and Abby needed to have a long, serious talk. They'd grown so close. He couldn't deny his feelings for her.

But he had to lay his doubts on the table if they had any possibility of a future. And he wasn't looking forward to it.

It was five long days and nights before Charlotte was fever-free and discharged, but finally, Garrett was on his way back to the cabin with Charlotte. Abby slid a chicken casserole into the oven. She'd come over with some groceries and the idea of cooking dinner so Garrett wouldn't have to stop with Charlotte on the way home.

Winter's last gasp had dropped the temperature into the fifties and rather than turn the heat on, she'd started a fire in the fireplace. With the place tidied, candles lit and Elvis asleep on the rag rug in front of the hearth, the small cabin felt cozy and homey.

Elvis lifted his head and woofed softly. Abby heard Garrett's SUV pull up in front. She checked the room one last time for anything out of place before she opened the door, skipping down the porch steps and grabbing his bag while he released the infant car seat and brought Charlotte in.

"It smells so good in here. Looks good, too. I might cry." Garrett laughed as he unbuckled Charlotte and lifted her into his arms. "I know we were only gone five days but it felt like a month."

He kissed Charlotte on the head and put her in her favorite swing. She seemed happy to be there, taking her pacifier immediately, her eyelids already drooping.

"Charlotte looks so much better." Abby handed Garrett a glass of tea.

He dropped onto the couch, stretching his legs out. "I'm so glad to be home."

"Me, too." She choked on the words, with a laugh. "I mean, I'm glad you're home, too."

"You didn't even get a breather when you got back from California." He smiled at her. "You must be tired."

"I am, but actually, being away gave me some time to think about things."

He raised an eyebrow. "Like what?"

"It's strange—I've been going from disaster to disaster for so long that it took me a while to realize that real life isn't just about triage and stopping the bleeding."

She could feel his eyes on her, but he didn't say anything. Looking into the fire where the flames leaped and glowed, she slowed her thoughts, just focusing on the moment together.

For the first time in days, they had nowhere to be. Nothing to do. No crisis. The hum of the baby swing, the peacefulness of the sleeping baby, the crackle and pop from the fireplace. These were things she'd missed as she'd bounced from job to job.

But Garrett didn't seem to want to talk tonight.

"Maybe we should talk about this later," she backpedaled.

From somewhere he dragged up a smile. "No, I want to hear what you're thinking."

Abby scratched her head. "I'm not sure I'm making sense, but when I went to California, I realized that I really have lived my life from one catastrophe to the next. All crisis management, all the time. I loved my job—I do love it. But real life should have ebb and flow. Sometimes things happen and you can work *through* them. You taught me that. You, Nash's mom Melanie, Brooklyn. You inspire me to be brave, too."

"You're already brave, Abby." He looked down, shifted away from her, glanced at his watch. "It's almost time for Charlotte's bottle. I need to get it ready."

In the kitchen, he pulled out a couple of bottles and a can of formula, before he braced his hands on the counter and let his head drop.

Wary now, Abby followed him. "What's going on? What aren't you telling me?"

"Nothing." He scowled. "It's just—you make a

difference in people's lives. Go places other people wouldn't dream of going. You got *shot* and still went back to work. If that's not brave, what is?"

"Staying." She slid her hands down his arms and fitted them into his hands. "For me, staying is what takes courage. I've lived so long in black and white I forgot there was a whole world of color in between. I want the color, Garrett. Laughs and family dinners and picnics in the park."

His eyes met hers and held as he slowly brought his head up. "Abby—"

"I don't know how to belong yet—I never have before. But I'd really like to figure it out. With you." Her lips trembled and she pressed them together, holding her breath as she waited for him to say something.

A note of hope crept into his voice. "You're planning to quit your job?"

"Not completely, no. I'll still be traveling some."

Shaking his head, he took a step back, away from her, putting his hands up between them. "I can't do this, Abby. You keep your feelings all tucked away in neat little packages. I'm not like that."

The words were a slap. "I don't even know what that means."

"You're just…calm." He made a motion somewhere in the direction of her midsection. "I don't know how you do it."

She narrowed her eyes, anxiety and awkwardness gone, replaced by anger. "You think I don't have feelings just because I don't wrap my compassion around me like armor?"

"That's not what I said."

"Maybe I hold them close, but I have *feelings*, Garrett. Deep feelings. For example, I—"

Love you.

She swallowed the words because she knew he wouldn't accept them. He obviously wasn't ready to hear them and she sure didn't want to put them out there just to get them pushed aside. "Okay, then. I'm going to go."

"I'm sorry, Abby. I want to believe we could make this work, but I can't live a life where I'm always waiting for you to run away when things get hard. I can't do that to Charlotte."

Her heart felt like it was literally breaking. She'd put her hopes on the line with him and he'd stepped on them. Ground them into dust, not because he didn't care about her, but because he didn't care enough to risk getting hurt.

"You can use Charlotte as an excuse, and you might even buy into it, but I'm not the one running here. You are." Picking up her purse and keys from the end table, she turned back to face him. "Your casserole will be done in ten minutes."

He was standing in the middle of the kitchen, grief etched on his face, his hands held out as if in appeal. "Abby, when you leave, you take my heart with you. I wouldn't survive if you didn't come back."

Abby shook her head. "I was wrong about you being brave. When you care about something, you fight for it. You don't give up because you're scared of what *might* happen. Come on, Elvis."

Abby walked out the door and closed it gently. She let Elvis into the backseat, got in her car and drove to the end of the driveway. Put it in Park, laid her head on the steering wheel and sobbed.

Elvis poked his head between the seats and licked her ear. She let out a strangled laugh, wrapping her arm around his neck. "I messed up, buddy."

Boy, did she. All those times she'd thought to herself that getting involved with Garrett was a bad idea? She should've listened to the voice of warning.

She picked up her phone and opened her text message app. Her thumb hovered over her boss's name. Surely there was a disaster somewhere in the world that could use her expertise.

Being in love was terrible. Maybe there was something essential missing from her because she didn't get it. If this was what being in love felt like, she wanted no part of it.

Chapter Seventeen

Three days after Abby walked out, Garrett scrubbed the feeding troughs in the barn with a stiff-bristled brush and hot soapy water. He'd gone through sadness and anger and was firmly in the self-delusion phase of grieving the loss of his relationship with Abby. It had hurt, no denying that. But he wasn't giving in to it. He'd done the right thing.

Any doubt he'd felt had been shoved down, patched and plastered over. He wasn't going to think about it.

While Garrett worked on the troughs, Devin was in one of the stalls, humming along to the country music station while he shoveled out the old straw, forking it into a wheelbarrow. Tanner worked behind them, making minor repairs. It would be a long day of mucking and maintenance, but it was a necessity on the farm if they wanted their animals to stay healthy.

Devin stopped singing. "Hey, Garrett, where's Abby? Lacey figured she'd be by to help with Charlotte today."

Garrett's hand paused midscrub at Devin's question. "Ah—she's not going to be coming around anymore."

Devin's head swiveled toward him. He leaned forward on the pitchfork. "What do you mean, she's not gonna be coming around here anymore?"

"I mean, we broke up. Except we weren't really together to start with so I don't even know if 'breaking up' is what you'd call it."

"Wow." Devin limped toward the bale of fresh hay and started sifting it onto the floor of the stall. "So after all that, she decided she wasn't going to stick around? That's kind of jerky."

Garrett paused again, a queasy feeling starting in his stomach. "That's not exactly what happened."

Tanner's voice came from the next stall over. "Look, I wasn't going to say anything because I figured it was none of my business. But she was sitting at the end of the driveway when I turned in the other night, crying her eyes out."

Now that was a piece of information Garrett didn't know. The patch job on his wall of denial was starting to crumble. He made a desperate gambit to shore it up. "She told me she'd decided to stay in Red Hill Springs, but she wasn't planning to quit her work in disaster areas."

"So?" Devin tossed the word over his shoulder as he moved to the back of the stall. "Tanner, there's a loose board in here."

"So, it's not a great way to build a relationship if one person is jetting off to disaster areas all the time. There's no way that was going to end good. Right?"

"I got it. You ended things with her so you wouldn't get hurt." Tanner calmly pounded the loose nail back into the wall with one hand and sanded down the splintered area around it with the other.

"Well, yeah. And Charlotte, too. I have someone else to think about besides myself right now." He rinsed out the trough with a bucket of clean water, watching it drain onto the dirt floor of the barn.

Devin shook his head. "Nope. I'm not buying it. You're making assumptions based on fear about what you think she's going to do. You don't know."

Garrett rolled his eyes. "We should've never let you go to therapy."

Tanner cleared his throat with a pointed look at Garrett, who squirmed under his older brother's scrutiny.

"Sorry," he muttered to Devin.

"No problem." Devin shrugged. "I know from personal experience how bad it stinks to be called out on something like this, but this is on you, bro. You broke her heart and you did it because you were scared."

His self-delusion buckling under the weight of Devin's words, Garrett stammered out an excuse. "I don't think—I mean, yeah, I was scared. But with good reason. It wasn't going to work out."

"What wasn't going to work out?" Lacey's voice came from the door.

"Garrett broke up with Abby." Devin's smile split his face as he tattled on Garrett to Lacey. He was actually enjoying this.

"What?" Lacey plopped a large orange water cooler onto a table by the door, along with a stack of disposable cups. "Tell me everything. Start at the beginning."

Garrett looked at the ceiling, praying for guidance. He hadn't expected so many questions, which—in retrospect, knowing his family—was a miscalculation on his part. He might as well go through the whole thing and maybe then they would let it go. "Okay, so the other night when I brought Charlotte home from the hospital, Abby was here. She made a casserole and had the house all cleaned up and stuff."

"Oh, yeah," Devin said. "She's a horrible person."

Garrett scowled at him. "Do you want to hear the whole story or not?"

"My bad. Continue." Devin limped past Garrett and picked up a rake.

"So Abby cooked dinner and she said…" Lacey prompted.

"She said she'd realized that traveling from one disaster area to the next, she'd never learned to work through things. She'd never stayed anywhere. Never belonged anywhere. She wanted to try to figure out how." He paused, the next words hard to say. "With me."

Lacey's eyes were glossy with tears. "She told you she wanted to stay in Red Hill Springs?"

"Yeah." He put his brush down on the edge of the trough, beginning to realize he'd made a terrible mistake. Abby was amazing. She'd been here every step of the way for him with Charlotte. She understood him in a way no one else really did.

He didn't know why he was so confused. "But I asked her if she was going to keep doing disaster work and she said yes. After all we've been through as a family, I just can't risk…"

His voice trailed off. He shook his head.

Tanner's eyes were steady on his. "Can't risk loving her?"

Garrett nodded, the ache in his throat too large to speak around.

Devin dropped the hose and walked over, gripping Garrett's shoulder in one strong hand. "I hate to break it to you, but I think it's too late for that. I think you already do."

"I sent her away." His voice was a hoarse whisper.

Tanner nodded. "You did. And you have to own that, but it's not over. If you love her, don't let her get away without a fight."

"I have to go." He turned to Lacey. "Can you—"

"I'll watch Charlotte. You go fix this."

Garrett left the barn at a run. He had to find her. He'd made a terrible mistake.

What if he was already too late?

Garrett took the turn into Abby's driveway fast, his heart racing at a painful clip. The words *too late, too late, too late* were circling in an endless loop in his head.

He pulled up at the house, barreled out of the car and up the stairs to the front door. His feet stumbled to a stop as he saw a haphazard pile of baby things by the front door. Charlotte's bouncy seat and portable crib Abby had bought. A tote bag full of diapers and bibs and tiny pink clothes that tore at his heart.

The door was cracked and he pushed it open. He didn't even have to call out her name. The house was empty. All of the peace and light that Abby had brought was gone. The rental was spotless, not a speck of dust anywhere, and not a sign of life.

His shoulders dropped. He really had lost her. She was somewhere in the world, making a difference in the lives of children, but he had no way of knowing where.

"Garrett?" Jules Quinn walked in through the door with an armload of fluffy white towels. "If you're looking for Abby, she's already gone. I'm getting the place ready for new renters. They're coming in tomorrow."

"I figured." He looked around the living room, memories flooding over him of the time he'd spent here with Abby, learning how to be a dad, laughing and healing. Falling in love.

He'd really made a mess of things. His feelings had been so intense from the beginning with Abby, which he guessed should've been his first sign that things were different with her. No one else had even come close.

With a sigh, he started for the door.

"You might be able to find her at her new place."

He slowly turned back. "New place?"

Jules smiled. "She signed a lease on that little house on the river bluff, next door to Jordan and Ash."

Relief nearly buckled his knees. "She's staying."

With a laugh, Jules nudged him out the door. "I think you need to talk to her about that."

"I'm going right now. I thought I'd lost her. I'm not going to make that mistake again."

Abby toed open the old screen door that led to her new front porch. There was an ancient metal glider in desperate need of a paint job and a view of the river that was worth a lot more than she was paying in rent. She took in a deep breath and let it slowly out.

Garrett's rejection had crushed her, but she wasn't going to let that stop her. She'd found a home and a community in Red Hill Springs. For the first time, she could see past the awkward and past the hard. She could have roots here. People who cared about her, if she would let them in. And she was determined not to hide behind her calling anymore.

Elvis was happy to roll in the grass in the sunshine or chase the nasty tennis ball he'd unearthed from one of the flower beds. And until she could put her feelings for Garrett to rest, there were plenty of projects to be done. Projects that she could pour her blood, sweat and tears into.

Like the sunshine soaking into her skin, the babble of the river as it skimmed across the rocks was soothing. Peaceful. It may not be the life in Red Hill Springs that she'd imagined, but it was going to be good.

Behind her, she heard a car coming up the dirt road that led through the woods and to her house. Wynn had said she was stopping by this afternoon with a housewarming present, so when the car door slammed shut, Abby turned, mustering up her best smile.

Garrett stood there, leaning casually against his car in a position reminiscent of the day she'd left for California. She froze, her smile fading.

She wasn't ready to see him. She wasn't sure she could hold it together with him and she desperately wanted to hold it together.

He was wearing jeans and boots and a faded law school T-shirt. He looked good, relaxed, which for some reason made her angry. Her chest ached with the effort of not reacting. Elvis dropped the tennis ball and trotted over to stand beside her.

"Jules told me where I could find you. I hope it's okay that I came." He shoved his hands into his pockets. She could see the tension in his muscular arms and shoulders which made her feel marginally better.

"*Why* did you come, Garrett?"

He walked closer to her, his eyes on the grass, his long dark eyelashes a smudge against his tan skin. She hated that she noticed that. She wanted to hate him. No, that wasn't right. She didn't want to hate him. She wanted to feel nothing.

But she didn't. She hurt in a million places that she didn't even know she could hurt. In a way, though, maybe she should thank him. He'd broken her heart, but he'd also shown her that she was stronger than she knew. She was brave—brave enough to stay and she didn't need him to be the reason. It was enough that she wanted her roots to be here.

He stopped in front of her, hands still in his pockets. "I owe you an apology."

"Okay."

"I can't even say 'in my defense,' because I don't have a defense. I just messed up." He paused, his eyebrows drawing together. "When Charlotte got sick, all I could think about was how I couldn't protect her. And when Brooklyn came, it just made that feeling worse. I've gone all these years thinking that I'd come through my parents' deaths without any lasting scars. I was wrong."

She rubbed the spot between her eyes with her fingers and then dropped her hand. "I'm not sure what this has to do with me."

He squinted against the bright sun glinting off the water. "When my parents died, I lost my center, my safety. And I pushed down my feelings so much that I believed my own lies to myself, that I'd overcome it."

He was confirming what she'd instinctively understood about him—that he'd tried to control life in the only way he could. And in that regard, he wasn't so different from her. "You thought if somehow you could weight the scales toward the good, it would mitigate the bad?"

When he nodded, she said, "But life doesn't work that way. I can vouch for that."

"Yeah. I've kind of figured that out." He shook his head. "I love my brothers, don't get me wrong, but Charlotte... I've never felt love like that. She stole my heart without even trying and I let her, knowing I would never get it back, not in one piece."

Abby's eyes stung and she blinked back the tears. She would not shed them. Not in front of him.

Garrett let out a short mirthless laugh. "And then I met you. Before I could stop myself, I was falling for you. It was like realizing this solid rock I thought I'd been on all these years was really quicksand and I didn't even know it until I was halfway under."

Abby took a step back, away from him. She didn't want an explanation for why he couldn't be with her, not when she knew that at the end of it, he would still walk away. "Garrett, you don't have to do this. It's fine. I'm fine."

"I do have to do this, though. Because the other night, when you said you wanted to stay in Red Hill Springs, that you wanted to figure it out with me... coming right on the heels of almost losing Charlotte, I couldn't see past how literally terrified I was."

She took a deep breath. "Did you know when I was a little girl, I always had a bag packed?"

"I didn't know that."

"I kept it under my bed in case I had to leave. My aunt wasn't unkind, she just didn't know how to deal with me, so I kept the bag ready and I learned not to count on anyone else. But that kind of independence comes at a cost."

Rubbing dampness away from his eyes with his thumb, Garrett voice was hoarse with emotion as he said, "Someone should've been there for you."

He was right. Someone should've been, but that wasn't her point. "I've unpacked my bag, Garrett. I'm staying in Red Hill Springs. I hope I don't cause you pain by being here, but I'm not leaving. Not this time."

Garrett held out his hands for hers, but she couldn't make herself reach for them.

He held them out anyway. "Abby, you are the most amazing, beautiful, perfect woman and when I said I wouldn't survive it if you didn't come back, I meant it. That night, I wasn't sure I could trust your feelings."

Her heart, which she thought had been broken, shattered into jagged pieces. She took another step back, resisting the urge to run into the house and slam the door and lock it. Once again, someone she cared about was looking at her and deciding she wasn't worth the trouble.

"I'm messing this up." He stabbed his fingers into his hair and the simple gesture reminded her: this was Garrett, the man who'd bought a ten-thousand-dollar stroller for a mom who couldn't afford it. The same man who'd found a baby on his doorstep and become a parent—a good one—in an instant. The same man who'd left chicken potpie on her doorstep when she'd been exhausted after a long day at work.

She stared at his hands—strong, work worn, open—then slowly slid hers into them.

He tightened his grip and swallowed hard. "That night, I didn't know if I could trust your feelings, but then I realized—I can trust mine. I love you. I love you so much that my heart is never going to be the same. And whether you're here or California or Timbuktu, that's not going to change."

The tears she'd refused to shed spilled down her face. "I love you, too."

"I know." His voice was full of wonder as he tugged her forward into his arms and his lips hovered over hers. "Just like I know I don't deserve you, but I promise, when you go away, I'll be right here waiting for you to come home."

He was so tantalizingly close, but she didn't make him close the distance. She brushed her lips across his, laughing against his mouth when he kissed her back.

Finally. *Finally.*

He lifted his head and tenderly touched his forehead to hers as he let out a long, slow breath of relief. "Oh, I almost forgot. I brought you something—a housewarming gift, you could say."

He went back to the car and reached through the open window, pulling out a kitten, cupping it in his hands. "She's still a little small, but she's feisty."

"Oh, Garrett, I love her." She reached for the calico kitten, who crawled up her shirt, purring as she dug in with her tiny claws. Abby laughed and put her down on the ground, where she stalked Elvis, her little tail sword straight. "Be nice, Frances."

Garrett looked down at her, his heart in his eyes. "I'm not a prize. I'm a little broken, a little bit cracked, but you—you light up all the dark places, for me and for Charlotte. And I want to spend the rest of my life making you as happy as you make us every day. Please marry me?"

"Yes!" Abby laughed and tilted her face up, pressing her lips against his as his arms closed around her, lifting her off her feet. "Yes. Yes. Yes."

She slid to the ground, wrapped her arms around him and tucked her head into the crook of his neck, where it fit perfectly.

And she realized that in this spot—right here in Garrett's arms—she'd found the place where she belonged.

Epilogue

Devin and Tanner stood to Garrett's left. Wynn and Lacey stood to Abby's right. The whole place smelled like flowers, which seemed somehow wrong to Garrett. Courtrooms were supposed to smell like old leather and wood polish.

Abby squeezed his hand and he looked down at her. She was dressed simply in a lace dress, a flower crown in her hair. And she was beautiful—her love for him, along with her healthy sense of humor, shining in her eyes.

At the judge's direction, Abby slid the heavy gold band onto the fourth finger of his left hand. "Garrett, I give you this ring as a sign of our constant faith and abiding love. With this ring, I thee wed."

And then it was his turn.

He took his mother's ring from Devin and slid it onto Abby's finger. His voice shook with emotion as he said, "I give you this ring as a sign of my solemn vow. With all that I have and all that I am, I will honor you. With this ring, I thee wed."

Wynn was openly sniffling as the judge said, "By

the power vested in me by the state of Alabama, I now declare you husband and wife. Garrett, you may kiss your bride."

Abby wasn't having any of that. She threw her arms around his neck and planted one on him. Wynn let out a whoop. The many people who filled the courtroom and spilled out into the hall clapped and cheered.

The judge rounded the bench and picked up her gavel, tapping it to get everyone's attention. "And now, we have one more very important matter to attend to. Abby and Garrett, please raise your right hands and repeat after me. I will tell the truth, the whole truth and nothing but the truth, so help me, God."

Garrett had heard those words hundreds of times, had said them nearly as many, before testifying as a guardian ad litem. But saying them today, on the most important day of his life, was different.

Weightier. He reached for his baby girl. Charlotte was starting to sit up now and when he settled her on his arm, she grabbed his face and squealed.

The judge laughed. "Abby and Garrett, will you provide a loving, lifelong home for Charlotte?"

Together, they answered. "Yes, we will."

"Will you confer upon her the same rights and benefits as you would a biological child, should you have one?"

Again, they answered yes.

"What name are you giving this child?"

Garrett looked down into Abby's eyes and back at the judge, with a smile. "Charlotte Abigail Cole."

Without warning, Charlotte dove forward into Abby's arms. Abby snuggled her close, eliciting a sigh from their audience as Charlotte laid her head on Abby's shoulder. Garrett put his arm around both of them and wondered for the millionth time how he could've possibly gotten so lucky.

"I don't have to ask Charlotte what she thinks about this situation. That's pretty obvious." The judge grinned down at them.

Garrett glanced back to the first row, where Brooklyn was sitting with Elvis. Her eyes were shiny, but she nodded. She was part of their family, too.

With a flourish, the judge signed the adoption decree on the desk in front of her. "I'm so honored to have been a part of the creation of a brand new family today. Congratulations to the newlyweds *and* to the newest member of the Cole family. I wish you all a very happy future together."

Later that night, after all the cake had been eaten and their friends had gone home, Abby brought the baby monitor out onto the porch where Garrett was waiting for her. They were planning to go on a honeymoon, but wanted to be with Charlotte tonight, on their very first night as a family.

Abby took Garrett's hand and drew him out into moonlight. It was a warm summer night, a multitude of stars brilliant against the black sky. Fireflies twinkled around them, winking off, only to reappear a few feet away. And the rustling of the river in the background was the only music they needed.

"It was a perfect day, Mrs. Cole. A dream come true." Garrett held out his arms and she stepped into them.

Swaying back and forth, she giggled as he whirled her around, bare feet spinning in the grass. When she was upright again, he wrapped his arms around her waist, pulling her close. "I never even dreamed anything like this would happen for me. I love you, Garrett."

"I love you, too." He pressed a kiss to her hair and rested his chin on her head with a contented sigh.

And, as she stood in his arms, with their baby sleeping safely inside, she could only think how blessed she was that out of all the places on the planet, she chose this one.

God had brought their family together here.

Right where they all belonged.

* * * * *

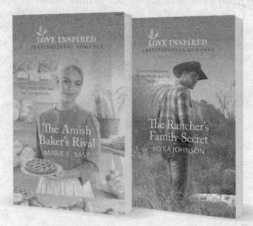

"Time to get back to work," Marshall ordered, and the other men pushed their chairs back and started filing out the door.

"But, *Groossdaadi*, Peter's not done with his pie yet," Susannah pointed out. "And that's practically the main course of this meal."

Marshall glowered, but as he put his hat on, he told Peter, "We'll be in the north field."

"I'll be right out," Peter said, shoveling another bite into his mouth and triggering a coughing spasm.

"Take your time," Lydia told him once Marshall exited the house. "Sweet things are meant to be savored."

Susannah was still seated beside him and Peter thought he noticed her shake her head at her stepgrandmother, but maybe he'd imagined it. "This does taste *gut*," he agreed.

"*Jah*. But it's not as gut as the pies your *mamm* used to make," Susannah commented. "I mean, I really appreciate that Almeda made pies for us. But your *mamm*'s were extraordinarily *appenditlich*. Especially her *blohbier* pies."

"*Jah*. I remember that time you traded me your entire lunch for a second piece of her pie." Peter hadn't considered what he was disclosing until Susannah knocked her knee against his beneath the table. It was too late. Lydia's ears had already perked up.

"When was that?" she asked.

"It was on a *Sunndaag* last summer when some of us went on a picnic after *kurrich*," Susannah immediately said. Which was true, although "some of us" really meant "the two of us." Peter and Susannah had never picnicked with anyone else when they were courting; Sundays had been the only chance they had to be alone. Dorcas, the only person they'd told about their courtship, had frequently dropped off Susannah at the gorge, where Peter would be waiting for her.

"Ah, that's right. You and Dorcas loved going out to the gorge on *Sunndaag*," Lydia recalled. "I didn't realize you'd gone with a group."

Susannah started coughing into her napkin. Or was she trying not to laugh? Peter couldn't tell. *How could I have been so* dumm *as to blurt out something like that?* he lamented.

After Lydia excused herself, Peter mumbled quietly to Susannah, "Sorry about that. It just slipped out."

"It's okay. Sometimes things spring to my mind, too, and I say them without really thinking them through."

It felt strange to be sitting side by side with her, with no one else on the other side of the table. No one else in the room. It reminded Peter of when they'd sit on a rock by the creek in the gorge, dangling their feet into the water and chatting as they ate their sandwiches. And instead of pushing the romantic memory from his mind, Peter deliberately indulged it, lingering over his pie even though he knew Marshall would have something to say about his delay when he returned to the fields.

Susannah didn't seem in any hurry to get up, either. She was silent while he whittled his pie down to the last two bites. Then she asked, "How is your *mamm*? At the frolic, someone mentioned she's been...under the weather."

I'm sure they did, Peter thought, and instantly the nostalgic connection he felt with Susannah was replaced by insecurity about whatever rumors she'd heard about his mother. Peter could bear it if Marshall thought ill of him, but he didn't want Susannah to think his mother was lazy. "She's okay," he said and abruptly stood up, even as he was scooping the last bite of pie into his mouth. "I'd better get going or your *groossdaddi* won't let me take any more lunch breaks after this."

He'd only been half joking about Marshall, but Susannah replied, "Don't worry. Lydia would never let that happen." Standing, she caught his eye and added, "And neither would I."

Peering into her earnest golden-brown eyes, Peter was overcome with affection. *"Denki,"* he said and then forced himself to leave the house while his legs could still carry him out to the fields.

Don't miss
An Unexpected Amish Harvest *by Carrie Lighte,*
available September 2021 wherever
Love Inspired books and ebooks are sold.

LoveInspired.com

LOVE INSPIRED

INSPIRATIONAL ROMANCE

UPLIFTING STORIES OF FAITH, FORGIVENESS AND HOPE.

Join our social communities to connect with other readers who share your love!

Sign up for the Love Inspired newsletter at **LoveInspired.com** to be the first to find out about upcoming titles, special promotions and exclusive content.

CONNECT WITH US AT:

Facebook.com/LoveInspiredBooks

Twitter.com/LoveInspiredBks

Facebook.com/groups/HarlequinConnection

LISOCIAL2020

HARLEQUIN

Heartfelt or thrilling, passionate or uplifting—Harlequin is more than just happily-ever-after.

With twelve different series to choose from and new books available every month, you are sure to find stories that will move you, uplift you, inspire and delight you.

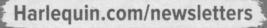

Get 4 FREE REWARDS!

We'll send you 2 FREE Books plus 2 FREE Mystery Gifts.

Love Inspired books feature uplifting stories where faith helps guide you through life's challenges and discover the promise of a new beginning.

FREE Value Over **$20**

YES! Please send me 2 FREE Love Inspired Romance novels and my 2 FREE mystery gifts (gifts are worth about $10 retail). After receiving them, if I don't wish to receive any more books, I can return the shipping statement marked "cancel." If I don't cancel, I will receive 6 brand-new novels every month and be billed just $5.24 each for the regular-print edition or $5.99 each for the larger-print edition in the U.S., or $5.74 each for the regular-print edition or $6.24 each for the larger-print edition in Canada. That's a savings of at least 13% off the cover price. It's quite a bargain! Shipping and handling is just 50¢ per book in the U.S. and $1.25 per book in Canada.* I understand that accepting the 2 free books and gifts places me under no obligation to buy anything. I can always return a shipment and cancel at any time. The free books and gifts are mine to keep no matter what I decide.

Choose one:
☐ **Love Inspired Romance Regular-Print** (105/305 IDN GNWC)
☐ **Love Inspired Romance Larger-Print** (122/322 IDN GNWC)

Name (please print)

Address   Apt. #

City   State/Province   Zip/Postal Code

Email: Please check this box ☐ if you would like to receive newsletters and promotional emails from Harlequin Enterprises ULC and its affiliates. You can unsubscribe anytime.

Mail to the Harlequin Reader Service:
IN U.S.A.: P.O. Box 1341, Buffalo, NY 14240-8531
IN CANADA: P.O. Box 603, Fort Erie, Ontario L2A 5X3

Want to try 2 free books from another series! Call 1-800-873-8635 or visit www.ReaderService.com.

---

*Terms and prices subject to change without notice. Prices do not include sales taxes, which will be charged (if applicable) based on your state or country of residence. Canadian residents will be charged applicable taxes. Offer not valid in Quebec. This offer is limited to one order per household. Books received may not be as shown. Not valid for current subscribers to Love Inspired Romance books. All orders subject to approval. Credit or debit balances in a customer's account(s) may be offset by any other outstanding balance owed by or to the customer. Please allow 4 to 6 weeks for delivery. Offer available while quantities last.

Your Privacy—Your information is being collected by Harlequin Enterprises ULC, operating as Harlequin Reader Service. For a complete summary of the information we collect, how we use this information and to whom it is disclosed, please visit our privacy notice located at corporate.harlequin.com/privacy-notice. From time to time we may also exchange your personal information with reputable third parties. If you wish to opt out of this sharing of your personal information, please visit readerservice.com/consumerschoice or call 1-800-873-8635. **Notice to California Residents**—Under California law, you have specific rights to control and access your data. For more information on these rights and how to exercise them, visit corporate.harlequin.com/california-privacy.

LIR21R